THE
FOREIGNERS

THE FOREIGNERS

James Lovegrove

VICTOR GOLLANCZ
LONDON

This edition published in Great Britain in 2000 by

Victor Gollancz
An imprint of Orion Books Ltd
Orion House, 5 Upper St Martin's Lane, London WC2H 9EA

To receive information on the Millennium list, e-mail us at:
smy@orionbooks.co.uk

ISBN 0 575 06894 9

Typeset by Deltaytype Ltd, Birkenhead, Merseyside

Printed in Great Britain by
Clays Ltd, St Ives, plc

For Lou

CONTENTS

An optimist is someone who knows exactly how sad and how challenging a place the world can be, and a pessimist is a man who finds it out anew every morning.

Peter Ustinov

So may the outward shows be least themselves –
The world is still deceiv'd with ornament.

Bassanio, *The Merchant of Venice*

PRELUDE

Some believed that they came from another solar system, after hearing the music issuing from the gold-plated disc on the *Voyager II* space probe; that they were drawn to Earth by the unearthly beauty of Bach's Brandenburg Concerto No. 2.

Others claimed that they hailed from a parallel dimension, an alternate universe that existed in concert with our own, its harmonious twin, the treble clef to our bass.

Still others maintained that they were humans from our furthest-flung future, as evolutionarily advanced from us as we were from the lower primates, and had travelled back in time to safeguard their own existence by ensuring humankind's survival, or else simply to spectate.

Others were of the opinion that they were nothing more (or less) than angels; while, according to yet a fifth popularly held school of thought, they had been present on Earth all along, cohabiting secretly and invisibly with us until the day arrived when they had no choice but to make their presence known – the day the Great Conductor gestured with His baton and brought them in.

The truth was there was no general agreement about the origins of the Foreigners. There could be none. In their strangeness, their sheer ineffability, they thwarted every human effort to define or decipher them.

What was universally acknowledged, however, was that from the moment the Foreigners first appeared – on city streets, inside public buildings, stalking with stiff yet stately grace across parkland and countryside – the world changed for the better. At a stroke, the nations of Earth set aside their disputes. Rapacious squabbles over land and resources subsided. Ethnic and religious differences ceased to be bones of contention. Crime rates plummeted. All the social tensions that had seemed to be pushing humankind ineluctably towards self-destruction were suddenly and miraculously obliterated.

Why should this have happened? Perhaps it was because there

was something about the Foreigners, something about their magnificent extraordinariness and extraordinary magnificence, that awakened in the soul a kind of gnostic joy. Or perhaps it was because humankind was aroused from its nihilism, its idle, solipsistic tendency towards self-destruction, by the sudden appearance of clear, incontrovertible proof that it was no longer alone in the universe. Or perhaps the reason was more mundane, to do with pheromones, something like that.

In truth, no one could say for sure, and no one wanted to delve too deeply into the matter for fear that questioning such a wonderful mystery might destroy it, like a child crushing a butterfly in his eagerness to capture it. It was enough merely to accept that, on the day the Foreigners came, the day of their Debut, a new age began. A plainer, cleaner, more honest age. An age of reasonableness and responsibility. An age not obsessed with speed or immediacy or short-term gratification. An age of calm heads and mutual trust. An age of mending fences and building bridges. An age when need was put before greed, less ousted excess, ethics replaced economics, parity supplanted poverty. An age of consensus rather than division, entente rather than factionalism, generosity rather than antipathy, benevolence rather than callousness.

The bad old ways were abandoned. The strong spared the weak. The rich helped the poor. Hope was embraced. The future became something to look forward to, not dread.

Or, at least, so it seemed.
So everyone said.

OVERTURE

The rioting had lasted for two days, mob and police locked in a dance of surge and containment, the streets of central London their ballroom. Back and forth, to and fro, the two groups – the one dark blue and regimented, the other multi-coloured and chaotic – had met and clinched, then disengaged and retreated to lick wounds. During the night an uneasy truce had prevailed. In the glow of impromptu fires stoked with looted newspapers, torn-down tree branches, prised-off car tyres and the wood and cardboard placards that betokened the riot's origins as a demon-stration, the two sides had sat and watched each other warily like pugilists between rounds. Their members sleeping in shifts, they had waited, and at dawn the anger had begun again.

By noon on the second day the police were exhausted, while the mob, fuelled by rage and fear, remained as fresh as ever. The mob's numbers seemed limitless, drawing upon the reserves of a city of frightened millions. The police had finite resources. Already they were deploying officers who did not belong on the front line: desk sergeants and detectives and older, less agile coppers. If matters were not resolved soon, forces from other regions might have to be asked for help – those regions, that is, that weren't having civil-unrest problems of their own. The army might even have to be called in.

All that day there were running battles, scuffles in side streets, assaults, arrests. A hail of makeshift weapons rained down on the police – bottles, half-bricks, broken paving stones, sections of uprooted railing, lengths of scaffolding. Every now and then a cloud of CS gas would blossom and rioters would scatter like spurned lovers, covering reddened, tear-streaked faces. Every now and then could be heard the duff detonations of plastic bullets being fired. Every now and then water cannon would emit a cataract roar. Overhead, helicopters clattered and tinny tannoy voices repeatedly exhorted the rioters to disperse and go back to their homes. But these distant, echoing pleas were constantly drowned out by the babel howl of the mob, an eerie, senseless concatenation of words without meaning, the cry of the crowd-animal.

Detective Sergeant Jack Parry of the London Metropolitan Police joined the fray during a lull on that second evening. Stepping down nervously from the back of a van with cage-covered windows, he and a dozen other men and women were directed to join several more groups of recently arrived reinforcements, all gathered together on Pall Mall. Clad in flame-retardant jumpsuits, Kevlar vests and helmets with shatterproof visors, and wielding batons and transparent shields, they looked less like people and more like large, well-armoured insects – dehumanized, identical, alien.

After several minutes of milling confusion, the reinforcements were organized into phalanxes by senior officers with megaphones and ordered to march towards Trafalgar Square. They had been told earlier that their presence alone might be enough to quell the rioting. A fresh influx of police looking sufficiently intimidating might just bring the mob to heel. They none of them believed this, however, and inwardly they prepared themselves for violence.

And not long after they entered Trafalgar Square violence came. The mob, spotting the reinforcements, extended itself toward them like an amoeba stretching out a hungry pseudopod. Civilians and police mingled. Across road and pavement, in and around the fountains, between Landseer's lions, law and disorder clashed. Batons and lengths of two-by-four were wielded with equal ferocity. Then, from the direction of Charing Cross Road, a horseback charge of mounted police scissored the two sides apart, and each withdrew to an opposite corner of the square to regroup and retrench.

The summer evening sky was a bruise of fire smoke and pollution. Parry, dripping with sweat, surveyed the mob as it seethed less than a hundred metres away from him, ready to surge forward again at any moment. He saw wide white eyes and bared white teeth and he heard unintelligible yelling and he loathed these people, loathed them as any terrified combatant loathes the enemy . . . yet, somewhere deep down, he felt a kinship with them as well. They were just human beings, after all. Ordinary, scared human beings.

Then, after an interval that seemed far briefer than it actually was, the mob launched yet another attack. Most of the rioters had long since forgotten what had originally brought them here, the nature of the protest that had been their initial purpose for gathering. They had found a focus for their fury and fear. It was them versus the authorities, simple as that.

They came baying across the square, weapons brandished, faces fixed in masks of hatred and glee. Their opponents responded instinctively. Shields up, batons raised, they charged to greet them. The two groups converged and commingled. Parry, suddenly in the thick of it, did the only thing he could do and lashed out with his baton, clubbing and cudgelling. Blood sprayed across his shield and spattered in fine droplets across his visor. The baton rose and fell, breaking faces, transforming rage to shock and pain.

There was a weird, calm dreaminess to it all. Parry could hear nothing except his breathing, hoarse inside the helmet. He could see nothing except the people around him, whom he instantly bracketed into either of two categories, those who were on his side and those who were not, those he should hit and those he should not. His world had irised down to just those two alternatives: targets and non-targets.

Then she appeared in front of him. A woman. Not even a woman, really. Still in her teens. A girl. She had a brick in her hand, but she looked as if she had no idea what to do with it. She looked lost, buffeted on all sides, desperate and confused. Her hair was raggedly short. She was wearing jeans and a combat-green vest. Her left shoulder was gashed and bleeding.

She stumbled towards Parry, not seeing him, colliding with him . . .

And the baton came down. Almost of its own accord. His arm felt as if it was operating independently of the rest of his body. He had no control over it. The baton cracked down on the girl's skull and she fell, raising her hands to protect herself. And Parry knew he should stop there, she was no threat to him, there was no need to hit her again, but he could not help it. The baton continued to batter the girl relentlessly, coming down, coming down, as she cowered on her knees, hapless and helpless, and she was screaming – he could see her mouth working, even though he could not hear her – and still he kept on bludgeoning her, making her less human and more contemptible with each blow, reducing her to a writhing, shrieking, crimson-streaked *thing* . . .

. . . and seventeen years later, on a freezing April afternoon, Captain Jack Parry of the Foreign Policy Police, New Venice division, stood on almost the exact same spot in Trafalgar Square, staring at the ground at his feet and shivering. He was wrapped in several thicknesses of clothing, including a woollen overcoat he had purchased that morning from an Oxford Street department store, but still he shivered. Deep inner trembles radiated out from his solar plexus, racking him through and through.

What he had done! What he had *done*!

It took a greater effort than Parry would have believed possible to straighten up, steel himself with a deep intake of breath, come to his senses, return to the present.

The present:

A half-dozen gamey-looking pigeons were waddling expectantly around him, their plumage the same shades of grey and white as the quids of turd they squirted out so casually on to the ground, without breaking stride. A similar number of tourists dotted the pedestrianized portions of the square, all of them huddled within rainproofs or overcoats. From a layer of cloud like penicillin mould a slow sleet was falling, each wet flake appearing to melt and vanish before it hit the ground. The British Isles had lost the warming embrocation of the Gulf Stream several years ago and now endured a climate appropriate to their location in the same band of latitude as Moscow and Labrador. This was London in spring. Spring in London.

Welcome home, Jack.

The memory of the riot still writhed and sparked and spat at the back of Parry's brain like a downed power cable. He had hoped that a visit to Trafalgar Square would be a pilgrimage of sorts, a chance to make peace with a piece of his past. He had not counted on being rocketed back so vividly and shockingly to the events of that evening, the square itself – little changed in seventeen years – triggering the recollection, as though stone and brick, like elephants, never forgot, nor ever allowed *you* to forget. Even now, his mind was fast-forwarding through the rest of his involvement in the riot. The continuing conflict. The onset of night. The sense that the police were gradually gaining control of the situation. The mob starting to flag. The last few vicious pushes into their midst. The rioters finally recognizing that the only rewards for their outrage were pain and more pain, and admitting defeat, scuttling away in twos and threes. The mopping-up operations around midnight. The sense of Pyrrhic victory back at the station. The exhausted faces of his colleagues, looking at one another in the hope of absolution but finding only disgust and flinching-eyed shame. It was all there, stored perfectly in his head. If he had thought that coming back here after all this time might somehow lay the unquiet ghost of the riot to rest, or at least show how faint and faded it had become over the years, he had been sorely mistaken.

With a heavy sigh, Parry squared his shoulders and strode over to examine the circular brass plaque that was set into the plinth of Nelson's Column. Squinting down, he read the inscription on the plaque, a few short lines commemorating the thirty-two lives lost on or near this site during the Hunger Riots. Thirty-two men and women, police and civilian, but none of them named. The plaque gave only the number – the quantity of the quenched, the total of the totalled.

Had she been among them? The young woman, the girl – had she been one of those thirty-two?

The hell of it was there was no way he would ever know. At the time another rioter had grabbed him while he was beating her and he had turned his attention to this new threat, forgetting the girl in an instant. Had she crawled away to safety, or perhaps been hauled away by one of the mob? Or had she simply lain where she was, insensible, possibly dying, to be trampled on by all and sundry?

It did not do to speculate. He could only hope. Hope that, whoever she was, she was alive and well. Hope that, wherever she was, she had forgiven him.

He turned away from the plaque and with slow, trudging footsteps made his way north towards the West End.

He had been back in London for a little over twenty-four hours now, and the capital remained as inhospitable as when he had arrived. He had spent the whole morning strolling around, trying to rediscover the city on foot, but finding instead that he had a new city to discover, one that no longer matched the memory-maps in his mind. As though to express displeasure at his long absence, London had rearranged itself in all manner of subtle, confusing ways. Old short cuts were no longer open to him. Old haunts turned out to be further apart or closer together than he remembered. Buildings that had been landmarks in his life had been altered beyond recognition. Some had disappeared altogether.

London's inhabitants seemed different, too, their faces more pinched, their attitudes less open, as though they had shrivelled inside themselves. The taxi driver who had ferried Parry into town from the airport yesterday, the staff at the hotel where he was staying, the sales assistant at the department store where he had bought the overcoat, the waitress who had served him a lunchtime sandwich at a Soho café – all of them exhibited a sullen closedness which he did not recognize and did not like. But he thought he understood the reason for it. England was seldom visited by Foreigners. The golden giants disliked cold climates and so a few came here in midsummer but none at any other time of year. The country was deprived of the full effect of their benignant presence and it showed. It showed.

Leicester Square was busier than Trafalgar Square. There were vagrants aplenty, and young people too, both groups in their different ways killing time. Sketch artists wearing fingerless gloves offered passers-by the opportunity to have their portraits done in charcoal, perhaps with a celebrity drawn in beside them, or a Foreigner. Cafés tried to entice customers to sit at outdoor tables by means of powerful gas heaters. Parry found the smell of burning fossil fuel both noxious and oddly nostalgic.

He was drawn towards a crowd that had gathered in a loose circle around a Foreigner. He was curious to know what a Foreigner was doing here and why people were standing watching it. When he came close enough to have a proper look, however, he realized that the golden giant was in fact a mime perched on short stilts and dressed in a home-made Foreign outfit of mask, gloves and robe.

The mime's imitation of a Foreigner's distinctive gait was well observed and convincing. Had his (or it could have been her) costume been of better quality, he might even have been able to pass himself off as one of the golden giants. Still – and Parry did not think this was just his imagination – there was something missing from the mime's performance, some hard to define element that rendered his mimicry imperfect.

Perfection. That was it. That was the missing element. Whenever Parry looked at a real Foreigner, he knew he was in the presence of something wondrous, something superior, something utterly free from human taint. He could not explain how he knew that any more than he could explain how he knew that a night sky full of stars was awe-inspiring or the sight of a mountain majestic. Some things just were what they were, and Foreigners were sublime.

And this Foreigner was not. This 'Foreigner' was a tawdry imitation, and the longer Parry observed its antics the more peeved he found himself becoming. He was almost childlishly gratified to note that the beret which the mime had laid out on the ground for donations contained nothing but a few copper coins and an International Currency card which was showing its red expiry message.

Deciding that he had had enough of London for one day, and that London had had enough of him, Parry headed for a nearby taxi rank, where a dozen black cabs waited for fares, comp-res engines humming two-note intervals as they idled. The driver of the first cab in line pressed a dashboard button that opened the passenger door automatically and thus saved him from having to wind down his window and do the job manually. Parry bundled himself into the cab's well-heated interior.

'Where to, mate?'

'The Elgar.'

The driver engaged gear and the taxi whirred off sedately. As they wound around Piccadilly and up towards Regent Street, he broached a conversation.

'Been away?'

'Hm? Oh. Yes.'

'Quite some while, by the looks of things.'

Parry said nothing, which the taxi driver chose to interpret as an invitation to continue.

'Only that doesn't look like the kind of tan you get from a fortnight on a beach at Bridgeville.'

'No,' said Parry, glancing reflexively at the back of one nut-brown hand.

'Got out, did you?' the taxi driver said and, when his passenger was hesitant about answering, grinned knowingly into the rear-view mirror. 'Don't blame you. I would, too. Like a shot. Tomorrow! If it wasn't for the bloody Exit Levy . . . If it wasn't so sodding hard for a working man to get an emigration permit . . .'

And for the rest of the journey the driver continued in this vein, expounding alternately on the wisdom of leaving England and the impracticability of doing so. Parry, whose input was not necessarily being solicited, only half-listened.

The Elgar in Bayswater was one of the first hotels to have been constructed in Britain after the arrival of the Foreigners. Parry remembered it freshly finished – a cylindrical tower of up-thrusting, sky-aspiring optimism, a monument of the new era, proud and gleaming and clean. The building where the taxi deposited him was a haggard version of its former self, drab and dilapidated and not a little forbidding, somehow reminiscent of Soviet-bloc ministry offices. In its corridors, lightbulbs had burned out in their ceiling recesses and no one had bothered to replace them. The central hearing was turned up so high that the air smelled singed and was hard to breathe (Parry had tried opening the windows of his room for ventilation and found they would not budge). In his en-suite bathroom lukewarm yellowy water flowed sluggishly from stiff-turning taps. The lifts were as cranky and unreliable as the staff. He had been pleasantly surprised that the wallscreen and telephone both worked.

That evening, after an indifferent supper in the hotel's restaurant, Parry set about phoning up old friends, people he had had little or no contact with since emigrating. He was dismayed to discover that two of them had passed away and no one had seen fit to inform him about their deaths. As for the rest, they sounded glad to hear from him and made the appropriate noises about meeting up for a drink or something, but, when it came to fixing a time and place, became vague and evasive. In each case, Parry did not press the matter. He said where he was staying and how long he intended to be there. If anybody decided renewing old acquaintance was not such a bad idea after all, they would know where to contact him.

One of his friends, a colleague from Parry's days with the Met, did agree to go out for a drink with him, and accordingly they rendezvoused the following evening at a pub near the friend's house in Tottenham. It started out well, the two of them reminiscing pleasantly, recalling the characters they had known, both force and criminal; the practical jokes that had been played on various individuals at the station; the collars they had made, some of them hilarious, some hair-raising, some both. Gradually, however, the old friend became increasingly morose and sour, and by his fourth pint of bitter – for which, like the preceding three, he had been content to let Parry pay – he had become openly hostile and was verbally attacking Parry, accusing him of selling out, the rat leaving the sinking ship and all that. Then he broke off and, astonishingly, burst into tears. A grown man, a senior police officer, still serving, just a few years from retirement age, he blubbered as helplessly as an infant, his beer slopping in his hand as the sobs racked him. After a while, when he had cried himself out, he wiped his eyes and apologized ('I was well out of order') and then began berating himself. He should have left, too, you see. While he had still had the opportunity. Before the government brought the gates down. Should have upped stumps and headed

14

south, same as Parry had done. It was the missus's fault. She had refused to go. Said what would they want to do that for? All their friends and family were here, all their kids' friends. He should have overruled her, or ignored her, and gone anyway. And now it was too late. These days only the really rich could afford to leave and how many of *them* hadn't? Precious few. Precious fucking few.

The following morning Parry travelled to Kennington to revisit the house where he had been born and brought up.

Kennington being one of London's worst-flooded areas, the street could be reached only by means of a complicated system of walkways rigged up from duckboards and scaffold. Counting along the row of terraced two-up-two-downs, he halted outside his childhood home. Its lower storey was submerged in freezing, waist-deep Thames water, and its front garden, in common with that of every other house in the street, was a rectangular pond, with just the top run of enclosing brick wall proud above the water's surface. The front door was a decayed tooth.

Hunkering down, Parry peered through the ground-floor windows' paneless frames to the drowned living room. The wallpaper, what was left of it, the few soggy scraps that still clung in place, was the gold-on-white *fleur de lis* design he remembered from his youth – a design which, despite costing little per roll, his mother had considered classy. The patio doors that used to give on to the back garden were gone. He could just make out a rotten stump that was all that remained of the cooking-apple tree which had once flourished at the far end of the garden. He remembered the day he had climbed to the tree's topmost branches in order to retrieve his sister's beloved beanbag rabbit, which he had hurled up there for reasons that were lost in the mists of time and the mire of childhood motives. He had managed to reach the rabbit and toss it down to Carol, but during his descent he had lost his footing and fallen to the ground, fracturing his collarbone.

An aluminium ladder running from the walkway to the top of the porch indicated that people had made their home in the house's upper storey. Parry debated whether to clamber up, knock on the window and ask if he might take a look round inside. He decided against the idea. No matter how polite he was, it was doubtful the homeowners would let him in. The inhabitants of London's inundated boroughs were, as a rule, prickly types. It required a certain stoicism, to be sure, to endure the mud, the perpetual reek of stagnancy, the rat and frog infestations, the summer outbreaks of cryptosporidiosis, the ever-present, all-pervasive damp, and the myriad other inconveniences of living in the middle of what was essentially an urban lake. It also required a certain self-righteous masochism that seldom went hand in hand with kindness toward strangers. After loitering outside the house for several minutes, Parry simply turned and walked away.

The next morning he headed north to York.

The journey took six hours, station to station. The train, trundling unhurriedly along tracks raised up on a chunky crystech viaduct, wound through what remained of Lincolnshire (frost-fretted marshes, barren and brown) and meandered across the Humber floodplains. Parry gazed out at passing fields of sparse, struggling crops and at snowbound towns and villages where people, fattened by layers of clothing, waded around as laboriously as deep-sea divers.

Carol was waiting for him on the concourse at York station. Parry was startled by how old his younger sister looked, her hair greyed and her face grooved by the passage of years and the raising of two children. She, too, was unable to mask her surprise at the alterations that age had worked on him. The first thing she did after embracing him was reach up and playfully rub the scrubby strip of bristles that adorned the otherwise hairless top of his scalp. 'Just like Dad,' she said, laughing. 'Nearly all gone.' Later, at her house, he found the most recent photograph of him she owned. It sat in a tortoiseshell frame on the mantelshelf, a snapshot taken when he was in his early thirties, not long before he left for New Venice. At that age, his face was still unlined and, from certain angles, it was not noticeable that his hair had begun to recede.

He and Carol had had only sporadic communication since his move to New Venice – the occasional phone-call, e-cards on anniversaries. He had expected they would have a lot to say to each other but this turned out not to be the case. Carol's life was domestic squabbles, the benchmarks of her children's growth, and a hundred other small, private achievements. His life was Foreigners and Sirens and well-heeled tourists and the formalities and peculiarities of FPP work and the shimmering Shangri-La remoteness of New Venice. The disparity between their experiences yawned between them, until Carol found it necessary to apologize for the ordinariness of her existence and Parry for the exoticism of his, and in order to avoid further awkwardness they were reduced to talking in phatic platitudes – enquiries about health, remarks about the house, observations about recent events in the news, that sort of thing – as though the conversation had travelled backwards, ending where it ought to have begun. The bond they had shared in childhood had already grown weak by the time Carol decamped from London to York to be with her husband, Patrick, and to be closer to her and Parry's parents. Now Parry sensed that it was all but gone, a vestigial link attenuated to an almost invisible thinness.

It was a relief, then, when the children came home from school and filled the house with their noise and fluster and impatience. Parry had known Tom and Cecilia as toddlers. Meeting them after such a long interval – Tom was now sixteen, his sister fifteen – was like meeting two new people for the first time, two strangers who happened to be close relatives of his. Both youngsters, after a few searching glances, decided to be unimpressed by their uncle, who up until this moment had been something of a fabled figure, a creature of family myth. Perhaps they had expected him to be taller, more imposing, less wiry, not so bald. He was a Foreign Policy Policeman, after all. Upholder of fairness and justice and decency. Watchman on the walls of the world. But in no way at all did he resemble the square-jawed, teeth-gritting, fully thatched actors who played FPP officers in television dramas such as *TRUST!* and *Resort-City Beat*.

They were equally unimpressed by the present he had brought for them, a replica Foreign statuette with 'A Gift from New Venice' stamped on to its base. The instant he produced it from his suitcase, they knew it was a fake because it was not singing in his hand. They accepted it with grudging gratitude. The word 'Thanks' had to be physically dislodged from Tom by a nudge from his mother.

The two days Parry spent in York with Carol and family were, for the most part, a trial. In particular, Parry found Carol's husband Patrick, a doctor at a local hospital, hard to deal with. Patrick insisted on harping on about his job at every opportunity he could, claiming that medical practitioners of every variety were more vital than ever in this country in this day and age, when the predominant causes of death were no longer cancer and coronary but the more readily preventable and treatable conditions of hypothermia and pneumonia. Each time Patrick spoke in this manner about the importance of his vocation, Parry could not help but notice an aggrieved undertone in his voice, and he knew that what he was hearing was, thinly disguised, the same resentment he had discerned in most of the Londoners he had encountered – the resentment which his old friend from the Met had given voice to in his outburst at the Tottenham pub. It was as though those remaining in England considered themselves a besieged army whose ranks had been dangerously depleted by deserters.

As for the children, his nephew Parry dismissed almost straight away. There would never be any empathy between him and Tom. Beneath the teenage obnoxiousness and self-absorbtion there was nothing, no spark, no encouraging glimpses of the adult in embryo. Cecilia, on the other hand, for particular reasons, interested him. She was a pretty girl, but over-conscious about her appearance. She appeared not to have much of an appetite on her, nor much to say for herself. Even at her tender age she seemed aware that she would be able to obtain almost anything she wanted in life simply by keeping quiet and staying slim and looking good. And he was unable to prevent himself measuring her up against another fifteen-year-old Cecilia he knew. That other Cecilia was lively, bright-eyed, level-headed and smart, and had enough self-confidence not to care what anyone thought of her. Again and again he found himself measuring the two of them against each other. Again and again his niece came off worse from the comparison.

One thing occurred during his time at Carol's that hinted to Parry that he was not entirely cut adrift from his family. He and Carol made a pilgrimage to their parents' graves, driving out of York to the small village to which their mother and father had moved after their father had been laid off at work and taken early retirement. Their mother had been a Yorkshire lass and had always vowed she would return some day to her native county.

John Edward Parry and Theresa Mary Parry lay buried side by side, within arm's reach of each other, in a churchyard on a high plot of land surrounded by drystone-walled fields. The death dates on their headstones were separated by just a few months. Parry's father had passed away while on a trip to the shops with his wife. Parry's mother was driving and had thought her husband had simply fallen asleep beside her. He had become a terrible one for napping. Forever nodding off at inopportune moments! Only when they reached their destination and she was unable to wake him up did the awful truth dawn on her.

They had been devoted to each other. Her grief had brought a swift decline.

At the graveside, Carol tutted and crouched down to pluck

weeds – hawkbit, plantain, cat's ear, clover – from the grass. Parry, after wondering for a moment why she would undertake such a futile task, bent down to help her. Then, standing up and lowering their heads, brother and sister silently paid their respects, while a raw wind scoured in at them from across the fields, gusting and buffeting. And as they stood there, Parry felt Carol's hand grope for his and felt her gloved fingers squeeze themselves around his gloved fingers, and the contact generated warmth, and all at once he saw in his mind's eye the four of them – himself, Carol, their mother, their father – as four corners of a rectangle, the living at one end, the deceased at the other, joined to one another by slender etched lines of remembrance. And he understood that these were connections that could never truly be erased, not by time, not by distance, nor by any other alteration of circumstances, not even by that ultimate alteration of circumstances, death.

The next morning, as scheduled, he returned to London.

With the children at school and Patrick at the hospital, only Carol was there to see him off at York station. A peck on both cheeks, an embrace too light and short-lived to be called a hug, and then Parry hefted up his suitcase and, inclined against its weight, lumbered towards the ticket barrier. When he was through, he set the case down and turned to look for Carol. She was still there on the concourse, watching him, smiling. Without thinking he raised his hands to chest height and clasped them together in FAREWELL. It was an automatic, reflexive gesture. He had forgotten that hand-symbols, so prevalent in New Venice, particularly among FPP officers, were not in common use in places like England. Carol's smile faltered and she gave a curt, embarrassed wave, and before he could offer her any form of apology, she about-faced and strode away, her arms folded, her shoulders hunched against the chill, wraith-wisps of breath vapour skeining around her ear. Annoyed with himself, Parry watched her go. Later, on the train, he wondered whether that would be the last time he ever laid eyes on Carol and whether he minded, and he decided, with a saddeningly slight twinge of regret, that the answers were probably yes and probably no.

That night at the Elgar he stayed in and watched TV, restlessly and ruthlessly channel-hopping. Among the many programmes he dipped in and out of was a re-run of an edition of *Calliope* that he did not recall having seen before. It included an interview with a Frenchwoman who was convinced, against all reason, that she had had a month-long love affair with a Foreigner. There was also a feature on a pressure group that was campaigning for all the calendars of the world to be reset and retroactively synchronized so that they all began the year of the Debut, which would be known as I AP, *Anno Peregrinorum*. Parry's opinion of the Frenchwoman was that she was a semitone short of the full octave, and as for the calendar pressure group, he wished it well but held out little hope of success for its campaign. In the political and business spheres the will was there for this unification of dating systems, but religious leaders of every persuasion were dead-set against it. Pope, archbishop, rabbi, imam, lama, all were of one accord, united on this issue as on no other: their calendars were not for changing. And, given that there is nobody more intransigent than an intransigent religious leader, Parry knew that in the face of such vehement and vocal opposition the campaign was destined to fail.

He also watched a whole episode of *Resort-City Beat*, something he had never done in New Venice. America's long-running cop opera and *TRUST!*, its somewhat more staid English equivalent, were consigned to late-night slots on NVTV, New Venice's small but influential television station, and regarded with a certain condescending disdain. Over here in England, both were peak-time, mainstream viewing and enjoyed by millions who, not realizing how unrealistic their protagonists and plotlines were, had no reason to consider them anything other than an authentic representation of life in a resort-city.

Throughout the episode Parry veered between amusement and exasperation, the latter mainly directed at the portrayal of Foreigners. Mask-makers and costumiers had recreated the look of golden giants wonderfully well, and some over-tall actors in stacked-sole shoes did a very creditable job, like the mime in Leicester Square, of rendering the Foreign gait and mannerisms accurately. Unfortunately, the televisual Foreigners did not behave like any Foreigners Parry had ever encountered. There was even a golden giant, nicknamed 'Goldie', who hung around the show's fictional FPP HQ and served as a kind of communal agony aunt, dispensing manufolded advice when consulted by the human characters. Absurd!

The final day of his trip to England Parry spent roaming London once more, absorbing last impressions of the capital to take back with him to New Venice. The city had not noticeably mellowed towards him. If anything, it was unfriendlier than before, as if punishing him because it knew he was about to abandon it again. It assailed him with fast-moving businesspeople, striding along barking staccato sentences into their barely visible cellphone headsets, like the world's best-dressed lunatics. It accosted him with skinny, wizened prostitutes who stepped out from doorways to ask if he had the time. It threatened him with cursing beggars and passing pedestrians who bumped shoulders with him – sometimes deliberately, it seemed.

There had been a snowfall in the south of the country while Parry was up in York, and though most of the snow had melted, some persisted on the pavements in hard, icy spatter-patterns that crunched like peanut brittle underfoot and were treacherous. The temperature had dropped further and the wind came at Parry around street corners like a hawk, sinking talons into his bones. Before moving to New Venice he might have been able to weather such weather conditions with a manful shrug, but twelve years of living in a subtropical climate, twelve years of year-round warmth, had lowered his tolerance, thinned his skin, considerably.

He stuck it out as long as he could, but eventually, in need of warmth, he ducked inside the British Museum and wandered its well-heated galleries and aisles for a grateful hour or so. The museum boasted a collection of (genuine) Foreign statuettes, allegedly the only complete chromatic scale in existence, which it had put together assiduously and at no small expense.

The figurines were displayed in a semi-circle, starting on the left at one metre tall and decreasing in size at regular increments, the rightmost one being no larger than a grown man's handspan. There were ninety-six of them all told – Parry counted, just to be sure – and apart from size and the position of their hands they were all identical, like a set of impossibly intricate *matrioshka* dolls. All were made of a smoky yellow crystalline material, within which tiny flecks of gold glinted like mica in sunlit granite, and all had slender limbs, high, hunched shoulders and upturned, expression-less faces whose features were less well delineated than a human's but better defined than the vague, nubby contours of a Foreigner's mask. The fingers of each were folded into a different configuration, exhibiting the entire range of what were known officially as Verhulst manifolds, more often just as manufolds, and most commonly as hand-symbols.

A crimson velvet rope cordoned the statuettes off from the public, and a set of notices were ranged around the display, each bearing the same message:

Parry had to ask himself whether it had occurred to the museum's curators that this edict entirely defeated the purpose of the statuettes' existence.

He endured one last night of the Elgar's coarsely starched sheets, and after breakfast the next morning packed his suitcase and went downstairs to check out.

'Leaving us then, sir?' asked the concierge, a slovenly, acne-pocked post-adolescent who had been treating Parry throughout his stay at the hotel with a mixture of curiosity and contempt, as though he were a three-legged dog.

'Yes,' Parry replied. 'I'm going home.'

He did not think anything about the remark – *I'm going home* – until an hour later, when he was travelling by taxi to Heathrow. Then he was struck by the significance, not of what he had said, but of the way in which he had said it.

Of course he had referred to New Venice before now as home, but always it had been with a certain irony, a certain incredulity even. On this occasion the word had tripped easily, thoughtlessly, from his lips, without having to be smiled around or stammered over or half-apologized for or bracketed in inverted commas, and all at once Parry knew that what had been an otherwise frustrating and disheartening seven days had had one redeeming feature. The coldness (both meteorological and metaphorical) that he had encountered in England confirmed what he had for a while been suspecting was true. His motherland was inimical to him now. The bonds of nationality and blood no longer held him to this place. He had become a stranger, an outsider, an alien, in the country of his birth.

With the glad heart of a returning prodigal, Parry boarded the *Jessye Norman*, the airship that was to take him back to the city he had come to regard as – and at last knew for certain was – where he wanted to be and where he belonged.

FIRST MOVEMENT

1 AIR

Overnight, through the buoyant, throbbing dark, the *Jessye Norman* nosed southwards across continental Europe. Parry, tucked away in her belly along with three hundred other passengers, found sleep difficult to come by. It had been the same a week ago, coming the opposite way: the bed hard and narrow, the cabin windowless and claustrophobic. It seemed like only moments after he finally dropped off that a chime began sounding repeatedly in the corridor outside – a soft, sonorous sequence of four notes, awakening, awakening.

Washed and dressed, he went blearily to the port-side viewing lounge, to take breakfast four kilometres above the Mediterranean. The sun, rising over Gibraltar, steeped the lounge in golden light. As he nibbled a croissant and drained cup after cup of tea at a table by himself, Parry cast a bloodshot gaze over his fellow travellers. The flight had originated in New York and almost everyone on it was American. Those who had joined at its stopovers in Halifax, Reykjavik and London accounted for no more than a twentieth of the onboard complement.

To amuse himself, he decided to play a little game. Which of the people eating and drinking and chatting around him were genuine holidaymakers, and which were coming to New Venice to try their luck as Sirens? It was impossible to tell from appearances alone, but therein lay the fun.

For instance, that fat man over there tucking heartily into a heaped plateful of bacon, sausages, eggs, fried bread and mushrooms – his was an opera maestro's fig-shaped figure if ever there was one. And those two women over there, shuttling snippets of conversation between them, elaborating on each other's remarks – Parry could picture them engaged in a duet, each threading her melody line around the other's. As for those four clean-cut, crewcut young fellows sharing a table together, it was easy to imagine them bunching together with beatific smiles as they crooned sweet barbershop harmonies. And that man with the three prepubescent boys might be a father with his three sons, but equally he might be a choirmaster shepherding three of his purest-throated trebles.

An announcement from the captain over the airship's internal PA system broke in on all conversations and thoughts, commandeering attention.

'Good morning, ladies and gentlemen. We hope you-all had a pleasant night's sleep and are enjoying your breakfast.' The voice was deep and reassuringly sincere, with a down-home Texan tinge. The sentences undulated like rolling hills. 'We're presently cruising at an altitude of approximately four thousand metres and, as I'm sure you're aware, it's a gorgeous day outside. You might like to know that our final destination is just coming into view ahead. Please feel free to go take a look, but' – a folksy chuckle – 'my co-pilots and I would appreciate it if you-all wouldn't rush at once, so's we have time to compensate for the shift in weight distribution.'

The passengers bore the captain's warning in mind as they rose from their tables and crossed over to the sloping observation windows. Keen though they were for a first glimpse of the place to which the majority of them had spent more than forty-eight hours travelling, they were equally (and sensibly) keen not to risk unbalancing the airship. They moved sleepwalker-slow, and only when they reached the windows did they allow their excitement to manifest, making animated gestures and vying with one another to come up with the most effusive epithets, the loudest oohs and aahs.

Parry remained seated, waiting till some of the tourists began to drift back to their meals, having seen as much as they wanted to for now. Then he stood and ambled over to join the crowd at the window handrail.

Ahead, roughly ten kilometres away, set amid a sheen of gleaming sea, lay New Venice.

From this height and distance, the resort-city resembled nothing in the world so much as a snowflake – a gigantic snowflake that had somehow fallen from the clear, cloudless sky to alight, unmelted, pristine, fantastically intricate, on the ocean's surface. Distinguishable were the fine dendritic patterns of the quays at the city's periphery and the gently shelving inclines of its glassy beaches, laced with breaking waves. Also distinguishable were the honeycombs of the outlying residential estates and the spikes and spires of hotels and apartment complexes, which grew taller and clustered closer together the more central their location. All the buildings were as white as wedding cakes, and between them could be discerned numerous intersecting, criss-crossing azure threads of canal. To the south, the mainland was a jagged-edged strip of terracotta, fading into horizon-haze. Over everything arched a sky like a dome of polished sapphire.

Gazing down at the city, Parry was struck by its apparent fragility. As a resident, he was confident of its permanence, its intrinsic solidity. Up here, though, from this Olympian vantage point, all he could think was how delicate it looked, how vulnerable, how evanescent. A breath could have demolished it. How could he have left it to fend for itself without him, even for just a week? His responsibility was to New Venice's inhabitants – its citizens, the tourists and Sirens and Foreigners who visited it – but all of a sudden he was conscious of another, perhaps greater responsibility: to the city itself, the stone and stucco and glass and concrete of its structures, the crystech foundations on which it rested. The emotion was strong in his chest, a tugging ache, fond and profound, and he thought to himself: This must be how a father feels, watching over his child.

The *Jessye Norman* skirted anti-clockwise around the city's western edge and with a hiss of vented hydrogen commenced her descent to the airport. The thrumming whine from her engine nacelles changed pitch, rising and falling in fits and starts, as captain and crew made the complicated manoeuvres and fine adjustments necessary to bring their craft in to dock at the assigned mooring mast. Tacking and turning with a grace that belied her leviathan bulk, the *Jessye Norman* took her place alongside a dozen other airships, her stars-and-stripes livery settling in beside representations of the flags of a dozen other nations. Ground crew secured her nosecone and tailfin cables, and she was reeled down to the landing area. Gangways swung down from the base of her passenger section and the passengers began filing out, ushered on their way by the flight attendants, who smilingly wished them farewell and a pleasant vacation.

Inside the terminal building, the majority of the disembarked were presented with a choice. Those willing to have their passport cards checked and their entry into the city recorded could join one queue; those not wishing to do so could join another queue and undergo a brief but pertinent questioning by a Customs official. Parry was one of a mere handful entitled to take a third option and enter the fast-track channel reserved for resident New Venetians. At the automated barrier he showed his passport card to an electronic eye. At a subsequent barrier a Customs official checked him over with an electronic wand for personal telecommunications devices. Cellphones and any other items of technology utilizing microwaves were not allowed in resort-cities out of respect for Foreigners, who appeared to find proximity to microwave emissions disagreeable. It was one of the many courtesies that resort-cities extended to the golden giants.

Because Heathrow had been the flight's last stopover, Parry's suitcase was among the first to be offloaded and appear on the luggage carousel. Heaving it off the circling conveyor belt, he made for the doors that led to the main concourse.

Beyond the doors, a pack of people waited to pounce. No sooner had Parry entered the concourse than he was beset by taxi-gondoliers touting for custom, holiday reps wanting to know if he was with their tour companies, hotel scouts eagerly thrusting brochures and discount vouchers at him, and guides, both official and unlicensed, offering to show him the sights. They would not have accosted him, any of them, had he been in uniform. As it was, incognito in civvies, he lowered his head and bulled his way through the clamouring throng, muttering polite but firm rejections as he went. The idea of taking a taxi-gondola home was tempting, but one of the canal-bus routes from the airport had a stop directly outside his condominium. Besides, taxi-gondolas were principally for tourists and Foreigners, and were expensive. The canal-buses were free.

The concourse was huge, and walled and roofed with glass, like a cross between a conservatory and a cathedral. Echoing through its vastness, female voices intoned the phrase 'Welcome to New Venice' in every known language. Reinforcing this aural message visually, and serving as a centrepiece, was a five-metre-high sculpture atop a chunky octagonal pedestal. The sculpture, fashioned from white crystech with an alabaster-like lustre, consisted of a pair of hands clasped together, palm pressed to palm, fingers spaced out, thumbs crossed.

Beside it Parry spied a pair of FPP officers. At first all he could make out of them was their cream-coloured uniforms, and he assumed they were there to keep an eye on the crowd and ensure that newly arrived holidaymakers were not unduly harassed or hassled. As he drew nearer to them, however, he discerned that one

28

of the FPP officers was a large man, broad-shouldered and strawberry-blond, and that the other was a petite, olive-complexioned woman whose dark hair was pinned tightly up at the back. He recognized them then. Lieutenant Pål Johansen and Sergeant Rachel Avni. Both worked in his district, under his direct command . . . and both of them had faces as grim as any gravedigger's. Their expressions eased a little when they caught sight of him heading towards them. They were here for him. They had been waiting for him.

Reaching the sculpture, Parry set down his suitcase and, facing his two subordinates, put his hands together in the same configuration as the crystech hands – SALUTATION. Johansen and Avni reciprocated.

'Well I never,' Parry said, with a breeziness that he neither meant to sound convincing nor felt inside. 'A reception committee. To what do I owe the honour?'

'First of all, did you have an enjoyable holiday, sir?' Avni asked.

'It fulfilled its function. Come on. Stop pissing about. What's going on? Why are you two here?'

'Boss . . .' Johansen scratched a thumbnail back and forth across the small fold of skin where his meaty forehead met the bridge of his squat, squared-off nose. 'Something bad's happened.'

'I gathered that.' Initially Parry had thought that some administrative problem must have cropped up while he was away, some tangled bureaucratic knot that only he could unravel. Now, he knew that a far more serious reason had brought Johansen and Avni here.

Anna? Had something happened to Anna?

'We have a dead Siren,' said Johansen.

Relief. Guilty relief. Not Anna. Anna was OK.

'A dead Siren? Is that all?'

Johansen hesitated. 'And a lost Foreigner.'

'Oh Christ,' said Parry.

'Yeah.' Johansen plucked Parry's suitcase from the ground as though it weighed nothing. 'Precisely. Oh Christ.'

2 ORGAN STOP

The FPP launch burred along, wavelets lapping and slapping its bows. Avni was at the helm. With her spine straight and her head held erect, she looked every inch the proud Israeli sabra as she steered the boat around slower-moving vessels, unerringly negotiating the city's waterway maze. She had the throttle wide open and was pushing the launch close to its maximum speed of ten knots. All the same, Parry found himself wishing they could go faster. For once, the restrictions imposed on the rapidity of travel by the limited power output of complementary-resonance cells, instead of cheering him, chafed. The scene of the incident, the Amadeus Hotel, was still a good quarter of an hour away, and he wanted to be there *now*. Johansen had filled him in briefly on what he could expect to find when they got there, but this served only to exacerbate his impatience. The sooner they reached the hotel, the sooner he could see for himself what had happened and begin the process of repairing the damage. That was what he desired most at this moment: to restore order to the world, to right the imbalance that had been caused by an appalling, unthinkable wrong.

He turned to Johansen, who was sitting beside him in the stern of the launch. The Norwegian had his sun-honeyed face raised to the breeze, and in this position every sinewy striation in his thick neck was visible, like the grain in wood. Parry observed that the lieutenant's jacket and trousers were too tight in several places, the sleeves riding up under his armpits, the seams along his thighs stretched taut. FPP uniforms were individually tailored, but Johansen's addiction to pumping weights and augmenting his physique to more and yet more outlandish proportions meant that he outgrew each new outfit within a matter of months. He looked schoolboyish in the ill-fitting suit, and in certain respects he *was* as unsophisticated as a schoolboy. He was also, like many habitual gym-goers, prone to favouring development of the body at the expense of development of the brain. Set against that, however, he had clear, straightforward thought processes and an engaging sense of humour, and was as loyal as the day is long. It was for these virtues that Parry, upon his promotion to captaincy two years earlier, had personally selected Johansen as his second-in-command.

'What time were we notified?' he asked.

'Avni says the call came in just after seven a.m.'

Avni was in charge of the small-hours shift for Parry's district. Any call made to the South-West's operations room between midnight and eight was handled by her personally.

'And naturally she contacted Captain van Wyk right away.'

'Um, no, not exactly, boss. She contacted me, wanting to know if your flight had landed yet.'

'And you told her that it hadn't.'

Johansen offered his senior officer a sheepish, lopsided smile. 'I have a confession to make.'

Parry already had a good idea what Johansen was going to say. 'Van Wyk doesn't know anything about this yet, does he?'

Johansen glanced at his wristwatch. 'He's probably just arriving at HQ now. I've left him an "Urgent" e-memo on his work board, but as you're going to be the first senior officer on the scene, it'll become your case. And strictly speaking, it's *your* wedge. Captain van Wyk was only minding the South-West for you while you were away.'

'He's going to be mightily pissed off he wasn't called at home, Pål.'

'Oh yes, boss. Mightily.'

'You must realize how this is going to look. It's going to look like you're getting your own back.'

Originally Parry had deputized Johansen to mind his district while he was on holiday. Van Wyk, upon learning of this, had remonstrated with Commissioner Quesnel, saying a mere lieutenant was neither worthy of nor suited to such responsibility. So great was the fuss van Wyk had kicked up, so ferocious his indignation, that in the end Quesnel had bowed to pressure and granted van Wyk himself jurisdiction over the district for the week. She had told Parry she had done this in order to preserve the peace and he had wanted to believe her. He had not wanted to think that she was simply playing favourites.

Johansen shrugged his gargantuan shoulders. 'I know.'

'I bet you anything Captain van Wyk reports you to the commissioner.'

'And she'll tell me off and there'll be an official reprimand on my conduct record. That's a price I'm prepared to pay. *You* have got to be in charge of this, boss. What we have here is too important to let a *dritt-hode* like Captain van Wyk loose on it.'

Parry, in spite of himself and the gravity of the situation, found it hard to keep a straight face. 'I have no idea what *dritt-hode* means, Pål, but I'm not sure I should be hearing you using it with reference to a superior officer.'

'It means "sweet-natured and wonderful person".'

'Really. And not something like "shit-head"?'

'No, boss.'

'Oh well, that's OK then.'

Johansen had done the right thing, the sensible thing, by keeping van Wyk out of the picture. It was not that Parry had an inflated opinion of his own abilities, rather that he had a clear understanding of Captain Raymond van Wyk's shortcomings. The fact that Johansen's deliberate error of omission would almost certainly leave van Wyk irate and fuming was, however, not a little gratifying, and Parry would not have been human if he had been unable to enjoy a brief moment of *schadenfreude* at the expense of a man he distrusted and disliked. Not wishing Johansen to see the glee in his eyes – he did not want to appear to be condoning the lieutenant's actions – he turned his head away and devoted his attention to the passing scenery.

On a palm-shaded esplanade, souvenir vendors were setting out their stalls, while municipal cleansing operatives clad in white turbans and djellabas stood doubled over, hand-pulling weeds from flowerbeds. On the staggered balconies of a ziggurat-like hotel, newly arisen tourists were taking breakfast and the morning air. At a canalside café, waiters were ministering to patrons seated at white wrought-iron tables in white wrought-iron chairs, surrounded by white planter troughs that effervesced with bougainvillaea and hibiscus. Avni steered left and the launch passed under a footbridge, a broad, graceful arc of chalk-pale stone that afforded coolness and a momentary respite from the sun's glare. Beyond the bridge they overtook two taxi-gondoliers who raised a hand from their steering-poles in salute. Parry saw a seagull perched on the backrest of a public bench. Next to it, with no more than half a metre between them, was a blue-backed, golden-breasted parrot. The grey-garbed scavenger and the tropical dandy were busily preening, each minding its own business, neither acknowledging the other, peaceably co-existing. Then there was a brief, glinting glimpse of something tall and golden-robed making its way across a distant plaza, something moving in a series of forward-bent lurches that somehow managed to appear both effortful and graceful. The Foreigner was gone almost the instant he caught sight of it, vanishing around the corner of a building, but when he closed his eyes it was retained on his retinas, a temporary after-image, a tiny blue ghost.

He thought of the fake Foreigner in Leicester Square. Already his holiday in England was starting to seem like a dream, a fugue state into which he had temporarily fallen. He could hardly believe he had been away at all. Perhaps this had something to do with the fact that he had been back in New Venice barely half an hour and was already at work again (and, moreover, on his way to the scene of a serious Foreigner-related incident). Perhaps, in order to address itself fully to the exigencies of the present, his mind considered it necessary to draw a veil over the immediate past. Or was it that, like the amnesia of trauma, the holiday was an experience he was better off forgetting?

'Nearly there,' said Johansen, pointing ahead.

Moments later, Avni pulled in alongside the Amadeus's landing jetty. Once the boat had been secured, all three FPP officers crossed the jetty and entered the hotel's lobby.

To judge by the tranquil atmosphere in the lobby, you would never have suspected that anything untoward had recently occurred on the premises. A janitor was swabbing the floor, bent over his mop, slowly and methodically slopping suds. A porter stood to attention beside a large ornamental earthenware urn, his brass-buttoned chest puffed out, his white-gloved hands tucked behind his back, his gaze focused on nothing in particular. At the reception counter, one concierge was taking a reservation over the phone while another was giving a pair of guests advice on shopping in the city, marking the locations of the best arcades on a map. Other guests, seated in armchairs around low tables, were perusing international newspapers or working at portable home boards or chatting. Voices were subdued, little louder than the background exhalation of the air-conditioning.

The entrance of two FPP officers, accompanied by a rather unremarkable-looking man in plain clothes, caused a few heads to turn, a few brows to furrow in mild curiosity, and even a couple of hearts – the kind that automatically grew nervous in the presence of authority – to quicken. Fascinated and furtive eyes watched the trio's progress across the lobby, and *pianissimo* speculations passed between neighbours as to the reason for the FPP's presence here. The assumption most readily made was that the unremarkable-looking civilian was a Siren who felt he had not been sufficiently remunerated for his services. The FPP had been summoned to negotiate a settlement between him and the Foreigner who had hired him.

The moment the concierge on the phone caught sight of the FPP officers, she curtailed her conversation and hurried off to fetch the manager.

He, Klaus Lechner, a short, stiff-necked, dapper Austrian, took a moment to recognize his district captain out of uniform. When Parry offered him SALUTATION, however, Lechner quickly returned it, and followed it with an under-and-over clench of both fists, GRATITUDE.

'This way, please,' he said, and led Parry, Johansen and Avni towards a lift. Lechner was doing his best to maintain an impression of business-as-usual calm, but his efforts were belied by the film of sweat on his forehead and the thumbprint-sized spot of choleric magenta on each cheek. Once he was alone in the lift with the three FPP officers and ascending to the eleventh floor, his façade of composure slipped completely.

'I still can't believe this,' he groaned. 'In *my* hotel! The Amadeus has won awards, you know. Stars for its catering. It's mentioned in all the best guides. So far this year two hundred and fifty-two Foreigners have taken advantage of our premium-rate rooms. We're not the Hannon or the Shibata Excelsior, but we hold our own respectably well. If word of this gets out . . .' He turned and fixed Parry with an imploring stare. 'But you'll see that it won't, won't you, Captain? I mean, no one *has* to know. You can keep the news people from finding out, can't you? Surely?'

'Since a Foreigner is involved, Mr Lechner,' Parry replied evenly, 'it's possible that under the terms of the Foreign Policy Constitution we have legitimate grounds for keeping the location of this incident secret. But I can't promise anything. To a large extent it depends on your staff.'

'My staff are utterly reliable.'

'Let's hope so. How many of them actually know what's gone on here?'

'The concierge downstairs. Another concierge, the one who found them. That's all.'

'It would be good for you if you could keep it that way.'

The lift slowed, bounced to a halt and unrolled its doors.

Officer Yoshitaka Hosokawa had been posted by Johansen to stand guard outside Room 1114. Hosokawa and Avni had been the first FPP officers on the scene and, according to Avni, the young Japanese had taken one look at what was in the room and sprinted to the bathroom to vomit. 'College boy,' she had commented to Parry with a disparaging sniff. 'And what's worse, he all but begged to come along. He was there when I took the call and he pleaded to go with me.'

'Well, you can't fault his enthusiasm,' had been Parry's reply.

Hosokawa was somewhat green-faced still, but snapped to attention as Parry approached, and even braved a smile. Parry directed a quick SALUTATION to him while Lechner set about unlocking the door using a master key-unit. Hosokawa responded with the complex interlacing of fingers that signified RESPECT, the customary manufold greeting in Oriental countries. Verbally he added, 'Good to have you back, sir.'

The door to every room in the hotel was secured with a sonic code that consisted of an individual phrase of music from a symphony movement (the symphony, for security reasons, being changed on a regular basis). Key-units specific to the room played just the single phrase, but the master key-unit played a compressed, ultra-fast version of the entire movement, blurting through from beginning to end in a matter of seconds. Lechner held the small black plastic lozenge up to the door's sensor and pressed a button, and the master key-unit emitted a faint, rippling squeal. Registering that amid all the other note combinations the appropriate phrase had been played, the heavy door unlocked itself and swung inwards.

'If it's all right with you, Captain Parry, I won't go in,' said Lechner, averting his gaze from the interior of the room. 'I've seen them once already. It was enough.'

'Of course,' Parry replied. 'No need for you to hang around outside. Just be somewhere where we can find you if we need you.'

'My office? It's on the ground floor.'

'That's fine.'

'Um, Captain?' said Hosokawa. 'If it's all right with you, I'd prefer not to go back in either.'

Parry heard Avni snort softly, and he directed a reproving glance at her. To Hosokawa, he manufolded INDULGENCE. Hosokawa returned a heartfelt GRATITUDE.

Turning, Parry entered the room, followed by Johansen and Avni. Lechner leaned in and pulled the door to behind them.

Everything in a premium-rate hotel room was built to Foreign scale, which meant larger by a sixth. The bed was a sixth bigger than king-size, the ceiling a sixth higher than average, the chairs a sixth more voluminous. It was hard, when walking in, not to feel as though you had suddenly shrunk by the same fraction. Invariably there was a moment of disorientation as your brain adjusted to the perceived change in spatial relationships around you. This reaction was more pronounced in adults than in children, since children were still growing and used to a world in which proportions were flexible. Some adults, indeed, found Foreign-scale rooms impossible to cope with and could not remain in one without suffering, sometimes violently, from dizziness and nausea.

The trick, Parry had learned, was to close your eyes as you entered and imagine the room and its furnishings to be even larger than they were. That way everything would seem normal-sized when you reopened your eyes.

As usual, the tactic worked. The sight that confronted Parry next, however, was enough to leave anyone feeling ill.

The body was sprawled, face-up, by the foot of the bed. The four limbs were bent and splayed, describing a shape not unlike a swastika. The front of the white T-shirt the body was wearing was soaked with blood. Blood also soaked the carpet around the head, lending it a sinister dark-crimson halo. The rear portion of the head was gone, destroyed, so that the corpse's cranium appeared to be half-embedded in the floor. The hair was matted with blood and clotted with soft lumps of yellow-grey tissue. More tissue, and more blood, splash-patterned the wall nearby. A gun, a large-calibre semi-automatic, lay on the carpet a few millimetres from the fingertips of the body's right hand. A faint whiff of gunpowder was detectable in the air; also a sharp, clean, meaty smell reminiscent of butcher's shops.

Johansen and Avni remained by the door, giving their captain space to step forward and inspect the body more closely. Breathing through his mouth, Parry did so.

He had been a young man. Early twenties, was Parry's guess. Thick black hair, strong nose, cleft chin. He had almost certainly

36

been handsome. An eye-twinkler. A charmer. But death had undone his glamour. His face was now sagging, slack-jawed, dull. That was the thing about the violently killed, in Parry's experience. They never looked at repose, and they seldom looked horrified or traumatized. For the most part the violently killed simply looked *stupid*, their eyelids half-closed, their expressions stultified, as though death were the most boring surprise imaginable. Or maybe it was simply that stupidity was the natural state of human beings, revealed once and for all when life was gone.

As far as Parry could ascertain, two rounds had been fired into the young man. One had entered his chest through the left half of his ribcage, just to the side of his sternum. Presumably its intended target had been the heart, but it must have missed, otherwise there would have been considerably more blood from the wound. The other round had been fired inside the young man's mouth, angled up into the skull. If there were further injuries to the body, Parry could not see them.

He turned to Johansen. 'Do we have a name?'

'We didn't find any personal effects on the body.'

'What about the room key?'

'There.' The lieutenant pointed to the bedside table.

'And you've notified the mainland criminalists, I take it?'

'They're on their way, along with the medical examiner. Boss? There's also . . . you know. The other one. Over there.' Johansen gestured towards the far corner of the room, where, beside the windows, whose curtains were still drawn, there lay a rumpled puddle of silky, glistening material. Parry had already registered this peripherally but, unwilling and unprepared to devote full attention to it yet, had chosen to concentrate on the body first. Now, drawing a deep, self-mastering breath, he stepped carefully around the dead young man and approached the windows.

The puddle of material was unmistakably the golden robe of a Foreigner. Partly hidden among its folds were a pair of matching golden gloves. Next to it, a few centimetres from the high, ruched collar, was the shining aureate ovoid of a Foreign mask, resting on its side.

Just items of clothing, mere inanimate artefacts – yet what they represented, what their presence in the room implied, made them just as disconcerting as the shattered, gory, defunct human being nearby, if not more so.

'Sir?' said Avni, after Parry had gazed down at the Foreign

remains for a silent minute. 'What's your take on this? What do you think went on here?'

Parry slid a hand backwards across his scalp until he found a patch of hair to scratch ruminatively. 'I think it's safe to assume that Pål's correct and that our friend there' – he indicated the body – 'is a Siren. Why else would somebody be in a Foreigner's hotel room if not to sing? The question is, did he top himself, as it looks like he did, or . . .?'

Murder.

That was the word Parry was trying to keep out of his brain and off his lips. Ever since Johansen had described the scene to him, he had acknowledged that homicide was a possible explanation, but he refused to accept it was the likeliest explanation. Murder? In this day and age? In this city? Inconceivable.

Yet there it was, the stark and bloody evidence in front of him. A life brutally terminated. And he had to consider the possibility that someone, some lunatic, had killed the Siren. Abhorrent though it was, he had to allow the idea head-space.

'Well,' he said, 'we'll leave it to the criminalists and the medical examiner to tell us more. That's what they get paid for.'

'And what about the Foreigner?' said Johansen. 'That's the other question. What happened to *it*? There's no damage that I can see to the clothing.'

'Maybe the sound of the gun?' Avni offered.

'Maybe,' said Parry, nodding. It had been observed that Foreigners became distressed by sudden loud noises, particularly percussive ones – although Parry had never heard of a Foreign loss being caused as a result.

'Or maybe the Siren killed the Foreigner first, then himself,' suggested Johansen.

'With what?' said Parry. 'I don't see any weapon here apart from the gun. Anyway, like I said, all that's for the criminalists to determine, if they can. Our job is to do . . . well, as much as the Constitution lets us. Which is figure out why the hell this has happened, whatever this is, and do everything we can to prevent it from happening again.' He smacked his hands together. 'All right. Rachel, I want you and Yoshi to interview every human guest on this floor. Find out if anyone saw or heard anything, anything at all. I doubt the shots were audible. These premium-rate rooms are fully soundproofed. All the same, it's worth asking. And Rachel?'

Go easy on Yoshi. Please. We were all young and inexperienced at one time or other.'

'Yes, but not all of us think our shit doesn't stink.'

'Nevertheless.'

Avni nodded, reluctantly.

Parry turned to Johansen. 'As for you, Pål – get a full statement off the concierge who found the bodies.' *Get a full statement.* Jesus, it was like being a proper copper again. And not in a good way. 'Also, track down whoever was on duty in the lobby last night and get a statement off them too. And find out what time these two came in.'

'No problem, boss.'

'I'm going to stay here and have a nose around, see if I can turn up anything before the criminalists arrive.' Parry looked away from the two officers, then looked back. 'Oh, and by the way. You don't need me to tell you this, but I'm going to anyway. Be polite. Be discreet. Let's keep the ripples to a minimum, eh?'

Johansen and Avni both manufolded ACCEPTANCE, and Parry replied with GRATITUDE.

3 STUDY

Parry had a quarter of an hour by himself in Room 1114 before the medical examiner and criminalists arrived. During that time he was able to confirm for himself Johansen's statement that the Siren was carrying no form of identification on him. Checking through the corpse's cold pockets, he found nothing except an International Currency card. He activated the IC card's tiny liquid-crystal readout and saw that it contained the equivalent of a pocketful of loose change, enough for, perhaps, a taxi-gondola ride home.

The absence of personal effects was unsurprising. Sirens preferred to travel light. A refusal to carry personal items while working was almost a badge of their trade. It made them seem – to themselves, at any rate – a breed apart, an élite, divorced from the need for mundane human paraphernalia. Part of the attraction of their job was the sense it gave of being closer than anyone else to the golden giants, of being favoured above the rest of humankind. Anonymity enhanced that feeling of superiority. Not only that, lack of ID made it harder to keep track of them. The FPP's global database of known Sirens was pitifully incomplete, accounting for perhaps a quarter of the estimated number of full-time Sirens on the planet. It suited Sirens that way. They liked to be able to come and go between resort-cities without being subject to special entry levies at Customs, the only practical method of taxing their income. Footloose and financially free was the Siren lifestyle, and if some people, including Parry, were of the opinion that in this respect Sirens were taking advantage of the resort-cities' liberalism, nevertheless it had to be accepted that singing was what the Foreigners seemed to like the most about Earth, what kept them coming here, and thus there was no alternative but to turn a blind eye to Sirens' less public-spirited practices.

Parry had a look round the room's en-suite bathroom in the hope of finding something there, anything, that might tell him more about what had happened the night before. The bath, shower cubicle, lavatory and basin – all designed for a being of Foreign proportions – were pristine, most likely having never been used for their proper purpose since their installation. The complimentary soaps, shampoos and teeth-cleaning implements were still in their cellophane wrappers and had probably not been replaced in months. Almost from the outset it had become clear that Foreigners had no toilet needs, or at least none that matched those of humans, yet premium-rate hotel rooms continued to be built with fully-fitted bathrooms, more out of a kind of stubborn courtesy than anything. In this particular bathroom nothing looked suspicious and nothing appeared to be out of place, apart from the paper hygiene seal on the lavatory, which Hosokawa had snapped aside before throwing up into the bowl. Hosokawa had flushed his vomit away, but spatters of it remained around the lavatory rim and a whiff of stomach juices was discernible in the dry, bleach-scented air. Parry remembered Avni's dismissive comment a few moments ago. Hosokawa might think his shit didn't stink, but his other digestive products certainly did.

Returning to the main room, Parry went back over to the Foreign clothing. Staring down, he tried to reconcile the inert, deflated thing in front of him with the glorious beings which swayed so sweetly and strangely through the world's squares and thoroughfares. It was difficult to believe that these items of clothing had once draped a living Foreigner, in the same way that it was difficult to believe that a conch shell had once housed a living, ambulatory gastropod. Both were discarded casings, spotless and empty and lovely, retaining no trace of the creatures that had inhabited them.

Foreigners, in the normal course of events, arrived from wherever they came from and returned there without anyone seeing them appear or disappear. They were able to transport themselves to and from Earth apparently at will, turning up fully garbed and departing the same way, and always choosing their moment so that there were no humans around, or looking in the right direction, to observe the act of matter-transference. They slipped back and forth between here and elsewhere as though they could simply open a fold in space and step through.

When, however, one of them fell victim to some violent trauma, only that which provided shape and substance beneath its gleaming apparel disappeared. The clothing itself stayed behind. People who had been on hand when such an event occurred spoke of the Foreigner losing solidity, seeming to melt away within its robe, incohering, dissipating, its gloves deflating and falling, its mask hitting the ground with a dull, ringing thud. 'Like a tent collapsing', was the somewhat bathetic description given by one of these eyewitnesses.

Not everyone was of the opinion that this sub-sartorial vanishing constituted death. Some Xenologists posited that it might in fact be an emergency escape mechanism. If, as was commonly believed, Foreigners were beings composed of invisible energy, such as soundwaves perhaps, and wore their robes, gloves and masks while on Earth purely in order to make themselves apparent and comprehensible to humans, then conceivably the shedding of that clothing was a quick means of getting out of a hazardous situation, the Foreign equivalent of a lizard detaching its tail. The ambiguity of the phenomenon was reflected in the term used to describe it – a 'loss'.

It was possible, then, that the Foreigner that had worn this outfit might still be alive. Might still be in this room, even. Unheard, unseen. Watching.

A tingle ran, spiderlike, up the back of Parry's neck, and he could not help darting a glance over his shoulder.

No. Smarten up, Jack. You're being foolish.

Tugging a cotton handkerchief from his pocket and wrapping it around his hand, he bent down to pick up the mask. The makeshift glove served a twofold purpose. It prevented him leaving his fingerprints on the mask, of course, but it also meant that he was not actually touching the mask with his skin. Immediate physical contact with a Foreigner's clothing was, to him, akin to desecration.

He raised the mask until he and it were face to face. The pose was respectful, contemplative. Whether or not he was deliberately emulating Hamlet with Yorick's skull, not even he was sure.

He had held one of these masks before, but never under such circumstances. New Venice FPP had in its possession a half-dozen complete Foreign outfits, retrieved from the sites of previous losses. Among collectors, golden giants' robes, masks and gloves fetched astronomical prices, and in order to stem this opprobrious (though not actually illegal) trade the FPP did its best to ensure that all items of Foreign clothing that turned up in a resort-city – and thankfully, they did not turn up often – were kept at that resort-city's HQ in purpose-built storage units, tucked away out of sight so that they would never suffer the indignity of being displayed as trophies in some rich idiot's dining room.

In the past, Parry had visited the storage area and viewed the contents of the various drawers there, and even handled them, always with what he hoped was an appropriate reverence. He held this mask now with the same reverence. How light it was. The masks looked solid and you expected them to weigh several kilograms, but in fact they were hollow and no heavier than a soup bowl. Sealed seamlessly, with no aperture visible anywhere, they were clearly not conventional head-masks. They seemed props more than anything, devices intended to make Foreigners recognizably hominid. Hence the crude, quasi-human features – the pair of blind indentations for the eyes, the rounded peak of the nose, the bulging, bisected ellipse that represented lips, the crude corn-row corrugations that were roughly analogous to hair. They seemed an attempt by creatures, who, in their natural state, had nothing physiologically in common with their earthly hosts, to fit in, to look right, to be as similar and familiar as possible.

Parry stared at the mask's face until he became aware of his own face reflected in the mask's surface, golden-tinged and distorted. He turned the mask this way and that, watching, with a peculiar, furtive delight, as his mirrored face rippled and undulated, as though made of melting wax. Then, remembering himself, he swiftly set the mask down, returning it as close to its former position as he could manage.

He stood up again. Looked around again.

There was a general orderliness about the room that was in stark contrast to the appalling *dis*orderliness of the two sets of remains. The made bed. The drawn curtains. The fixtures and fittings, polished and dust-free. All the pieces of furniture in their rightful places, just so.

Hotel rooms never reflected the characters of those who inhabited them. They were merely stage sets through which guests flitted, and between uses they were tidied up, purged of all traces of previous tenancy, re-minted, rendered shipshape again, readied for reoccupation. In due course even this one, once the body and the Foreign garments had been taken away and the bloodstains had been swabbed off the wall and scrubbed out of the carpet, would be as new again. It would be as though nothing had occurred here.

New Venice was a city of transitory lives.

Transitory deaths, too.

A soft knock at the door announced the arrival of the criminalists. They were a pair of Moroccans, dapperly dressed and toting large steel equipment cases, and they entered the room as Parry had done, closing their eyes then reopening them. With them was another Moroccan, the medical examiner, a man whose dour, jowly demeanour put Parry in mind of an Arabic Alec Guinness. The medical examiner introduced himself as Dr Hussein Erraji.

'I think we've met before, actually, Doctor,' Parry said. 'An accidental drowning near the Exchange Bank, couple of years ago?'

'Ah yes. I remember. You were Captain Balfe's lieutenant.'

'Correct.'

'A good man, Captain Balfe.'

'The best.'

'And this' – Erraji glanced soberly around the room, stroking one corner of his thick moustache – 'is not so good.'

Parry gave a rueful nod.

At a gesture from Erraji, the criminalists set down their briefcases, undid the catches, opened the lids, and began unpacking the panoply of their grim craft: white overalls, camera, fingerprint-dusting kit, adhesive tape, scrapers, tweezers, small resealable polythene sample envelopes, clear plastic bags with which to sheathe the corpse's hands.

Erraji himself, meanwhile, sheathed his own hands in a pair of latex gloves.

'You will be wanting my report as soon as possible,' he said to Parry, snapping the left-hand glove in place.

'Please, yes.'

'The autopsy will have to wait till we get the body back to Tangier. This afternoon at the earliest, more likely tomorrow. But I could send you a copy of my preliminary findings before then. Say, around lunchtime?'

'I would be in your debt.'

Erraji pointed in the direction of the Siren's body. 'This is not something the Foreign Policy Police are particularly well equipped to deal with. Death in suspicious circumstances.'

'Believe me, I'm aware of that.'

'It might be better if the mainland authorities were to become involved.'

'Might be,' Parry agreed. 'But then the Foreign Policy Constitution is quite specific. Offshore resort-cities are exempt from outside jurisdiction.'

'I was merely making a point.'

'And I appreciate what you're saying. If it's any consolation, I used to be a detective sergeant in the London Met. I have had *some* experience in this sort of thing.'

'Then this should be just like old times for you.'

'God, I hope not,' said Parry, with a sardonic grimace. At that, Dr Erraji nearly – *nearly* – cracked a smile.

4   CROTCHET

The three Moroccans set to work, and Parry, content that the scene of the incident was in good hands, opened the door to leave.

And was confronted by a vision of pure fury.

Captain van Wyk was standing in the doorway with his fist raised, surely with the intention of knocking on the door but looking, equally, as though he was about to punch someone. His face was an alarming shade of plum. The whites of his eyes were crazed with engorged capillaries. His ears were vermilion to their very tips. His scalp, visible through his close-cropped flaxen hair, glowed bright red. It was as though the whole of his head had filled to bursting with blood, and the thought that sprang to Parry's mind was that his fellow FPP captain was about to fall down dead on the spot from a catastrophic cerebral aneurysm. That would be just what this corpse-ridden room needed – a third set of remains cluttering the floor.

Van Wyk had been taken aback by the sudden, unexpected opening of the door. Now, recovering his wits, he began to bellow.

'Captain Parry! What the *fuck* is this? What in the name of *fuck* is going on? Why is it that you were informed about this incident in person and I have to find out from a fucking e-memo on my work board?'

'Van Wyk,' said Parry, quickly latticing his fingers into the hand-symbol for TRANQUILLITY. 'Please. Not here.'

Van Wyk peered over Parry's shoulder. All three Moroccans, equipment in hand, were staring at him, startled. Immediately van Wyk composed himself and, flattening his hands together at chest height and bending his nose to his fingertips, said, '*Salaam*, gentlemen.' Then, grabbing Parry by the elbow and the door by the handle, he hauled the former out of the room and pulled shut the latter.

'Well?' he demanded, tugging Parry brusquely along the corridor. 'Can you explain Johansen's actions?' Anger made van Wyk's Afrikaans accent more pronounced, so that he chopped off words

46

and flattened vowels with greater than usual vehemence. 'Because I can tell you this for free, that muscle-bound Nordic oaf has fucked up big time! Flagrant bloody disobedience. Quesnel is going to hear about this, and you can bet your arse I'm going to push for a suspension, Parry. Without pay. You can bet your fucking arse, oh yes!'

By the time van Wyk finished this profanity-garnished speech, he and Parry had reached the end of the corridor, which gave directly on to a broad communal balcony. Emerging into the open air, the two men halted. New Venice lay spread out before them, bone-white and brilliant. The canals were busier than earlier and more pedestrians were out and about, enjoying the day while it was still pleasantly hot, before the shadows grew short and the sun bore down with its full ferocious force.

'Look, van Wyk,' Parry said, in a placatory tone, 'I'm not about to defend what Lieutenant Johansen did.'

'Too bloody right you're not.'

'But I wouldn't be surprised if he didn't do the wrong thing for all the right reasons. You have your own district to run, after all, and Johansen obviously felt you've got enough on your plate already without having to handle an incident like this in my wedge as well. He knew I was coming back this morning and, well, it may have been misguided of him, but I believe he had your best interests at heart.'

'Please do me the courtesy of at least pretending not to think I'm a moron,' van Wyk snorted. 'Johansen resents the fact that I prevented him from playing captain for a week. Also, because this is a major incident here, he didn't want me to take charge of it because he knew I'd deputize one of my own lieutenants as my second-in-command instead of him. He's an ambitious bastard, that Johansen, although I dare say you don't realize that.'

Van Wyk calling someone else ambitious? Here was a man who was seven years Parry's junior and yet of equal rank within the New Venice FPP. A man who had scaled the ladder of command in half the time it had taken Parry, powering his way upwards through a combination of obsequiousness, shameless self-promo-tion, good old-fashioned brown-nosing and, as even Parry had to admit, great efficiency, too. A man who rubbed everyone up the wrong way except the right people. A man who was so cosy with Commissioner Quesnel that he was known around Headquarters, scurrilously, as QT – short for Quesnel's Tampon.

47

Parry refrained from drawing van Wyk's attention to the irony, however. He also refrained from voicing the suspicion that what irked van Wyk most was not that Johansen had failed to observe proper procedure but that responsibility for the incident had, by fair means or foul, fallen to Parry rather than him.

Instead, adopting a conciliatory tone, he said, 'Well, what's done is done. Johansen acted in good faith and made a mistake. Feel free to report him if you wish, but the fact remains, for better or worse I'm in charge here, and I'd really appreciate it if you would respect that and give me the space and support I need.'

It was galling to have to abase himself before van Wyk, like a dog submissively showing another, more vicious dog its belly, but a good FPP officer was, if nothing else, a skilled and self-effacing diplomat.

'Yes, well,' said van Wyk. The colour was beginning to fade from his face. 'The point is rules, isn't it? Rules must be observed.'

'I couldn't agree more.'

'And trust.' Van Wyk pointed to his bronze lapel badge, with its engraved logo of a pair of hands intricately enfolded – right index finger curled over the lower joint of the left little finger, the other three fingers of each hand clasping the opposite hand, the thumbs tucked away – and, beneath this, the letters FPP. 'That's why we carry this around on our chests,' he said, and directed a sneer at Parry's civilian clothing. 'Those of us in uniform, that is. The manifold for TRUST. If FPP officers can't trust one another, what chance do we have of the public and Foreigners trusting *us*?'

'Quite.'

'All right. Very well.' Van Wyk was still annoyed, but at least he had had a chance to vent his feelings. 'This is your show then, Parry. Make sure you run it well. After all, we can't have Foreigners getting into their heads that New Venice is a dangerous place, can we? Not unless we want to end up like Koh Farang.'

'Absolutely not.'

'Now *there* was an object lesson in the inadequacy of the Constitution.' Van Wyk jabbed an emphatic finger at Parry. 'A quick, hard crackdown on the perpetrators would have sorted everything out in no time. Round them up and chuck them out of town, that would have been the way to do it. But of course that wasn't possible, was it? Instead our people had to fuss about trying to get them to make a formal apology to the golden giants. An apology, for God's sake!'

By now van Wyk's face was merely a deep rose-pink and he was speaking at near-normal volume. So as not to antagonize him afresh, Parry worded his reply carefully. 'If an occasional failure is the price that has to be paid for retaining the moral high ground, then so be it. Better that than a return to the bad old days.'

'None the less, sometimes you need to deal with people roughly to get results. Sometimes you have to do the wrong thing for all the right reasons.'

'You know I have to disagree with you there.'

'Really? And yet isn't that how you yourself, just a moment ago, described Lieutenant Johansen's little slip up?' Van Wyk's grin was broad and smug. Trap sprung. Point scored.

'Apples and oranges.' The rejoinder sounded lame, even to Parry himself. 'You're not comparing like with like.'

'Am I not? Really? Well, perhaps. But the fact is Koh Farang put the wind up a lot of people, Parry. A lot of important people. You'd do well to bear that in mind.'

Forcing on a smile of egregious sincerity, Parry said, 'I will, van Wyk. Thank you.'

Van Wyk, satisfied that he had made his point, offered Parry FAREWELL and a nod, and headed back indoors and off along the corridor towards the lift.

Parry, turning, strolled over to the balcony's edge. There he rested his forearms on the parapet and contemplated the view.

His eyes were on New Venice, but his mind was on Koh Farang.

A year and a half ago there had been a string of brutal assaults against Foreigners visiting Thailand's main offshore resort-city. The culprits were members of an eschatological sect who were aggrieved that the coming of the golden giants had cheated them of the climactic global orgy of death and destruction which they had been looking forward to and which, for a while, had indeed seemed close to becoming a reality. Forced to rethink its beliefs, the sect had fixated on the Foreigners, deciding that they were agents of a worldwide occult conspiracy and that their purpose on Earth was to brainwash and subjugate the masses, starting with Sirens and continuing from there. In order to free humankind, the sect appointed itself the task of purging Earth of the golden giants, starting with Koh Farang. Their strategy was crude but effective. A sect member, posing as a Siren, would hook a Foreigner with his singing. An accomplice, in the guise of a *tuk-tuk* driver, would then transport both of them to the Foreigner's hotel, but along a route that took them through a dark secluded alleyway where other sect members would be lying in wait. The ambushers would leap out, haul the Foreigner out of the *tuk-tuk*, and set about it with baseball bats until it collapsed within its clothing and was lost. After seven or eight such attacks, the golden giants began giving Koh Farang a wide berth, and nowadays the humanmade atoll stood all but empty, a husk of itself, its purpose gone, inhabited by just a few solitary individuals who wandered the dusty, litter-strewn streets in a daze, like the survivors of an air raid or an earthquake.

Could a similar fate befall New Venice? Could it, too, become a pariah place, shunned for fear that the disaster it had suffered might somehow be contagious?

Parry could not see that happening. He could not see a set of circumstances which might lead to disarray in the ordered, stable city in front of him. He could not see how, even with one of their number lost in this very hotel, Foreigners would begin to shy away from New Venice in large numbers.

He could not envisage such an outcome mainly because he was scared to do so.

5 NOTES

In his office at FPP HQ, Parry ate a lunch of grilled chicken salad and went over every piece of information so far accumulated about the Amadeus Hotel incident, typing notes into a case-folder on his work board. Outside his window the light was infernally dazzling. The sun was at its zenith, shade was at a premium, and anyone with any sense was indoors. This was the period of the day when, on canals and plazas, activity ceased; New Venice was still; Sol was dominant.

The morning's questioning had yielded precious few additional facts. According to Johansen, the Foreigner had checked into Room 1114 the previous day at around four p.m. What time it went out to search for a Siren was unclear. One Foreigner crossing a lobby looked indistinguishable from another, after all. Likewise, what time it returned with the young man in tow was also unclear. The concierge on night duty reckoned that a Siren matching the young man's description *might* have turned up with a Foreigner at around midnight, but could not say so with any certainty. The concierge had cultivated the habit, as had most hotel employees, of discreetly ignoring Sirens and their comings and goings. What he could say with confidence was that an electronic request for an early morning wake-up call had come down from Room 1114 shortly after half-past one. The hotel's computer records confirmed this, logging the message at one thirty-seven a.m.

The wake-up call had been timed for seven a.m. At the appointed hour, the computer rang the room three times at five-minute intervals. When, after the third attempt, the wake-up call was still not acknowledged, one of the early-shift concierges went upstairs with a master key-unit. She was the one who had found the bodies.

Johansen reported that the woman was coping well. She had been an accident and emergency nurse before moving to New Venice, had seen similar and worse scenes in her time, and so was sanguine about the sight of blood. Trauma counselling had been offered to her but would most likely be unnecessary.

As for Avni and Hosokawa, they had drawn a blank in their interviews with other guests on the eleventh floor. Of the half-dozen humans staying in standard-rate rooms on that floor, not one had seen or heard anything out of the ordinary during the night.

The lack of corroborating evidence almost made Parry wish for closed-circuit surveillance in New Venice. Almost. But then he had never been in favour of video cameras as a law-enforcement tool. They undermined public trust and made police officers lazy, turning them into glorified security guards. The red diode, in his view, was no substitute for the blue lamp.

So this was all he knew, all he had to go on: sometime between one thirty-seven and seven a.m., a Foreigner and a Siren had taken their own lives – or had had them taken.

There was more to it, though. Something was nagging at him, some small but crucial anomaly. What? What was it? He didn't know. He knew only that, like a splinter embedded in the skin, too deep for tweezers, he should not worry at it and risk driving it further in. Left alone, it would eventually work its way up to the surface of its own accord.

He was just finishing off the salad when a fanfare announced the arrival of Dr Erraji's preliminary report at his work board.

The report (which bore all the hallmarks of having been run through a Chambers language-enhancement program in order to polish up the doctor's written English, rendering it more fluent and idiomatic) augmented slightly, but not by much, the sum total of Parry's knowledge about the incident. Erraji narrowed down the time of death, at least as far as the Siren was concerned, to between one and two in the morning. He added that gunshot residue tests on swabs taken from the deceased's right hand indicated that it had held and fired the gun at least once, suggesting that the Siren's fatal wounds might well be self-inflicted. If so, then the shot to the chest must have come first (and, to judge by the starring of the skin around the entrance wound, had been fired with the muzzle of the gun in close contact with the victim). The shot to the head, fired inside the buccal cavity, had therefore been second. The reverse order, Erraji remarked dryly, was highly improbable.

'Given that two shots were fired rather than one,' he wrote, 'it may be that a third party was responsible. The shot to the chest sufficiently debilitated the victim to allow the killer to wrap the victim's hand around the gun when firing the second. The resulting gunshot residue on the deceased's skin would create the appearance of self-termination and disguise the truth of the crime. Placing the gun next to the deceased's hand would compound this impression. However, I submit that there is a stronger case for arguing that this death is what it seems to be, a suicide. Assuming the deceased was sufficiently determined to end his life, having failed to secure that goal with the first shot he could still have retained the necessary self-awareness and presence of mind to administer the second shot in a manner more certain to bring success.'

Parry highlighted the last two sentences onscreen, and read on.

The gun, Erraji said, was of German manufacture, a Köchel and Haas 9mm. recoilless semi-automatic, roughly twenty years old, not in the best condition but still serviceable. The serial number had been filed off and the trigger mechanism showed no indication of having been fitted at any time with a government-issue locking bolt. Both these facts pointed to a black market provenance. Only two bullets in the clip had been used. Ballistics analysis would verify whether or not they were same two bullets that had been discharged into the young man, but in all likelihood they were.

As for the Foreigner, its garments would undergo atomic fluorescence spectrometry to determine their authenticity. Other than that, there was very little that could be done in the way of analysis. If the garments were of non-terrestrial origin, then it had to be inferred that the Foreigner they had clad was no longer in existence. 'I could,' Erraji commented, 'embark here on a foray of speculation into the nature of Foreign corporeality, but it would profit neither of us. Whether Foreigners are beings of solid sound energy, or they are made of flesh and blood and organs like us, or of some other substance with no earthly analogue, makes no difference from a medical point of view. Until there is proof, there is only conjecture, and if, as a medical man, conjecture is all I have to offer, then I am better off offering nothing at all.'

Reading these words, Parry half-smiled. He knew how Erraji felt. Still, after all these years, the Foreigners were pure enigma. Humankind, for all its ingenuity, for all its scientific prowess, remained at a loss to fathom them. Reams of Xenological theory had been written, but the list of proven facts about the golden giants would have left room to spare on the back of the proverbial postage stamp. That, to Parry, was part of their charm. The Foreigners reminded a race which could split atoms, chart invisible stars and rearrange the insides of living cells that there were things it might never comprehend, answers it might never learn, goals it might never achieve. They were a salutary reminder against hubris, wandering about in plain view, there for all to see.

'As for the actual cause of the Foreign loss,' Erraji continued, 'again I have only conjecture. It is impossible even to determine whether, as at Koh Farang, a blunt instrument was used since the material from which Foreign robes are fabricated does not retain traces of substances with which it comes into contact. We simply do not find the usual hairs, carpet fibres, flecks of paint, foodstuffs, not even so much as a grain of pollen adhering to its surface. Perhaps Foreign clothing has been designed to repel all traces of its immediate environment in order to ensure its wearer's hygiene or safety. I do not know. In the end, all I can say is that your guess as to how the golden giant was lost is as good as mine.'

Parry copied Erraji's communication into the case-folder, then took off his reading spectacles and rubbed his eyes. He felt weary and bleary, his brain blunted and not operating at its best.

A cup of tea. That might help.

As he was leaving his office, he was intercepted in the corridor by Hosokawa.

'Sir,' said the young Japanese, fixing his hands into RESPECT, 'I was wondering if I might have a word.'

'Certainly. Didn't you come off shift at eight?'

'I've been putting in a few hours' extra duty on the front desk.'

'Good lad. I'm on my way to the commissary. Mind walking with me?'

Hosokawa fell in step beside him. He was a smooth-faced, graceful and slightly fey young man, with chisel-sharp cheekbones and a millimetre-perfect haircut. Parry knew that he had a good brain and admired him for his keenness, but also felt (though not as strongly as Avni) that Hosokawa's youth and relative rawness meant he was not ideally suited to the role of Foreign Policy Policeman. Hosokawa had been one of the beneficiaries of a recent FPP Council initiative to recruit from outside the sphere of law enforcement and thus broaden the FPP's demographic composition. A university education and a head full of noble intentions were, however, no substitute for experience of life. In Parry's view, to be a good FPP officer you needed to have knocked around a bit. You needed to understand people, and *like* people. Hosokawa gave little indication of affinity for his fellow humans. He gave off, in common with many of the well-educated, an air of diffidence bordering on scorn. But he was determined to do well at the job and in the end that quality, Parry was sure, would prove to be his saving grace.

'It's about the incident this morning, of course,' Hosokawa said, adding, 'the deaths, I mean,' in case Parry might think he was referring to his regurgitant reaction to the sight of the Siren's body.

'Yes?'

'I was prevented from mentioning this to you by, um, circumstances at the time, but the scene in that room reminded me of a tradition we have in my homeland. Well, not a tradition exactly. More a bad habit. We call it *shinju*.'

As they reached the lift, the doors slid open. Parry stepped inside. Hosokawa, after hesitating a moment, as if expecting an invitation, followed him in.

'*Shinju*,' Parry said, pressing the button for Floor E, two floors down, 'that is?'

'When lovers, teenagers usually, find that their families disapprove of their liaison and want them to split up, they make a pact and kill themselves together. That is *shinju*.'

The doors kissed shut and the lift began to descend.

'A lovers' suicide pact? You think that was what we saw at the Amadeus?'

'It appeared to me as if it might have been, yes – although of course I didn't have a long look around the room.'

Parry summoned up the scene in his mind: Room 1114, the empty Foreign clothing, the messy gangle of human remains. Was it possible? Had these two members of utterly different species fallen in love and, recognizing the impossibility of their situation, taken their own lives? Found perfect consummation in death?

A note – F above middle C – bonged from the speaker on the lift-button panel, announcing that they were passing the third floor.

He shook his head. No, it didn't seem right. If nothing else, the relationship between a Foreigner and a Siren was supposed to be business. Strictly business. The Siren provided a service and the Foreigner paid for it. Handsomely, usually.

But there had been cases, hadn't there? Instances of Sirens and Foreigners forming strong bonds, becoming almost inseparable for a while, travelling together, sightseeing together (at the Foreigner's expense, naturally). The Siren becoming a sort of paid companion, on hand to sing whenever the golden giant required. Between two humans it was feasible that such a relationship might develop into love. But between a *Foreigner* and a human?

E above middle C chimed out from the speaker, and the lift sighed to a halt.

'It's an interesting theory, Yoshi,' Parry said as the doors opened. He stepped out, turned and signed GRATITUDE. 'Thank you for mentioning it.'

A smile twitched the corners of Hosokawa's mouth and he manufolded ACCEPTANCE and RESPECT to his captain.

Deep in thought, Parry strolled along the corridor to the commissary. There, he ordered a tea (milk, no sugar) from Carmen behind the serving counter.

'You'll be wantin' some ginger cake with that,' Carmen said. This was neither a question nor a suggestion. Carmen, a bulbous, ebullient Barbadian, had made it her mission in life to encourage everyone she met, especially those like Parry who erred on the skinny side, to eat more. She was a doctor dispensing her own prescription for happiness – food.

'You can put a slice on my saucer, but you know it'll only stay there.'

Carmen expressed her disapproval, sucking her tongue against the sides of her mouth. 'How you speck to find a woman want to be your wife, Captain, you stay so bony?'

'It's a risk I'm prepared to take.'

The tea was handed to him with a slice of ginger cake duly lodged beside the cup.

It was while he was in the lift on the way back up to his office that Parry realized abruptly what had been bothering him about the incident, the nagging anomaly. It was, now that he saw it, kick-yourself obvious.

The wake-up call. Why had someone in Room 1114 requested a seven a.m. wake-up call? If the death and loss really were suicides, surely the last thing on anyone's mind yesterday night would be making sure they got up on time the following morning. Which meant either that suicide had been a last-minute decision, or else that the suicidees wanted to be discovered.

If the latter, why? To make a point? And, if so, *what* point? Besides, they would have been discovered soon enough even without the wake-up call. At some stage during the day a chambermaid would have gone into the room to clean it. So, apart from ensuring that their remains were found earlier than they otherwise might have been, the wake-up call had no clear purpose.

That was, if the incident had been a double suicide. If it had been a double murder, then presumably the request for the wake-up call had been made before the perpetrator attacked. Or else the perpetrator was eager for his or her handiwork to be made known.

Parry re-entered his office, fully intending to sit down and mull over the problem further and at the same time enjoy the tea. No sooner had he set the cup down on his desk, however, than Johansen appeared in the doorway.

'Boss? Commissioner wants to see you.'

The lieutenant was looking haggard, like someone who has just witnessed a serious car crash.

'I take it she's just been talking to *you*,' Parry said.

Johansen gave a pained smile. 'I hate it how she speaks so softly when she's angry. I'd much prefer it if she would yell.'

'Suspension?'

'Oh no. Like I thought, a reprimand on my file.'

'Well, that's something.'

One in the eye for van Wyk, he thought.

With a forlorn glance at the tea, which was too hot to drink now and would be too cold to drink by the time he returned, Parry left his office again.

6 BRASS

Quesnel's office, on Floor Upper C, was dominated by a vast circular window behind the commissioner's desk which provided a view of the Fourth Canal, one of the eight main aqueous arteries which radiated out, spoke-fashion, from Hub Lagoon, dividing the city up into eight arc-shaped districts. The entire length of the canal was visible, stretching all the way to the sea and traversed at intervals by footbridges that diminished with perspective until the most distant appeared as slender as a strand of spider's silk. Set into the centre of the window was a stained-glass representation of the FPP logo picked out in shades of gold – TRUST superimposed over the city.

Quesnel rose from her chair as Parry entered. She was a tall woman, strong-jawed and handsome, who never wore anything but the bare minimum of make-up. Her ash-grey hair hung in a collar-length ponytail, fastened at the back by a tortoiseshell clip, and her eyes were such a sparkling, startling blue that it was often assumed, by those who did not know her well, that she wore tinted contact lenses. Quesnel, however, would have been the last person to indulge in such cosmetic vanities. She was of straight-talking, no-frills Canadian stock, a former RCMP colonel who had been brought up by strict French Catholic parents in Saskatchewan, not far from the training facility at Regina where she had undergone her initiation into the mysteries of Mountie craft.

All Parry knew about Quesnel's private life, other than the foregoing, was that she had a husband who lived somewhere near Montreal. Though not divorced, it was clear she had no intention of returning to the fellow at any stage or of inviting him to join her in New Venice, and Parry suspected that whatever had gone awry with her marriage she herself was in no small part to blame for. Céleste Quesnel was not a forgiving person. She demanded high standards from those around her and was swift to chide when they were not met – although, to her credit, the highest standards of all were those she demanded from herself.

'Jack, come on in,' she said affably. 'Normally I'd want to know what you're doing out of uniform, but Lieutenant Johansen explained everything to me. Tell me how your trip went.'

'It was fine. Cold, but' – he searched for a euphemism – 'rewarding.'

'Doesn't sound like fun.'

'I wasn't expecting windsurfing and margaritas.'

'So you're glad to be back.'

'Delighted.'

'Though I guess this business at the Amadeus ain't exactly the ideal homecoming.'

'I don't know. There's nothing quite like diving in headlong after a break, is there? To get you back into the swing of things.'

Quesnel laughed. 'Sit down, Jack.'

Parry positioned himself in the padded, leather-upholstered swivel chair that faced the commissioner's desk, which was a vast chunky lozenge of crystech the colour of lapis lazuli, complete with an inbuilt work board. Quesnel, still standing, paused the work board and pushed the screen flat into its recess so that they would not be interrupted.

'So,' she said, 'tell me what you've got so far.'

Parry recited every detail he could remember about the lost Foreigner and dead Siren. 'Pending full reports from the medical examiner and the forensics labs in Tangier, that's it.'

'Not a lot.'

'Johansen and I will go out this evening before Sirensong to ask around. We probably won't have much joy, but at least we can try.'

'What about Xenophobes? You thought about making enquiries in that direction at all?'

'With the greatest of respect, ma'am, this doesn't have any of the hallmarks of a Xenophobe action.'

'Not even a Triple-X action?'

'I assumed that's who you were referring to.'

'And you think they weren't responsible because . . . ?'

'Because it happened somewhere private, not somewhere public. When Triple-Xers commit one of their atrocities, they do it in a way that'll get as much attention as possible – like the fire-bomb attack on the Bridgeville Hilton last September. Besides, Captain Roldán negotiated the repatriation of a Triple-X cell just a couple of months ago, didn't he? And there's no intelligence to suggest that any of them have crept back into the city.'

'They may have. It doesn't take many to form a Triple-X cell. Two people, three – that's all.'

'I take your point, ma'am. I'm just not convinced this is the sort of thing Xenophobes, even militant-extremist Xenophobes, would do.'

'Well, if that's your considered opinion, Jack, I'm happy to go along with it. But I'm going to have to push you a bit here.' Quesnel perched one buttock on the edge of her desk and leaned towards Parry. 'If this isn't terrorism, what is it?'

Parry hesitated. 'I wish I could lie and tell you I have an idea, ma'am, but the truth is I don't. We've come across lost Foreigners before, of course, and dead Sirens, but not often, and never together like this, in the same room at the same time. Bad enough that we have a human fatality. But what were the Foreign remains doing there? Why was it lost? *How* was it lost?'

'Too many questions, Jack. I need statements of fact.'

'Foreigners, ma'am.' Parry gave a hapless shrug. 'They're one big question mark.'

The commissioner stood up and strode over to the window. 'I appreciate your difficulties,' she said, looking out, 'but I have to have something to tell the FPP Council and our NACA Liaison, something more than mere speculation. So let me ask you straight. What happened in that room?'

'Ma'am, I really cannot say at present. Perhaps once I have more on the Siren, his personality, his history, then I can start piecing together a theory. Until then . . .' He shrugged.

'Fair enough. But in your opinion, was this incident a one-off, or are we looking at the start of something, some kind of pattern or trend?'

'Again, ma'am, I really can't say.' Parry injected a note of bemused exasperation into the reply. Surely the commissioner must appreciate that she was seeking an assurance from him that he could not give.

Quesnel turned and fixed him with her blazing blue eyes. 'Jack, this is me you're dealing with, not some hack from the *Clarion*. I want to know your real thoughts on this, not what you think I ought to hear.'

'Yes, ma'am. Sorry, ma'am.'

'So?'

'So you want to know if this was a one-off?'

'Yes.'

'Commissioner—' the awkwardness of his position necessitated a thicker than usual lacquer of politeness— 'I can't predict that we won't find the remains of a Siren and a Foreigner together in a room again at some point in the future. I can only say that at this stage there is no obvious indication that the incident, whatever it was, will be repeated.'

'Jack.' Quesnel's eyes were blazing more intensely than ever.

Oh God, Parry thought. Here it comes. The wrath of Quesnel. She didn't use up her quota for the day on Johansen. There's still some left over for me.

A pair of fine, curved creases (like opening and closing parentheses) formed on either side of her mouth as Quesnel smiled. 'You're so *English* when you get wound up, you know that? Listen, I didn't mean to put you on the spot. It's just that, you know how nervous the Council has been lately.'

'Since Koh Farang.'

'Since Koh Farang. So when I conference with them on this, which I'm due to in about an hour, I'd like to be able to tell them that one of my most trusted and respected captains is confident it was an isolated event.'

'But now, because you can't tell them that . . . ?'

'I won't.'

'That's a promise?'

There was a note of rebuke in Quesnel's reply. 'You know it is.'

'Yes. Of course, ma'am. I'm sorry.'

'No need. Sometimes I forget how hot you are on this honesty thing.'

'Aren't we all?'

'I'd sure as hell like to think so. But you more than most, Jack.'

'It's no secret that I believe we have a duty, now that the Foreigners are here, to be the best that we can be,' Parry said. 'They've given us so much. Most of all a second chance – a second chance we didn't really deserve. The least we can do is show our gratitude by behaving well towards them *and* towards one another. And they're so skittish, that's the other thing. Like rabbits or deer. You get the feeling that they could bolt at the slightest provocation. Simply turn and run and never be seen again. They'd wipe this city from their tourist brochures.'

'And we'd all be out of a job.'

'That's not why it would be a tragedy, ma'am. I don't care about our jobs. I care about New Venice. I care about what it represents. A step forward for humanity, a new way of doing things, a glimpse of how the entire world could be.'

'That's an awful lot of significance to put on just a town, Jack.'

'Maybe so. But this *is* a special place. I think you know that too. And it would be a hell of a shame to see it go the way of Koh Farang.'

'You think that might happen because of this Amadeus thing?'

'No. But it might happen if we're not constantly vigilant. I don't mean just the FPP. I mean everyone here. The Foreigners are a kind of, I don't know, living litmus test for our behaviour. As long as they keep coming here, it means that we're still managing to do something right.'

'Or simply that we have good Sirens.'

'If you wish to be cynical, yes. I'd rather think that the Sirens are just the icing on the cake, that it's New Venice itself that attracts Foreigners. The beauty of it, the architecture, the atmosphere. People are happy here, visitors and residents. They're courteous, they're welcoming. And I'd like to believe that Foreigners are drawn to that and that the presence of the FPP guarantees that they'll continue to come.'

Quesnel smiled, shaking her head. 'Jack, you truly are one of the most – well, I would say naïve, but I know you're not that. Virtuous. One of the most virtuous people I've ever come across.'

Parry manufolded ACCEPTANCE – both palms spread out, fingers latticed, thumb tips touching. 'No one quite so virtuous as the reformed sinner, is there?'

'Don't ask me, ask St Paul.'

'There you go. Case in point.'

'Yup.' Quesnel nodded. 'And I have to say, I'm not unhappy that it was you who got to be in charge of this situation, Jack. I think it's going to need your delicate touch.'

This oblique reference to van Wyk surprised and pleased Parry. 'I'm going to do the best I can, ma'am.'

'Of course you are. But in the meantime, while you're investigating, I feel we should keep a tight lid on this thing. Measure Seven of the Constitution. It's not in the public's interest to know about this right away. We don't want people jumping to conclusions. We especially don't want Sirens getting twitchy. If the Sirens get twitchy, they might start to leave. They're as skittish in their way as Foreigners, don't you think?'

'They're certainly not too fussed which resort-city they stay at. One's as good as another to them.'

'Exactly. Also, we want to keep the Xenophobes especially Toroa MacLeod out of our hair.'

'Unless they already know what's happened.'

'Well spotted, Jack. They make a squeak before we've gone public on this, and it'll tell us one of two things. Either they have well-plugged-in spies, or . . .'

'Or they had a hand in it.'

'Bingo. We'll see if we can't trip them up here.'

'Agreed.'

'Everything's clear, then?'

'Clear as crystech.'

'Good.' Quesnel pressed the spring catch of her work-board screen, which gently rose from her desktop until it was a few degrees from vertical. Parry took this as a signal that the interview was at an end. He stood up.

'Squirt me over a copy of your case-folder on this one, will you?' Quesnel said.

'Of course.'

'Oh, and Jack?'

Parry paused, halfway to the door.

'Do me a favour. Stay virtuous.'

INTERLUDE

One Decade Ago . . .

You've been avoiding the casket all day. Others have been going up and paying their respects, but you have been nervous, scared even, about approaching it. You've no desire to look at him close up. You've glimpsed his face, his hands, from across the room. You don't like the thought of seeing him lying there, full-length, in a suit he never wore while he was alive. It would make it too real for you, too final. And so you've kept coming up with excuses to stay out of the room, to hang around in the kitchen area and hallway. Sooner or later you're going to have to pluck up the courage and walk over to him and say goodbye, but not yet. Not just yet.

People have been coming in and out of the house since morning, drinking coffee, eating food, talking with your mother, offering their condolences. Your mother's completely out of it, zombified, so it's been up to you to play the host. Everyone's been telling you how brave you are, how well you're handling your loss. Everyone's been saying to you if there's anything they can do, anything at all to help, just let them know.

You think to yourself: Yeah, you can bring my dead dad back to life. But you say to them: Thanks, no, there's nothing you can do, but thank you for asking.

You are learning something here. How to think one thing and say the opposite. Separate your behaviour from your feelings. And somehow you sense that this will prove a valuable lesson.

Talk drifts to and fro with the visitors. You hear them say what a talented man your father was. You hear them say he didn't get the breaks he deserved. You hear them say it was a case of bad timing. Your father didn't know how to move with the times. Too proud, too stubborn. You hear them say what a waste, what a shame. One man, some record company executive your father knew, a slimy creep, you overhear saying that your dad and his kind are extinct. Like the dinosaurs, a meteor has come and wiped them out. The comment wasn't intended for your ears, but still you have to fight the urge to go over and punch the guy's lights out. Your father was worth ten of him. A hundred of him. You're only fourteen years of age, but you feel you could happily kill the record company executive.

Finally the time comes. You know you can't put it off any longer. The room has emptied. The room is quiet. Slowly you venture towards the casket, which sits on trestles in one corner. Tentatively you present yourself before the body of your father.

Everyone who has seen him has said what a good job the morticians have done. So serene, they've said. So lifelike.

But he doesn't look lifelike to you. His cheeks were never that rosy, his skin that pale, his lips that red. What everyone means, you think, is that the morticians have covered up his injuries well. His shirt collar is pulled up right under his chin. You'd never know he hanged himself. You'd never know that the steel guitar string he used for a noose all but severed his head from his neck.

He always said he wanted to be buried with his Feldman Starshine, his prize possession, but in his suicide note he stipulated that the guitar was to be sold off to pay for the funeral and this party. So he lies there with nothing in his arms, just a corpse in a suit. Your mother has, however, stuck one of his guitar picks between his right thumb and forefinger. The small triangle of black plastic is her small tribute. She's also placed a folded, handwritten note in the casket with him. You don't need to read it to know what it says. Its content can be summarized in one word:

Why?

You stare at him, so calm in repose, so empty, so erased. You feel that someone must be responsible for this. Someone else, not him. It can't be his fault. Someone drove him to failure. Someone drove him to despair.

Tell me who it was, Dad, you say in your head. You're trembling, close to tears. Tell me who it was and I'll get them for you.

Of course, no answer comes.

You want something to remember him by. Not just him, but this moment. You want a tangible souvenir of this sombre occasion and of the vow you have, without realizing, just made.

You pluck the pick from his fingers.

No one'll notice, and even if they do, no one'll say anything. It's a funeral. No one's going to raise a fuss at a funeral over something like a guitar pick.

Later that day, when your father has been buried, you sit in your bedroom with the pick in your hand. Something similarly small and hard has lodged itself in your heart. You feel it there, scratching, chafing away, like a piece of grit inside an oyster. In time, a casing will accrete over it. A pearl will form. A dark, solid, powerful pearl at the centre of your heart that will enable you to do anything and not feel guilty about it. A pearl that will liberate you from conscience and shame.

You smile to yourself.
Let it itch.

SECOND MOVEMENT

7 FLAT

There was some paper mail in Parry's box in the hallway of his condominium. Nothing personal, just circulars that met – most of them barely – the conditions for candour and non-intrusiveness laid down in the Unsolicited Correspondence Act. Parry consigned them to the recycling chute immediately upon entering his apartment. His home board was fitted with a filter that performed the equivalent function automatically for electronic junk mail. He checked the screen. The home board had recorded forty-seven hours of television while he was away, using its knowledge of his viewing preferences to select the kind of material it thought he would want to watch. He scanned the list of programme titles and was surprised by some of the choices it had made. The TV stations must be up to their old tricks again, getting 'generous' with their content-parameter calibrations. The International Broadcast Commission would bring them back into line soon enough.

Parry pressed the 'Erase All' command. When was he going to have the time to sit through, or even sift through, forty-seven hours of TV?

The home board also held a grand total of two phone messages for him. The first had come in at seven forty-eight that morning. Caller's location: the Amadeus Hotel. Parry played it. It was Johansen saying that if for any reason he and Avni missed Parry at the airport, Parry was to go directly to the Amadeus. Drop everything. Don't even pause. Get to the Amadeus a.s.a.p.

The second message was from Anna and had come in during the afternoon. That one Parry did not play straight away, but left for later.

He unpacked his suitcases, which Avni had kindly dropped off for him, and changed out of his travelling clothes into a sweatshirt and shorts. Avni had switched his air-conditioning back on, but the apartment, though cool, nevertheless felt stuffy and unstirred. He slid open the balcony windows to let in some fresh air.

The fire had faded from the day. Evening sea breezes licked

lukewarmly around buildings and along canals, carrying snatches of sound from various sources: a cheerful cry from a bridge, friend hailing friend; the rumbling drone of a far-off airship; the mournful yowl of a Burmese cat that belonged to one of Parry's neighbours; a low conversation from a nearby balcony; the splash of somebody diving into a rooftop swimming pool; children giggling. It was not always easy to tell which direction which sound was coming from. Acoustics were deceptive in a city with water for roads.

Parry went back to his home board and summoned up Music mode. A long list of music-consumption presets presented itself onscreen, with his top ten predilections named first and high-lighted:

```
                   Reflective
                  Celebratory
           Invigorating (Vintage)
               Mellow Surrender
              Upbeat (Classical)
               Upbeat (Vintage)
                    Solitude
       Brass Band Bonanza (Vintage)
      Brass Band Melancholia (Vintage)
               Close-Harmony Chants
```

What did he fancy? Something rousing. Lack of sleep was catching up with him, tugging at him like a child who wants to leave. He needed a mental perk. He selected 'Invigorating (Vintage)', and straight away the room was filled with the strains of a tune he recognized from his youth but could not name, a jaunty pop ditty from the days when music was predominantly a personality-based commodity, sold by artist rather than type. The lyric was typically inane, a paean to an unnamed second-person lover of unspecified sex which did not shrink from such time-honoured imagery as stolen hearts and stars in heaven or the almost obligatory rhyming of 'maybe' with 'baby' and 'waiting' with 'anticipating'. None the less Parry stood and listened to the words with an undue raptness, remembering how sophisticated and adult such sentiments had seemed to his adolescent self, when pop songs were like guidebooks to a strange and exciting world he knew he was soon to enter.

The next song the home board selected dated back even further, to his father's youth, and was a rocking little number pumped along by a distorted, churning guitar figure and some powerhouse drums. Just the sort of thing, in fact, that the old man had liked to put on the stereo and sing along to in order to amuse his children.

John Parry had been tone-deaf (a trait he had bequeathed genetically to his son, along with baldness and lack of physical stature). When it came to entertaining his offspring, however, he never let his inability to hold a tune stand in his way. On the contrary, he used to make a virtue of it. He would prance about the living room, croaking hoarsely in a very rough approximation of a melody, and if the song was hard rock he would shake his head as though it were graced with a heavy metaller's long flowing locks and not a band of close-cropped hair that petered out above the level of his ears. Normally he was a reserved man, some might say even staid, and therefore when he let his hair down (so to speak) in this way, it was doubly hilarious, and his antics would leave his son and daughter helpless on the floor, doubled over, clutching their sides, laughing so hard they thought they might be sick. Things became even funnier still if their mother decided to join in by playing the put-upon, long-suffering wife, coming into the room and clucking her tongue and shaking her head despairingly at her husband's undignified behaviour.

You know you're old, Parry thought with a wistful smile, when pop music does nothing more for you than stir up memories.

As the song ground towards its fade-out and another one began, he settled down on a bare area of the living-room floor to commence his daily exercise routine. A hundred press-ups. A hundred sit-ups. Another hundred press-ups. Another hundred sit-ups, this time diagonal ones, fifty with the left elbow to the right knee, fifty vice versa.

Flushed and perspiring, he went to the kitchen and charged a glass from the refrigerator's reservoir of chilled water. As he drank the water he toyed with the notion of playing Anna's message, but again refrained. It would be a pleasure to hear her voice, but deferring the moment, revelling in the anticipation, was a pleasure in itself.

He was aware that it was sad and not a little desperate to be making such a big deal over a recording of the voice of a woman who had made it clear to him, without actually saying as much, that she no longer loved him, at least not in the way she used to. It was the kind of behaviour you might reasonably expect from a heartbroken teenager but not from a been-around-the-block bloke who was pushing fifty. All the same, he could not help himself, and indeed he would have thought less of himself if receiving a message from Anna had left him feeling incurious or indifferent.

He took a long, hard shower, then shaved off his five o'clock shadow, and completed his toilet by trimming his nostrils and ears with a pen-size electric clipper. The fact that hair no longer grew where he wanted it to, on the top of his head, but flourished luxuriantly in areas where it was undesirable, such as inside his ears and across his lower back, was, in his view, one of the greatest of the many iniquities of ageing. Greater than the decay in his close vision. Greater than the unavoidable trip to the lavatory in the early morning (he knew now why they were called the wee small hours). Greater than the accumulating scrawny sagginess of his physique, something his exercise routine could retard but not reverse. Greater, even, than the occasional aggravating lapses of short-term memory. Greater than all of these, but not perhaps as great as the sense of time accelerating as he got older, each year seeming to pass more quickly than the previous one; the feeling that he was being hastened faster and faster towards the dark, ineluctable conclusion of his life. He had only just turned forty-nine. He had a good three, four decades in him yet, almost as much time again as he had already had. But he knew that the years remaining to him, however many they were, were going to whisk by with alarming speed, and somewhere near the end of them senility awaited, that clouded twilight of incontinence, incoherence and general decrepitude. And this was an uncomfortable fact that one could only cope with by ignoring it, and so, as usual, he told himself not to think about it.

Back in his bedroom, he took his uniform out of the wardrobe and put it on carefully and methodically, taking his time. White shirt. Umber tie. Cream jacket and trousers. Brown shoes. Bronze lapel badge. He examined himself in the full-length wall mirror. It was good to have the kit on once more. Good to feel the cotton of the suit hanging lightly on his body. Good to be wearing the outward emblem of his vocation, especially after a day spent working in civvies. He knew from his time with the Met how much the uniform was a part of the job. You were a copper constantly, waking, sleeping, twenty-four hours a day, but never more so than when you were wearing the navy blue. That was when people looked at you differently and you knew they were seeing what you stood for rather than who you were. There might be respect in their eyes, there might be resentment, but either way they were responding to something larger, something more important, than the person in front of them. And pretty soon you yourself came to invest the uniform with the same significance. It was more than just clothing. When you were in it, you stood straighter, your mind was sharper, your senses more acute, your sense of self worth elevated.

Now at last, suited and booted, Parry felt ready for Anna's message. He approached his home board and, with something of a ceremonial flourish, selected Play Message 2.

'Jack, it's Anna. Hope you had a good time in England. Maybe you can let me know how it went when you've got a moment. Cissy says to say, "Good morrow, good sir." That's it, really. 'Bye.'

Formal. That was his initial impression. Anna using her clipped voice, the one she normally reserved for domestic staff and official purposes. Not unfriendly by any means, but making it clear that there were things to be done, and done quickly and efficiently. Her accent straying out of its native Eastern Europe towards the southeast of England. Funny how upper-class Home Counties pronunciation continued to be perceived as the stamp of authority wherever and whenever English was spoken. Still, even at the tail-end of England's long slow decline in international standing.

He played the message again.

There was more to it, of course. 'It's Anna.' A year or so ago she would have said, 'It's me', or even not announced herself at all, knowing he would recognize her voice instantly. The change was small but telling. Then there was that slight pause between 'Maybe you can let me know how it went' and 'when you've got a moment', suggesting that the subordinate clause was an afterthought, appended in order to make the first part of the sentence seem less of an exhortation, less keen. Greater warmth of tone suffused 'Cissy says to say, "Good morrow, good sir",' for with Cecilia they were on safer ground. Cecilia's affection for Parry was unproblematic. There was no need for evasion or tiptoeing when she was the topic of conversation. With 'That's it, really', however, Anna was trying to reassert her distance from him, becoming curt again. Too curt, he thought. Overcompensating. The same went for that final ''Bye'. It was barely a word, barely a syllable even. A slamming door. A falling curtain. The snipping of a thread.

Parry played the message a third time. Having analysed its discrete nuances, he now listened to it as a whole again in order to assess what his response should be. Ringing Anna back straight away was his instinctive urge, but reason dictated caution. That 'when you've got a moment' was not merely a qualifier, it was advisory, a warning. Anna was not asking him to find a window in his busy schedule to call her, she was intimating that he should ensure, or at least pretend, that his schedule was so busy and window-free that he would be incapable of calling her for a while. He was to leave it a day or two, perhaps even as much as a week. He was to act as if contacting her was of no importance to him, something to do only if he found himself at a loose end. She thought this would be good for him. It would teach him continence. Self-restraint. She was trying to wean him off her.

The trouble was, if she really wanted to wean him off her then she ought not to have rung him at all. He saw from the screen that the call had come in shortly after three p.m. That was a bit of a giveaway, in that Anna could not have been aware that he had been at work today. His leave was supposed to last till tomorrow morning. Officially he was still on holiday and she had known that. Therefore she must have expected that there was a good chance she would get to talk to him in person, and he could only interpret this as a positive sign, a tiny but encouraging indication that his patience was at long last bearing fruit. He did not believe that Anna was on the point of breaking down and recanting. No, not yet. After all she had said to him, after all her adamant declarations in the wake of her husband's death that they could not continue their affair, he could not see her suddenly caving in – telling him that she had been wrong and begging him to take her back if he would have her. He was enough of a realist for that. Still, the message and its timing gave him cause to feel faintly hopeful. Maybe the months of waiting, of holding back and biding his time, had not been in vain after all. Maybe Anna was beginning to realize that the embers of their affair were not as cold as she had thought. Maybe, in spite of herself, she, too, wanted to see them stirred, relit, rekindled.

It was getting on for seven p.m. The refrigerator was nearly empty, but from the few items in it and the non-perishables in the kitchen cupboards Parry was able to cobble together a reasonably nutritious and edible supper. He had learned to manage without a microwave oven, that godsend for all bachelors. He had, in his way, become a not unproficient chef.

By seven forty-five he was back downstairs and waiting on the condominium's jetty for Johansen to pick him up.

8 CHORUS

Armed with hardcopies of a morgue-slab head-and-shoulders photograph of the dead Siren, Parry and Johansen cruised the sites where Sirens were wont to gather of an evening.

At the Medina Maroc, no one recognized the face in the picture, which Erraji had cleaned up and composed so that now the dead young man looked merely as if he were fast asleep.

Likewise at the Place des Fontaines, no one could be found who claimed acquaintance with the young man. Parry and Johansen showed the picture to Sirens who were sitting perched on the rims of the basins of the plaza's eponymous fountains, where the air was cooled by the action of water splashing in cascades and shallow rippling rills over inner-illuminated crystech boulders. One after another the Sirens denied having ever seen or met anyone even resembling the man in the photograph.

At St Cecilia's Square the story was repeated. None of the occupants of the tables of the cafés and bars lining its periphery could help. Whenever there was a language barrier to be circumvented, Parry and Johansen had only to present the photograph and solicitously form the hand-symbol for ENTREATY. It made no difference. In reply, all they got was the silent Esperanto of shrugs and shaken heads.

At the Weillplatz, Johansen thought he had struck lucky when a fellow Scandinavian, a slim Swede roughly the same age as the dead Siren, seemed convinced that the young man in the picture was a resident of the hotel at which he himself was staying. However, when the Swede fetched a friend and compatriot with whom he shared a room and showed him the picture, the other Swede said that he knew the man his room-mate was talking about and that he bore no more than a passing likeness to the person in the photograph. Shorter, fatter, broader – only the hair and the colouring were the same.

It was close to ten o'clock when Parry and Johansen pulled up alongside what they fully expected to be their last port of call that evening, the Esplanade of Glass. Sirensong was due to begin at any moment, and once it was under way they would have little chance of obtaining a useful response to their enquiries.

While Johansen tethered the launch to an FPP-only mooring post, Parry leapt nimbly ashore and climbed the steps to the esplanade. With Sirensong so close, the atmosphere here was one of jittery carnival, both festive and restive. People, many of them in costumes or in national dress (or a parody thereof), milled about, greeting, talking, laughing, but at the same time warily eyeing up the competition. Waiters scurried. Bottle necks clinked against the rims of tumblers and wine glasses. Cappuccino machines coughed and spluttered. The occasional aromatic waft of marijuana smoke reached Parry's nostrils, and an old instinct, no longer valid, had to be suppressed. Here and there voices could be heard warming up, running through scales and arpeggios that sounded like rising and falling chants of self-assertion, egocentric mantras of *me-me-me-me-me-me meee*. Taxi-gondolas thronged the canal, dropping off fare after fare, and a handful of FPP officers were busy ushering tourists away from the scene. The tourists, hoping to capture Sirensong with their cameras and palmcorders, were reluctant to leave, but could not hold out long in the face of reason and reasonability, the two main weapons of the FPP.

Parry set to working his way through the crowd, accosting everyone he could, loners, pairs, groups, showing the photograph and asking over and over whether anyone knew the man in it. Johansen did the same, moving in the opposite direction from Parry so that they could cover as much ground as possible in the scant time that remained to them. None of the Sirens was so incautious or impolite as to shrink away when approached by an FPP officer, and each took an obligingly long and careful look at the picture, but it was obvious that their minds were on other things, and this, coupled with the habitual guardedness of many Sirens towards the FPP, meant that neither Parry nor Johansen believed they were going to have any more success here than they had had at their four previous destinations. Even if someone did recognize the dead man, it was unlikely that he or she was going to admit it, not now, not with Foreigners imminent. Who in their right mind was going to risk missing out on an evening's work because they had been stuck talking to the Foreign Policy Police when the Foreigners showed up?

Still the two men persevered, feeling it was better to try and fail than simply not try at all. And in the end, much to Parry's surprise, their persistence was rewarded.

The Esplanade of Glass took its name from the crystech sculptures positioned at intervals across its length and breadth. Modelled on the minimalist principle of reiterative musical motifs, the sculptures consisted of hexagonal columns of transparent crystal arranged in rows and tiers and, like the fountains of the Place des Fontaines, lit from beneath so that they glowed. Although all apparently identical, each of the rows of columns was subtly distinct. The gradations in height differed minutely from one to the next, and the stepped parabola each described was unique. Grown into shape by means of pure sound, crafted through tonality and frequency, the sculptures were proof of the versatility of crystech as an architectural material. Its applications could be immense and functional, as when it was providing foundations for construction or forging bridges between islands or fashioning midair walkways between the upper floors of buildings in waterlogged cities, but they could be small-scale and aesthetic too.

It was a castrato standing next to one of these sculptures who at last put a name to the dead Siren's face.

'That's Daryl,' the castrato said. 'Daryl . . . Anderson, I think his surname is. No, Henderson. That's it. Daryl Henderson.'

'You're sure?' said Parry.

The castrato nodded. He was a Scot, pale-skinned, shaven-scalped, soft with fat. A plethora of piercings glinted around his head. Mascara made black stars of his eyelashes. A tongue-stud flickered as he spoke. 'Aye.' He squinted at the picture again. 'Definitely him. He's an Aussie. Nice fellow. I saw him just the other night, actually, over at St Cecilia's.'

'The other night? Can you be a bit more specific? Might it have been last night by any chance?'

'No. No. Couple of nights ago at least. Maybe three.' The castrato flicked a glance over Parry's shoulder. No Foreigners coming. 'Aye, three nights ago.'

'And your name is?'

'Do I have to tell you?'

'No, but it would help me greatly if you did.'

'Only, I don't want to end up on the Siren register just 'cause I was doing you a favour, you know, helping out.'

'You have my word that won't happen.'

The castrato eyed Parry carefully. 'Well, if you can't trust the FPP . . .' he said finally. 'Hamish Dillon. D-I-L-L-O-N.'

Parry had out a pencil and his small spiral-bound notebook, two items of stationery he had constantly carried with him since his early days as a junior constable in the Met. He had already jotted down the dead Siren's name. Now he made a note of the castrato's, adding after it 'Falsetto?' He crossed the word out. Dillon's speaking voice sounded authentically high-pitched, and genuine castrati did tend to run to fat. Not only that, but another, more irrefutable proof of surgical subtraction floated in formaldehyde in a hermetically sealed glass jar which hung on a chain around Dillon's neck. Falsetti trying to pass themselves off as castrati used skilfully crafted rubber replicas, but the pallid, shrivelled, preserved testicles in Dillon's jar looked real to Parry. All too wince-inducingly real.

'And you know this Henderson well?' he asked.

'I know him to talk to. We were at the Conservatorio together. Different classes, though. He was a bass-baritone.'

Parry wrote down 'Conservatorio di Musica Straniera'.

'And when you met him the other night, how did he seem to you?'

'Seem?'

'His behaviour. His attitude.'

'Oh. Normal, I suppose. We didn't have a chat as such. Just hello, how's it going, that type of thing. That's all.'

'You wouldn't happen to know where he was staying in New Venice?'

'No idea.' Dillon checked over Parry's shoulder again. Then a thought occurred to him. 'Hang on a second. Shit.' He examined the picture, then peered up at Parry. '"*Was* staying". The poor wee bastard's dead, isn't he?'

Not all the Sirens to whom Parry and Johansen had so far shown the photograph had spotted this. To the ones that had the two FPP officers had given the explanation that Parry now gave to Dillon. 'We found his body this morning. We believe he may have met with an accident. We couldn't identify him, so that's why we've been asking around.' A lie, yes, but Quesnel had stipulated that the incident at the Amadeus was to be kept out of the public domain for the time being, and Parry could understand her reasoning. The prepenultimate of the nine measures of the Foreign Policy Constitution stated that *Openness and accountability for all its actions shall be among the avowed aims of the Foreign Policy Police, and in all dealings with humans and Foreigners its officers shall be wholly honest and without evasion, except in those circumstances in which it is deemed either by a senior officer or by the Council that the public interest is better served by the suppression of certain information until such time as said information may safely be revealed without fear of causing prejudice or concern and regardless upon the expiry of a period of 60 (sixty) days after said information is originally discovered.* In other words, a small white lie was permissible if it was for the greater good, which in this instance it surely was.

'An accident,' said Dillon morosely. 'Christ. Poor Daryl.'

'I'm sorry to have had to break the bad news.'

'Not your fault. He wasn't like a friend or anything. It's just, well . . . someone you know, you know?'

'I understand. One last thing. Can you tell me where you're staying? I don't think it's very likely but I may need to contact you again.'

'I'm at the . . .' Dillon hooked his thumbs together with his hands twisted away from each other, forming the S-like configuration for EXCELLENCE, which a certain Japanese megacorporation had co-opted as its company logo.

Parry wrote down 'Shibata Excelsior' and connected the words with an arrow to Dillon's name.

'Thank you very much for your help, Mr Dillon,' he said, shutting and stowing away the notebook.

'No problem. Glad to—'

Dillon broke off. A thrill was running through the crowd like an electric current. Conversations were dying away, joints and cigarettes were being stubbed out, cups and glasses drained. Everyone was looking towards the canal's edge, craning their necks for a glimpse.

They were coming. Foreigners were coming.

Parry stepped back, giving Dillon room. This was nothing to do with him now. He had no place here any more except, perhaps, as an observer. This, now, was a time for Foreigner and Sirens. For manufolds and vocal preening. For the hooking of clients and the selling of selves.

Sirensong.

The sound began near the water. A dozen throats all at once opened, a dozen voices began to fashion impromptu arias, a dozen mouths shaped fas and las and oohs and mmms. The noise massed and swelled, catching from person to person like fire. Now two dozen were singing. Now fifty. The volume increased with each Siren who joined in and increased further as those who were already singing sang louder to be heard above the newcomers. Soon every Siren on the Esplanade of Glass was vocalizing at the top of his or her lungs, vying with one another, trying to outdo one another.

It was birdsong bursting raucously from the dawn treetops. It was the horny caterwaul of back-alley toms and queens. It was wolves in ancient forests, keening for territory and the companion-ship of the pack. It was the grumble and mourn of whales summoning mates across thousands of miles of ocean. It was the late-night howl of city dogs, setting one another off in canine canon.

Language ceased to be relevant. Into simple syllables or nonsense phrases the Sirens projected everything that they had hoped or felt or believed or desired. Some of them swaying, some stock-still, some with their eyes tight shut, they sang and sang and sang. It was unintelligible. It was cacophony. It was exquisite. It was deafening.

Here were a trio of Bulgarian women in peasant costume, their hair braided, their bosoms a-heave as they knitted together strange chords with uncanny, even eerie accuracy.

Here was a Mongolian throat-singer, emitting multiple notes in a buzzing, inhuman drone from somewhere deep, dark and cavern-ous within his ribcage.

Here were a quintet of Gregorian monks, or men dressed as Gregorian monks, habited and tonsured, intoning melismatic plainsong.

Here was a choirboy chaperoned by a watchful mother, cherubic in cassock and surplice as he generated variations on the soaring melody of Allegri's Miserere.

Here was a Native American in full tribal regalia, his feathered headdress quivering as he let forth a languid, chanting wail.

Here was a blues singer with a voice as muddy as a silted-up delta, grunting out twelve-bar phrases and no doubt giving thanks for every cigarette he had ever smoked and every shot of whisky he had ever downed and every woman who had ever done him wrong.

Here was an Arab Muslim who must once have been a muezzin, his cry rhythmic and hypnotic, the sound of minarets against a sky greyed by daybreak or dusk.

Here was a willowy, anaemic folk artiste, her timbre gauzy and ethereal, dreaming of unicorns and meadows as she plucked her notes from the air.

Here was a wizened, wise-eyed, bandy-legged jazzbo, scatting his way through *doo-wops* and *shoo-bops* and *oo-be-doo yeahs*, shuffling his feet and brisking his wrinkled, monkey-paw hands.

Here was a busty, blowsy veteran of a million stage musicals, a trouper who knew all about giving it some oomph, putting every-thing she had into it, stopping the show.

Here was a yodeller in Tyrolean hat and *lederhosen*, the noise he made as slippery and gap-riddled as Swiss cheese.

Here, and here, and here, were Elvis look-alikes, whole hunks a' burnin' love, pausing to murmur *thangyewvermuch* every so often as they hummed, twitched and quivered their way through sweaty rock'n'roll riffs.

Here was a dozen-strong gospel choir, all happiness and handclaps and hallelujah harmonies.

Here was a whistler, cheeks pinched and lips pursed, warble-twittering like a canary and hoping against hope that tonight he would have the good fortune to encounter one of those rare Foreigners with a taste for his specialist wares – whistling in the dark, in more ways than one.

Here they all were, men, women and children, clamouring clamorously: and here, now, among them, came the objects of their bids for attention.

Each stood a head higher than any human present (with the exception of Johansen, who was something of a golden giant himself). Each moved in a series of short, gliding lurches, bent-backed like a penitent priest, the hem of its robe swishing along the ground. Each gleamed in the effulgence of the crystech sculptures, whose patterns of soft light added to the unearthliness of its appearance, making it radiant, angelic. Each turned now this way, now that, as a voice or combination of voices grabbed its interest, twisting its whole body round until its mask faced in the right direction and inclining slightly towards the Siren or Sirens concerned, who in response upped the volume and introduced trills and grace notes and generally redoubled their efforts to impress. Each seemed capable of singling out the sound of individuals or groups from the overall medley with unerring precision, and each acted like a shopper sampling goods, listening to one kind of singing for a while, then moving on and listening to another, and then another, then another.

An alien race. You could never forget that. As the Foreigners infiltrated the Siren crowd, fanning out across the Esplanade of Glass, weaving among the massed humans, it was impossible not to feel a small shiver of excitement. At least for Parry it was. Some Sirens acted blasé about the golden giants, claiming to regard them as nothing more than two-and-a-half-metres-tall sources of income, but for Parry they were never anything less than objects of wonder. Several of them swept by him, just centimetres away, easily within reach. He could have held out a hand and brushed their robes with his fingertips had he wanted to, had he not known that they shied away from physical contact with humans, seeming to dislike it. An alien race. Beings who, through their arrival, had pulled human-kind back from the brink of self-annihilation. Strange saviours, worthy of respect, to be begrudged nothing.

After several minutes of browsing, the Foreigners began making selections. Gravitating towards the voice or voices that most took their fancy, they commenced the process of negotiation. Delving into a slit in its robes, each produced a handful of gemstones, which the individual Siren, or whichever one was the elected representative of a group, was invited to examine. If the jewels did not, by the look of them, match up to expectation, the Siren would form DISAPPOINTMENT. The Foreigner might then return the jewels to the slit in its robes and walk away, or else it might rummage again in its 'pocket' and pull out larger gemstones, or a greater number of gemstones of a similar size to the first ones. The Siren could either accept this better offer or refuse it and hold out for a further increase. Few did, since Foreigners seldom made a third offer for a Siren's services, and the second offer was normally overgenerous anyway. On the other hand, a third offer could be astonishingly lucrative, and if the Siren was feeling confident that the Foreigner concerned was more than usually keen, then the gamble could be well worth taking. AGREEMENT was signalled by holding the right hand down with the palm out and the index and middle fingers of the left hand pressed horizontally across.

Should the negotiation fall through, the Siren could try to regain the Foreigner's patronage by forming the hand-symbol for REGRET. If the Foreigner responded with FORGIVENESS, then all was well, but if the Foreigner, too, manually expressed REGRET, then the Siren had forfeited that particular golden giant's custom for the night. All was not lost, however, as Sirensong could last for anything up to four hours and there would be further waves of Foreigners later, if not at the Esplanade of Glass then at other venues across New Venice. Inevitably there would be some Sirens who would return to their hotels or apartments unsuccessful and empty-handed, by virtue of simple mathematics: there were many more of them touting for business than there were Foreigners to provide it. As a rule, however, with diligence and a bit of effort a Siren who could sing well could almost always gain employment before Sirensong drew to a close.

The chorus of voices dwindled as Foreigners made their choices. With the Sirens they had hired filing after them like ducklings behind their mothers, they headed for the taxi-gondolas waiting along the esplanade's edge. Soon all the golden giants were gone and the conventional human hubbub that had prevailed prior to their arrival resumed, albeit less loudly, the number of Sirens present having been reduced by almost half.

Parry and Johansen met up again by the canal.

'Next time we do this, I'm bringing along some cotton wool,' the lieutenant said, gouging one ear with a forefinger.

'If there is a next time, it won't be for a while.' Parry filled Johansen in on what he had learned from the Scottish castrato.

'The Conservatorio. So he was properly trained, this Henderson. A pro.'

'Which ought to make it easier finding out which hotel he was staying at. We'll do a ring round, starting at the top and working downwards. My guess is he was at one of the five-star jobs, the plush ones.'

'You think we should begin that now?'

Johansen's tone implied he was hoping the answer was no. He looked tired. Parry *was* tired, and stifled a yawn as he said, 'Leaving it a few hours won't hurt. Let's call it a night and start again tomorrow, bright and early. Well, early anyway.'

Johansen gave Parry a lift home in the launch. Before clambering into bed, Parry played Anna's message one more time. Her words, a small spark of hope, were something to curl around beneath the covers and nurture snugly, smugly, as he sank into sleep.

9 SUITE

Another day, another hotel room.

Parry's guess had been on the mark. Daryl Henderson had been a resident of the Top A (strictly speaking still was, since he had yet to check out officially). The hotel, one of New Venice's most expansive and expensive, was situated on the perimeter of the Hub Lagoon, and Henderson's fifteenth-floor suite had an enviable view not only of that octagonal stretch of azure water but also of five of the city's main radial canals, thinning into the distance. Mid-morning heat made the world outside the suite's windows waver and shimmer, but inside the three large interconnecting rooms, with their decor of marble and glass and silk and pine, all was glacially cool.

In the drawer of Henderson's bedside table Parry found nothing except the obligatory Gideon's Bible. The closets held Henderson's clothes, laundered and folded or hung. His shoes were arranged in racked rows, the leather pairs professionally polished and gleaming like the carapaces of beetles. The bed was made, plump as an iced bun, one corner of the covers turned back, a foil-wrapped chocolate on the pillow. The suite was ready for the return of its paying occupant, who, of course, would not be coming back; and again, in this room where Henderson had lived, Parry got the same impression as in the room at the Amadeus where Henderson had died – that sense of people passing through and leaving nothing behind, not even a memory of themselves.

Questioning the chambermaid responsible for this floor revealed no evidence that Henderson had been in a disturbed or unstable frame of mind before departing for Sirensong. The woman, an Algerian, told Parry in halting, French-accented English that she remembered Henderson passing her in the corridor on his way out that evening and wishing her goodnight. As far as she could recall, there had been nothing out of the ordinary about his appearance or manner. He had left the suite in no untidier a state than usual, and she had definitely not found any kind of note. A resident of the Top A for several months now, Henderson had always had a smile and a greeting for her. A good-looking boy, she said. Not the sort you would want your daughter to marry. A Siren, if you please! But still, a nice young man.

From the hotel manager Parry learned that Henderson was in credit for his accommodation until the end of the month. That was why none of the hotel staff had been concerned about his absence for the past two nights. Naturally, as long as the rooms were paid for, a guest was free to stay there or not stay there as he or she wished.

Parry prevailed upon the manager to show him the contents of the safety deposit box for Henderson's room. In it were a passport card, a cloth-wrapped Foreign statuette approximately twenty centimetres high and several small velvet bags full of glittering, uncut foreign currency. Parry took the passport card and, without much difficulty, persuaded the manager to keep custody of the valuables until they could be sent to Henderson's next of kin.

Leaving the Top A, Parry made his way back to FPP Headquarters on foot. In the course of the ten-minute journey he traversed two bridges and three plazas, and all the while he brooded on the conundrum facing him.

The more he was discovering about Daryl Henderson, the less simple the case was becoming (not that it had been simple to start with). Henderson's actions prior to his death were uncharacteristic of a suicidal person. The Scottish castrato, Dillon, had described him as 'normal' when they had last met; the chambermaid had noticed no change in his customary friendliness towards her. Henderson was prospering from singing, as most graduates of the Conservatorio did. He was not in arrears with his hotel bill – the opposite, in fact. Nor did he appear to be the kind of person who made enemies, at least not easily. Although that was not to say that someone might not have targeted him for murder. Someone jealous of his looks, perhaps? His success? Someone like a fellow Siren?

But increasingly murder was looking like a less feasible explanation for the deaths. Parry knew that when you have a murder you have to look for a motive, and the motive in this instance was elusive to the point of imperceptibility. If someone wanted to kill Henderson, why had the Foreigner had to die too? Because it was a witness to the deed? But how would it possibly have been able to testify against the killer? And if this someone harboured a grudge against both the Foreigner and Henderson – again, why? What could the two of them together have done to offend? Might Henderson have hooked a Foreigner that another Siren considered belonged exclusively to him? It was hardly a murder-worthy transgression.

And that, there, was the crux of the matter. What, in this day and age, was a murder-worthy transgression? If the statistics were anything to go by, almost nothing. Since the Debut, the world had seen a spectacular drop in homicide figures. Where once the annual toll in a major metropolis might have been in the hundreds, now it was in single figures. In New Venice itself there had not been a murder in nine years. Nine years! Sometimes even Parry found this hard to believe, yet if anything typified the post-Foreign era it was the rarity of crime, both petty and serious. People were more even-tempered nowadays and less avaricious. A dispute that once might have been settled with violence was now settled amicably, or more likely would not arise. Consequently, the worst violent crime of all, murder, had become the almost exclusive province of zealots and the clinically insane. And what had happened in Room 1114 did not look like the handiwork of either.

For all these reasons Parry was inclining away from murder as an explanation for the deaths and looking favourably on Hosokawa's *shinju* theory. Perhaps Henderson had been singing to one particular golden giant on a regular basis for some time. Although the Foreigner had checked into the Amadeus on the same night on which it and Henderson had died, that did not mean the two of them had not been companions for a while. Foreigners were known to chop and change between hotels. They were peripatetic creatures. Like all good tourists, they liked to keep moving.

So, pursuing this idea: Henderson and the Foreigner had grown close and had come to the decision that the gulf between their races, which normally only hand-symbols and singing could bridge, could be fully and permanently elided if they were both to die. Their final night together, then, had been their mutual swansong. Henderson had purchased the gun, brought it along with him to the Amadeus, given the vocal performance of his life, then shot himself while, simultaneously, the Foreigner had ended its existence by whatever method Foreigners did such a thing. And the wake-up call? Just making sure that they would be found.

This explanation was more straightforward than murder and had fewer ramifications. It meant that no third party was involved; no one was targeting Sirens and Foreigners; there was no killer stalking New Venice. Foreign Policy was better designed to deal with a tragic but self-contained event such as suicide than it was to deal with a murder investigation. Which, in itself, was no reason to favour the *shinju* theory over any other. But the theory did seem to fit the facts as well as, if not better than, any other.

By the time he emerged on to the acacia-fringed Piazza di Verdi, Parry's head was beginning to ache, both from the heat of the sun drumming down on his pate and from the effort of trying to make sense of so much contradictory and inconclusive information. There were too many variables, that was the problem. Too many unknown factors. He was trying to solve a problem of which one vital component was an insoluble mystery: the lost Foreigner. Without the Foreigner, the case would have been far more straightforward. But then that was false logic. Without the Foreigner there would not have been a case, as such, at all.

FPP HQ was situated on the piazza's north side. It was Parry's not entirely unserious belief that New Venice's architects must have dreamed the building up on a Friday afternoon. How else to explain the crenellations that crowned its eight-storey bulk, or the profusion of asymmetrically positioned windows, or the central spired turret, the finials and baroque curlicues and odd protuberances of masonry? The architecture had about it that end-of-the-working-week feeling, an air of unconstrained ideas and devil-may-care expectation. Even the entrance seemed intended to raise a smile, resembling as it did the fascia of an old Art Deco wireless set, with, where the speaker grilles would have been, tall panes of glass inset with doors. FPP HQ was a building designed to welcome rather than impose. It was also a building without any locks, inside or out, other than the bolts on the doors to its toilet cubicles. It was, in short, accessible in every way.

Parry bee-lined towards it across the piazza, jogged up the sugar-cube front steps, and entered the enclosed chill of the airy white atrium. Offering a SALUTATION to the officer on duty at the horseshoe-shaped front desk, he crossed to the lifts and was soon ascending from Floor Lower C to Floor G. In his office, he activated his work board. No sooner had the screen illuminated itself than the computer emitted the orchestral phrase – predictably, the opening phrase of Beethoven's Fifth – which signified an urgent message was waiting. Parry hit Play and heard Quesnel's voice.

'Jack. I got word you may have identified the dead Siren. Come up and see me as soon as you get in.'

This morning the commissioner was not alone. Entering her office, Parry was dismayed (though somehow not surprised) to find van Wyk with her. Seated in the swivel chair that he himself had occupied the previous day, the Afrikaner was looking as contented as a cream-fed cat. His hands were laced in his lap and there was a smile on his face that said that he felt right at home here and that it would be only a matter of time before his backside was resting just as comfortably in the chair on the *other* side of the desk.

'Ma'am,' Parry said to her, with a SALUTATION. 'Captain van Wyk.'

'Jack, thanks for coming. Pull up a seat.' Quesnel indicated a plain steel chair in the corner of the room. Parry fetched it, positioned it at the same distance from the desk as van Wyk's plusher perch, and lowered himself on to it, trying not to feel as though the inferior chair represented some sort of demotion.

'Ray's asked if he can sit in and hear what you've found out,' Quesnel said. 'You don't mind, do you?'

Of course I bloody mind.

'Fine by me,' Parry said with a shrug.

'So, what *have* you found out? Who *was* this Siren?'

Parry took out Henderson's passport card and handed it to her across the desk. 'A twenty-four-year-old Australian, name of Daryl Henderson. Conservatorio trained. Making a very tidy living for himself.'

'Till his brains got blown out,' muttered van Wyk.

Quesnel scrutinized the picture on the passport card. 'It's a shame. Waste of a good-looking young guy. So, what else do we know about him?'

Parry had run some checks before heading out to the Top A. 'He's not on the Siren register, he has no criminal record and he has family in Melbourne. I haven't yet notified them about his death.'

'Leave that to me,' said Quesnel.

Parry signed GRATITUDE.

'Anything else?'

'I'm beginning to develop a theory as to what might have happened. It's extremely tentative as yet.'

'Give it to us anyway.'

Parry shot a sidelong glance at van Wyk. His fellow captain had one pale eyebrow raised.

'As a matter of fact, I can't claim full credit for this,' he said. 'One of my junior officers, Yoshi Hosokawa, suggested it to me.'

Nice one, Jack. In case they laugh, make sure there's someone else to shift the blame on to.

'Officer Hosokawa pointed out that the situation in the room at the Amadeus resembles what's known in his native country as a *shinju*. It's a kind of shared suicide. A lovers' death pact. Two individuals find themselves so in love, and the course of their love so full of obstacles, that the only way out they can see is to kill themselves.'

He looked at Quesnel. She was nodding. He looked at van Wyk. The eyebrow remained aloft.

'And that', he said, 'could be what Henderson and the Foreigner did the night before last.'

Quesnel hmm'ed for a moment. Then: 'How would a Siren and a Foreigner communicate such an idea to each other? Not through hand-symbols, surely. I can't think how they would manage it that way.'

'Through singing?' Parry ventured.

He heard van Wyk snort.

'It's not inconceivable. If a melody – a certain set of notes expressed in a certain way – can carry a specific emotional resonance, then why not? Why couldn't a Siren use his voice to convey a desire or an intention to a Foreigner? All the Foreigner would have to do in return is sign ACCEPTANCE or REGRET, depending on how it felt.'

'Yes, well, I guess it *is* possible,' Quesnel said. 'I certainly don't have any more of a problem with that idea than I do with the idea of Sirens and Foreigners falling in love. I mean, I know it's happened, but . . .'

'Precisely,' said Parry. 'It *has* happened. And a shared suicide logically represents one possible outcome of that. Not a desirable one by any means, but a possible one.'

'So let me get this right, Parry,' van Wyk said. 'You're claiming it was some kind of *folie à deux*?'

'Something like that, yes.'

'Forgive me, but isn't that just a little, well, farfetched?'

'It does demand a slight stretch of the imagination.'

'A *leap* of the imagination, I'd say. Céleste, I hope I'm not speaking out of turn here, but I mean, really, if this *shogun* theory is the best explanation that Captain Parry can—'

'*Shinju*.' Parry articulated the word with condescending exactness.

'Of course. I beg your pardon. Let me make a mental note of that. *Shinju*. If this *shinju* theory is the best explanation he can come up

93

with, surely it's time someone else should be appointed to help him. Someone who can bring a fresh perspective to the matter.'

'And what fresh perspective might this "someone" bring, Ray?' Quesnel enquired.

'He wouldn't waste time following up the suicide angle, for one thing. It's quite obvious that we're looking at homicide here. Homicide dressed up as suicide in order to throw us off the scent.'

'Captain van Wyk, with the greatest respect,' Parry said, 'I have not discounted the possibility of this being homicide, not to mention Xenocide. If, however, you had considered the case as carefully as I have over the past twenty-four hours, and if you bear in mind how rare an occurrence murder actually is, you'll realize that the *shinju* theory comes out, on balance, as the likelier explanation.'

'A lot depends,' Quesnel interposed, 'on whether or not something similar happens again.'

'I agree,' said Parry.

Van Wyk gave a very good impression of someone looking aghast. 'You mean to say you think there is a chance this might be murder but you're going to wait and see if it happens again before you commit yourself? A bizarre tactic.'

'I'm not saying I *want* there to be another of these things. Of course I don't.'

'Then it's up to you to ensure that there *isn't* another one.'

'Thank you for that sterling piece of advice. I'd never have thought of it myself.'

'Jack . . .' admonished Quesnel.

Parry manufolded APOLOGY. 'Forgive me, ma'am. Captain van Wyk is, of course, correct. Unfortunately, as we're all aware, the way things stand our options are somewhat limited. We could, I suppose, interview as many Sirens as possible, establish which of them, if any, have formed personal attachments with Foreigners and then monitor those Sirens closely.'

'But?'

'But that would not only entail the co-operation of the Siren community as a whole, which we're unlikely to get, but it would require a massive mobilization of FPP personnel and resources and may, perhaps, clue Sirens in on the fact that something's up and send them running. More to the point, any kind of monitoring is expressly forbidden under Measure Three of the Constitution. We cannot perform surveillance on individuals or groups of individuals. It would be a gross infringement of their personal rights.'

'Not even if we consider Measure Nine?' said van Wyk.

'Is the public good being jeopardized? As yet, no. The public doesn't even know about this incident yet, so its "good" cannot be said to be under threat. It would be a different matter if, for some reason related to the *shinju*, Foreigners began deserting the city. Then, under Nine, we would have the right to take more drastic preventative steps. But the Audit Bureau hasn't logged a sudden dramatic fall in Foreign population density, has it?'

Quesnel shook her head.

'Then there we are,' Parry said decisively. 'Nine is invalid.'

And just as well. Of all the measures of the Constitution, Nine was the one with the most potential for abuse. Within its wording – its reference to the somewhat nebulous notion of the general well-being of the resort-city community – it had the power to undo the strictures of the other eight. Proposed by the FPP Council and ratified by the UN for addition to the Constitution as a direct consequence of the Koh Farang débacle, Nine was a classic case of a statute cobbled together in an emergency, one that had not been thoroughly thought through, more flaw than law.

'But all this still assumes that the incident was a double suicide,' said van Wyk.

'Indeed.'

'And if it was a double murder? If the perpetrator is still lurking within the city? What about that?'

'Then we track the guilty party down using whatever means the Constitution allows, and when we find whoever it is we turn him over to the mainland authorities. They may not have any jurisdiction here, but the UN will issue a special cross-border mandate for prosecution. No one gets away with murder, even in a resort-city.'

'But you really don't believe it *was* murder, do you?'

'I'm keeping an open mind.'

'So while you prevaricate, or as you put it "keep an open mind", a murderer could even as we speak be boarding an airship, getting away scot-free. Worse, he could still be here, planning his next outrage.'

'If the perpetrator were intending to leave the city, he would be long gone by now,' Parry said. 'In which case we're too late anyway.'

'And you're content just to let this happen?'

'Like I said, there are limits. A resort-city is not a conventional city and we are not a conventional police force.'

'More's the pity.'

'No. No.' Parry could feel his temper rising, and his voice with it. He told himself to remain calm. Van Wyk's intention was obvious. In order to persuade Quesnel that the investigation would be better off in *his* hands, he was trying to provoke Parry into an irritable outburst and so make him appear unfit for the task. Parry refused to give him the satisfaction of succeeding. 'On the contrary: so much the better. That is what makes a resort-city special. It's outside the jurisdiction of any nation and it has few laws of its own. It operates on the principle of trust.' He tapped his badge. 'Trust between people. Trust between humans and Foreigners. Trust between the city's inhabitants and the FPP. And it *works*.'

'It works until that trust is abused.'

'And that's what we're here for. To make sure it isn't abused. Not through the powers we have, which we all know are limited. Simply by our presence. People here know that and Foreigners, I'm sure, are aware of it too. You've probably heard me say this before, but resort-cities seem to me to be, aside from everything else, an experiment. They're prototypes of the way every country in the world could one day be run, watched over by a force of men and women, like you and me and the commissioner, whose purpose is to serve as figureheads. If that system works here and in other resort-cities, then people will see that it might work elsewhere. And one day perhaps even figureheads won't be necessary. One day, thanks to us, police forces and armies and systems of authority will be things of the past.'

'Your idealism is highly commendable, Parry,' said van Wyk. 'It is also entirely disproved by the present circumstances. And I have to disagree with you about the FPP. Where you see figureheads, I see watchdogs without teeth. We're fine, we do the job we're supposed to, until we need to bite. Then we're utterly ineffective.'

'But I don't believe that we do need to bite, or ever will. And I believe that this incident isn't anywhere near as sinister as you seem to think it is.'

'Believe, or hope?'

Parry, to his own surprise, hesitated before answering. 'Believe.'

'You're staking quite a lot on this optimism of yours.'

'Perhaps I am.'

'Then you're either a far better man than I or a fool.'

Parry flashed a quick smile. 'I think we both know the answer to that one, van Wyk.'

'Oh, I hope we do, Parry, I hope we do.'

'OK, boys, that's enough,' Quesnel said firmly. 'I'm sure we all feel better for having gotten some stuff off our chests, but the problem remains. We have a dead Siren and a lost Foreigner and we're still not entirely clear how they wound up that way in a hotel room together. Now, Jack, as you know, I spoke with the FPP Council and Mr al-Shadhuli yesterday. The conclusion we reached between us is that the FPP can't continue to sit on this incident much longer. I know Measure Seven gives us sixty days, but the Council, the NACA Liaison and I all feel that long before then somebody – somebody who works at the Amadeus, somebody from the forensics laboratories at Tangier, maybe even somebody within our own ranks – will have spilled the beans to the media. Measure Seven is designed to make the FPP transparent in its dealings and that's a good thing. Trouble is, whenever we make use of the sixty-day provision, we end up looking secretive, all the more so with an incident as disturbing as the one we have here. For which reason, the Council has instructed me to make a formal statement to the local media.'

Parry stifled a groan. 'When?'

'The Council were pressing for today. I managed to get them to agree to Thursday morning, first thing. I thought you could do with the couple of extra days.'

'I could. I'm grateful.'

'Now, how sure are you about this *shinju* thing? Because if the idea does have some foundation, then that can only be good. Better than the alternative, anyhow.'

'I can think of a couple of people it might be useful to talk to.'

'Excellent. Then talk to them.'

'Céleste . . .'

Quesnel swivelled her head to fix her glittering blue gaze on van Wyk. 'Yes, Ray?'

Van Wyk was on the point of lodging an objection, but then appeared to think better of it. 'No. Nothing.'

'No, if you want to say something . . .'

'No, you've made your decision. Far be it from me to quibble.'

'Then that's settled. Jack, I will of course need a full report of your findings. Tomorrow afternoon at the latest. That OK?'

Parry signed ACCEPTANCE and stood up to go. As he did so, he caught van Wyk's eye. The Afrikaner had a sullen look about him that was in marked contrast to the smugness he had been exuding earlier when Parry came in. He glared at Parry, nodding his head shallowly and rhythmically, his eyes narrowed in cool appraisal.

Parry, feeling triumphant and also feeling guilty about feeling triumphant, left the room.

10   Call and Response

Back in his office Parry obtained the number for the Conservatorio di Musica Straniera in Rome from the international directory database and dialled it. A receptionist answered in Italian but upon hearing Parry's '*Buon giorno, signorina*', switched smoothly to English, sensing that the caller had reached the limit of his conversational ability in her language.

'How may I help you, sir?' she enquired.

'I'd like to speak to Professor Franchetti, please.'

'I am sorry, the professor is busy now. Perhaps if you could ring back another time. Or would you prefer to speak to the admissions tutor?'

'My name is Jack Parry. I'm a captain with the New Venice FPP, and it's a matter of Foreign Policy that I would like to discuss with Professor Franchetti.'

'Ah. A moment, sir, while I check.'

Check his credentials on her work board, or check whether Franchetti was prepared to talk to him? Probably both, Parry thought. He drummed his fingers on his desk. At least, thank God, he wasn't being forced to listen to a selection of pop classics or classical pops while he was on hold. The aural torture of call-waiting music had been outlawed under the Fairness in Telecommunications Act, as had automated touch-tone switchboards with their pre-recorded messages and their branching, seemingly interminable labyrinths of options.

The receptionist came back on the line. 'I will put you through to *il professore* right away, Captain.'

A moment later a man's voice said, 'Massimo Franchetti here. This is Captain . . . Parry? Did I get that right?'

'Quite right, Professor. Jack Parry, New Venice FPP. Is this an inconvenient moment to talk?'

'No. But you must forgive if my English is not so good.'

'Your English sounds infinitely better than my Italian.'

'Ha! You are kind to say so.'

With a few surreptitious keystrokes Parry summoned up a digital still of his interlocutor. No doubt Franchetti was doing the same at his end of the line. The founder and senior tutor of the Conservatorio, if his caller-ID picture was current, was perhaps ten years Parry's senior, with a pugilist's face, ribbed and scowly, reminiscent of a clenched fist. His eyebrows were bushy and black, and his hair was silvery and swept back in a thick, leonine mane. Parry had observed that it was common for middle-aged men who were untouched by the blight of baldness to wear their hair like this, long and bouffant, as if to drive home the point that they possessed in abundance what the majority of their peers lacked. Not that this was a sensitive topic with him or anything.

'And how may I help the FPP, Captain?' Franchetti asked.

'It's about a former pupil of yours, Daryl Henderson.'

'Daryl Henderson, Daryl Henderson . . . Ah, of course. Daryl. I remember. He graduate from the Conservatorio two year ago. A bass-baritone. A fine voice, perfect pitch – although he like too much the vibrato. I have to train him to use it – how do you say? – sparingly. *Gli Stranieri*, they like the vibrato, but it is best saved for the climax. Until then it is like too much chocolate. Too sweet.'

'He was a good student, then?'

'At the Conservatorio we take only the best,' Franchetti said, with both pride and a touch of righteousness. 'This is why our fees are high, to keep away the time-wasters. We accept only Sirens who have proved they can earn much money already by singing, and we make them even better. Like a trophy, we give them a polish so that they shine.'

'Forgive me, Professor. When I said "good", I meant was he well behaved?'

'Well behaved? Daryl? I do not remember that he is not. No, a pleasant boy, Daryl. Friendly. A bit coarse, like many of his countrymen. Rough at the edges, is that not the phrase? But I like him very much. Everybody at the Conservatorio like him.'

'No psychological problems, then.'

'Why, Captain? What has he done?'

Parry could see no harm in telling Franchetti a portion of the truth. 'I'm sorry to say, Professor, that the day before yesterday Daryl Henderson died.'

There was a moment of silence from the other end of the line. Then Franchetti said, 'Poor Daryl. I am sorry to hear this.'

'We believe he may have killed himself. Would that surprise you?'

'For him to kill himself? Perhaps. Daryl, he is a sensible boy. But then . . .'

The professor seemed in no hurry to finish the sentence.

'Signor Franchetti?'

'Captain, how much you know about singing?'

'Me personally, not a great deal. Can't hold a tune to save my life. Voice like a cement mixer. But I imagine you're referring to singing for Foreigners, in which case the answer is I've a pretty good idea what's involved.'

'The theory, yes, is very simple. Foreigners love the sound of the human singing voice. It arouse them to a passion. Some say the thrill for them, it is sexual, but I am of the opinion it is spiritual. They are moved by singing in the same way that you or I may be moved by a symphony or a melody. It excite them in the heart, in the soul. And there are certain phrases and techniques which, used skilfully, used *judiciously*' – Franchetti was satisfied to have hit on this adverb – 'will enhance this pleasure for them. This is what we are teaching at the Conservatorio, along with projection from the diaphragm, breath control, the traditional skills. Sometimes my pupils have raw talent but no delicacy, no finesse. That is what they can learn here. Finesse.'

'Forgive me, but how is this relevant to Daryl Henderson?'

'A moment, Captain. I come to that. For the Siren, you see, there are many things to learn, many things to remember, and so, many pressures. It is hard work, to sing like that every day. To sing for your supper. Hard on the body, hard on the mind. You must have the fire inside you, which burns in your song. The Foreigners can tell if you do not feel completely what you sing. And always there is the need for approval. Nothing is more important for a Siren than a Foreigner to appreciate your work, and nothing is worse than a Foreigner, when you have finished singing for it, to make the DISAPPOINTMENT with the hands. Many Sirens, they are sensitive. It is an intimate act, singing. Rejection can go deep, like a knife.'

'You mean Henderson could have been failing at his job? Losing his touch?'

'A number of times I have former pupils come back to me and tell me they have no more the ability to sing. Sometimes it is the physical difficulties – the nodules on the throat, that sort of thing. But sometimes it is the mental difficulties. For some reason they cannot delight Foreigners any more. They have no more the feeling for it. The fire is gone. They cannot project any more how they feel into how they sing. They are devastated. Some of them I can help, some I cannot. It is like any artistic talent, you know? Sometimes it will just go away and never return.'

'That's interesting, Professor,' said Parry, 'although I have to say that, from all appearances, Daryl Henderson was doing perfectly well as a Siren. If he was losing his knack for singing, his financial circumstances certainly wouldn't seem to indicate it.'

He could almost hear Franchetti's shrug. 'I simply suggest a reason why a Siren may kill himself, Captain. Many Sirens start out well balanced, but the singing can make them – what is the word? Highly strung.'

'I understand. Fair enough. Let's try another tack, then. Do you think that a Siren, in the course of his job, could become inordinately attached to Foreigners? Maybe to one Foreigner in particular?'

'Yes, yes, it has happened. You must know that.'

'Actually, yes, I do. But would you have any idea how it might come about?'

'Hmmmm.'

Parry pictured *il professore*, half the length of the Mediterranean away, running his fingers ruminatively through his luxuriant silvery locks.

'It is a strange business, singing,' Franchetti said, eventually. 'As I told you earlier, it is intimate. Maybe more intimate even than the sexual intercourse. It is the giving, not of body, but of soul. I am a Siren once myself, in the early days. One of the first, as you must know. A pioneer.'

Parry did not know this but said, 'Of course,' as if he did.

'I see how Foreigners respond to a good voice and the right techniques, how they twitch, they tremble, they sway. Watching this, making them do this, I feel almost embarrassed, as if I see more than I should. As if I see them bare. Not nude, not like that. As if I see inside them to who they really are. When they listen to singing the Foreigners show much of themselves, and when you see a creature revealed in that way, exposed in that way, you feel either compassion or contempt. The more gentle Siren, the more sensitive, he will feel compassion. And compassion may develop to something stronger, who knows? The Foreigners are not human, Captain. This is an obvious thing to say, but it is important. They are not human – but sometimes we may mistake them for human. I am not sure I make myself clear with this.'

'We see them in human terms, is that what you mean? Anthropomorphize them.'

'Yes, that is the word. A complicated word with a simple meaning. We do it to animals, we do it to Foreigners – interpret their actions according to our own behaving. We cannot help it. This is the way our brains work. And so it is possible that a Siren can think he or she is more deeply involved with a *Straniero* than is true. It is a question of reading signs, or rather *mis*reading them.'

'Interesting. And might it not be possible for a Foreigner to fall for a human in the same way? As we anthropomorphize them, could they not . . . "Foreignerize" us?'

'A good question, and of course one I cannot answer. Can Foreigners deceive themselves just as we humans can? I do not know. Somehow, speculating on such things, it seem to reduce the Foreigners.'

'I agree. It seems to demean them.'

'Demean them, yes! Demean them.' Franchetti chuckled. 'I am discovering, Captain Parry, that you are charmed by the Foreigners.'

'I'm afraid I am, a bit,' Parry confessed.

'No! Do not be afraid to be charmed. Never be afraid of that. *I giganti aurei* have brought back magic to the world. This is a good thing and must be preserved at all costs.'

'And preserving it is what the FPP's here for, Professor.'

Parry was not sure whether Franchetti heard this remark (which, even to his own ears, sounded somewhat glib). Someone at the other end of the line had started talking to the professor in Italian and Franchetti had moved his mouth away from the telephone receiver in order to reply in the same language. A moment later his voice returned, loud and clear again, speaking English. 'Captain? I regret that I must go. I have a pupil waiting. Please, I hope that I have been of some help to you.'

'You have. Thank you, Professor. I'm grateful for your time.'

'*Prego.* Call me again if you would like to talk some more.'

'I will. Goodbye.'

'*Ciao.*'

Parry hung up and stood up. It was nigh on noon. He walked out of his office and down a short corridor to his district's operations room. Here several dozen FPP officers worked within low-partitioned cubicles, answering calls and logging reports. At present the majority of them were elsewhere, either out on patrol or taking an early lunch, but Johansen, as Parry had hoped, was at his desk.

Someone, in all probability Johansen himself, had tacked a printout copy of the Norwegian flag to the back of his chair with, beneath it in 36-point capitals, the slogan 'NORWEGIAN FROM HELL'. Johansen hailed from the city of Trondheim, but there was not nearly so much comic mileage to be derived from that as there was from claiming he was from Hell, a small town twenty-five kilometres east of Trondheim and notable for not much other than its name.

'Pål?'

Johansen glanced up from his work board. On the screen were the FPP Council Audit Bureau figures showing the results of the latest survey of Foreign population density in resort-cities. The only method anyone had been able to work out for gauging the number of Foreigners present on Earth was to take regular satellite photographs of specific open-air sites in resort-cities and then literally count heads among the crowds, distinguishing golden masks from human crania. The resulting totals were then tabulated in the form of graphs, all of which, allowing for minor fluctuations, demonstrated an upward trend, the notable exception being the graph for Koh Farang, which showed a line as flat as a dead man's ECG readout.

'Not gone for your usual lunchtime gym session?' Parry asked. 'With all the other physical jerks?'

'Ha ha. You know what, boss, every time you crack that joke I like it a little bit more.'

'Yes. Sorry. But you're not doing anything important right now.'

'Nothing that can't wait. Why?'

'Fancy a little trip?'

'Sure. Where to?'

'You remember that Frenchwoman who was on *Calliope* a few months back? The one who said she'd had an affair with a Foreigner?'

'Yeah. Calliope went too easy on her, I thought.'

'She goes easy on everyone. That's why she's so popular. Can you remember what the Frenchwoman was called?'

'No, but we can look it up.'

Johansen turned back to his work board and hammered out a

two-fingered tattoo on the keys. Soon, with the help of FPP privileges, he had accessed the NVTV database. Once there, it was a simple matter to pull up a list of the names of all the guests who had appeared over the past year on New Venice's top-rated, world-syndicated television talk show.

Bending and squinting, Parry scanned the list, knowing he would recognise the woman's name when he saw it. 'There she is.' He pointed to the screen. 'That's her. Viola d'Indy.'

'So what do you want with her anyway?' Johansen asked. 'She's a complete fruit-and-nut case.'

'Never mind. Pull up her address from the directory. We're going to pay her a visit.'

11 RHAPSODY

The Sea-Hive was one of New Venice's cheap areas, although in a resort-city 'cheap' was a relative concept. Anywhere else in the world the Sea-Hive's rents and utility costs would have been considered on the steep side. Here they were deemed reasonable, even for an area whose purpose was to provide accommodation for those in the service industries and the lower echelons of the hotel trade.

The Sea-Hive's condominium blocks shouldered together in squat, hexagonal configurations, overshadowing narrow canals. It was in one of these blocks that Viola d'Indy lived, on the bottom floor, in a one-bedroom waterside apartment with a galley kitchen, a tiny terrace and furniture supplied by the landlord.

Viola was a petite, pale-skinned woman who held herself with a kind of febrile, pinched rigidity. Her hair was cut in a Louise Brooks bob and dyed a lustreless black. Her chin was small, her nose emphatic, and her eyes were like a doll's, glassy and over-large for her face. Ringed with kohl, they rarely blinked, although her hands, as if to compensate for her eyelids' immobility, were constantly aflutter, darting here and there as she spoke like two white flesh moths. She was wearing a knee-length dress of cerise-coloured crushed velvet, accessorized with trainers and sweatsocks, a hoopla of bangles on either forearm and a black silk scarf wrapped dramatically around her neck. She smoked FAVOURITE cigarettes in quick, nervous bursts, each slender, gold-banded tube spending the majority of its life smouldering on the rim of an ashtray.

'This was nearly two years ago,' she said to Parry, while beyond the living-room windows a canal-bus lumbered by, filling the salt-clouded panes with its bumbling bulk. Seconds after the double-decker boat had passed, its wash hit the outer wall of the apartment and waves thumped and bumped against the building with diminishing intensity until the canal calmed again. 'My life has not been so wonderful since. But the time I had with him was very special. A golden memory.'

'Him?' said Parry. Out of the corner of his eye he saw Johansen looking surprised, too.

'Oh yes. Without a doubt he was a him.' Viola coughed into a loosely clenched, jangling hand. 'Excuse me.'

'So there were certain aspects of this Foreigner's behaviour that enabled you to determine its sex?' Parry managed to keep all but a tiny trace of scepticism out of his voice.

'Doh-Fa-Sol. His name was Doh-Fa-Sol.' She crooned the three notes in a husky, harsh coloratura. 'He liked me calling him that. It was his favourite sequence. And in answer to your question, I don't know how I know, I only know that I do know. And yes, I've read Vieuxtemps of course.'

She waved a hand in the direction of a stack of bound downloads on the smoked-glass coffee table. The topmost of them was François-Joseph Vieuxtemps's *Foreigners Are Neither from Venus Nor from Mars*. Current claimant for the never-too-hotly-contested title of World's Most Famous Belgian, Vieuxtemps was a behavioural psychologist and latterly Xenologist who had been studying Foreigners since the Debut. His book, which had become an international bestseller in both onscreen and hardcopy formats, asserted among other things that golden giants were asexual and exhibited no traits that could be distinctly defined as masculine or feminine.

'All I can say is, Monsieur Vieuxtemps clearly has not spent time in close contact with a Foreigner,' Viola continued. 'He should have consulted me. I would have told him that what may not be perceived by the eyes may be perceived with the heart.'

'And how long were you and – I won't attempt to sing his name – Doh-Fa-Sol together, Mademoiselle d'Indy?'

'Five weeks and three days, Captain, although I am sure that I sang for him at least twice before I knew who he was, if you see what I mean. He was checking me out, you see. Anonymously. He was interested in me from the start, but he was shy and it took him a while to pluck up the courage to ask me to be his companion.'

'Which he did how?'

'Like so.' Viola slotted her hands together, index and middle fingers extended, other fingers bunched, thumbs tip-to-tip and forming an O. COMRADESHIP. 'It was beautiful, that moment. I shall never forget it. I cried because I felt so honoured, so chosen.'

She picked up her cigarette and lifted it to her lips for the briefest of drags before returning it to the ashtray. 'And for thirty-eight days I was in heaven. We met up regularly, Doh-Fa-Sol and I, even went on day trips together. A bus tour up the coast. A cruise around Old Venice. Have you ever visited Old Venice, Captain?'

'I've seen pictures.'

'Pictures don't do it justice. It's quite remarkable. The ruins – like coral reefs. And every evening I would sing to him. My voice – such raptures I would send him into with my voice! It's not what it used to be. These damned cigarettes are taking their toll, and I keep meaning to give up, but you know . . . But Doh-Fa-Sol *adored* my voice. I could leave him weak and shuddering with my song. I swear, as I left his room he would be barely able to stand. And I myself . . .' A blush deepened the redness of the rouge on her cheeks. 'Well, Captain, I won't go into the matter too deeply, but there were occasions when I even brought myself . . . pleasure. I did not have to touch myself. I only had to sing and to see what my singing did to Doh-Fa-Sol. That was enough.'

Parry averted his eyes from Viola's unwavering gaze. Her frankness made him uncomfortable.

'Did he give you all those?' Johansen asked, nodding in the direction of a wood-laminate sideboard on which was arrayed a collection of Foreign statuettes, some fifteen of them in all. The rest of the room was shabby, grubby, in need of a thorough clean, but the statuettes had been kept scrupulously dusted. They were without question the most valuable items Viola d'Indy possessed, perhaps the only valuable items she possessed. Everything else in her apartment, including her, had seen better days.

'Some,' she replied. 'The rest I bought after . . .' She faltered, then collected herself. 'After it was over. I spent almost all my savings on them. They make me think of him.'

So saying, she rose and approached the statuettes and, choosing a medium-sized one, laid her fingertips lightly on it. Straight away a mid-register note vibrated out, ceasing abruptly the instant Viola took her hand away. She touched the statuette again, this time running her fingers down its length, and the note issued forth again, its upper harmonics deepening as she traced a line from the statuette's shoulders to its feet. Lowering her arm, she returned with a wistful air to her seat.

'Wonderful, *n'est-ce pas?*' she said. 'It always cheers me up to hear one sing. I imagine you, Captain, must have several at home yourself.'

Parry, smiling, shook his head. 'No.'

'But surely an FPP captain has done plenty of things to make Foreigners grateful.'

'Obviously not grateful enough to reward me with a statuette.'

'And you haven't bought one second-hand?'

'On my salary?' Parry said, and laughed. 'Anyway, Mademoiselle d'Indy. Perhaps if we could get back to your relationship with this Foreigner . . .'

'What else is there to tell?' Viola heaved a tragic sigh. 'It was love, pure and simple. A time of utter happiness for me. Occasionally, when we were in public together, I would catch people giving me this sort of look.' She mimed *ugh*. 'But that was only when we were outside New Venice. In a resort-city everybody is more tolerant, are they not? Besides, what did I care what others thought? They could not know, could not understand, what Doh-Fa-Sol and I had together. We were joined at the heart. Different species, joined at the heart. United by our love.'

'I suppose, then, that you must know of other Sirens who've formed such close relationships with golden giants.'

Viola's current FAVOURITE had smouldered down to the filter on the ashtray rim. She picked up the packet with its gold hand-symbol logo, tapped out a fresh cigarette and lit it. 'Not until *Calliope*,' she said. 'In fact, that was one of the main reasons I did the show – to find out if there were others like me out there. I couldn't believe, you see, that I was the only one. And sure enough, after the interview aired, dozens of Sirens from all over the world got in touch with me to say that they, too, had been involved with Foreigners. None of them, I have to say, seemed to have enjoyed quite such an intensity of passion as I did with Doh-Fa-Sol.' Now she blinked – a slow, deliberate meshing of the eyelashes, profoundly smug. 'But then I suspect, deep down, that for them the money was a factor, however strenuously they denied it.'

'But *you* were paid for your companionship.' Parry gestured towards the statuettes.

'Doh-Fa-Sol insisted. But I would willingly have accompanied him for free.'

Parry took out his notebook and pencil. 'Then, mademoiselle, perhaps I could ask you if the name . . .' He thumbed through the notebook until he found the page he wanted. It was an entirely superfluous action, a piece of stage business intended to give the impression of method and orderliness. 'The name Daryl Henderson means anything to you?'

Viola thought for a moment. 'No. I don't know anyone by that name.'

'You're sure?'

'*Absolument.*'

'He wasn't one of the Sirens who contacted you after *Calliope*?'

Viola shook her head. 'No. Definitely no. I would remember.'

It had been worth a try. 'Well, mademoiselle,' Parry stowed away the notebook, 'you've been extremely helpful, and we wouldn't want to take up any more of your time . . .'

'Don't you want to know how it ended?'

Parry, having half-risen, lowered himself back into his chair. No harm in letting her finish her story. It obviously mattered to her, unburdening herself of the tale in its entirety.

'He left,' she said simply. 'Without warning. Without excuse or explanation. One evening I went to Sirensong and he did not come. I went to the last hotel he had been staying at and he was no longer there. And more days passed, and he did not come to Sirensong, and I soon understood that he had gone home. Do I hate him for that? Yes and no. Yes, because it was cowardly, but no, because it was a typically male thing to do, so in that sense he wasn't to blame. He couldn't help himself. He'd decided our time together was up and that was that. Men brood silently on things, arrive at sudden decisions, and then act on them. That's just how they are. I know this from experience. And a male Foreigner is no different.'

'Foreigners come, Foreigners go, Mademoiselle d'Indy,' Parry pointed out. 'We don't know how and we don't know why.'

'Naturally you leap to his defence, Captain.' Somehow the weariness in Viola's voice was more scathing than bitterness would have been. 'You are, after all, a man.'

Gender loyalty was not at issue here. Parry simply did not like hearing someone ascribe common human failings to a Foreigner. 'But they're not like us,' he said. 'They have their own motives. Perhaps you ought to give it – him – the benefit of the doubt.'

'Oh, I have. You see, he's coming back for me.'

'He is?'

'I'm certain of it. Doh-Fa-Sol didn't abandon me. He hasn't forgotten me. I know this, and so every night I go out to Sirensong and sing. The way my voice is these days . . . well, let's just say I don't get many takers. But that's not the point. That's not why I do it. I keep going out there because one day Doh-Fa-Sol will come back and he'll be looking for me and he'll hear me and find me . . . and then we'll be together again for ever.'

The rapturous conviction of these last few words crumbled into a series of rough, racking coughs.

Yes, that's just what'll happen, Parry thought. If the cigarettes don't kill you first.

'Love, Captain,' Viola said. She had to wrench the words out between coughs and gulps for air. 'It's the final thing. The only thing. It's all that we have. When everything else has gone, love is all that matters. For you, for me, for everyone – even for Foreigners.'

12 PROMENADE

Viola's tussive utterance was still resonating in Parry's head as he and Johansen returned to the jetty where their launch was moored. He had no idea why a few comments made by a desperate and bereft woman should have lodged themselves in his brain and be screaming significance at him. What Viola had said about love had been no more profound or insightful than the lyrics of the song he had heard on his home board yesterday evening. Crude aphorisms, nothing more. Clichés.

Yet he could not deny that there were certain parallels between Viola pining for her lost Foreigner and his own situation with Anna. The Frenchwoman had convinced herself that her Doh-Fa-Sol was going to return for her. She had to believe this. It was all she had left to cling to, all that gave her life shape and aim. And likewise was there not an element of necessary self-delusion in *his* conviction that Anna would eventually, if he hung on long enough, consent to a resumption of their relationship?

Well, no. For one thing, unlike Viola and her Foreigner, he and Anna still communicated with each other. Infrequently, to be sure. A phone call once a fortnight on average. But at least they had contact. And not only that, they met up in person every now and again, for a drink, sometimes a meal, and on those occasions they would have conversations, long ones – although admittedly nothing of much substance was ever said. They would talk trivial events to death, smothering inconsequentialities beneath an excess weight of words, while the important stuff, the subjects Parry felt they should be discussing, went, by silent agreement, unspoken. There were questions that he needed answered, but he was afraid to ask them, afraid that asking them would contravene the terms of the relationship as it now stood, terms he had not set and did not know, and meanwhile Anna, obstinate Anna, had no intention of volunteering an explanation for why she had abruptly and unilaterally called off their affair after her husband's death, and thus a great deal remained unresolved between them . . . and this he knew now (although he had endured months of anguish before reaching this conclusion) was not altogether bad. What was unresolved was unfinished and what was unfinished might be restarted. As long as he and Anna still had a friendship – and they did, albeit an awkward one, with a significant region of its established territory cordoned off and marked taboo and always to be carefully circumnavigated – then there was always a chance that one day, once again, that friendship could become something more. That was what made their phone conversations and dinner dates endurable. That was how he could bear to be physically close to Anna but not at liberty to touch her and could accept a peck on the cheek instead of the kiss on the lips that he craved, because in proximity and dry gestures of affection, wintry echoes of summer plenty, there was always the promise of regeneration, spring's eternal hope.

Johansen took the helm of the launch while Parry loosed the mooring ropes. It took about a quarter of a minute, from the moment Johansen turned the ignition key, for the comp-res power cell to achieve full output. A duotone whine from beneath the engine housing grew louder as the power cell's pair of crystals were exposed to each other and a charge accumulated between them. The same system, on a considerably vaster scale, operated in the mainland hum farms that supplied the city's electricity – power born of mutual excitation.

There was no earthly reason, at least none that any terrestrial physicist had been able to ascertain, why complementary resonance should work – why two crystals, vibrating out of sync, should generate energy, spontaneously, out of nothing, with apparently no undesirable by-products and without being subject to the laws of entropy. Like crystech, comp-res was an inexplicable miracle in everyday use, and Parry was not alone in regarding it with a kind of superstitious awe. He believed – and he knew it was wholly irrational, but since when had that stopped anyone holding a belief? – that to question how comp-res operated was to risk causing it to cease functioning, in the same way that a gambler, the moment he begins to ask himself why he is on a winning streak, may find Lady Luck turning her back on him. It was better, in the Foreign era, simply to accept some things for what they were. Including, of course, Foreigners themselves.

When the output indicator light glowed green on the dashboard display, Johansen engaged the throttle. Pausing to let a taxi-gondola go past, he steered away from the jetty and began threading the launch through the interstices of the Sea-Hive, aiming for the nearest main thoroughfare, the Second Canal.

'Well, boss?' he said over his shoulder to Parry. 'Waste of time, or did you get something useful out of that?'

Parry seesawed a hand in midair. 'What's *your* opinion of her?'

'With all due respect to the lady, I think she's – as you would say – barking mad.'

'You think she made the whole thing up?'

'She probably *believes* she hung out with the same Foreigner time and time again, but it could have been a dozen different ones.'

'And all these other people who got in touch with her?'

'Again, barking mad. All of them. Woof woof!'

Parry nodded. He knew Johansen was probably right. The trouble was, in spite of Viola's manifestly neurotic traits, he had found her strangely plausible.

'Listen, Pål,' he said, 'would you mind pulling up at the next public jetty we come to?'

'Sure,' said Johansen, puzzled.

A minute later he brought the launch in to a gliding halt behind a tethered private cruiser.

Parry stepped out on to the jetty. 'You go on back to HQ. Anyone asks where I am, tell them I'm, I don't know, making further enquiries or something.'

'Right. What *are* you doing?'

'Going for a wander. I need to think and walking usually helps.'

'Oh. OK.' Johansen grinned amenably, offered his captain a non-regulation salute, and reversed the launch into the centre of the canal, a liquid blister of backwash welling at the boat's stern. 'See you later, then.'

Parry waved him off and started walking.

The sun-starved backwaters of the Sea-Hive were soon behind him and he was once more in the embrace of New Venice proper, the New Venice of the brochures and the television adverts, the New Venice of bright, open spaces, of walkways and bridges and tiered hotels and shopping arcades and outdoor restaurants and ambling, perambulating tourists. As though a tourist himself, he strolled without direction, his only criterion being that, on this typically blazing-hot afternoon, he remain in shade as much as possible. This was not difficult, since wherever he went there was shelter of some sort to pass under: an awning, a parade of palms, an avenue of stone arches thatched between with vines, the cantilevered overhang of a balcony, a chessboard arrangement of large pyramidal parasols. New Venice had been designed so that pedestrians could avoid the sun if they chose to. It was a nice touch, courteous and pragmatic, typical of the city's creators.

They, a team of Italy's most prominent architects, had intended that their Venice be in every respect a worthy successor to the home of Casanova and Canaletto. To this end they had drafted and crafted a city where humans and Foreigners alike could find beauty and refinement and repose. Originally their plans had called for New Venice to be sited a kilometre off the Tuscan coast, in the Ligurian Sea (and not far from the port of Livorno, which had its own area called Venezia Nuova – hence the Anglicized name, to avoid confusion). Shortly before the first crystech foundation could be seeded in the ocean bed, however, the architects discovered that the finance for building the city was not in place. Owing to egregious bureaucratic mismanagement, the funds they had been promised by their nation's government did not exist, and when this became public knowledge a political scandal ensued that saw the whole of Italy up in arms, the people, the Mafia (then wheezing its last), even the Vatican, all decrying the incompetence of the country's elected officials and all offering different and contradictory suggestions for rectifying the problem. There were resignations and re-elections and recriminations, but by the time the dust had settled, the architects were long gone, having stormed off in disgust and sold their blueprints to the North African Countries Alliance. Italy's loss was NACA's gain, as New Venice – the name, at the behest of its creators, retained – arose from the southern Mediterranean, swiftly and ably erected by a workforce only too eager to bring into being this source of prestige and income for their homelands. Since then Italy had made a number of further attempts at constructing its own resort-city, to be called either New Venice II or, even more clumsily, New New Venice, but so far each of these projects had collapsed in ignominious failure. For this Parry was glad. In his opinion New Venice was, and should remain, unique. It was not the first-ever resort-city (that was Gaijin Hello Friendly Island, erected on top of Japan's enormous coastal reefs of consumer waste), nor was it the largest (that honour went to Bridgeville, which sprawlingly straddled the remnants of the Florida Keys). It was, however, the most elegant. Everything about it had been put together with an eye for the overall composition.

Even the spaces between buildings, those empty polygons of sky, seemed to have a structural and aesthetic purpose. No shape was random. Nothing stood that did not complement something else. All was in harmony. A city of light and air and order that had transcended its chaotic genesis to emerge supreme, redeemed – what better emblem of the Foreign era could there be?

It would have been nice to think that New Venice's architectural majesty was somehow conducive to bringing out the best in its inhabitants and visitors, and on the whole perhaps it was. But as he walked, choosing his turns on impulse, drifting, diverting, doubling back, going wherever the whim took him, all around him Parry saw – possibly because he was in a mood to notice such things – little instances of disagreement and misunderstanding that seemed somehow all the more unsightly for being set against such a splendid backdrop.

He walked and he saw a tourist couple arguing with a restaurant waiter over an error on their bill. The tourists – snowy-haired Americans, their matching pastel-and-tartan leisurewear outfits marking them out as irremediably wedlocked – addressed the waiter in loud bullying voices, repeating themselves incessantly, taking it in turns to harangue him, tag-team intimidation. 'But *surely* you *realize* . . . ?' 'But *couldn't* you *tell* . . . ?' 'But *what* kind of *idiot* . . . ?' 'But *what* sort of *math* do they *teach* at . . . ?' In return the waiter, a gawky North African post-adolescent, kept nodding and writhing and saying sorry in English and wringing APOLOGY from his hands. His contrition was acute, but the American couple kept up their verbal barrage regardless. A disproportionate amount of discomfort had to be inflicted before they could consider the matter settled to their satisfaction.

He walked on and he saw a Jehovah's Witness standing at the confluence of three avenues, silent and imperious beneath a banner that read, 'Sing to the Lord a New Song'. In the man's hand was a copy of the latest edition of the *Watch Tower*, in which, if previous issues Parry had read were anything to go by, resort-cities were described as Babylons, Sirens as whores, and Foreigners as harbingers of the Last Days, an omen of the onset of End-Time. The Jehovah's Witness was entitled to stage his protest on condition that he talked to no one and did not force his magazine on passers-by but rather let people take copies from him if they wanted to. Accordingly, while the fervent blaze in his eyes spoke volumes, his lips stayed firmly sealed.

Parry walked on and he saw a Foreigner, wandering on its own, being approached by a young woman who, without warning, burst into song, leaning seductively towards the golden giant as she trilled questing, exploratory arpeggios. The Foreigner appeared taken aback and, with an awkward, flustered inclination of its head, formed the hand-symbol for REJECTION, rapidly following it with GRATITUDE. The Siren immediately stopped singing, signed APOLOGY, and backed away. The Foreigner, having taken a moment to compose itself, continued on its journey. Had the woman persisted with her attempt to hook the golden giant, Parry would have intervened and requested her to desist.

He walked on and he saw a vagrant being accosted by two of his fellow FPP officers (he was in another captain's district, so he knew the officers' faces but not their names). The vagrant was a Berber, dressed in a vivid blue woollen cloak and a short white conical hat, his face as arid and lined as a desert, his limbs skinny like tree branches. Obviously, in common with many on the mainland who begged for a living, the Berber saw nothing wrong in hopping aboard the commuter ferry to New Venice and trying his luck here, where money flowed in abundance, hoping that a tourist would take pity on him and donate a nearly extinct IC card, perhaps, or a tiny fleck of Foreign currency. He offered no resistance when the FPP officers took him by the elbows and helped him to his feet. Murmuring docilely in Riffian, he allowed himself to be escorted to a waiting launch. He would be kept in a holding chamber at HQ and returned to the mainland later that day.

Parry walked on and he saw a shop window that had been broken either by a vandal or, more likely, by someone accidentally falling against it. Cracks radiated from a point of impact at shoulder height, and over this a crystech patch like a smooth puddle of ice had been applied so that no shards would fall out. Behind the damaged glass there was a display of novelty merchandise: ornamental swords, New Venice snowstorm globes, Foreigner bean-toys in velvety golden plush, T-shirts with the faces of famous composers printed on them, ikons of St Cecilia. It was from a shop such as this that Parry had bought the fake Foreign statuette that had so underwhelmed his nephew and niece.

He walked on and he saw other such vignettes of life in New Venice, other tiny human blemishes that in most cities would have passed unnoticed but here stood out like coffee stains on a white damask tablecloth, and all the while he thought of Anna, and of

Viola d'Indy, and of dead Daryl Henderson. He thought of language, and how words could sometimes convey less than silence. He thought of music, and how, with or without lyrics, it could often convey more than language. He thought of the myriad daily misunderstandings that occurred between people as the cogs of communication hiccuped and juddered and mismeshed and occasionally whirled free, turning nothing except themselves. He thought of hand-symbols, which the Foreigners had taught the world so that they and humans could converse, and which humans had adopted in order to converse with each other – the closest thing to a pan-global vocabulary since the Tower of Babel fell, more widespread and successful than Interlingua or Interglossa or Esperanto had ever been, and yet, with a repertoire of only ninety-six terms, still basic, a toddler's tongue. He thought of the purity of emotional connection that both Professor Franchetti and Viola d'Indy had described when talking about singing, and he tried to imagine Henderson moaning love and sorrow to his Foreigner, the charmer charmed, the handsome youth who could have had any woman (or perhaps man) he wanted but who, it appeared, had fallen hopelessly, helplessly, for a non-human entity.

Parry walked until, almost to his surprise, he found himself at Crystal Beach on the westernmost limits of the city. Blinking as though coming round from a trance, he saw that the sun was on the wane, losing its shape a few degrees above the horizon, sagging and turning red from the effort of shining all day. According to his watch, the time was a few minutes short of half-past five. Incredibly, he had wandered, deep in thought, for nearly four hours.

Hungry, he bought a lamb pitta sandwich from a vendor's stall on the promenade and descended steps to the beach's long, gently shelving slope. The crystalline surface underfoot was milled and grained so as to provide traction, its texture not unlike that of corduroy. Here and there sections of the beach were elevated to horizontal, creating platforms for deckchairs and sun-loungers. Parry made his way towards the waterline. Halting a metre or so from the sloshing breakers, he removed his jacket, folded it to form a neat cushion, and sat on it. Elbows propped on knees, he munched the sandwich, pausing every so often to wipe a dribble of mint dressing from his chin.

Bathers yelped and frolicked in the glittering shallows, and beyond the buoys of the shark-nets windsurfers exploited what little late-afternoon wind there was, yanking on their sails while their boards splashed sedately across the waves. Pleasure yachts bobbed at anchor in the middle distance, while far off, where sea ended and sky began, chrome-tinged cloud banks were amassing. On the beach itself hundreds of sunbathers basked, prone or supine or sitting upright or lying on their sides reading, their bronzed skins glistening with oils, and there were people strolling, languid in the deepening light, and there were Foreigners about, too, picking their way around and among the mobile and immobile humans. It was rare to find a Foreigner standing still. Always, when out in the open, golden giants seemed to be on their way to somewhere, peering around them with their masks' empty eyes as they went, somehow seeing, or at least appearing to see. These ones gazed at the sunbathers and the sea-bathers and the ocean and the sky and the gloaming fade of the day, all with equal fascination. They steered clear of the water, and sometimes clustered together in groups of two or three to share a few silent moments of travelling companionship before dispersing and going their separate ways again. It struck Parry that, here on the beach, they were turning fewer heads than usual, and he wondered why, till the answer, an obvious one, occurred to him. Most of the people around him had sunglasses on and so could stare without appearing to stare. They looked as sightless as the Foreigners, but from behind their blank black lenses could see just as much.

When his sandwich was finished, and its greaseproof-paper wrapper had been wadded up and tucked into his shirt pocket for later disposal, Parry licked his lips and closed his eyes and listened for a while to the cream and purl of the surf. He might have nodded off briefly. When he opened his eyes again, he saw that the sun was bloated, old now, very low, ripe for immersion. It was time to make a decision. Quesnel needed an explanation for the death of Daryl Henderson and the loss of the Foreigner with him. She needed something to give to the media, something for the newspapers and TV networks and internetworks to disseminate, something that was straightforward and reassuring and readily digestible. She needed to let everyone know that all was well in New Venice. It was not enough that the world was running on a more-or-less even keel these days. It must be *seen* to be doing so.

He could tell her that he thought the deaths were murders, and she could say so on air, and what then? Uproar. NACA would demand action. The FPP would be under pressure to find the culprit or culprits, and of course its officers would do their best, but the FPP was largely a symbolic organization, bound by strict rules and protocols, there to reassure more by its presence than by anything it could do. Hampered by the measures of the Constitution and hamstrung by the lack of evidence pertaining to the incident, the FPP would flounder around, much to the delight of its opponents, Xenophobes in particular, who would not hesitate to make political capital out of its misfortunes. Meanwhile there would be consternation in the city, perhaps even panic, not least among Sirens, seeing as it was one of their number who was dead. Sirens were the direct interface between humans and Foreigners. If they were alarmed, their alarm would be conveyed, inadvertently or otherwise, to the Foreigners they sang for. So far the golden giants appeared unaware of – or, if aware, unconcerned by – the loss at the Amadeus. He doubted they would remain so calm if the Sirens they hired had their minds on other things and gave vocal performances that were anxious and preoccupied and anything less than wholeheartedly enthusiastic.

On the other hand, there was the *shinju* theory. It was credible and to a certain extent comprehensible. Love was so broad and fundamental an emotion, encompassing so many extremes, that almost anything could be and had been committed in its name. Love was a motive everyone was familiar with, even if everyone might not always understand or sympathize with it.

He considered what the reaction might be. Naturally there would be those who would not take kindly to the idea of a human and a Foreigner falling in love, and not just falling in love but killing themselves for love. Anthropocentric moralists, religious extremists, Xenophobes – they would all feel the need to voice their discontent and disapproval, and their grumbles would be patiently heard out. However, within and outside New Venice the vast majority of people would, he believed, he hoped, respond to the content of Quesnel's statement with a tolerant shrug. These things happened, they would say. *C'est la vie. Que sera sera. Mai pen rai.* So it goes.

Murder or suicide? The latter was, in so many ways, the lesser of two evils.

He had distinct reservations about offering Quesnel what was still essentially a guess rather than a solid, tested, testified fact. All he had to back up the *shinju* theory was anecdotal and circumstantial evidence, and that made him uneasy. The copper in him, the

Hendon-trained boy in blue, wanted eyewitness testimonial, signed statements, corroboration, previous, form. In the absence of those he felt edgy and adrift.

He told himself he still had a day left. Perhaps something would turn up tomorrow, something that would either confirm or disprove once and for all that the incident at the Amadeus had been a shared suicide rather than a joint homicide/Xenocide.

13 QUAVER

The following day, however, Parry made no further progress on the case, and all that turned up was Dr Erraji's full report which, for all its depth of detail, shed scant new light on the matter. The medical examiner was now able to state that the Foreign clothing found with Daryl Henderson was genuine. A sample of the robe subjected to vaporization in an acetylene flame had emitted the light-wavelength signature unique to Foreign cloth. As for the criminalists, they had uncovered a multitude of fingerprints all over the room, superimposed and subimposed, partial and latent and complete, far too many to make sense of. The only fingerprints on the gun, however, were those of the deceased.

The transcript of the medical examiner's postmortem monologue little improved Parry's understanding of the case, even though he read through the text several times. He had not perused such a document in quite some time, but it came back to him quickly enough – the dryly macabre terminology of forensic pathology, that dark necrotic fustian. There they all were, his old friends autolysis, serology, and the triumvirate he used to refer to blackly as the Mortis Brothers – Rigor, Algor and Livor.

For all its precision and detail, however, the transcript left him none the wiser as to the state of the mind that had inhabited the dead Siren's dissected body. Erraji was unable to penetrate Henderson's motives with his scalpel and his bone saw. He could make Y-incisions but not why-incisions.

By afternoon's end Parry had made up his mind once and for all to deem the deaths suicides. In a report on the investigation that ended up being ten pages long, he outlined the conversations with Professor Franchetti and Viola d'Indy that had helped him arrive at this conclusion, and he suggested that Quesnel might consider using the term *shinju* in her press statement, as it offered a factual, if somewhat exotic, precedent. Throughout, he was at pains to employ the most cautious syntax he could, entwining countless ifs and maybes and perhaps into the text until it ended up a veritable cat's cradle of caveats and conditionals. He was sure the commissioner would take the hint and phrase her statement similarly.

Three e-messages from Quesnel came through to his work board while he was putting the report together. The first was a polite nudge: 'Any time you're ready with that report, Jack, fire it my way.' The second was a sharp dig in the ribs: 'I'm looking forward to seeing that report real soon, Jack.' The third was nothing short of an order: 'The report, Jack. Now.' When that one arrived, Parry knew he had probably about quarter of an hour before Quesnel came down and visited him in person. Quickly he applied the finishing touches to what he had written, trimming away excess adjectives, honing, paring, tightening.

The report lay ready on the screen. He summoned up Transmit mode and inputted 'Internal/Quesnel'.

The Send icon was highlighted. Parry's forefinger hovered over the Enter key.

Even now, when he could not afford to hesitate, he had misgivings. A vague, deep-seated unease, something that was almost a presentiment of unwelcome consequences, kept his finger from descending. He told himself he was being daft. He told himself he was being paranoid. What was the worst that could happen? Somehow, somewhere down the line, he would be proved wrong? He had covered his backside. He had given himself a sizeable margin for error. Maybe that was what was troubling him, the very elasticity of the report's wording. There *was* something a bit snaky and evasive about his refusal to commit a definite, unqualified assertion to the page. Maybe he should have greater confidence in his opinions.

But there was no time to rewrite, no time to revise. What was done was done. Should anything negative come of this, he would simply have to live with it.

His finger stabbed down.

14 REVEILLE

The mechanism of the musical box lay spread out on the black velvet cloth like stars in the night sky, spangled constellations of cog wheels and damper wires and gearing and springs and screws. Close by, also on the living-room table, the musical box itself rested with its lid open, displaying its eviscerated interior. Next to it a pair of plastic figures – a dancing couple, each no taller than a matchstick – lay on their sides, locked in a ballroom embrace. When the musical box worked, the figures rotated together and, once every revolution, the male dancer would raise the female dancer aloft. As he did this, her legs, which were attached by pins, would quiver as if in delight.

It was a Sunday afternoon. Parry's father was hunched over the tabletop, bow-backed, frowning, a man intent. He and his son were alone in the house. Where Mum and Carol had gone, Parry had no idea.

Outside, visible both through the front windows and the glass doors that gave on to the back patio, there was dreary, insistent rain. The rain must have been falling for days, because the patio was awash, the rear lawn had become a swamp, and the branches of the cooking-apple tree were drooping and dripping heavily. There was time in the tick of the rain on glass, like a clock gone wrong, quarter-seconds passing at irregular speed. Parry could also hear, distantly, the shouts of a crowd, and a rumbling as of something immense and mechanical, something hideously huge, approaching.

'You see, Jack?' said his father, not looking up, pointing to the musical-box components with a pair of tweezers.

Parry moved closer to the table.

'You see what I'm talking about? Anyone can do it. It's easy. Taking apart is easy. A few twists of the screwdriver and it all comes to pieces.'

This was his father's spare-time hobby, mending novelty musical boxes. He advertised in the local paper and in a specialist magazine that dealt with clockwork memorabilia, and from all over the country they would be sent to him, frozen and silent in padded parcels: ballerinas and alpine chalets and merry-go-rounds and trains on circular tracks and beer steins that played tunes when you lifted their lids, all of which, for a surprisingly modest fee, because he loved the work and would have done the work for love, he would make turn and tinkle and ting once more. He had a job on the production line at a nearby car plant, but when he wasn't taking part in the assembly of automobiles, he would be disassembling and reassembling musical boxes. He would scrub rust off the chromatic tines of the comb with wire-wool; make sure the pinned brass barrel revolved properly; oil and if necessary replace the mainspring and the fan governor. With tiny elven tools grasped in his coarse car-builder's hands, he would restore voices to these toys that had been struck dumb by age or corrosion or neglect. He was self-taught, having served an amateur apprenticeship on a wrist-watch he had owned as a boy, dismantling it out of curiosity and forcing himself to figure out how to put it together again. It was rare that he received a musical box so broken that he could not repair it.

'The difficult bit,' he told his son, 'is rebuilding.'

When *is* this, Parry wondered. How old am I?

'That's the trick of it,' his father went on. He was wearing his close-work spectacles. Their steel rims glinted in the dull post-meridian light. Their lenses flashed with reflected silver. His bald scalp glowed like polished pink marble. 'Construction is always harder than destruction.'

Somewhere nearby a telephone was trilling. A fruity electric burble.

'You might be able to see all the pieces,' Parry's father said, waving a hand across the velvet cloth, 'but that doesn't necessarily mean that you can fit them all together correctly.'

The phone was still ringing. Someone ought to get it, Parry thought. Maybe *I* should.

Still in the living room of his parents' old house, where there was gold-on-white *fleur de lis* paper on the walls and where the back garden was now knee-deep in rainwater, Parry reached out an arm. He reached out an arm because he had realized that the phone that was ringing was the bedside extension in his apartment in New Venice and it was early morning and he was still asleep, and as he fumbled for the receiver, his father and the wet Sunday afternoon and the dismantled musical box began to fade as though retreating down a long tunnel, hollowing into oblivion. Then Parry was sitting up in bed with the receiver to his ear, and the voice at the other end belonged to Sergeant Shankar from his district. Shankar and Avni alternated on the midnight-to-morning shift, each taking three days on, three days off.

'Captain, so sorry to disturb you.'

'What time is it, Ranjit?'

'Coming up to six. You had better get down to the Ponte da Ponte.'

'Why?'

'A body, sir. A floater.'

15   BRIDGE PASSAGE

The sky was overcast, the air warm and clammy like an infection. Rain had been forecast and Parry could tell that, when it came, it would be one of those tepid, tiresome subtropical drizzles that wavered in and out of existence all day long.

The concept of *rain* triggered a vague, dim inkling of a memory – something to do with the dream which Sergeant Shankar's call had interrupted. But almost as soon as he had swung his legs out from under the bedcovers Parry had forgotten what the dream was about and he knew that trying to remember now would be futile, not to mention a waste of mental energy, in which resource he was distinctly lacking at this early hour.

He was standing at the midpoint of the Ponte da Ponte, which spanned one of New Venice's subsidiary canals. Below, a pair of FPP officers in a launch were recovering the body of the drowned woman. She was floating belly-up, her face canted backwards below the water's surface and her limp arms slowly wafting as though, pathetically, she was attempting to swim. Trapped air bloated her skirt, which pulsed like a jellyfish, revealing brief, unerotic glimpses of underwear. She was tethered in place by the buckle of one of her shoes, which had snagged on a clump of kelp that flourished on the bridge's central pile.

With the aid of boathooks the two FPP officers succeeded in disentangling her, then pulled her towards them and, with a shivery, inexpert roughness, hauled her into the launch. She rolled aboard, slithering over the gunwales and fetching up at the officers' feet with no more grace or dignity than a haul of fish. Face-down, drenched and slippery, her legs crossed, her arms akimbo, her hair in Medusan tangles, her head twisted at an ugly, ungainly angle, she lay. Her flesh was mottled pink and grey, the two colours together reminding Parry of poached salmon. Her skin looked fibrous and swollen, like sodden blotting paper.

On the banks of the canal and on the balconies of the hotels that rose on either side, there were onlookers, perhaps a dozen of them all told. Their expressions, as far as Parry could make out, were of frank fascination. None of them was being furtive in their interest. None of them was flinching in horror. Perhaps they felt that because the drowned woman was dead she could not be offended by their stares. One onlooker – a stocky man on a ninth-floor balcony, wearing nothing but a pair of mauve Y-fronts – was even filming the event with a palmcorder. That would be something to show the folks back home, Parry thought sourly. *Here's us lounging by the poolside. Here's us at Crystal Beach. Oh, and here's a corpse being pulled from the water. And here's us having cocktails at the* . . .

Shankar approached Parry along the bridge. He was a tubby Hindu with cottage-loaf cheeks and eyes that were tawny shading to orange. His face looked pale, which Parry put down to either the weak dawn light or the gruesome nature of the business that had brought them here, most likely a combination of the two.

'Her neck is broken, I think,' Shankar said.

Parry nodded. 'She must have fallen.'

'Or thrown herself.'

'Or thrown herself.' Parry spoke the words distantly, dismissively. He was keen to believe that the woman's death had been nothing more than an accident. She had slipped from a bridge, or stumbled off a boat, or been perched on the balustrade of a balcony and inadvertently overbalanced. Fate alone had been responsible. No human volition had been involved.

'From some considerable height, I would say,' Shankar added, peering up at the overshadowing cliffs of hotel as though by some sixth sense he might be able to pinpoint the very spot from which the woman had plummeted. Parry, by contrast, looked down, scanning the torpid turquoise waters of the canal, as if an answer were more likely to be found where the woman had finished up.

As carefully as parents putting a child to bed, the FPP officers in the launch draped a tarpaulin over the body.

And then Parry heard Shankar utter a soft, surprised 'Oh.'

He glanced round at the sergeant, raising first his head, then an eyebrow.

Shankar was holding up a hand, pointing. 'I may be mistaken, sir, but isn't that . . . ?'

'Isn't that what?'

'Look, sir.'

Parry followed the line of Shankar's finger. He needed spectacles for reading, there was nothing wrong with his long vision.

'You mean that bloke with the palmcorder?' he said, and tutted. 'I know. Some people.'

'No, sir. One floor down from him, four balconies along to the left.'

Parry tracked accordingly. He squinted.

'I can't see what you're referring to.'

Then he could.

Through the balustrade of the balcony that Shankar had indicated, Parry made out what looked like a pile of discarded laundry. It might have been a swimming towel that had been hung up to dry on the balustrade and slithered off . . . except that the material was golden and, even on this grey morning, glistered.

'Which hotel is that?' Parry asked, in a low, hard voice.

'The Debussy, sir.'

Three minutes later Parry and Shankar were in the lobby of the Debussy, demanding a master key-unit from the concierge. Two minutes after that they were up on the eighth floor, moving swiftly along a corridor, counting doors as they went. The odd-numbered rooms to their left were those with a view of the canal and the Ponte da Ponte. So intent were they on locating the correct door that when a thickset man in a hotel bathrobe came sauntering past with his hands behind his back, they paid him little attention. Parry noted the man peripherally and thought there was something faintly familiar about him, but he had more important things on his mind.

They reached the seventh door from the end of the corridor – the door which, by their reckoning, belonged to the room on whose balcony they had spotted what appeared to be a Foreign robe. The room was number 879.

'Get ready to apologize,' Parry said to Shankar. 'We may be about to wake some poor bugger up.' He knew, though, with a dull, aching certainty, that the room itself would be empty and that the remains of its erstwhile Foreign occupant were lying outside. And the drowned woman? Had she, too, been in this room? Something – some instinctive dread – said she had.

He knocked. No reply from within.

The key-unit chirruped and the door opened.

Inside there were Foreign-scale furniture and hotel-perfect tidiness.

The curtains were open.

On the balcony lay the Foreign robe.

And on the room's dressing table there was a small evening bag with a long thin strap, the kind a woman might carry to a gala function or a nightclub. Parry picked it up and opened it. It contained lipstick, a powder compact, a panty-liner in its paper packet, a passport card, and an old-fashioned velvet drawstring purse in which there was both an IC card and a few Foreign jewels.

Parry had only caught a brief glimpse of the face of the drowned woman, but as soon as he saw the photo on the passport card he had no doubt.

The drowned woman and the woman in the photo were one and the same.

16 INTERPRETATION

At first, Parry was suffused with a deep and grating sense of injustice. That this should have happened twice in his district within the space of a few days was outrageous – a personal insult, almost. He felt like someone whose home has been burgled and then, while there are boards still up on the broken window, burgled again.

These feelings soon subsided and his professionalism reasserted itself. He looked again at the passport card.

'Dagmar Pfitzner,' he said. 'German citizen. Age thirty-eight.'

'A Siren?' said Shankar.

'Hard to believe otherwise. One of those rare Sirens who carry personal effects on them. Bet you anything she's registered, too. When it comes to being law-abiding, the Germans can teach us all a thing or two.'

Parry returned the passport card to the evening bag, then went to the windows, which were wide open. He stepped out on to the balcony in order to inspect the Foreign remains. The individual items – robe, mask, gloves – were identical to those at the Amadeus but strewn in a different pattern. One of the gloves was stretched out flat on the balcony tiles, as though the Foreigner had been reaching for something when it died. The other was tangled in amongst the folds of the robe. The mask lay in one corner, and Parry pictured it rolling there like a head severed by an axeman, fetching up on its side to face the blank wall.

Grasping the balustrade rail, he glanced over. It was a straight drop to the canal, fifty metres or more. Down there the FPP launch was pulling away from the Ponte da Ponte with its dead human cargo. The boat was small enough for him to have blocked it from sight with a hand held out flat.

As he watched the launch chunter off, he heard a disturbance within the room behind him. Shankar was addressing someone loudly: 'Please, sir, I must ask you to leave. This is a crime scene. You are not allowed to do that in here.'

Parry turned.

Shankar was talking to the man they had passed in the corridor, and now Parry realized why he had seemed familiar. He was also the man who had been filming with a palmcorder from the floor above, the man with the mauve underpants. He had the palmcorder in his hand now, and it was trained on Parry and the Foreign garments. Shankar was tapping the man's shoulder and continuing to remonstrate with him, but the man kept on filming blithely, panning between Parry and the Foreign remains, adjusting focus with a twitch of his forefinger.

'Sir,' Parry said, stepping off the balcony, back into the room, 'would you kindly do as my colleague says? You're interfering with a Foreign Policy Police investigation.'

'Captain, I'm very sorry,' Shankar said. 'It's my fault. I left the door ajar. He walked right in.'

'That's OK, Sergeant.' Parry moved a couple of paces closer to the man with the palmcorder.

The man was powerfully built, his body bulking out the bathrobe. His face was so solidly fat that what would otherwise have been wrinkles across the forehead were deep seams, and his mouth was a surly batrachian pout. His visible eye, the one not obscured by the palmcorder, was closed, so Parry had no choice but to direct his comments to the lens of the palmcorder itself.

'Sir,' he said, 'please, I implore you. Turn the camera off. Now.'

There was implacable obstinacy, not only in the blank blue-brown gaze of the lens but in the attitude of the man himself, his stance, his silence. He was not about to stop doing anything for anybody.

None the less Parry persisted. He had no choice. 'Sir, I must demand that you switch off the palmcorder this instant.'

'Please, my friend,' said Shankar, 'you must do as the captain says.'

But still the man did not respond and Shankar, piqued by his stubbornness, made a grab for the palmcorder. He succeeded in knocking it away from the man's eye, and the man, letting out a growl, retaliated by seizing Shankar's collar with his free hand and giving the sergeant a mighty shove that sent him staggering backwards. The back of Shankar's knee collided with the edge of the bed and he tumbled to the floor. The man wheeled round and made for the door.

Pausing only to check that Shankar was not seriously hurt, Parry set off in pursuit.

The palmcorder man was surprisingly fleet of foot for someone of such a physique. When Parry emerged from the room, he was already halfway down the corridor, propelling himself along with bounding thrusts of his stumpy legs. Parry sprinted off in pursuit. The man passed the lifts and, at the end of the corridor, barged through a pair of fire-doors and turned a corner. The fire-doors did not have time to swing shut before Parry had reached them and lunged through. Skidding, he veered left as the man had done, then halted. The man was gone. The corridor stretched ahead, empty.

Parry loped along it, wondering if his quarry had taken refuge in one of the rooms on either side. No, that was impossible, unless he had a master key-unit, which he surely did not.

Twenty metres on from the fire-doors, Parry came to a half-glassed door marked 'Staircase'. He pushed it open just in time to hear the corresponding door on the next floor up hiss shut on its hydraulic hinge.

Galvanized back into action, he bounded up after the man, taking the stairs three at a time, and yanked the door open. Turning right, he headed along the corridor and thrust through the fire-doors which, according to a plaque on the wall, led to Rooms 960–990. The man was nowhere to be seen, but that did not matter. It was obvious now where he had fled to. Parry recalled that the balcony on the floor below with the Foreign remains on it was four along from the balcony on which he had first sighted the man. If the Foreigner's room was 879, then the man's room had to be – a quick spot of mental arithmetic – number 971. Parry offered up a brief prayer of thanks for the mathematical rectitude of the hotel's designers.

Outside 971, he brandished the master key-unit. The door clunked open. Tensing in anticipation of hostility, if not actual assault, he entered.

The man was in the middle of the room, bent double, red-faced, heaving for breath. He was still clutching the palmcorder. Beside him, with a solicitous hand on his back, stood a woman. She was of a similar age and proportions, short, rotund, in her fifties. She was wearing a bra and a nylon petticoat, and she was staring over her shoulder at Parry with a mixture of shock and indignation.

Immediately Parry manufolded APOLOGY, to which the woman's only response was to swivel round and lodge her fists on the shelves

133

of her hips, which caused great swags of doughy flesh to clump down from her upper arms. Her eyes were small and spaced too close together, and her cheeks and the yoke of her shoulders were rosily radiant with sunburn. Her huge breasts, slung within the conical confines of the bra's cups, jutted forward like a pair of warheads, minatory and military. She made no effort to cover herself. She knew how intimidating she could look, even in her underwear.

'Yes?' she said. 'Excuse me?'

Her accent was Russian, Parry guessed, and the guess was confirmed by a glimpse of a New Venice guidebook sitting on the dressing table – the cover text was in Cyrillic script – and by the sight of a Schebalin portable home board plugged into the bedside phone socket. The brand had few devotees outside Russia.

'Captain Parry, Foreign Policy Police,' he said.

'I can see you are FPP. Why are you chasing my husband?'

Parry was about to reply when the man grunted something in his native tongue. His wife asked him a question, which he answered with a gasped torrent of words, then wiped sweat from his brow and resumed panting.

'Misha says that he has done nothing wrong,' the woman told Parry. 'He was making a video film and one of your men attacked him.'

'*Da*,' said the man. 'Attack.'

'Please inform your husband, Mrs . . . Excuse me, I don't know your name.'

'Dargomyzhsky. Irina Dargomyzhsky. My husband is Mikhail.'

'Please inform your husband, Mrs Dargomyzhsky, that he intruded on a situation of a highly sensitive nature and filmed footage of something I would prefer he had not.'

Irina Dargomyzhsky explained this to her husband, and translated his reply. 'Misha says he by chance passed the room you were in. The door was open. Out of curiosity he looked in. He happened to have his palmcorder on him, so he started to film. The other officer with you attacked him. You were both talking to him but he did not know what you were saying. His English', she added, 'almost does not exist.'

That last part, at least, sounded true. As for the rest, Parry knew Dargomyzhsky had not passed the room 'by chance'. He had been prowling the eighth-floor corridor, having observed Parry's and Shankar's keen interest in one of the balconies on that floor, and perhaps having also spied the Foreign clothing on that balcony. He had scented an opportunity and decided to exploit it.

Biting back an exasperated sigh, Parry said, 'I admit that, in order to stop him filming, my sergeant acted in a somewhat intemperate manner and I apologize for that. If your husband wishes to file a complaint about the sergeant's conduct, then he is free to do so through the appropriate channels. What I have to know, Mrs Dargomyzhsky, is what your husband intends to do with the footage he has obtained.'

Mrs Dargomyzhsky passed Parry's question on.

'He will sell it to a television station.'

Which was precisely what Parry had expected, and feared.

Mikhail Dargomyzhsky spoke again. He had got his wind back by now.

'It will make much money,' his wife said. 'The woman's body alone will make money, but the remains of a Foreigner, too – a television station will pay plenty for this.'

Parry took a deep breath, ordering himself to remain calm, remain civil. 'I understand that, Mrs Dargomyzhsky, and you are probably aware that as an FPP officer I have no legal authority to force you and your husband to hand over the palmcorder disc to me. I can only ask – beg – that you do. The footage on that disc, if aired on television, may significantly compromise an ongoing FPP investigation.'

'Can the Foreign Policy Police offer more money for it than a television station?' was Dargomyzhsky's reply, transmitted via his wife.

'Your only compensation would be the gratitude of the New Venice FPP and the satisfaction of knowing that you have helped the cause of Foreign–human relations.'

When his wife told him this, Dargomyzhsky simply laughed. His subsequent speech was couched in such a sneering tone, Parry almost did not need to have it rendered into English.

'Misha says that gratitude will not pay us back the cost of this holiday, and he does not care about Foreign–human relations. We are from Kiev. Foreigners do not often visit there. What difference does it make to us how well they get on with humans?'

'Because,' said Parry, and he was about to launch into an impassioned homily concerning the many reasons why the people of Earth, all of them, of every nationality, had a vested interest in retaining the good will of the golden giants, not to mention a moral duty to do so. Then he thought: Why bother? Whatever he said, it was unlikely to have any impact on the couple, least of all on Mr Dargomyzhsky, who would be receiving the speech second-hand through his wife. Dargomyzhsky was dead-set on making a fast buck from his palmcorder footage, and no amount of reasoned, sincere argument was going to dissuade him.

So instead Parry simply said, with as much rancour as he would permit himself, and a little more than perhaps was Constitutional, 'Well, no doubt you'll feel very proud of yourselves, both of you, as you cash the TV station's cheque. I expect you'll feel a real sense of achievement, knowing you've behaved in a way the rest of us grew out of years ago.'

'You want to shame me into changing my mind?' was Dargomyzhsky's wife's rendition of his reply. 'I am Russian. A good Russian capitalist. When it comes to money I know no shame.'

'I was trying to appeal to your better nature,' Parry said. 'To your conscience.'

Dargomyzhsky pushed past his wife and barked several sentences of Russian at Parry, punctuating them with chopping forward thrusts of his hand. According to Mrs Dargomyzhsky, he was accusing Parry of putting far too much store by a conscience. If a conscience was what made Parry so sensitive towards the Foreigners' needs that he had become, effectively, their lapdog, then a conscience was surely a bad thing. Was Parry forgetting which race was here on this planet first? Why should humans have to put Foreign interests before their own every time? Why was it up to humans to adapt their ways to suit Foreigners and not the other way round?

The contempt in Dargomyzhsky's words and tone was somehow, paradoxically, the greater for being relayed in such a calm, neutral manner by his wife. Parry wondered how it could be – how Dargomyzhsky could so wholeheartedly believe that he was in the right and Parry was in the wrong. Surely, by any objective standard, the reverse was true?

He and Dargomyzhsky stood there, glaring at each other, and suddenly the urge to punch the Russian was immense. Parry could feel his right hand itching to clench and swing. It would be great, wouldn't it? So satisfying to plant a fist into that fat, belligerent face.

In the old days, even as a copper, he might have done it, and sod the consequences. Now, though, he knew he had to restrain himself. In this world, as a member of the new and improved human race, you were expected to act at all times with forbearance, not least if you worked for the FPP.

'I regret this encounter,' Parry said as he turned on his heel and exited the Dargomyzhskys' room.

He hoped that in Russian, as in English, the word *regret* could convey both apology and distaste.

17 DISCORDANCE

Parry's return journey from the ninth floor to the eighth was as slow and ruminative as the journey from the eighth floor to the ninth had been swift and purposeful. All the way, he simmered with anger. Dargomyzhsky's refusal to budge over the issue of the palmcorder disc seemed to him the worst kind of arrogance. It was as though the man felt he had a God-given right to make money from the footage he had filmed. *A good Russian capitalist.* Like that was something to be proud of.

But then – a small, reasonable voice in a corner of Parry's mind pointed out – Dargomyzhsky was not entirely to blame for the way he was. Prior to the Debut, the West had spent many years and a great deal of money enticing Dargomyzhsky and his countrymen into the embrace of capitalism, like a suitor wooing a lover, offering all manner of bribes and blandishments. After some initial wariness, and a few misunderstandings and false starts, the Russians had taken to enterprise culture with a vengeance, and soon the grasping, voracious Russian businessman had become a stock figure of caricature. Free-Market Fyodor. Boris Gotenough. Ivan Awful-Lot. And then the Foreigners had come and the world had moved on.

Or had it? Capitalism, after all, had not vanished with the coming of the golden giants. International trade accords had been put in place to make the distribution of wealth among nations fairer, and there were strict controls over monopolies and firm guidelines on wages and workers' benefits, but money – the creating of it, the obtaining of it, the augmenting of it – still made the world go round. If anything, the presence of the Foreigners had lent further legitimacy to the pursuit of financial gain. You only had to think of Sirens, and of resort-cities, and of the many crystech pioneers who had amassed fortunes from a technological process they did not themselves invent. Hector Fuentes for one. Anna's late husband. The self-styled Crystech Caballero.

And thinking of Fuentes, Parry was unable to prevent a twinge of sullen resentment from attaching itself to his general state of irritability. Alive, Fuentes had been one of those men you either admired or tried hard *not* to admire. Parry had had no particular dislike of him then. Now, however, Fuentes exerted an unwelcome hold over him, for his death had not, as it ought to have done, freed Anna to carry on her affair with him openly. Rather, for reasons unknown to him, it had had the opposite effect of forcing her to draw back and say that they could not see each other ever again except as friends. ('Good friends', she insisted, as though that made a difference.)

These thoughts threatened to drag him down into deeper realms of bitterness, and so, with some effort, he refocused his mind on Dargomyzhsky.

It was, he decided, not Dargomyzhsky's desire to make money that annoyed him. A certain acquisitiveness was innate in everyone. It was just that Dargomyzhsky's greed had been so naked, so unprincipled. That was what left such an unpleasant taste in the mouth.

Re-entering Room 879, he found Shankar sitting on the corner of the bed, nursing a bumped elbow.

'You all right?'

Shankar performed that characteristic Indian head-wobble which signifies neither *yes* nor *no* but a little of both. 'I'm fine, I think.'

'You shouldn't have touched him.'

'I know, Captain. I was most remiss. Would it help if I went and apologized to him?'

'Doubt it.'

'May I ask what happened? Did you catch up with him? You don't have the disc on you, I see.'

Parry supplied a terse précis of his full and frank exchange of views with Dargomyzhsky, then exhaled a long, remorseful sigh. 'This is going to screw things up pretty badly for us. All I can try and do is limit the damage.'

'How?'

'The commissioner's due to hold a press conference on the Amadeus incident in about' – Parry glanced at his watch – 'an hour. I'm going to have to ask her to cancel it.'

'Cancel it, sir? Why?'

'Quesnel is going to stand up in front of the assembled media hounds and break the news about death and loss at the Amadeus,' said Parry, heading over to the room's bedside telephone. 'She's going to want to play it down, emphasize that it's an exceptional case, unprecedented, with any luck unique. A few hours later, Dargomyzhsky's footage goes out on air. At best, we're going to look like we've been caught on the hop. At worst, we're going to come across as a bunch of inept morons who don't have the faintest idea what's going on in our own city.'

'From what the Russian filmed, it's not obvious that the Pfitzner woman and the Foreign remains are connected.'

'News people are good at making connections. You and I were down on the bridge, then up in this room. That's a pretty major clue right there. Add to that the fact that Quesnel will have just told everyone about the discovery of the remains of a Foreigner and a Siren together, and it's likely that, even if the Foreign loss and Siren death here *weren't* related to each other, the media will assume they were.'

He picked up the telephone handset, pressed 0 for an outside line, and tapped in the number for HQ.

'FPP Headquarters, front desk,' said a voice on the line.

'Captain Parry here. Yoshi?'

'Good morning, sir.'

'Morning. Would you put me through to the commissioner's office?'

'Of course, sir. The body they found. Is it another—?'

'Just put me through, Yoshi.'

'I don't think she's in yet, sir.'

'Doesn't matter.'

The dial tone for Quesnel's work board burred three times, then gave way to a click of connection.

'This is the voicemail of Commissioner Quesnel. Speak.'

'Ma'am, Parry here. I'm at the Debussy. We've come across another pair of remains, human and Foreign. Very similar circumstances to the last pair. Unfortunately something's, um, something's come up that means we're not going to be able to keep this one under wraps. I'll explain why later, in person. Suffice to say it's beyond my control, I can't do anything to prevent it, and I strongly suggest that you abort the press conference. Postpone it at least, until we can figure out some kind of revised plan of action.' He laid his finger on the disconnecting switch. 'Best try her at home as well. Just to be on the safe side.'

'You have Commissioner Quesnel's home number?'

Parry gave an ironic smirk. 'Captain's privilege.'

Quesnel's home board was in answer mode as well. She must be in transit between there and Headquarters. There was no point, then, leaving the same message at her apartment, where she would not pick it up until long after it would be of any use. Parry replaced the receiver and sat for a while with his hands braced on his knees, staring at the Foreign garments out on the balcony.

'Sir?' prompted Shankar, after his superior officer had been silent for a good couple of minutes.

'Yes?'

'I was wondering if you might have any instructions.'

'We should give this place the once-over, I suppose, and call in the criminalists, for all the help they'll be.' Parry rubbed a hand wearily up and down his face. 'Christ, how shittily have I handled this?'

'Captain, you aren't to blame for anything that's happened this morning. It was simply bad luck and bad timing.'

'Good of you to say that, Ranjit, but I should have looked more carefully when I saw Dargomyzhsky lurking in the corridor, I should have made sure the door was shut, generally I should have been a bit more on the ball. Quesnel's going to have my bollocks for earrings over this.'

'And very fetching they'll look on her, I'm sure. But really, sir, this is not your fault, any of it.'

Parry nodded noncommittally. 'Well, maybe not. But someone has to carry the can.'

'Captain's privilege?'

'Precisely.' Parry slapped the tops of his thighs and got to his feet. 'Oh well. On with the job. At least the worst has happened. I mean, things can't get much more ballsed-up than this, can they?'

An hour later he discovered that things, in fact, could.

He and Shankar had searched the room, not expecting to turn up anything useful and, sure enough, not doing so, and now they were awaiting the criminalists. Parry doubted that *their* examination of the room would prove any more fruitful than his and Shankar's, but formalities had to be observed, and going through the motions, futile though it might be, was invariably better than doing nothing at all.

The telephone rang. Thinking it was the concierge down in the lobby calling to let him know the criminalists were here, Parry picked up the receiver.

'Boss?' It was Johansen. 'I had a hunch you'd still be there. I got the room number off reception. You wouldn't happen to be near a TV set, would you?'

'I would. Why?'

'You may want to check out News Network 24.'

Parry took the remote control from the bedside table and aimed it at the television unit in the corner of the room, thumbing the Current Affairs button. The wallscreen sprang into life, and he scrolled through the onscreen options menu until 'News Network 24' was highlighted. He pressed Select, and immediately the screen was filled with a shaky, grainy palmcorder image of a smallish, balding man in FPP uniform. The man was standing in a hotel room, speaking directly to camera, his features underexposed and shadowy against a background flare of daylight. Superimposed on this, tucked in the bottom left-hand corner of the screen, was the blockish, lapidary NN24 logo accompanied by the word 'Exclusive'.

'Jesus, that's me,' Parry said, and there were several weird moments of dislocation as he watched a news broadcast showing him standing and talking in the very same room in which he was now watching a news broadcast showing him standing and talking in the very same room in which . . . and so on, like a never-ending recursive loop, a mirror reflecting a mirror.

All at once the palmcorder image swerved diagonally downwards, and there was a hectic, juddering montage of carpet and feet, accompanied by the sounds of a scuffle and someone falling to the floor. Then the film clip ended abruptly in a hissing snowstorm of static and the image cut to an anchorwoman, composed and immaculately coiffed at her desk, who informed viewers that the amateur video they had just seen had been recorded a little over an hour ago at the Debussy Hotel, and showed not just the retrieval of a corpse from a canal but what was clearly a set of Foreign remains on one of the hotel's balconies. As the anchorwoman spoke, a composite illustration came up behind her, a rectangle divided in half by an angled line, on one side of which was a captured still of Dagmar Pfitzner's floating body, on the other a captured still of the Foreign garments. The shout-line beneath the illustration was grimly clever, if perhaps predictable: 'Death in New Venice'.

'Fast work,' Shankar commented, and Parry thought of the portable home board he had seen in the Dargomyzhskys' room.

Dargomyzhsky must have squirted the footage to the network over the phone-lines.

'Jack,' said Johansen on the phone, 'would I be wrong in thinking that this incident looks much like the one at the Amadeus?'

'I'm afraid you wouldn't.'

'Oh dear, this is not good.'

'Really, Pål. You don't say.'

'No, I mean, this is *truly* not good, because the commissioner is downstairs right now telling a couple of dozen reporters about the Amadeus.'

Parry thought he must have misheard. 'Run that by me again.'

'The press conference, boss. It was scheduled for this morning, remember?'

'I *know* it was scheduled for this morning. I rang and left Quesnel a message an hour ago advising her to cancel it.'

'Obviously she didn't take the advice.'

And as if to confirm the truth of Johansen's words, the anchorwoman announced that they were now going over live to New Venice FPP Headquarters, where Commissioner Céleste Quesnel was making an official statement about another human death and Foreign loss which had occurred earlier during the week (the anchorwoman laid a heavy, insinuating emphasis on the word *another*).

And there was Quesnel in the atrium of FPP HQ with a cluster of microphones in front of her, squinting a little against the glare of the news-crew arc lights but still managing to look assured and assuring as she spoke about the simultaneous suicides of Daryl Henderson and a Foreigner who had engaged Henderson's services as a Siren.

And there, just behind her and to the side, half out of shot and slightly out of focus, was Raymond van Wyk, his head bowed, his expression suitably solemn and self-effacing (van Wyk always knew the right pose to strike when there were cameras around).

And the commissioner was describing the discovery of the human and Foreign remains in a hotel room – she could not, for reasons of confidentiality, say which hotel – and then she was using the word '*shinju*' and then the phrase 'a rare and unique event, unlikely to be repeated'.

And Parry looked on agog, with a sensation in the pit of his stomach like a bolus of molten lead sinking and hardening, as

Quesnel continued with her statement, delivering the sentences with such rhetorical fluency that you would never guess, unless you knew, that she was speaking without notes.

And she was saying how proud New Venice was of its reputation for safety – safety for its human inhabitants, of course, but especially for its Foreign visitors – and how there was no cause for anyone to be concerned by this unfortunate and tragic and, most of all, isolated occurrence.

And meanwhile, outside on the balcony, the Foreign remains lay, huddled and empty.

And now, furtively, like a secret leaking out, a soft, steady rain began to fall.

18 FURORE

In the aftermath of the morning's events, Parry learned two things: first, that sometimes it is worse *not* to be made a scapegoat than to be made a scapegoat; and second, that whoever said there was no such thing as bad publicity deserves a damned good kicking.

As he had anticipated, it did not take long for the ladies and gentlemen of the news media to conclude that the incident at the Debussy Hotel was cast from the same mould as the earlier incident described by Commissioner Quesnel. For a couple of hours speculation was rife on News Network 24 that the scenes Mikhail Dargomyzhsky had filmed constituted evidence of a second *shinju*. With each quarter-hourly headline update the similarities between the two incidents were stressed with greater and greater emphasis, until eventually, by that alchemical journalistic process in which opinion transmutes into fact without the catalyst of official verification, the Debussy deaths were being referred to simply as a double suicide, no longer prefixed by moderating adjectives such as 'probable' or 'alleged'. Soon NN24's exclusive was being reported on by all the other international twenty-four-hour news channels, which covered not only the story itself but also the story of the breaking of the story, in a kind of self-referential, postmodern approach to current events, news about news.

As the morning wore on, various talking heads were brought in to analyse and comment on Quesnel's press statement, Dargomyzhsky's footage and the phenomenon of *shinju*. Among them was François-Joseph Vieuxtemps, the Xenologist. Never one to shy away from an opportunity to go on television and plug his book, Vieuxtemps was the guest of no fewer than three different channels, and on each said virtually the same thing, namely that he had suspected for some while that just because Foreigners were genderless beings, this did not mean they were incapable of forming quasi-sexual attachments with humans, and that although he had not explicitly stated as much in *Foreigners Are Neither from*

Venus Nor from Mars, although, indeed, the book might seem to make claims to the contrary, the inferences were there in the text for the intelligent reader to draw. The book was, of course, available from all the usual outlets.

Sirens were interviewed, too, and while most of them insisted that singing was merely a means of earning money and engendered little sense of kinship or empathy with the golden giants, one or two claimed that on occasion they had, through the act of singing, felt in some way *connected* with a Foreigner and had experienced feelings which, between humans, would have been called love, or at the very least affection.

Viola d'Indy had a taste of the limelight again as her views on the topic were sought. With the same wide-eyed candour she had exhibited during her meeting with Parry and Johansen, she told of her romance with the Foreigner she had dubbed Doh-Fa-Sol, and her tale was greeted with a lack of scepticism that some might say was healthy and others remarkable.

Xenophobes were also encouraged to air their opinions, and Toroa MacLeod, spokesperson for the New Venice branch of the movement, was particularly vehement in his condemnation of the deaths. 'How else are we to regard this,' he said, the intricate patterning of dark-blue tattoos on his face tightening in a scowl, 'but as yet one more example of the corrosive effects of Foreign culture on our own? I'm also appalled that the FPP is seeking to "exoticize" the phenomenon by giving it a Japanese name – a cheap tactic, redolent of all the old prejudices about the brutal, inscrutable, sexually perverted East.'

Poor old Klaus Lechner was dragged in front of the cameras. It had not taken long for investigative reporters to ascertain which hotel had been the site of the first two deaths, and while Lechner made a valiant stab at defending the good name of the Amadeus, you could tell by his eyes that he knew he was going to be losing custom as a result of this unfavourable exposure, and possibly his job.

And while all this was unfolding Parry was summoned to Quesnel's office and subjected to an icy dressing-down. Standing still in the centre of the room with his shoulders slightly hunched, he watched as Quesnel paced back and forth in front of him and listened as she addressed him in witheringly subdued tones about the need for discipline and efficiency within the FPP, the need for proper understanding between the various different sections of the division, and the need for the channels of communication up and down the chain of command to be open and clear and direct. She had just had a very thorny conversation with Dagmar Pfitzner's mother in Stuttgart, trying to explain to her why her daughter's death had been broadcast on television before Frau Pfitzner herself was notified about it. Before that she had fielded a long phone call from NACA Liaison al-Shadhuli, who wanted to know, quite rightly, what the hell was going on. She had been made to look a fool on TV, the FPP had been seen to exhibit a level of competence that would have embarrassed the Keystone Kops, and as far as she could see the blame for all these things rested with just one person – Jack Parry.

Parry did not interrupt her to remonstrate, merely stood there and passively endured his chastisement, knowing that Quesnel had to vent her spleen on someone and that, since he was to a certain extent guilty as charged, the someone might as well be him. When, however, Quesnel finished her tirade and asked him if he had anything to say in his defence, he responded with a straightforward, blow-by-blow account of the morning's events, relating everything he had seen and done since Shankar's pre-dawn phone call. Quesnel heard him out till he reached the part where, unable to convince Dargomyzhsky to surrender the palmcorder disc, he had made the decision to call her and suggest she cancel the press conference.

'But obviously you forgot,' she said.

'Forgot?'

'About calling me.'

Parry frowned and shook his head. 'No. No, ma'am, I have to say that I phoned from the Debussy and left a message on your work board.'

'Jack.' Quesnel sounded disappointed. 'You, of all people.'

'Ma'am?'

She spelled it out to him, as though to a child. 'You didn't leave any message. Why make out as if you did?'

'Begging your pardon, ma'am, but I definitely rang and I definitely left a message.'

Quesnel's eyes narrowed. 'At what time, exactly?'

'At least an hour before the press conference. I called you at home as well. You weren't in.'

The commissioner looked puzzled now. 'An hour before the press conference? Are you sure?'

'Quite sure, ma'am. Sergeant Shankar can back me up. And Officer Hosokawa, who was on front-desk duty. In fact, surely Hosokawa told you when you came in that a body had been found.'

'Hosokawa? He wasn't on the desk when I came in. Someone else was. The Hungarian kid. What's his name? Kadosa.'

'And Kadosa didn't say anything?'

'Not a word. Guess he didn't know.'

'But still, you checked your work board.'

'First thing I did when I came in. Must have been about twenty minutes after you say you rang. There were no messages then.' She went to her desk and summoned up her voicemail records. 'Nope, nothing on here from before ten o'clock today.'

'I swear to you I made that call.'

'And I believe you, Jack. It must have been a software glitch. Goddamn it.'

'Of course, I should have tried you again, to make sure you'd got the message. The thing is, I'd no idea Dargomyzhsky would get his footage on air so quickly.'

'Way I understand it, NN24 was the first channel Dargomyzhsky approached and he accepted their first offer. Seems they paid him a fraction of what he could have got if he'd tried another couple of other channels and opened up a bidding war. That's some consolation, I hope.'

'It is,' said Parry, nodding. 'Some.' So, *not* such a good Russian capitalist, he thought. Or could it be that Dargomyzhsky had had an attack of conscience at the last minute? Maybe something Parry said to him had sunk in, so that he had deliberately taken far less for the footage than it could have earned him. Guilt and gilt – uneasy bedfellows.

'Anyway,' said Quesnel, 'the upshot is that you did warn me about what had happened at the Debussy, even if the message somehow went astray. I'm really glad to know that, Jack. I shouldn't have doubted you, but, well, I did, and it was a mistake. Sorry.'

Parry quickly deflected the apology, feeling unworthy of it. 'We're still left with an almighty gaffe, ma'am, for which I hold myself principally responsible. If there was some way I could make amends – perhaps by making a press statement of my own?'

'Very noble of you, but I don't see what it would achieve.'

'Share out the blame a bit.'

'This is where the buck stops,' Quesnel said, tapping her chest.

'But we should at least let people know that I'm the one who briefed you on the Amadeus deaths, the one who didn't foresee a second similar set of deaths coming.'

'Jack, why are you giving yourself such a hard time over this? I thought it was us Catholics who're supposed to have a lock on the whole guilt-trip thing. Besides, you went out of your way in your report to say you weren't a hundred per cent sure about your findings.'

'I was hoping', Parry said, doing his utmost not to sound accusatory, 'that my lack of certainty would be infectious.'

Quesnel regarded him levelly, though not with any hostility, across her desk. 'Jack, you know as well as I do that when you're dealing with the press, even these days, you can't give them uncertainties and likelihoods. Journalists are predators. They scent weakness. If they think you're not being wholly honest with them, if they think you're covering something up, they home in and attack. Give them a few plain, straightforward, solid-sounding facts, and they go home happy. That's how you have to treat them, for everybody's good, and OK, in this instance it didn't work out, but that's my problem and I'll deal with it. What *you* have to do is get to the bottom of these goddamn deaths. Find out why we've had two sets of Foreign and Siren remains turn up within the space of a week and what we can do to stop it happening a third time. Because, I tell you, I'm beginning to think that Ray's right and this business is even worse than it looks.'

'You think someone's doing this to them? A killer?'

'Don't you?'

'I just can't see why.'

'Neither can I. But maybe we're dealing with someone who doesn't need a reason, or at least a reason you or I or anyone sensible can understand. Someone, like those guys at Koh Farang, who simply wants Foreigners out of this city and doesn't mind if humans get hurt in the process. I hope that isn't so. Every shred of me wants it not to be so. But I'm beginning to think we have to consider it, at least.'

Parry nodded slowly.

'Of course, for the time being, we can't admit that to anyone,' Quesnel went on. 'There'll be speculation, I'm sure, but as long as it remains speculation it can't do much damage. Now, I've a second press conference coming up in about an hour's time. Thought I should try and salvage *something* from this shambles. And actually, if you really do want to make amends, Jack, there's some salvaging you can do, too.'

'What sort?'

'I got a request earlier from Toroa MacLeod.'

'What does he want?' said Parry with a sigh.

'It so happens, you.'

19 COUNTERPOINT

It had stopped raining. A low leaden layer of cloud still glowered overhead but for the time being the drizzle was holding off.

Thankful for small mercies, Parry killed the launch's engine, tied up, and stepped ashore on to the canalside walkway.

The walkway ran alongside a wall into which wrought-iron gates were set at regular intervals. The gate directly in front of him was distinct from all the others in that its bars were fashioned to incorporate a simplified representation of a Mercator projection of the Earth. Outside it, behind him, a small launch was tethered, doubtless the Xenophobes' private transport. Through the gate he saw a long, narrow garden consisting of a lawn, a few cypresses, some flowerbeds thick with cordylines and spiky orange strelitzia, and a winding gravel path that led to the front door of a house. The house was one of a long, staggered row of identical residences, all tall and white and softly contoured, their corners and edges chamfered, like dice.

Immediately to the right of the gate was an intercom unit, mounted flush into the wall. Above it was a brass plaque inscribed with the words 'Free World House' and, in smaller letters, 'Xenophobe League, New Venice Chapter'. This was not merely the Xenophobes' base of operations in New Venice. It was also, since few of them could otherwise afford to live in a resort-city, their private lodgings.

Parry pressed the bell-button on the intercom unit and waited, rocking back and forth on his heels.

No one addressed him from the intercom speaker. Instead, he heard soft, rapid footsteps pattering towards him along the path, and the next moment he was facing a pair of Alsatians through the bars of the gate. Ears pricked, tails high, the dogs looked alert and distinctly unfriendly. Then there was a buzz from the intercom and the gate clanked open, swinging inwards.

'Pinkerton and Butterfly will escort you to the house,' said a voice from the speaker. The accent was Antipodean but Parry was almost certain that the voice did not belong to MacLeod. 'Stick to the path and they won't attack.'

Parry eyed the dogs warily. They looked back at him, their gazes jet-black and hostile.

Sod this, he thought. And sod *you*, MacLeod. Any chance you were going to get a sympathetic hearing from me – gone, mate.

He took a deep breath and, reasoning that no one, not even a Xenophobe, would be so stupid as to employ a pair of guard dogs that were anything but immaculately trained, stepped through the gateway.

Immediately one of the Alsatians fell in behind him while the other turned and began trotting ahead. Parry followed the one in front – Pinkerton, to judge by the unneutered rear view – all the while keeping a wary eye on the one behind; and like this, a dog sandwich with a man as the filling, they wended their way along the sinuous turns of the path to the front door.

At the door Pinkerton moved out of Parry's way and joined Butterfly at his rear. Both Alsatians sat down on their haunches, keeping their attention fixed on him. He fancied he saw disappointment in their faces. They would have loved it if he had ignored the advice and strayed from the path.

The door was opened by an Australian aborigine dressed in chinos and a denim workshirt.

'G'day,' he said. This was the man who had addressed Parry over the intercom. With a flick of his fingers he invited Parry in.

Parry entered a broad, cool hallway, tiled with pine parquet in a zigzag pattern. All around, on all four walls, were displayed hand-crafted artefacts from all over the world. There were ceremonial items: a medicine bag, a rainstick, tribal masks of threatening mien. There were musical instruments: a didgeridoo, a set of panpipes, different kinds of drum. There were ornaments: a scrimshawed narwhal horn, a bark scroll decorated with finger-painted representations of animals, dozens of figures and figurines carved from a range of materials (bone, coral, stone, wood). And there were weapons: a reed blowpipe with jaguar-claw darts, an assegai and shield, several sets of bows and arrows, a knobkerrie and, next to it, another kind of club, one with a short stubby handle and a head that was flat and oval with incurving indentations on both sides, so that in outline it resembled nothing on earth so much as a violin. The overall impression was of a museum, but the items were not tagged with identifying labels and there was none of the dustiness, the mustiness, traditionally associated with museums. This was a commemoration, then. A reminder.

'This way,' said the aborigine.

He led Parry across the hallway and up a flight of uncarpeted wooden stairs. On the landing Parry glanced through an open doorway and saw what looked like an administrative office. A Native American woman was busy at a work board, typing away. She was young and forceful-looking, her hair hanging either side of her face in two long plaits, her skin the colour of bloodstained earth. At a second desk in the room, a Mexican Indian was talking on the phone in mellifluent Spanish, reclining in his chair with his ankles crossed on the desktop. A water cooler and a coffee percolator stood in one corner, and a large cork board hung on the wall, festooned with thumbtacked memos and newspaper clippings. Parry surmised that this was where most of the chapter's fund-raising took place, a vital function for the Xenophobe movement, since maintaining a presence in every major capital and every resort-city did not come cheap.

On the next flight of stairs there was a Tibetan monk, polishing the banisters. He stopped work and, clutching his cloth and can of polish to his saffron robes, stood back to let the aborigine and Parry pass. Bliss-eyed, he bowed his shaven head to them both, then resumed his labours.

On the second-storey landing, the aborigine knocked on a door.

'Yes?' said a voice within.

'Mate, it's the FPP fella.'

'OK.'

The aborigine opened the door and stepped aside to allow Parry to go in.

The room would have been, had this house been a family residence, the master bedroom. The Xenophobes had made of it a kind of conference-room-cum-recreation-lounge. In the middle there was a rectangular arrangement of sofas and armchairs of canvas and chromed tubular steel, centred around a wooden coffee-table on which there was a glass ashtray, a bowl of pot-pourri and a stack of vintage copies of National Geographic, neatly fanned, their page edges almost as yellow as the border on their covers. A fully equipped home-entertainment stack occupied the far corner, linked to a wallscreen. Bamboo Venetian blinds filtered the sunshine. Downlighters recessed into the ceiling cast a flat, even brightness.

Toroa MacLeod was sitting in one of the armchairs with the entertainment stack's remote control in his left hand. He was watching the live transmission of Quesnel's second press statement on NN24. As soon as Parry entered, he aimed the control at the entertainment stack, muted the volume and rose from his seat, right hand extended.

Never having met MacLeod in the flesh, Parry was surprised at how short the man was. On television he seemed a giant, but in fact he had only a couple of centimetres of height on Parry himself. He was broad, though, solidly built, and his hand had a dry-palmed grip of some strength – enough strength to imply that a great deal more was being held in reserve.

'Captain Parry,' he said. His voice was broad and solidly built, too, richly reverberant, commanding. 'A pleasure to meet you at last. Although I must admit, I'm a little surprised you came.'

So am I, Parry nearly replied, but instead said, 'Well, that's what the FPP's here for. To listen to people, to hear out complaints. As long as it involves Foreigners, it matters to us.'

'And how do you know my reason for asking you here involves the *Pakeha?*'

'If it doesn't, Mr MacLeod, then you're wasting my time and yours.'

MacLeod chuckled and turned to the aborigine, who was still standing by the door. 'Greg, would you mind bringing Captain Parry and myself some coffee? No, wait. Make that tea.' He looked at Parry. 'You almost certainly prefer tea, don't you, Captain? And I'm sure that, for an FPP officer on duty, an alcoholic beverage is out of the question.'

Parry knew it would be rude not to accept the offer of hospitality, even though it came from a Xenophobe. Besides, right then a cup of tea seemed a very refreshing proposition indeed. 'Tea would be nice. Thank you.'

'Thanks, Greg,' said MacLeod.

'No worries.'

The aborigine exited and MacLeod gestured to one of the sofas, inviting Parry to sit. Parry did, and MacLeod resumed his place in his armchair.

'You mind if we watch the rest of this?' he said, pointing to the wallscreen. 'I do enjoy watching our commissioner squirm.'

Parry was on the point of manufolding INDULGENCE, but

checked himself and offered the standard terrestrial be-my-guest gesture instead.

MacLeod upped the volume, and Quesnel's voice filled the room.

'. . . incident at the Debussy Hotel is currently under investigation and therefore it's impossible for me to comment in detail on it. However, the FPP is indebted to News Network 24 for drawing our attention to the circumstantial resemblance between this Siren death and Foreign loss and those at the Amadeus. While it's too early yet to establish a direct link between the two incidents, the similarities would lead us to believe that they *are* related. I must stress, however, that there is no cause for concern at this time, nor any reason why anyone in New Venice should not feel safe to go about his or her business . . .'

Quesnel was saying nothing particularly surprising or revelatory, but then it wasn't the content of her speech that was so important as the fact that she was there, on people's screens at work and at home, looking measured and gracious and sounding suitably worried, yes, but also sounding quite determined to see the problem resolved as soon as possible.

Parry surreptitiously turned his attention to MacLeod, while the Xenophobe's gaze was fixed on the wallscreen, and studied him.

Lieutenant Johansen had the edge on MacLeod in terms of sheer meaty bulk, but the Norwegian's physique seemed vain and inflated by comparison. On MacLeod, every muscle, every sinew, looked taut with purpose. He was wearing a tight-fitting sleeveless T-shirt, and the biceps and forearm flexors and extensors, sheathed beneath his ochre skin, were like knotted nests of pythons. His hair he wore swept upwards in a short, stiff brush cut, and his nose was the characteristic Maori shape, flat with wide, uptilted nostrils. His eyes were small, hard black pearls, and the sharp, fierce contours of his face were emphasized by its tattoos, which, up close, were intricate and even more intimidating than they looked on television. Across his lobey forehead ran two mirror-image sets of thick, fanning lines, like a simple sketch of a bird's wings, each emanating from the inner tip of an eyebrow. On either flank of his nose there were intricate spirals, and these unravelled and flowed into a series of parallel arcs that spread out sideways and traced the hollows of his cheeks all the way down to the jaw. Beneath his lower lip were a pair of paisley shapes, head-to-head, and on each of the two bumps of his cleft chin there was another small spiral. The lines were ingrained in a dye that was the purple of thunderclouds, the deep blue of a stormy sea.

So much for the man's appearance. As for his character, what Parry knew was patchy at best, derived mainly from a news profile that had been aired a few months back, shortly after MacLeod arrived in New Venice to assume the reins of the local chapter from his predecessor, Augustus Kyagambiddwa, who had resigned the post following the unearthing and successful ousting of the Triple-X cell. The venerable Kyagambiddwa had been shocked to learn that Triple-X had infiltrated the city. A man of principle, he had ascertained the names and whereabouts of the cell's members, submitted these to the FPP and then done the honourable thing by quitting as head of the chapter.

The profile had made much of MacLeod's impoverished upbringing in the suburban slums of Auckland and of the fact that he had won a scholarship to read law at Victoria University in Wellington, where he had excelled both academically and on the rugby field, in the latter case to the extent of earning himself a try-out for the All Blacks. It also mentioned that he had been a committed civil rights activist and had campaigned tirelessly throughout his student days for all of the land appropriated from the Maori by British settlers to be restored to its rightful owners, a dream which had finally become a reality not long after MacLeod graduated, when, in the spirit of euphoria that had swept the world in the wake of the Debut, the Christchurch Covenant was signed, giving the Maori everything that they had been asking for.

MacLeod's subsequent espousal of Xenophobia seemed to Parry an act of stunning ingratitude. It was baffling to him that someone could turn on the very race whose advent had brought about so many positive changes in the world, including one that directly benefited him and his people. The reason, he supposed, was that MacLeod was one of those men who enjoyed sparring, be it verbally or physically. He knew this because he had read MacLeod's police records and learned (something the news profile had *not* mentioned) that MacLeod had been arrested several times during his student-activist days and been indicted for affray, assault on a police officer, and incitement to violence. These were all crimes committed on the picket lines, crimes of rashness and passion, and Parry was not so naïve as to think that the New Zealand police were not at least partly responsible. He was only too aware how heavy-handed tactics intended to calm civil unrest can often have the opposite effect. None the less MacLeod seemed to him the type who adopted a cause not so much because he believed in it but because he was innately aggressive and needed a legitimizing outlet, a channel sanctioned by a higher authority, through which to vent that aggression.

'That will be all for now,' said Quesnel. 'Thank you.'

Camera flashbulbs sparked as the commissioner stepped away from the press microphones. Questions were shouted at her, but she pretended not to hear them.

MacLeod switched the television off and turned to Parry.

'Well, there we go, eh? A skilful performance. Neither excuse nor apology but a little bit of both. Well done, Céleste.'

'If you've invited me here, Mr MacLeod, just so that I can listen to you mock the commissioner, then I think there's no reason for me to stay.' Parry made as if to stand.

MacLeod made a calming gesture, as though patting a cushion.

'Forgive me, Captain. Sit back down. I'm sorry. Sincerely. I didn't mean to offend you.'

'So,' said Parry, satisfied that the point had been made, 'why am I here? What is it you want to talk about?'

'These incidents, of course. The ones you're investigating. These deaths.'

Parry withheld a sigh. 'Mr MacLeod, if you want to find out about an investigation the FPP is involved in, you're perfectly at liberty to apply to our information department. The FPP are obliged to release all evidence concerning an investigation no later than sixty days after the initial event.'

'I know, I know. Measure Seven of the revered Foreign Policy Constitution. But the thing is, Captain, I'd prefer not to have to wait for the FPP to decide on my behalf when I can and cannot know about what's going on in this town. And rather than be spoon-fed, I'd like to get my information straight from the horse's mouth.'

'I don't have to tell you anything if I don't want to.'

'But I think you will want to.'

'Oh, you do?'

'Because I can help you.'

'You can help me? How can you help me? And, more to the point, *why* would you?'

'Perhaps I phrased that wrong. I can . . . not hinder you.'

Parry frowned, then nodded. 'I get it. I play along and the Xenophobes won't make life difficult for the FPP.'

'I myself wouldn't put it quite so crudely, but basically, yes. I hardly need tell you, Captain, that I'm capable of inconveniencing you and your colleagues in all sorts of ways. I can make it my mission to denounce and disparage you at every turn, and there's no shortage of forums available to me for that purpose – television, radio, newspapers, the e-ther. One of the few redeeming features of the age in which we live is that it's no longer considered merely polite to listen to alternative, counter-orthodox viewpoints, it's considered nothing short of mandatory. Then there's the personal influence I wield. I have the ear of a number of well-regarded and powerful individuals, as I'm sure you're aware.'

'I'm aware that your movement has some very wealthy backers,' said Parry, and, to illustrate his point, indicated their surroundings. 'A piece of prime real estate in a resort-city does not come cheap.'

'Then you know that such individuals can bring significant pressure to bear on governments, who in turn can lean on the Foreign Policy Council – which, after all, depends on the international community for its funding – and it in turn can lean on you.'

Parry gave a dismissive shake of his head. 'I'd believe that kind of talk if this was, say, twenty years ago. Back then that was the way things worked. But life's different now. Big business doesn't run and ruin the world any more. We've cleaned up our act.'

'You'd like to think so, wouldn't you?'

'I know so, Mr MacLeod. And it seems to me that you're laying down some pretty heavy threats for someone who claims he just wants a bit of fast-track information.'

'Merely setting out my stall. Letting you know who you're dealing with.'

'I already know who I'm dealing with,' Parry said, and arranged his mouth into something that was three parts grin to one part sneer.

Greg re-entered the room with a tea tray, which he placed on the table between Parry and MacLeod. MacLeod thanked him and Parry made a point of thanking him, too.

'He's not a servant, of course,' MacLeod said after Greg had left the room.

'I never assumed he was.'

'Oh really?'

'No,' said Parry. 'And I know what you're up to. I'm a white

Westerner. If someone of ethnic background fetches me tea, I automatically think he's staff.'

'You're a white Westerner who used to be a London policeman.'

'Yes, that's right. All blacks are wogs.'

'Your choice of words is quite revealing. You're clearly a man who calls a spade a spade.'

'Very funny. Now listen here, MacLeod . . .'

Parry stopped, having noticed the amusement twinkling in the Xenophobe's eyes.

'You see?' said MacLeod, pointing at him. 'You see how easy it is for me to snare you, Captain? Trip you up? And if I can do that here, when it's just the two of us chatting, think how much more effectively and devastatingly I can do it in the public arena.'

'I resent being called a racist,' Parry said aridly. 'I resent someone even thinking I'm one.'

'Yet it's an easy brush with which to tar you, not least because you work for an organization which predominantly recruits people like you – whites from Anglophone, Christian countries.'

'The FPP is far more ethnically and religiously diverse than most people appreciate.'

'But the general perception is that you're a bunch of white Westerners who've taken it upon themselves to tell the rest of the world how to behave. Which is pretty much how things were before the Debut, when the West was the world's self-appointed policeman. The names may have changed, but the cultural imperialism stays the same.'

'That isn't the general perception from where *I'm* looking.'

'Hardly surprising, given that you're on the inside looking out. And by the way, just so you know, no one here at Free World House is a servant to anyone else. Greg wouldn't have brought us tea if he didn't want to. We all work in equal partnership here. As a Xenophobe, you see, you contribute in whatever way you can. If you haven't got money, then you donate time and labour. It's a very human way of doing things. Human helping human.'

'An object lesson to us all.'

'We like to think so,' said MacLeod, overlooking the sarcasm in Parry's voice. 'How do you take your tea?'

'Milk, no sugar.'

A few moments later Parry was taking an exploratory sip of an aromatic brown brew – Darjeeling, he thought. Not his preferred leaf, but the tannin/caffeine hit came quickly and he revelled in its suffusing warmth.

'And now,' said MacLeod, settling back in his seat, 'these incidents. These *shinjus*, as you're calling them.' He spoke the term with distaste. 'What's going on, eh?'

Parry debated how much to tell him, and whether to tell him anything at all. MacLeod had no right to know any more than any other member of the public. Then again, this was a chance for the FPP to put its side of the story. If he was straight with MacLeod, MacLeod might appreciate it and return the favour by refraining from causing trouble. Courtesy bred courtesy, did it not? And if, by such an honourable means, he was able to draw the teeth of one of New Venice FPP's most vocal opponents, then that was a double victory – a moral as well as a practical one.

So he gave MacLeod a simplified version of the discovery of Henderson's corpse and the Foreign remains at the Amadeus, and of his enquiries among Sirens, and of the sequence of events that morning at the Ponte da Ponte and the Debussy that had led to the unearthing of the second *shinju* and its subsequent exposure on television.

'Yes, I felt you came across very well in that footage.'

Parry looked at MacLeod askance.

'No, I mean it,' the Xenophobe said, with apparent sincerity. 'Reasonable, unflustered, polite but firm. A good advert for your organization. If only all FPP officers were like you, eh?'

All at once Parry felt charm exuding from MacLeod in waves, like some pulsing, invisible radiation MacLeod was able to emit at will in order to alter people at a cellular level, mutate them into allies. It required a conscious effort to resist the flattery, to contain the urge to warm to the man. He reminded himself that he was talking to a Xenophobe, someone determined not to accept Foreigners for the miracle they were, a professional Doubting Thomas. At his most charitable, he could admire MacLeod for the strength of his convictions, but further than that he could not – must not – permit his sympathies to extend.

'They *are* all like me,' Parry replied, then thought of van Wyk. Well, almost all.

'And what does Commissioner Quesnel have to say about these two incidents?'

'You just saw.'

'What does she *really* have to say?'

'That they need to be looked into and, if possible, prevented from recurring.'

'But how can you prevent something like this from recurring?' MacLeod said, spreading out his hands. 'If this *shinju* is an act consented to by both parties, if neither has been coerced into it by the other, then surely it's a matter of free will. And the FPP, to the best of my knowledge, doesn't yet have powers to curb expressions of free will. Or could it be that there's more going on here than meets the eye?' He tapped an index finger meditatively against one of the paisley shapes on his chin. 'Could it be that the FPP thinks Xenophobes are in some way involved?'

'Absolutely not.'

'Yet, Captain, you agreed to come and see me when asked. Agreed very readily. Could it be that you're here to sniff around? Ask a few pertinent questions? See if I forget myself and let slip some vital, incriminating clue?'

'No one in the FPP has so much as mentioned the possibility of Xenophobe involvement in these deaths.' Of course, that was not entirely true, but he could not see what right MacLeod had to know about an opinion privately expressed by the commissioner.

'What about Triple-X?' said MacLeod.

'I don't get what you're driving at.'

'I'm not driving at anything in particular. I'm simply curious to know how the FPP's minds are working. Normally the first people to get the blame when something bad happens to *Pakeha* are Xenophobes.'

'Not true.'

'No? How about at Koh Farang? Your colleagues there started out by pointing the finger squarely at the local Xenophobe chapter.'

'The real culprits were found soon enough.'

'Only after several innocent people had been taken into custody.'

'They were released.'

'And exonerated?'

'I believe so, yes.'

'You believe wrong. Nothing was said. No apology was offered to them, either publicly or in private. Not even a grudging admission that the FPP had made a mistake.'

'A lot of mistakes were made at Koh Farang. Hopefully we've learned from them.'

'Hopefully.'

'Anyway, what does someone like you, Mr MacLeod, care about Triple-X? The legitimate Xenophobe movement does everything it can to distance itself from their actions.'

'A good point, Captain. Naturally, I can't condone indiscriminate bombing and killing.'

Parry felt that MacLeod had laid a certain subtle emphasis on *indiscriminate*, but the stress on the word had been so faint – barely a feather's weight of extra breath – that he might well have imagined it.

'Such things are even more offensive to public opinion nowadays than they used to be,' MacLeod continued. 'However, I also believe that the FPP shouldn't be allowed to arrest individuals purely on the grounds that they have a genuine or even a suspected affiliation with any movement, political, religious or otherwise.'

'I agree. As I said, mistakes were made and Koh Farang paid the price. This isn't a perfect world, Mr MacLeod, and it would be a whole lot worse if we pretended it was.'

'Well put. But I'm afraid I would go further than you, Captain. I would say that this is a world as far from being perfect as it's possible to get.'

'That is – respectfully, Mr MacLeod – rubbish. You only have to look at the improvements the Foreigners have brought. Not just crystech and comp-res, though God knows the latter was the answer to our prayers. The *social* improvements. It's an objective, statistically supported fact that since the Foreigners came the planet has been more peaceful than at any time in recorded history.'

'Or have we just lulled ourselves into a false sense of security?' said MacLeod. '*I* think so. I don't believe we've changed all that much. Certainly not deep down, where it counts.'

'On that, I'd agree with you. The potential is always there that we'll slide back into the chaos that existed before the Debut. We've attained a general standard of decent behaviour – of civilization, in the truest sense of the word – because the Foreigners are here, but we can't and won't maintain it without constant, rigorous self-assessment and vigilance. And that's part of my job, perhaps the most important part of it: keeping everyone up to scratch, by the application of Foreign Policy and by example.'

'How very impressive. "By the application of Foreign Policy and by example." And here I was thinking you were nothing more than a glorified holiday rep.'

The charm was being deployed once again. Parry was meant to

take the comment as nothing more than good-natured ribbing, the kind that was acceptable between friends.

'Well, that's in the job description, too,' he replied, with a laugh that no one could mistake for genuine. 'Frankly, it's good to be employed doing something that demands so many diverse skills. I could, after all, simply complain for a living, as some people do.'

'Captain.' Suddenly no longer amused, MacLeod leaned forwards in his seat and laid his cup and saucer down on the coffee-table. 'I am not a man to fuck with, and neither, I suspect, are you. So let's be honest with each other.'

'Suits me.'

'Does the FPP believe the Xenophobes have any connection with these deaths?'

'*Do* you?'

'No.'

'Then you have no reason to be worried.'

'I'm not. It's just that, as I said before, when something goes wrong in a resort-city, it's usually the Xenophobes who are the first to get the blame.'

'The FPP hasn't come knocking on your door yet. As things stand, I see no reason to believe that we will.'

'I have your word on that?'

'That we won't have cause to come and visit you? No, you do not. I don't give guarantees I may not be able to keep.'

'Well.' MacLeod closed his eyes and opened them again, a slow basilisk blink. 'Well, that's honest of you, I suppose.'

'I thought that was what you wanted.'

'Yes. True. And in that same spirit, Captain, I have to tell you that if there are any more of these deaths, I will have no choice but to be savage in my criticism of them and of the FPP. That isn't a threat, merely a statement of fact. The Xenophobe movement cannot be seen to sit back in silence while this planet's indigenous culture is further eroded.'

'But—'

'These deaths,' MacLeod continued, steamrollering through Parry's objection, 'would not have occurred if the *Pakeha* were not here and if their influence were not so pervasive and if people were not so willing to indulge them in their whims and ways. Two human beings have lost their lives so far and God knows how many more may follow. As long as we keep subordinating ourselves to the Foreigners, then such things will keep on happening, and as a descendant of a race who for two centuries were stripped of their land and their dignity and their identity by the forcible imposition of another race's culture, I will do everything in my power to see that the fate that befell my forebears does not befall the world.'

MacLeod's black-pearl eyes glittered with a dark fervour as he spoke, and Parry was not sure whether what he was witnessing was a genuine outburst of feeling or a taste of what could be expected from MacLeod if the deaths continued. In spite of himself, he could not help but be impressed and even a little stirred by MacLeod's rhetoric. The man was talking nonsense, of course. Single-issue pressure groups, by their very nature, could present only one side of any debate and that made them emotive but otherwise invalid arguers. All the same, when a case was put with as much fire and eloquence as MacLeod had just displayed, it was hard not to be swayed.

'You've made your feelings known, Mr MacLeod,' he said, setting his empty cup down next to the Xenophobe's, 'and I'm grateful for the opportunity to have heard them. But I have, as you can imagine, many other important matters to attend to . . .'

'Yes. Yes, of course, Captain Parry.' All at once, MacLeod was again the serene, genial fellow he had been when Parry came in. 'Let me walk with you to the front door.'

Pinkerton and Butterfly were waiting patiently out front. When Parry and MacLeod emerged from the house the Alsatians sprang to their feet and fixed their gazes on MacLeod's face, ready to receive a command. The worst thing about the dogs, Parry decided, eyeing them, was their silence. As a courtesy to neighbours, guard dogs in residential areas were trained not to bark. Even when attacking intruders, they were obliged to do it with barely a snarl, in order to avoid disturbing other humans in the vicinity. A sign of the times, that . . . though possibly not the most exemplary one.

'Are they really necessary?' he asked MacLeod, indicating the dogs.

'Everyone's entitled to a certain level of security, aren't they, Captain?' said MacLeod, misconstruing the question, perhaps deliberately. 'Even we Xenophobes?'

'Well, yes, but what I meant is, is it really necessary for the dogs to come with me to the front gate?'

'I wouldn't dream of letting you leave the premises unaccompanied. That would be very bad form.' The absence of any expression on the Xenophobe's face or inflection in his voice was, to Parry, worse than open mockery would have been. 'Remember: stay on the path and there won't be any trouble.'

The two men shook hands again.

'*Kia ora*, Captain,' MacLeod said.

A memory from childhood flashed incongruously into Parry's head – the taste of a stickily sickly brand of orange squash. 'Beg pardon?'

'It means "good luck".' MacLeod nodded at Pinkerton and Butterfly.

'Oh,' said Parry, and, unamused, added, 'thank you.'

MacLeod stepped back inside the house and closed the door, and Parry turned and set off along the path. As before, one of the Alsatians fell in step in front of him, the other behind.

Near the gate, Parry decided to risk a little experiment. Gradually he veered towards the edge of the path. Nothing happened until the side of his shoe brushed a blade of grass. Then Butterfly let out a warning growl behind him and Pinkerton whipped his head round to see what was going on.

For the last few metres of the journey, Parry stuck firmly and squarely to the centre of the path.

INTERLUDE

One Year Ago . . .

The call comes in the middle of the night.

'Do you know who I am?'

'Sure. We've met.'

'I have a proposition for you.'

'But I hardly know you!' Not bad for three-thirty in the morning and just woken up.

'Listen carefully. Listen seriously.' The caller pauses for breath. A third of a world away, you hear him wheezing. 'I know what sort of person you are. I think we have a sympathy on certain issues. What would you say if I told you I could provide you with the means of making a heart's desire come true?'

'I'd say keep talking.'

And he does. In fits and starts, in halting breathless bursts, he explains what he would like done and how he would like it done. At the end, he says, 'Well? What do you think?'

'I don't know,' you say, but you're intrigued. In fact, quietly, you're thrilled. You're already pretty sure what your answer's going to be. 'There's a lot of risk. I mean, crazy risk.'

'And a lot of reward.'

'That, too.'

'The one is often, I've found, the result of the other. If you succeed, believe me you will never have to worry about money ever again.'

'And if I fail?'

'Do you honestly think you will?'

He's got you there. Failure has never been in your vocabulary. In spite of the life you've chosen for yourself, and in fact because of it, you have become obstinate to the point of idiocy. The greater the odds stacked against you, the deeper you dig your heels in, refusing to be cowed or bowed. Fighting the tide of the times has become your mission, your crusade. You pursue it with a near-religious zeal, and every setback renews your fire. Every time you get knocked down, you're up again in an instant, ready for some more.

And here is a chance to strike such a blow. Such a spectacular act of retaliation.

How can you say no?

THIRD MOVEMENT

20 RECAPITULATION

An e-card from Cecilia Fuentes was waiting for Parry on his home board when he got in that evening. On the front was an image screen-grabbed from the newscast of the Dargomyzhsky footage: himself in Room 879 at the Debussy, staring importunately into the camera. A speech bubble had been added, issuing from his mouth, empty except for the word 'PLAY'. With a certain bemused trepidation Parry clicked on the bubble, and the image unfroze and began to move. The hands gestured and the lips shaped words, but the accompanying voice on the soundtrack was not his. Instead, Cecilia had overdubbed a recording of her own voice, pitched gruffly and using her best (or, depending on how you look at it, her worst) fake British accent, so that what Parry saw was himself uttering the following:

'Prithee and forsooth, sirrah, wouldst thou kindly desist from yonder knavish shenanigans?'

In spite of himself, in spite of the day's many tribulations and aggravations, Parry could not resist a smile.

He entered a command and the e-card flipped over. On its reverse there was a short text-message:

```
Greetings, Bold Sir Jack!

So, now that you're an internationally famous TV
star and you've probably already got an agent and
an entourage and a ton of groupies hanging around
you, you won't want to be consorting with lowly
varlets like me and Ma. Still, if you don't mind
slumming it for an evening, Ma's having one of her
superduper soirées tomorrow, and frankly I'll be
bored out of my skull if you don't come. It's short
notice, I realize, but I only got a look at the
guest list this morning and was shocked and
appalled to find your name not on it. So how about
```

it, brave English knight? Little bit of a do at the
Fuentes homestead? Don't say no.
                              - the Lady Cecilia

Again Parry smiled, although this time with a touch of condescension.
Anna's daughter was no fool, but life was still enviably uncomplicated
in her teenage world. It was not the first time she had tried something
like this. Last Christmas she had made sure he received an invitation
to the annual Fuentes banquet. He had accepted. He had also been
persuaded, with a little more difficulty, to attend Cecilia's fifteenth
birthday party in March. He had no doubt that on this occasion, just
as on the previous two, she genuinely wanted to see him and would be
glad of his presence among the partygoers. At the same time, her
ulterior motive could not be more obvious, nor her attempt at deceit
more transparent. To Cecilia, the logic was simple. Her mother was a
widow. Her mother needed a man in her life. Parry, her mother's
closest unattached male friend, was clearly the best candidate. The
more often the two of them were brought together, the more likely
they were to realize this.

Cecilia had no way of knowing that her mother and Parry had
already been more than friends – much more. All she saw was two
adults who seemed to get along well, who were right for each
other, who could make each other happy, and she wanted them to
be in love.

It was ingenuous. It was touching. It made Parry's heart leap and
ache at the same time.

It was also an opportunity he ought to take advantage of, but
could not bring himself to. Would it really be appropriate for an
FPP captain embroiled in a difficult and high-profile Foreign case to
turn up at a social function? He did not think so.

That, though, was not the only reason he was reluctant to
attend. The other reason was that he did not want Anna to think
him desperate for the least excuse to see her. He was playing the
long game here, the subtle game, the waiting game. When Anna
found out that Cecilia had invited him to the party and he had not
gone, that would surely be a point in his favour.

He sat down and composed a reply:

Milady Cecilia,

I'm afraid that you're right. As an international
celebrity I'm simply far too important to mingle
with common peasants like you and your mother and

speak with the sort of loathsomely ordinary people you consort with. Thus I will not be attending your mother's modest little get-together tomorrow evening.

                                                           - Bold Sir Jack

He reread what he had written and decided a postscript was in order.

P.S. Actually, Cecilia, I've just got too much on at the moment, as I'm sure you can understand. Another time, maybe?

Having fired the message off to the Fuentes home board, he got up and threw open the balcony windows. It had rained again for a spell during the afternoon. Amoebiform splotches of unevaporated water spotted the tiles of the balcony, and a glaucous haze of humidity hung in the air, so that the buildings on the other side of the canal, some twenty metres away, looked out of focus, at one remove from reality. On his way home he had glimpsed fewer than usual Foreigners out and about – they were less inclined to venture from their hotels when the conditions were damp – and he predicted that Sirensong would be slow tonight.

He settled down to his evening exercises. For background noise he switched the television on, selecting Current Affairs with the remote control. His home board had collated for him all the news items from the past twenty-four hours that pertained to subjects he was interested in or it thought he might be interested in.

The *shinju* deaths were still garnering attention, but they had been toppled from the headline slot by the announcement that last year the global mean temperature had for the first time fallen instead of risen. Admittedly, the drop was only .26 of a degree Celsius and, as an interviewed climatologist pointed out, it was too soon to say whether this was the beginning of a reversal of the warming trend. It was a hopeful sign none the less, suggesting that the increasingly widespread use of crystech power sources in place of fossil fuels might at last be starting to have a remedial effect on the wounded ecosphere.

Parry was halfway through his hundred sit-ups when an item came on that really made him sit up. It was introduced by an NN24 newscaster as a profile of the FPP officer at the centre of the *shinju* investigation, and it opened with a composite shot of his own caller-ID photo framed within the FPP's TRUST logo. Grabbing the remote control, Parry upped the volume and watched as his life and career to date were condensed to a handful of sentences and a few stock library images.

For the most part the profile was an accurate summation, although it did contain a couple of minor factual errors. It stated that he had been born and brought up in Kensington, not Kennington, and that he had achieved the rank of Detective Inspector in the Met, when he had only made Detective Sergeant. Neither mistake, however, reflected badly on him – if anything, the reverse – and, overall, the tone of the piece was positive. He was described as one of the FPP's finest assets (not the sort of evaluation with which he could sensibly quibble) and he was tipped as a potential future commissioner, which was a nice enough prediction to hear even though one unlikely to come true, given that van Wyk was in pole position for the job and moreover that, even if Parry *was* offered the commissionership, he would probably turn it down. The burdens of captaincy were sufficiently onerous for him, thank you very much.

The next thing to appear onscreen was an image of Anna arriving at a New Venice nightclub, dressed in white capri pants and a cornflower-blue cotton shirt knotted at the waist, and managing to look, in this simple, navel-revealing outfit, sexier and more glamorous than most women did in full evening regalia.

Instantly, Parry's every sense was on high alert. What was Anna doing in a profile about *him*? What did NN24 know about him and her? What were they going to say? There was nothing that could be stated as fact – no proof of impropriety, no evidence that they had a relationship that was anything other than platonic. Yet there was always innuendo. Implications could be made and the viewers left to draw their own conclusions.

Dread nettled in his belly.

Then the truth dawned on him. The profile of him was over. This was another item altogether, a society-column piece about some sort of concert Anna had attended last night. The segue had been swift, and he had not noticed it. The fact that the two items had been placed next to each other was coincidence, nothing more. A quirk of the shuffle. A gift from the cosmic trickster.

Parry grabbed the TV remote, hit Pause, and waited for his stomach to settle down. The onscreen image of Anna stood frozen in mid-step, her head canted, her teeth surrounding a laugh like a string of pearls.

Anna had long been a media favourite, but now more so than ever. There was no shortage of rich and famous and beautiful women in the world, or, for that matter, in New Venice, but having been visited by tragedy – the untimely death of her husband from cancer – Anna had been elevated to a rarer category, that of people whose otherwise idyllic lives have been blighted by a cruel twist of fate. The public preferred the rich and famous and beautiful to have suffered in some way. Envy of the better-off was supposed to be a thing of the past, but it was still comforting for the average man or woman to know that even those who seemed to have it all were not immune to random misfortune. It was proof, if proof were needed, that absolute happiness was not a natural human state. Foreigners were the ones who were sublime, golden, apparently carefree. People of Earth? Not so.

Sitting on the floor, forearms resting on knees, Parry shook his head and wondered at himself. How could he have thought that his and Anna's affair was about to be revealed on air? Ridiculous. They had gone to inordinate lengths to ensure it remained a secret. No one else knew about it, and even if someone by some extraordinary chance *did*, that hypothetical individual would surely have blabbed, were he or she going to, long before now.

No, he was confident the affair was buried treasure, locked safely away in the minds and memories of just two people. He had been haunted by an old fear, that was all. The fear of discovery that had prowled around him and Anna throughout the year-long duration of their affair. The sense of danger that had sometimes added savour to, and sometimes soured, their love.

From their very first tryst (and he liked to think of their irregular, infrequent assignations as trysts – the word having an old-fashioned ring to it, and an echo of Gallic sadness) Parry had been dogged constantly by thoughts of what would happen if someone were to find out. Anna was a high-profile figure, held up by all as a paragon of womanhood and wifeliness. She was noted for her charitable works, her fund-raising dinners, her vocal support of good causes, her involvement in city life. If word got out that she had taken a lover, and moreover that her lover was a captain in the FPP, another relatively high-profile figure who in all respects was supposed to be above reproach, then the media would have a field day. Anna would be publicly shamed and his career would be over.

Even if Quesnel did not demand his resignation, which she would, he himself would feel impelled to tender it.

Those had been the risks, and they had both been aware of them. By pursuing the affair, they had been putting at stake nothing less than their reputations and their futures, and from the vantage-point of hindsight Parry could see that it had been a kind of madness that had gripped them, and could see that part of the excitement, a small but significant part, had been how much they stood to lose should they be caught and exposed. If the value of an abstract thing can be gauged only by the severity of the consequences of its removal, then his and Anna's adultery had carried a very high price tag indeed.

They had first met a little over three years ago, while Parry was still a lieutenant. His superior, the softly spoken Seamus Balfe, had appointed him to the Civic Committee in place of Lieutenant van Wyk, who had just been promoted to captain of the North-West district. The Civic Committee convened on a quarterly basis to discuss Foreign Policy issues from the perspective of New Venetian residents. Nothing much was ever achieved at these meetings, but that was not really the point of them. They enabled the residents to keep a closer eye on the FPP and the FPP to show that it was happy to submit itself to scrutiny. The benefits to both sides were primarily therapeutic.

Parry knew this, but anything that fostered mutual understanding between citizens and law enforcement was, he believed, worthwhile. He also knew, even before he attended a meeting, that his role on the committee was to make up FPP numbers. Commissioner Quesnel would be doing most of the talking. He was there to back her up if necessary and smile reassuringly throughout.

He could remember the date of that first meeting, November 12th, and even that it was a Thursday. He could also remember vividly following Quesnel into the conference chamber at HQ and setting eyes on Anna for the first time.

Of course he had known who she was, but recognizing one of New Venice's better-known faces and encountering in the flesh one of the most breathtakingly beautiful women he had ever seen were two entirely different things.

There were three other residents' representatives at the conference table, three other New Venetians of equal social standing to Anna, but it was only Anna whom Parry really noticed and, during the course of the meeting, only Anna whom he really paid any attention to. He could not remember at all what issues were discussed that evening, but he could recall without difficulty the way Anna had gestured when developing a point (describing a kind of horizontal spiral with her hand) and the way she had held her head on one side while listening to someone else speaking and the way she had taken sips of mineral water, pursing her mouth delicately so as not to leave lipstick marks on the glass. Most of all he remembered how, at one stage in the proceedings, her eye had caught his across the table and she had offered him a calm, easy smile. She was a woman accustomed to being stared at by men and gracious enough not to resent it.

When the meeting was finished, during a period of informal chat before everyone departed, she came over to Parry, who was standing alone.

'I didn't feel we were properly introduced,' she said. 'Anna Fuentes.'

She held out her hand. Parry, on the point of manufolding SALUTATION, hastily untangled his fingers. 'Of course you are,' he said, clumsily.

Her hand felt soft. Not pliant, but gentle, accommodating.

'And you,' she said, disengaging her grip from his, 'are Jack Parry, and you have far too nice eyes for a policeman.'

He spluttered a reply: 'Well, you know, I don't really consider myself a policeman. Not any more. An FPP officer is sort of a, well, a moral guardian. If that doesn't sound too pompous.'

'It does,' Anna said, laughing.

He felt himself blush.

'A little bit,' she amended, kindly. 'But it's good that you take your job so seriously. People in this city can be so frivolous at times.'

'Thank you.'

'May I make one small personal suggestion?'

Parry hesitated, then manufolded INDULGENCE.

'You'll forgive me, I hope. It's probably not my place to comment on such things, but your hair . . .' She winced, as if at her own presumption. 'Sorry, this will sound rude, but I think it would look so much better if you did not do *this* with it.' She mimed brushing forwards over the top of her head. 'A little bit of thinning is nothing to be ashamed of. If you were just to cut it short all over, it would look so much better. More distinguished.' She examined his expression. 'But I've hurt your feelings, haven't I?'

'No,' he said quickly. 'Not at all.'

'Perhaps you wear it that way because that's how your wife likes it.'

'I don't have a wife.'

'Girlfriend, then.'

'Nor one of those.'

'Boyfriend?'

'Not my thing.'

'I didn't think so. So you're unattached, Captain. That surprises me. A man like you, with such nice eyes.'

Parry mumbled some elliptical comment about work commitments and the dearth of single women in resort-cities, and then, to his relief, one of the other residents came over to talk to them.

Three months later, at the next committee meeting, he was sporting an all-over Number Two crop.

'I was right, wasn't I?' Anna said after the meeting. 'It does look better, doesn't it?'

Parry nodded. He was almost boyishly proud of the haircut. At first glance in the mirror at the barber's, after he had undergone long, careful minutes of buzzing, tingling ministration with an electric razor, he had hated it. He had never before realized quite how knobbly and knurled and bumpy his head was, like a cauliflower floret. The haircut made him look like a mental patient, or a child-molester. At HQ, however, colleague after colleague had commented favourably on it, and their approval had won him over.

'You weren't offended, then?' Anna said. 'I was afraid you might not be here today. That nasty Fuentes woman had scared you away.'

'I think I'm made of sterner stuff than that,' he said.

'I think you are.' So saying, she reached up and briefly, gently, stroked the bristles at the nape of his neck. 'I do love the feel of close-cropped hair. It's a bit like velvet.'

Parry felt a tingle spread down his spine from the point where she had touched him. He darted a glance around. No one, thank God, was looking.

'And, you know,' Anna went on, 'it's much easier to trust a man who doesn't try to hide his imperfections.'

'Um,' said Parry.

There was no more to *that* conversation, but for several seconds after Parry's ineloquent monosyllable he and Anna gazed at each other, and her dark eyes, it seemed to him, were something you could fall into and keep falling into and never land, nor ever want to.

Another three months passed, during which Parry found himself looking forward to the next Civic Committee meeting. Looking forward to it with a ridiculous eagerness. Even counting down the days till it was due.

'I understand congratulations are in order,' Anna said, after the evening's business was done, 'Captain.'

'Not quite. Seamus Balfe doesn't retire for another two weeks.'

'Still. A well-deserved promotion.'

'Thank you.' Parry was convinced that Anna, although she could not know it, was in part responsible for his gaining the promotion. In some indefinable way she had changed him. Not just his haircut but his entire life had been improved by meeting her.

'Your own wedge,' she said.

'Yes. The South-West.'

'It means we won't be seeing each other at these meetings any more, doesn't it?'

'I'm afraid so.'

She lowered her gaze for a moment. 'I think that would be a pity.'

'Mrs Fuentes . . .'

She gave him a comical, cockeyed look. 'Is that how you've been thinking of me all this time? "Mrs Fuentes"?'

'No. No.' For the first time aloud he spoke her first name to her, as he had spoken it to her in his head countless times: 'Anna.'

'That's better. Yes?'

And his nerve failed him. No words would come out. He glanced down. Tugged awkwardly at a torn cuticle. Rubbed his left ear.

Anna took a quick look over her shoulder. Quesnel was talking to one of the residents. The other two residents were deep in conversation by the table.

'I have a feeling,' she said, 'that what I am about to say now could make our lives incredibly complicated.'

'Then perhaps you shouldn't say it.' But he wanted her to. Christ, he wanted her to!

'You're right. Perhaps I shouldn't.' She drew a breath. 'Jack, you know who I am. What I am. And I know who and what *you* are. Both of us have positions in life. A lot to lose. And yet . . .'

All at once Parry was flooded with a sense of certainty, of serenity, such as he had not felt in a long time.

'Who cares?' he said.

'Really?' Her eyes were wide – not with surprise but with amazement.

And he thought, how incredible that she should be amazed. This extraordinary woman. Anna Fuentes! And who am I? Nobody special. And yet she's amazed.

And if he had not been in love with her already, he would have fallen in love with her then.

In a low voice she told him where to be, when to be there, how to get in.

And three nights later he found himself at the side gate to the Fuentes compound. It was cool for June. A million stars scintillated overhead and the smell of the mainland – dust, earth, pollen – was thick in the air, borne over the city by the *imbat*, the local summer wind which blew onshore during the day then turned at sunset, like a tide, to blow offshore throughout the night. Behind him, canal waters lapped gently as, with tentative, half-disbelieving fingers, he inserted into the gate's lock the key that Anna had sent to his apartment. The gate unlatched itself. The gate swung open. With an anxious glance over his shoulder, he ventured in.

Her directions had been simple. *Go left. Follow the path towards the house.*

The path emerged on to a stretch of lawn. Ahead was the house, its white-stuccoed walls looming in the darkness, its ribbed red roof-tiles seamed with moonlight, its louvred window shutters sealed. He set off across the grass. His breath was coming in spurts, worry and anticipation together constricting his chest as he neared the house step by stealthy step, with doubts assailing him all the way, a series of *what if?* scenarios parading through his brain, taunting him, leering. What if, for all his caution, someone had spied him entering the compound? What if Hector Fuentes had unexpectedly curtailed his business trip to Bilbao and come home, not leaving Anna enough time to send a warning? Or what if Fuentes were to return, equally unexpectedly, in the next few hours and discover Parry on the premises? All the household domestic staff were supposed to have gone home for the evening, but what if for some reason one of them had stayed behind, unbeknown to Anna? Any of a dozen things could go wrong. Was he really prepared to jeopardize everything he had, just for this one woman? One woman whom, when all was said and done, he hardly knew?

What if he had made a mistake? What if this entire escapade was based on nothing more than a dreadful misapprehension on his part?

Then there she was, waiting for him on the terrace that fronted the south-facing side of the house, looking out for him, hugging herself, expectant. And as he came close he saw that her big dark eyes were thrilled and fear-filled, just as his own must be, and then she caught sight of him and let out a held breath and smiled, and oh Lord, he knew then that *anything* was worth her, *any* risk was worth this prize!

'You came,' she said.

'I know,' he grinned. 'I must be crazy.'

They kissed. Kissed again. *Kissed.* Clumsily at first, but then with greater sureness, greater urgency.

'What are we doing?' she said, pulling her head back, breathless.

'Does it matter?'

He felt the press of her body against his. He felt recklessness and arousal surging up together at once, two heads of the same beast.

She stepped back. She took him by the hand. She led him inside. Upstairs.

That first tryst had become the paradigm for the rest, the theme that each subsequent one had followed with minimal variations. He and Anna would bide their time until Fuentes went abroad on business somewhere and Cecilia was off at her boarding school in Geneva, and then Parry would enter the compound under cover of darkness and make his furtive approach across the garden to the house, and Anna would be there to greet him, and both of them would head indoors and upstairs to the bedroom to tumble into the heat and sweat and fervour of lovemaking . . .

. . . and afterwards there would be stillness, perhaps a gentle breeze lifting and impregnating the bedroom's muslin curtains, but other than that no movement, just a man and woman entwined in postcoital languor beneath a cotton bedsheet, bodies warmly fused by perspiration and exhaustion, each murmuring to the other in the silence, soft sentences, verbal caresses . . .

. . . and beneath it all, like a rheumatic ache, there would be the knowledge that he could not stay. Each time Parry longed for nothing on Earth so much as to fall asleep in Anna's embrace, but it would have been unwise to push their luck. And the knowledge of the necessity of leaving would intensify and grow more painful with every second that passed, as the time until he must make his departure slipped by with unkind swiftness . . .

And he remembered how, between trysts, he might see Anna on television or read about her in the lifestyle section of the New Venice edition of the *Resort-City Clarion*, and more often than not she would be on her husband's arm, radiant beside him, the very epitome of the multimillionaire's wife, and he would feel an unavoidable stab of jealousy for Hector Fuentes, who was better dressed and more sophisticated and far wealthier than he could ever hope to be and who – worse – could have Anna to himself whenever he wanted, could be seen out with her whenever he liked and bask at all times in the simple, miraculous fact that she was married to him and he to her.

Parry would feel this, but he would also feel, in his marrow, a quiet, ferocious glee, because he knew that there was a part of Anna to which Hector had no access. The part she had bequeathed to *him*. The hidden part of her that prompted her to tell him time and time again that she loved him, truly loved him, that he was the man her husband could never be . . .

And the man who could never be her husband. For Anna had made it plain the very first time they slept together that she would not leave Fuentes for Parry. He could not reasonably expect her to, she had said, and of course she was right. She had Cecilia to think about. She had obligations, responsibilities. She had a standard of living that nobody in their right mind would sacrifice, not even for love. It would have been outrageous for him to ask her to do so. Unconscionable.

But that did not stop him asking. Again and again, with a bull-headed, near-masochistic persistence. *Anna, leave him. Anna, forget the thousand and one reasons why you should stay with him. Anna, come and live with me.* She could only refuse, but he would ask anyway, wanting to hear himself say these things, and wanting to hear the note of strained, bitter regret in Anna's voice as she replied no, no, no . . .

Then Fuentes had fallen ill. A brain tumour. The best and most expensive oncologist in the world, Lü Pu-We, was flown over from Shanghai to attend to him. The prognosis was bleak. The tumour was inoperable. It had lurked undiscovered in Fuentes's head for too long, and was now too large to be removed safely. Nothing could be done for him except to make his last few weeks as comfortable as possible.

Anna told Parry, by telephone, that they must not see each other.

Of course not. He understood. She must look after her husband. *He* was her priority.

A month later he bumped into her at – of all places – the Chopin Mall, which, painfully punsome name notwithstanding, was one of New Venice's smarter retail arcades. He had gone there for one of his regular visits to Britten's for Britons, an emporium where expatriates could stock up (at regrettably high prices) on homeland staples such as Cheddar cheese and Marmite and pork sausages and decent tea. Anna had gone there to browse in a vintage bookstore. Hector liked her to read to him, she said, and she had been trying to find him something unusual and undigitized. She looked wan, worn, weighed down. Parry suggested they go for coffee.

'Someone might see us,' she said.

'So what? This was a chance encounter, and we know each other from the Civic Committee, don't we?'

She seemed too exhausted to submit any further protest. She seemed, in fact, grateful for the offer.

At a café overlooking the Eighth Canal, Parry drank tea while Anna, between sips of espresso, told him of the hell she was going through. Her husband was losing control of his bodily functions, and that was awful, but there were round-the-clock nursing staff on hand to deal with such things. What was worse, as far as she was concerned, was the way he was losing weight so rapidly, visibly shrinking from day to day. Dr Lü had told her to expect this, but still, it was as though the cancer was literally eating away at him from the inside, sucking at him like some horrible parasite, hollowing him out. Her only consolation was that Cecilia was away at school and so was being spared the sight of her father's slow, inexorable decline. 'With any luck,' she said, 'he'll be gone before term ends. Is that an awful thing to hope for?'

Parry assured her that it was not.

'You know, I can't stop blaming myself. Hector had been behaving erratically for a while. Short-tempered. Forgetting things. Dropping things. I should have forced him to go and see his doctor, but he kept insisting he was all right. That's his way. Nothing could ever go wrong with the great Hector Fuentes. But I should have ... should have ...'

She began to cry, and Parry passed her a paper napkin.

'I'm sorry,' she said, wiping her eyes. 'I know it's not my fault, not really. I'm just being stupid. But thank you for letting me unburden myself like this. Thank you for listening. I really appreciate it. Perhaps . . . perhaps we might do this again some time?'

And so they began to meet in public places – as friends, nothing more – even as Fuentes's condition worsened and the strain on Anna intensified. Towards the end, she became quite haggard and was sometimes scarcely able to string two sentences together, yet she was always grateful for Parry's sympathetic ear and Parry was always pleased to be able to lend it to her.

Fuentes died on a Saturday in April.

The funeral took place the following Tuesday. Parry was among the mourners, as was Quesnel. Quesnel was there because it was only right and proper that the city's FPP commissioner be on hand to pay her last respects to one of New Venice's most prominent and eminent residents. When she asked Parry why *he* was there, he fluently offered the excuse he had come up with. Someone had to keep an eye out for camera-hacks, didn't they? After all, the official news networks might always respect the privacy of individuals, but some of those e-ther journalists weren't so honourable, and it seemed a good idea to have a senior FPP officer on hand to intervene in case one of them tried to take footage of the ceremony and the Crystech Caballero's grieving relatives.

The service was held at White Quays, on the rim of the North-East District. The Quays were a fanned array of ctenoid jetties where rich folk berthed their pleasure yachts and cabin cruisers, immense spaceship-sleek vessels whose names – *The Lucky Toss, Filthy Lucre, My Peccadillo* – attested to a casual smugness about money. It was a breezy, balmy spring day. Clouds at full sail scudded across the sky, their shadows rippling after them over a finely striated sea like an expanse of etched green glass. A spare mooring had been set aside for the ceremony, and the majority of the mourners stood on the dock and looked on as, on the deck of a flat open barge, a Catholic priest intoned the last rites before a dozen members of Fuentes's immediate family. In front of them Fuentes's body lay linen-wrapped inside a canoe-like shell of amethyst-coloured crystech.

As the service concluded, a crystechnician stepped forward, unscrewed the lid of the soundproofed canister he was holding, and offered the open canister to each family member in turn. Each delved in and took out a handful of whitish-mauve granules, which he or she then scattered in sparkling drifts over the body. Anna and Cecilia were the last in line. This was the first time Parry had ever seen Anna's daughter in person, although from conversations with Anna he felt as though he knew her. She was some fifteen metres away from him and wearing a veil, but he could none the less make out dark-rimmed eyes and a face devoid of all expression. Unlike Anna, who looked tired and resigned, Cecilia had not had to watch Fuentes degenerate day by day, although she had been there at the end, helping her mother keep vigil through her father's last days and final night. Anna had begun to grieve for her husband before he was even dead. Cecilia had yet to overcome the shock of bereavement. But she was young. Youth meant resilience. She would come to terms with her loss soon enough, perhaps sooner than her mother.

When the last handful of crystech seeds had been scattered, the crystechnician approached Fuentes's body with a portable tone-generator. Kneeling, he aimed the directional speaker at Fuentes's granule-sprinkled remains and adjusted the pitch and envelope controls. With a twist of a potentiometer dial, a high clear whine began to emanate from the tone-generator, and all at once the crystals began to grow. Jewel-like clusters blossomed on the body, swelling up more rapidly where the granules were more densely sown. Like a gardener tending a plot, the crystechnician moved back and forth with the tone-generator. Where growth was happening too slowly, he stimulated it with blasts of sound at increased volume. Where it was happening too quickly, he inhibited it with stabs of white noise. The crystal clusters were by now extending glittering, spiky tendrils towards one another like frost in fast motion, coalescing, encasing the body and thickening upwards. Eventually Fuentes's mortal remains were sheathed evenly from head to toe in a block of gleaming see-through violet. A final sharp blurt of white noise terminated the growth altogether, and the job was done. The barge's engine started up, and soon Fuentes was being ferried out to sea and his final resting-place. Only his immediate family would be present as, somewhere out in international waters, his transparent coffin was eased overboard to slip beneath the waves.

It was later that day, at the wake at Casa Fuentes, that Parry and Cecilia actually met. Having offered formal condolences to Anna, he stood in a corner sipping a glass of white wine and debating whether to stay or go. Quesnel, to his relief, had elected not to attend the wake, otherwise he would have been hard pushed to justify his presence there as well. In her absence, however, there was no one he knew there, apart from Anna. Then Cecilia approached him – drawn to him, she would later say, through a combination of compassion and curiosity: she did not like to see people on their own at parties and she wondered if this FPP officer was the same FPP officer who, according to her mother, had been a pillar of strength during the past few difficult months.

They hit it off straight away. Cecilia, red-eyed and desolate, never the less had enough of her customary spark about her to find Parry's simply expressed sympathies touching and his obvious respect for her mother endearing. 'Ma says she really needed a friend like you,' she told him.

'She flatters me.'

'She says you've been her knight in shining armour.'

'I've only done what anyone would have done.' He felt a fraud as he said those words. He had only done what anyone would have done who was keen to appear supportive and caring. His motives had been anything but unselfish.

'All the same, I think I'll have to call you Sir Jack from now on. Like a knight. If you don't mind.'

And that was how he became a favourite of the daughter as well as the mother.

Things between him and Anna did not change straight away. He had not expected they would. She observed her period of mourning and behaved as a recently widowed woman should. Each time they met for a drink or dinner, however, he was pleased to note that a little bit more of her old self was coming back. Each time she was a little bit more the Anna she had been before her husband's illness. And each time he was encouraged that soon, soon, they would be able to pick up again where they left off.

A few weeks after the funeral the blow came.

It came one night in a crowded restaurant. Anna said she been putting off telling him. She said that she had been meaning to say what she was about to say for some while, but each time she had tried to broach the subject something had prevented her. The moment had never seemed quite right. She wanted him to be her friend, she said. She valued him highly as a friend. She knew her daughter liked him, too. Cissy spoke with amusement and pleasure about the e-communications the two of them had begun sending to each other, with their cod-Arthurian language and sentiments. And she and he could carry on with these public meetings, of course. She enjoyed them greatly. She loved his company.

'My company,' he said in a high, hoarse voice that he scarcely recognized as his own, 'but not me.'

'That's not it,' she said, and her gaze was both tender and bitter. 'That's not it at all. You . . . you wouldn't understand if I told you why, so it's better that I don't. Please, Jack. Will you please just accept what I'm offering?'

'There's no alternative?'

'No.'

'Until when?'

She shook her head sadly. 'I'm not promising you a when.'

'But there might be?'

'Jack. I can't give you a why, I can't give you a when. I'm simply asking you, as someone whom I . . . I respect highly – will you just be a friend?'

And of course, in the end, he had said yes. He had had to. A little of Anna was better than nothing of her at all.

Thinking about these things now put Parry in a sullen and disconsolate mood. He could not summon the enthusiasm to resume his sit-ups. All at once his apartment – the spacious weight of living alone – seemed oppressive, and he felt acutely his isolation as a permanent resident in a city of transients. Ninety per cent of New Venice's population was in a constant state of flux, tourists and Sirens and Foreigners coming and going. He was one of those rare people who had chosen to live here full-time, and now he was conscious of them all around him: strangers, a relentless, friendless surge. Suddenly he craved company. He picked up the phone and dialled Johansen's number. Not at home. He did not leave a message. Anna? No.

He wondered whether to ask Shankar out for a drink. He could pretend he wanted to discuss the morning's events at the Debussy. But the sergeant was a family man. He had a wife and three kids to whom he was devoted, and Parry could not in all conscience drag him away from an evening with them. How about one of other the officers in his district? No. It would seem odd if he asked any of them to meet him somewhere away from the workplace, out of uniform, out of hours. Odd and inappropriate. They did not know him socially. He was just the guvnor. Why did he know almost no one here who wasn't FPP?

In the end he decided to finish his exercises and go out anyway. Better to be among unfamiliar faces than to be among no faces at all.

21 MANUAL

He went to High C's, an open-air seafood restaurant on Copland Concourse. There, he ate a starter of crab *au gratin* followed by swordfish steak, listening all the while to the strains of piped Siren music, the preferred background accompaniment at any self-respecting eaterie. Afterwards he made his way to a cinema on the banks of the First Canal. He had no idea what film was playing there and was disappointed to find it was a new musical comedy entitled *Snatched!* Still, better than nothing. It would kill a couple of hours.

In the event, he enjoyed the film, which was based loosely on the *Body Snatchers* movies of old and even more loosely on the Jack Finney novel which had engendered them. Sharper and wittier than he was expecting, *Snatched!* was essentially a satire of pre-Foreign attitudes to creatures not of this world. It was set sometime during the latter half of the twentieth century in a generic Midwestern small town where the inhabitants were bitter, argumentative types who did not get on with one another, could never agree on anything and sang like geese. The only exception was the film's heroine, a spunky eleven-year-old girl whose sunny demeanour and superb soprano marked her out as an oddball and an outsider. She was one of the first to notice when certain of her neighbours began behaving out of character – laughing, treating others courteously, singing well – and in due course she discovered that an alien force was taking over the townsfolk one by one, assimilating them and improving them. No one would believe her about this. Eventually, however, the 'bad' townsfolk did become aware of the presence among them of the 'good' and, finding saintliness and tolerance unendurable, embarked on witch-hunts and pogroms. The conflict threatened to destroy the town but in the end was resolved when the girl, having nearly been killed by an irate mob brandishing torches and farming tools, sang about peace and understanding so beautifully that hearts melted and the 'bad' townsfolk saw the error of their ways and agreed to be assimilated and improved by the alien force too. A rousing, hand-holding, smiles-all-round singa-long finale ushered in the end-credits.

There were half a dozen Foreigners in the audience, all of them ensconced in the back rows of the auditorium, where the seats were larger (and more expensive). They sat evenly spaced out, no two of them adjacent, and Parry could not help but wonder what they made of the film. Did they understand the story? Did they get the jokes? Did they have even the first clue what was going on? A corner of the screen was set aside for a running commentary on the action with hand-symbols, but this *per se* was of limited assistance, able to illustrate the general tone of a scene but not much more. Perhaps the Foreigners simply enjoyed submitting themselves to indecipherable pieces of Earth culture, like occidental tourists watching kabuki theatre, at once intrigued and mystified by all the noise and colour and activity. It was hard to know for sure. For the most part the golden giants gazed at the screen, motionless, and could just as well have been serenely rapt as supremely bored. Only when the music struck up did they show any animation. The songs in particular – most of them old-fashioned songs with verse-structure and lyrics in keeping with the movie's period setting – set them swaying. They gesticulated and shuddered and rocked back and forth, sometimes so intensely that the swish and rustle of their robes was almost as loud as the soundtrack. (And when Parry heard the noise of this activity filling the auditorium it was difficult, even for him, not to think of old men and macintoshes.) Once the film was over, however, and the lights came up, the Foreigners rose and filed out as diffidently as a church congregation after the final catechism of a particularly unenthralling service.

In a slightly less gloomy frame of mind than earlier, Parry took a late canal-bus home. On the jetty outside his condominium he paused to watch an airship glide by overhead. With its balloon lit up from within and glowing, the airship made him think of a Chinese lantern drifting along a night-mirroring river. Its course took it directly in front of the moon, and for a few seconds the two gibbous globes of light, dirigible and planetoid satellite, seemingly drawn to each other by their apparent similarities, fused and became one. Then they parted again, the moon remaining fixed, the airship continuing on its way.

For some reason, Parry thought of himself and Anna.

It was then that a Foreigner came lumbering towards him,

appearing so suddenly and unexpectedly from the shadows beneath a nearby palm that he almost shed a skin.

His startlement turned to curiosity as the golden giant configured its gloved hands into TRUST. It had identified him as an FPP officer, even though he was in civvies. How was that possible? Unless it had been lying in wait for him. That was the only sensible explanation. The Foreigner knew a Foreign Policy Policeman lived here, knew that Parry was him, and wanted to speak to him.

He signed back TRUST, followed by SALUTATION.

The Foreigner returned the SALUTATION, then folded its fingers into the knotty-knuckled manufold for ENTREATY.

Parry signed ACCEPTANCE.

FINALITY, said the Foreigner.

Parry did not understand. He offered ENTREATY.

The Foreigner repeated FINALITY.

Parry was confused. He peered up, frowning, into the Foreigner's mask, hoping to find elucidation there. But of course that worked only with humans. In the glow of the courtesy light that hung above the condominium's front entrance, all he could make out in the Foreigner's 'face' was the reflection of his own face frowning back down at him, dimpled and distended by the contours of the mask's pseudo-physiognomy.

Then it came to him. FINALITY. The deaths. The Foreigner wanted to discuss the *shinju* deaths.

He signed ACCEPTANCE.

The Foreigner now offered RESOLUTION followed by ENTREATY.

Parry responded with PROBABILITY.

The Foreigner, with another ENTREATY, requested elucidation.

Parry thought for a moment, wondering how to put it. He used TRUST, then CURIOSITY, then URGENCY, then RESOLUTION, in the hope that this would convey that the FPP were looking into the deaths and were keen for the matter to be cleared up as soon as possible.

The more hand-symbols you used in conjunction, the greater room there was for misinterpretation. The Foreigner, however, appeared to understand. It signed ACCEPTANCE, then DOUBT.

Parry questioned the DOUBT with ENTREATY.

The Foreigner manufolded SUPERNAL and NEGATIVE. SUPERNAL stood for Foreign or Foreigner.

Parry signed ENTREATY.

The Foreigner repeated SUPERNAL, NEGATIVE.

So, the Foreigners regarded the *shinjus* as a bad thing. Was that it? Well, of course they would. But in that case, why was this Foreigner using NEGATIVE when it could have used CONCERN?

The Foreigner must have sensed that it was not getting its message across. It tried SUPERNAL, NEGATIVE once again, then added DIFFICULT.

Parry concurred. DIFFICULT.

The Foreigner offered TRUST, RESOLUTION, ENTREATY.

All Parry could do was restate his earlier declaration: TRUST, CURIOSITY, URGENCY, RESOLUTION.

The Foreigner hovered in front of him for a few moments more, as if engaged in inner debate, wondering whether to say more. Finally, offering him another SALUTATION, it turned away and lurched towards the jetty. Facing the canal, it fixed its hands in ENTREATY and began sidestepping back and forth, a few paces one way, a few paces the other, waiting for a taxi-gondola to come by.

It was still there at the canal's edge when Parry got upstairs to his apartment. He stood at his window for a while, watching it perform its peculiar crabwise to-and-fro shuffle, and he thought of the old joke, coined within days of the Debut, about how, like God in the hymn, Foreigners moved in a mysterious way.

A mysterious way indeed.

Several minutes passed with no sign of a vacant taxi-gondola, and Parry was on the point of phoning FPP HQ to send a launch to ferry the stranded Foreigner back to its hotel when, happily, a vacant taxi-gondola appeared. The gondolier hove to beside the Foreigner, and the golden giant delved into a pocket in its robes and produced the name-card for its hotel. The gondolier peered at the card, handed it back and signalled ACCEPTANCE. He steadied his craft by planting one foot on the jetty, and the Foreigner stepped stiffly aboard, adding so little weight to the gondola that it drew barely a centimetre of extra draught. A jewel flashed in the darkness, passing from the Foreigner's hand to the gondolier's then swiftly disappearing into a purse that hung about the gondolier's neck. The golden giant settled down on the cushions of the boat's shallow, forward-facing seat, the gondolier twisted the throttle on his steering-pole, and they were off, whirring away into the night.

Parry turned from the window and went to run himself a hot bath. Wallowing in the steaming, faintly briny water with a folded wet flannel laid across his eyes, he replayed in his mind the conversation he had had with the Foreigner. What the golden giant had been trying to tell him he was still not entirely sure, but he had the distinct impression that it had become exasperated at the end, either by his lack of comprehension or by its inability to communicate its message properly. But then what could you expect? Hand-symbols provided such a limited linguistic palette to work with. Even Professor Verhulst himself had been heard to complain that the manufold vocabulary ought to be at least five times as large – and this was the man who had helped codify hand-symbols in the first place!

The story of Jan Verhulst had provided the basis for a couple of telemovies, one big-screen biopic, several documentaries and a handful of books. Parry had seen the biopic and read the most credible of the books, Verhulst's own account – based on his personal diary – of the part he played in the development of hand-symbols. A musicologist at the University of Amsterdam, Verhulst had been generally regarded as a pre-eminent expert in his field. Before the Foreigners came he had also been something of a lost cause. The breadth of his knowledge of the classical canon was only equalled by the depth of his apathy towards the duties and responsibilities expected of him as an academic. Almost invariably he would arrive too early or late for lectures and tutorials and sometimes he would fail to arrive at all. He had a similar attitude toward the articles and theses commissioned from him by specialist magazines and learned journals. When he could be bothered to deliver them, they were of an abstruse and almost wilfully wayward nature.

All this he himself admitted in his book, with unusual candour for an autobiographer. He also described himself as a shambolic figure, something the biopic had made much of in its opening scenes, in order to engage the audience with his character and raise a few laughs. He favoured ill-fitting tweed jackets, and his hair and beard floated about his face in tangled twists and wisps like (to use his own words) mouse-brown candyfloss. Fond of cycling, he chose to pedal around on the heaviest and most primitive of bone-shakers, rattling across the Amsterdam cobbles with his head held high and his trousers clipped tightly at the ankles and his mind on almost anything except traffic and pedestrians. He was unmarried, unorthodox and unworldly. *Other*worldly, some said.

Which could well have been why the Foreigners chose him.

A month after the Foreigners' first appearance, while humankind was still getting over the shock and only just beginning to acclimatize to its new reality, Verhulst ambled into his study one morning to find one of the golden giants standing by his desk, apparently waiting for him. For several minutes Verhulst stared at the Foreigner across the room, and the Foreigner stared back. Verhulst could not fathom what the Foreigner wanted with him. It had been perceived that Foreigners understood and respected the distinction between public and private property, never trespassing on to the latter. Had this one lost its way? Or was a professor's study not considered a private place?

Verhulst was not perturbed by the golden giant. Rather, he was amused and fascinated by its presence, and, being an affable, trusting sort of person, he began to talk to it, chatting to it as though it were a stray cat. *What are you doing here, then? How did you get in?* That sort of thing. Meanwhile, the Foreigner continued to observe him silently with the empty eye-indentations of its mask.

Soon the one-sided conversation petered out and what happened next was something Verhulst would thereafter refer to, with typical humility, as his small stroke of accidental genius.

He decided to play the Foreigner some music.

After all, it had been noted that Foreigners gravitated towards places where music was playing, and here he was, a musicologist, in a room filled with sheet music, books about music, music on disc, a grand piano. Playing the Foreigner something seemed the most natural thing to do.

He chose Mozart. Why not start with the best? Symphony No.41 in C Major came to hand. Felicitously, the 'Jupiter' symphony. He slotted the disc into his stereo and pressed Play. The opening statement of the first movement, the allegro, issued from the speakers – the same chord repeated three times, the reiterations preceded by short rising glissandos.

Immediately, the Foreigner became animated. As the music picked up pace, filling the room, its whole body began shuddering and swaying in time to the lilt of the music, while its gloved fingers described spidery patterns in the air. Verhulst looked on in astonishment, wondering if the creature was in pain. But no, it was not pain, he decided, that was causing the Foreigner to move like that. It was pleasure.

When the allegro came to an end, Verhulst ejected the disc and excitedly cast about for another. He chose Beethoven's Ninth, inserted it into the stereo, and track-selected the last movement, the 'Ode to Joy'.

This time the Foreigner responded with less bodily activity but a notably greater intensity of appreciation. It clasped its hands together and, quivering like a tuning fork, twisted its fingers into an intricate digit-origami which it sustained throughout the entire length of the movement. When Verhulst, more than a little intrigued now, played the movement again, the same thing happened. The Foreigner wrapped its fingers together in the exact same position. Verhulst would shortly come to identify that particular interlacing of hands as the manifold for HAPPINESS.

The process of establishing all ninety-six hand-symbols began that day and took Verhulst and the Foreigner a further month and a half to complete. Once Verhulst had cottoned on to the fact that certain kinds of music elicited certain set configurations of the Foreigner's fingers, it was not hard for him to figure out that each configuration represented an emotional state corresponding to the sentiment the composer was intending to evoke. After that, all he had to do was ransack his own collection of discs and the university's music library for compositions and see which, if any, hand-symbol the Foreigner formed in response.

Not every piece of music elicited a hand-symbol. Some works the Foreigner appreciated without being moved to link its hands together, and some works it did not react to at all, remaining obdurately stock-still for their duration. Verhulst was quick to perceive a distinct preference on the golden giant's part for works featuring the human voice, which set it trembling and swaying more vigorously than did purely instrumental pieces. It enjoyed opera and chorales most of all. It also had a taste for sung jazz and a certain amount of pop music, although the more relentless, hardcore forms of dance music and heavy metal did not find great favour with it. It had an ear for a good voice, and a piece performed by one of the acknowledged recorded greats – Caruso, Callas, Schwarzkopf, Gobbi, Pavarotti – visibly stirred it more than the same piece performed by a lesser talent (although it exhibited what seemed to Verhulst a sneaking penchant for the crowd-pleasing stylistic excesses of Mario Lanza).

In very few instances was Verhulst able to determine right away the significance of a hand-symbol when he first beheld it, although he might make a guess which would later prove to have been on the mark. He had a feeling, for example, that the manifold the

Foreigner formed when heading the final chorus of the St Matthew Passion was REGRET, and that the meaning of the finger configuration it held during the introductory bars of 'Zadok the Priest' must be ANTICIPATION, and that the closing section of the *William Tell* overture inspired it to sign URGENCY, all three surmises being confirmed by subsequent data. Mostly, however, it was only through the slow, labour-intensive process of cataloguing which compositions incurred which hand-symbols that Verhulst was able to begin to interpret them.

On sheets of paper, each headed with a sketch of a different hand-symbol, Verhulst would log the title of every work or portion of a work which the Foreigner greeted with that particular hand-symbol. As these lists lengthened, he was pleased to discover a congruence of form and theme in each. Certain key signatures tended to group together, and the difference between the major and minor moods was reflected in the nature of the concepts they defined, words with positive connotations stemming predominantly from pieces in a major key, words with negative connotations predominantly from pieces in a minor key. Specific types of music recurred under each heading. Under SALUTATION, for example, were all sorts of liturgical works, aubades, and occasional pieces written for royalty. Under the hand-symbol which Verhulst came to understand represented ENTREATY were countless hymns and yearning arias. Under the hand-symbol for which he eventually could find no other name than NEGATIVE were funeral marches, winter songs, and a whole series of grumbling laments from the deep-indigo end of the blues spectrum. Painstakingly he fitted this peculiar vocabulary together, building it up in the manner of a lexicographer, music his etymology, compositions his supporting quotations.

Naturally he had to go to his head of department and request to be excused from his professorial duties while he and the Foreigner went about their work. He begged the head of department to keep quiet about the presence of a Foreigner on campus, but word leaked out and soon the entire music faculty, and then the entire university, was assisting Verhulst in his efforts, suggesting pieces he might like to try out on the golden giant. The change that had come over their colleague was the source of much comment and amazement among Verhulst's peers. Since the Foreigner had become a daily visitor to his study, Verhulst had ceased to be the distracted, absent-minded figure of yore. He was focused, a man with a purpose. It was as though his life till now had been a dormant state, as though he had been waiting, pupa-like, for this moment to emerge from his chrysalis. Every morning he would stride through the university's Oudemanhuispoort entrance with a stack of discs wedged between his hands and chin and with an unmistakable eagerness in his stride, and every morning the Foreigner would be there waiting for him when he opened his study door, ready to begin their work anew. Verhulst knew the task he was engaged in was important, and he rose to the challenge splendidly.

Within a month he had worked out definitions for almost all of the ninety-six hand-symbols the Foreigner had demonstrated. The last few days of their collaboration were spent fine-tuning those hand-symbols whose meanings remained nebulous or were not as precise as Verhulst wished. By the morning of the fortieth day since the Foreigner's first appearance in his study, Verhulst realized that their labours were almost complete. That evening he headed home, knowing somehow that he had seen the last of the golden giant. Sure enough, the following morning he arrived at his study to find the Foreigner not there. It had, however, left a gift for him. Standing on the lid of the piano was an object no one on Earth had seen before: a statuette made of a yellow, gold-flecked, marble-like substance, its hands interlaced in the formation that Verhulst knew signified GRATITUDE. When he finally nerved himself to touch the statuette, he was so startled by the note that sprang forth from it that he let out a shriek loud enough to be heard on the other side of the campus.

The official public unveiling of hand-symbols occurred a fortnight later. News of what Verhulst and the Foreigner were up to together had already leaked out, but Verhulst had kept mum about the actual nature of the communication that the Foreigner was teaching him, and so there was a huge sense of anticipation about the event. Parry remembered watching the broadcast and being impressed both by the simplicity of the hand-symbols themselves and by Verhulst's short speech detailing his part in their decoding. Others in Verhulst's position might have claimed an unwarranted proportion of the credit for themselves. After all, he was the only human witness to what had gone on in his study, and no one would have been any the wiser had he decided to lie, or at the very least gild the truth. However, Verhulst gave an utterly self-effacing account of events, famously describing himself as 'little more than an enlightened amanuensis'. In so doing, he endeared himself to a world that was just starting to look for honest role-models once more, heroes rather than media-generated celebrities.

Verhulst remained consistently modest in all the many interviews that followed, and international renown, a sizeable advance for his book and even a special Nobel failed to turn his head. This, coupled with his stereotypically professorial looks that no amount of PR ironing could unrumple, meant that he soon became to musicology what Einstein had become to physics – the friendly face of an academic discipline, brilliant yet approachable.

Verhulst was retired from academic life these days and, though in worldwide demand as a lecturer and after-dinner speaker, was content to live away from the limelight for the most part, enjoying long leisurely bicycle rides through the flat, regimented Netherlands landscape. His legacy, in the shape of the ninety-six finger formations that were taught in schools alongside reading and writing, would live on as long as Foreigners continued to visit the Earth, and his story had become something of a latterday fable – an archetypal example of the beneficially transformative influence of the golden giants.

Parry wrapped his toes around the bath plug's chain, yanked the plug out and lay there as the water swirled away, feeling his body grow heavier. When the bath was all but empty he climbed out and towelled himself dry, then cleaned his teeth and strode naked to the bedroom.

He had decided he would go to Anna's party after all. Partly this change of mind had been brought about by his encounter with the Foreigner and his contemplation of Jan Verhulst's story, both of which had reminded him that this was the Foreign era, an age when you should not feel you had to apologize for doing what you wanted to do. Mostly, though, he had changed his mind because he did not relish the prospect of spending another evening like this one, alone, bereft of human company and conversation. A night of drinking and socializing at Casa Fuentes? A chance to see Anna again? Why not? Why the hell not?

Before going to bed, he sent a second message to Cecilia.

```
On second thoughts, milady . . . If the invitation
still stands, I'd love to come.
```

22 DIALOGUE

No further *shinju* occurred that night. Throughout the next morning Parry kept expecting the call to come. *Sir, we've found another one.* Every time his work-board telephone rang, he picked up the receiver with an apprehensive hand, but every time it turned out to be routine business, the run-of-the-mill stuff of an FPP captain's day.

The great majority of his work was administration and personnel management. As a sergeant and then a lieutenant he had been more directly involved in the process of intercession between humans and Foreigners. For the most part this entailed nothing more than showing a high profile in public places, his presence a polite reminder to people to act conscientiously and courteously towards one another and, more importantly, towards the golden giants. Where necessary, however, he had taken an active hand in shielding Foreigners from abuse or exploitation, by cautioning vagrants who pestered them for handouts, by admonishing tourists who followed them around taking endless snapshots and video footage, and by extracting APOLOGY and recompense from hoteliers who had overcharged them, Sirens who had short-changed them and taxi-gondoliers who had taken them on circuitous 'scenic' routes. An FPP officer could not force people to comply with his or her demands, since the Foreign Policy Constitution did not endow the FPP with the right to incarcerate or fine. Successful resolution of a dispute lay in the individual officer's powers of persuasion, and Parry, in his less modest moments, considered that he had been quite adept at prevailing upon people's better natures. Now, his responsibility was making sure that the officers under his command performed their duties – the same duties he used to perform – to the best of their abilities. He watched the watchmen. Only in exceptional circumstances, such as when there was a human or Foreign fatality in his district, was he required to roll up his sleeves and become embroiled in the nitty-gritty of the job once again. It was ironic: he had always relished administering Foreign Policy where it counted, at street level, but nowadays he got a chance to do so only under the grimmest and most exacting conditions.

So the day rolled by and he found himself relaxing, the knot in his stomach unclenching, as the blow he dreaded failed to materialize. At lunch, in a mood of heady reprieve, he gave in to Carmen at the commissary and ordered a helping of ginger pudding to go with his main course of chicken and apricot *tajine* with couscous. Carmen rewarded him with a splendid vanilla smile.

He carried his tray of food to a corner table and was just tucking into the *tajine* when Quesnel appeared.

'Jack, mind if I join you?'

She set her tray down opposite his and sat. On the tray were a Caesar salad, an apple and a small bottle of carbonated mineral water. She glanced at Parry's somewhat heartier meal.

'Don't tell me you eat like that every day.'

'I would if Carmen had her way.'

'Yes, she's a one-woman pressure group, ain't she? And speaking of pressure groups: how was it at Free World House yesterday?'

Parry dabbed sauce from the corner of his mouth with a paper napkin. 'Dogged.'

'What did MacLeod want?'

'What do you think? To let us know he's there. He sees this situation as a marvellous opportunity to cause trouble, or, putting it generously, further his cause.'

'Predictable, I guess. Anything else?'

'He was sounding me out, trying to work out if we fancy the Xenophobes for the *shinjus* or not.'

'What did his attitude tell you? Does he know something we don't?'

'He didn't give much away, but then he doesn't strike me as the sort of person who *ever* gives much away.'

Quesnel speared a crouton, forked it into her mouth and munched it ruminatively. 'There has to be a reason why he was so keen to talk with you. I mean, over and above just wanting to make his number. You think he has Triple-X connections?'

'Hard to say. The line between the Xenophobes and Triple-X is so blurred sometimes I'm not sure it's even there at all. I suspect MacLeod may harbour Triple-X sympathies. But connections? I don't know.'

'You don't think he might even be a Triple-Xer himself?'

'What are you getting at, ma'am?'

'Really I'm just thinking out loud here. You see, let's assume the worst and say that the *shinjus* are murders not suicides and that they're Triple-X crimes. If MacLeod knows this, then there are two possible reasons why he's concerned about them – so concerned that he demands an audience with the officer investigating them. One reason's good and the other reason's bad. The good one is that he wants to emphasize the legitimate Xenophobe movement's disassociation from the Triple-Xers. He doesn't want to get dragged down by them like Kyagambiddwa did. The bad reason is that he's covertly trying to assist Triple-X by attempting to winkle out from us whether we've linked it to the deaths.'

'Respectfully, ma'am, the problem with this whole line of thinking is that Triple-Xers insist they aren't out to harm humans. It's one of the planks of their manifesto, or would be if they *had* a manifesto as such. They're on humankind's side, or so they always say. And here we have two dead Sirens.'

'True. But human lives *have* been lost in Triple-X attacks, have they not?'

Parry nodded. He could think of at least four instances off the top of his head. That fire-bomb at the Bridgeville Hilton, for starters. The bomb destroyed three Foreigners but also resulted in injury to a half-dozen human guests of the hotel and the death of a bellhop who had spotted an unattended suitcase and gone to pick it up, little realizing that it contained a paraffin-gel device set to detonate by remote signal.

Equally awful was the fragmentation-grenade attack on a beach near Nice which, in addition to shredding five golden giants, had killed two sunbathers and maimed four others.

Then there was the blaze at a hotel on Gaijin Hello Friendly Island in which thirteen people had suffered fatal burns or been asphyxiated by fumes. That was widely suspected to have been an arson attack and to have been instigated by a Triple-X cell, although neither suspicion was ever conclusively proved. (Ironically, if the fire *was* an attempt to incinerate Foreigners, it failed, since no charred Foreign remains were found at the scene.)

Last but not least, there was the incident on La Isla de Los Extranjeros off the coast of Costa Rica, when a rocket launcher had been fired at the window of a Foreign-scale hotel room. Falling débris from the explosion had smashed open the skull of the owner of a souvenir stall below.

'Of course,' Quesnel continued, 'humans are never the intended targets. They're, to use an ugly and hopefully obsolete phrase, "collateral damage". But given that media coverage of Triple-X actions is always more extensive and prolonged when there are human as well as Foreign casualties, you could be forgiven for thinking that Triple-Xers don't go out of their way to avoid causing human deaths. You could even be forgiven for thinking that they cause them deliberately.'

'And it isn't that big a step from killing people accidentally-on-purpose to killing people on purpose,' Parry said, nodding.

'Especially if those people are Sirens. It's no secret how Triple-Xers feel about Sirens. Their e-ther site's bad enough. "Unnatural hotel-room proclivities." "Grievous perversions of the human voice." Their pamphlets are worse. Last one I read, Sirens were likened to Nazi collaborators.'

The internetworks had a self-imposed code of conduct that was stringently exercised. Rhetoric liable to incite hatred or violence against individuals or types of individual was expressly forbidden, on pain of immediate site-closure, and so, within the e-ther, groups such as Triple-X had to settle for guarded, grumbling references of the kind just cited by Quesnel. There were, however, no such controls over the printed word. Being a neglected medium of dissemination and almost impossible to regulate, the printed word allowed unfettered expression of opinion, and Triple-X, in their secretly distributed, often quite professionally produced literature, took full advantage of that.

'I suppose,' Parry said, 'if there *was* any one class of human that Triple-X was likely to extend its campaign of violence to include, Sirens would be it. But why target Sirens and Foreigners together?'

'Two birds with one stone?'

'Well, maybe, but I wouldn't exactly consider the methods used in the *shinjus* to be "one stone". A gun killed Henderson, a fall from an eighth-storey balcony killed Dagmar Pfitzner, and while we've no idea what was responsible for the losses of the Foreigners with them, it certainly wasn't a gun or a fall. If it was the case that there'd just been a bomb in each of those rooms, then yes, I'd say this was Triple-X at work. An escalation of their typical *modus operandi*, but only a slight one. But if the *shinjus* aren't *shinjus*, if you see what I mean – if they're double murders dressed up as double suicides – then what is the point of them? What statement is Triple-X trying to make with them?'

23   BAR

He asked Johansen the same question a few hours later in a bar just off the Piazza Verdi. At quitting time Johansen had popped his head round the door to Parry's office and invited him out for an evening's carousing. 'And maybe we can find some nice tourist girls to chat up,' he had added. 'It's been a tough week, yeah? We should let off some steam.' Parry had declined the offer of a full night out on the razzle, but had agreed to accompany Johansen for at least one round of drinks, maybe two, before he headed off for his next social engagement, the party at Anna's. So they were sitting in a booth at the Bar Brindisi, a drinking establishment whose proximity to FPP HQ meant that the majority of its clientèle were FPP, and Parry had just finished filling his lieutenant in on his lunchtime conversation with the commissioner in the commissary.

'She didn't have an answer,' he said. 'How about you? Any suggestions?'

Johansen picked up an unshelled peanut from a bowl on the tabletop and crushed it in his fist. He shook fragments of pulverized shell into an ashtray and thumb-flicked the twin kernels one after another in quick succession into his mouth.

'It's tricky,' he said. 'Who knows what goes on inside the head of a Triple-Xer?'

'It would be cheap and easy for me to say, "Nothing", so I won't.'

'Admirable self-restraint, boss. OK, why not let's break this down into its basic components. What does Triple-X want?'

'To rid this world of all Foreigners.'

'And what do they do to achieve this goal?'

'They cause Foreign losses, usually by means of fire or high-explosive, with sometimes some human deaths as a side result.'

'And how else do they achieve their goal?'

'Propaganda. Graffiti and pamphlets and suchlike.'

'Yeah. They try and turn people's minds against the Foreigners.'

Parry took a sip of beer. The Bar Brindisi boasted a comprehensive range of drinks from around the world, including bitter ale hand-drawn and served in a straight glass at blood temperature. A pint of this was extremely expensive, but, to the perpetual mystification of the bar's Italian proprietor, his British customers couldn't seem to get enough of the stuff.

'Then the *shinjus* could be a way of combining the two things,' he said, 'or had you already thought of that?'

'I thought of it as I was asking you those questions.'

'Propaganda slayings.' Parry shook his head. 'Jesus. And hence the wake-up call at the first one. "Here it is, everyone. Come and have a look."'

Johansen nodded sombrely and took a sip of his cocktail, a Bellini.

'Sir?'

Parry turned.

Yoshi Hosokawa was standing beside the booth, dressed in civvies, a crisp T-shirt and a pair of pleated, slim-fit slacks. 'I apologize for interrupting. I was told at the operations room that I might find you here.'

'You're not interrupting. Come on, sit down.'

Johansen edged around the booth's plush horseshoe bench to make room.

'What'll you be having, Yoshi?' Parry indicated his and Johansen's glasses, which were nearly empty.

'Allow me to buy the round, sir.'

'Nonsense. My treat.'

'All right. Makino, please.'

Parry caught the bartender's eye and ordered Hosokawa's lager along with another pint of bitter for himself and another Bellini for Johansen.

'The lieutenant and I have been flogging our tired old brains over the *shinjus*,' he told Hosokawa. 'We'd welcome the input of a younger and sharper mind.'

Hosokawa gave a flattered bow and clenched his hands in GRATITUDE. 'As a matter of fact, it was about those that I wanted to talk to you.'

'I thought so. By the way, I've been meaning to ask. The other morning. When all that business was going on at the Debussy. You were on the front desk, right?'

'I took your call.'

'Yes. But then you weren't on the desk when the commissioner arrived a few minutes later. What happened there?'

'I'm afraid . . .' Hosokawa looked uncomfortable. There was even a hint of a blush. 'I had to relieve myself. The necessity came on me rather abruptly, so I called up and asked Kadosa to come down and sit in for me.'

'That was unfortunate timing. Maybe if you'd been there when . . . Well, never mind. Can't be helped.'

'If I'd been there when what, sir?'

'Doesn't matter. Spilt milk and all that. What is it you want to say? About the *shinjus*.'

'Sir, the word going around HQ is that they might be murders. Is that really true? Is that possible?'

'I think the fact there's been two of them now would seem to make it a little more likely.'

'Then could we be looking at something Triple-X have done?'

'The boss and I were just discussing that,' said Johansen. 'And we'd just come up with the idea that they're . . . How did you put it, boss?'

'Propaganda slayings.'

'Yeah. Propaganda slayings.'

'Well, now, that's what I thought, too,' said Hosokawa. 'There's something of a theatrical element to them, isn't there?'

'But then suicides can be theatrical also,' said Parry. 'Let's not forget that. You see, I'm not rejecting the possibility that these are still *shinjus*. Equally, it never hurts to explore another avenue of investigation. It may turn out to be a cul-de-sac, but you'll never know that unless you try.'

'A "cul-de-sac"?' said Hosokawa, with a frown.

'Don't ask,' said Johansen, shaking his head wearily. 'The boss doesn't speak proper English, not like you and me.'

Their drinks arrived and Parry handed the bartender an IC card for the cost of the round to be subtracted.

'Well, cheers,' said Parry.

'*Skål*,' said Johansen, raising his cocktail.

'*Kampai*,' said Hosokawa, doing the same with his lager.

The three of them clinked glasses.

'Now then,' Parry said, 'following this idea through. Let's try and put ourselves into the mind of a Triple-Xer, if we can. We hate Foreigners. We look down on Sirens as the lowest of the low. We decide we're going to kill a Siren and cause a Foreign loss and make it appear as if they took their own lives. Make it appear, as Yoshi here was helpfully on hand to observe, like a *shinju*. Simple question: why?'

'In order to discredit Foreigners,' said Johansen.

'Indeed. But how, precisely, does it do that?'

'Because,' said Hosokawa, 'it's drawing attention to an issue which a lot of people would prefer to ignore.'

'Yes, Yoshi, go on.'

If Hosokawa was flattered that the two most senior officers in his district were interested in his opinion, he gave no sign of it. 'I mean, most people love Foreigners, don't they? They love them because they're strange, they're beautiful. Because they brought humanity to its senses. Because they've chosen this planet to visit and everyone likes to feel chosen. People love them without knowing all the reasons quite why they love them. And yet there's this thing they use humans for that just doesn't sit right in many people's minds.'

'Singing.'

'That's it. Singing. It makes some of us a bit uncomfortable, doesn't it? Because of what it resembles. What it is similar to.'

The word did not need to be said but Johansen said it anyway: 'Prostitution.'

'We don't know, of course, that the golden giants' appreciation of singing is anything other than aesthetic,' Parry said, feeling that this point should be made, and indeed could not be made often enough.

'Of course, sir,' said Hosokawa. 'I wasn't suggesting for a moment that it *is* prostitution.'

'Yeah, boss. We're trying to think like Triple-Xers, remember.'

'Sorry. Yes.' Parry knocked back a deep draught of his bitter. 'Right, so Triple-X wants to tap into the public's unease, such as it is, about singing.'

'And a good way of going about that is to kill a Siren and a Foreigner in a hotel room together,' said Johansen. 'That way, there's no doubt as to what the pair of them were up to before they died.'

'And the suicide aspect?'

'Serves to heighten the "unnaturalness" of the act,' Hosokawa suggested.

'Not to mention makes the whole event much more headline-grabbing,' Johansen said.

'That's for sure,' said Parry, with a grimace. 'And at the same time as these *shinjus* are alarming humans, they're also alarming Foreigners.' Two birds with one stone. Just as Quesnel had said, albeit in a somewhat different manner. 'There's a definite logic there, yes. If you're a Triple-Xer, that is. You get to cause a Foreign loss, you get to kill a Siren, *and* you get to rub the public's noses in a practice about which a proportion of the population feel, to say the least, ambivalent. That's the why, then. That would be what Triple-X is trying to achieve. Now for the how.'

'I imagine it would be difficult, but not impossible, to get hold of a master key-unit and let yourself into a Foreigner's room,' said Hosokawa. 'You've seen that the room's occupant has gone out to Sirensong, and you know it'll be back in a few hours' time. You lie in wait, maybe in the bathroom. Eventually the Foreigner returns with a Siren. The singing starts, and then . . .'

'And then, catching them at a vulnerable moment, you do the deed,' said Parry, nodding. 'That's good, Yoshi.' He was impressed. Hosokawa might be green, but he had a sharp intuition. A couple of years, a few of the edges knocked off him, and he could definitely become an asset to the FPP. 'OK, down to the specifics. Daryl Henderson first. He and his Foreigner come into the room. He starts singing. You, Mr Triple-Xer – or, let's not be sexist here, *Ms* Triple-Xer – rush out of the bathroom, shoot Henderson once in the chest at close range, then, while he's dying or even already dead, wrap his hand around the gun, put the barrel in his mouth and make him blow his brains out. Possible, agreed?'

Johansen and Hosokawa nodded.

'Then Dagmar Pfitzner. Say she goes out on the balcony at the Debussy to get some fresh air. Perhaps she's getting ready to sing, perhaps she's just finished. Either way, she's out there taking a breather. The Foreigner's with her. You sneak up from behind and manhandle her over the balustrade. You've caught her unawares. She's no time to put up a resistance. She falls and hits the canal and cracks her neck. Both feasible scenarios, particularly if you have the element of surprise on your side. There's still one big glaring problem.'

'The Foreigner,' said Johansen.

'Indeed. In each case, how do you kill the Foreigner?'

'What if you don't?' said Hosokawa. 'What if, when they saw their Sirens being attacked, the Foreigners simply panicked and made an emergency escape?'

'Ah yes. Trouble is, how could you, as this hypothetical Triple-X killer, guarantee that that's what they're going to do? If your plan is to leave a human body and a set of Foreign remains in the room, you can't just hope that the Foreigner's going to oblige by pulling the ripcord. In order to be sure of its loss, you've got to kill it. Or at any rate have some surefire method of making it shed its clothing.'

'Turn off the air-conditioning?' said Johansen. 'That always gets *me* down to my underwear in no time.'

'Ho ho, Pål. Very droll.'

Hosokawa said, eyes narrowing in thought, 'Is there, sir, to your knowledge, a weapon capable of causing a Foreign loss? I mean, other than a bomb or an incendiary device or beating them with a club. Something that disposes of Foreigners without damaging their clothing?'

'None that I'm aware of.'

'But someone could have developed such a weapon.'

'Who? Who in their right mind would?'

'Triple-X,' said Johansen matter-of-factly.

This Parry acknowledged with the slowest, most reluctant of nods. 'I'm sure they'd *want* to create a weapon like that, but technologically it's beyond their capabilities. They're basement terrorists. Their bombs are always home-made, and if they use anything sophisticated, then it's something they've purchased off an arms dealer.'

'Then maybe somebody else has developed an anti-Foreign weapon and sold it to Triple-X,' said Hosokawa.

'But again, who would do such a thing?'

'I agree, sir, it's not a pleasant thought, but you must be prepared to consider it. There may be somebody out there, some maverick scientist, engineer, whatever, who's seen that the market exists for a portable, no-mess anti-Foreign weapon and built one.'

Parry sighed. 'Well, I admit it's a possibility. But I don't like it. Why can't the explanation be a little more straightforward? I mean, the perpetrators at Koh Farang used planks and baseball bats. Perfectly effective.'

'The least complicated answer is usually the right one,' Johansen added. 'If you ask me, this anti-Foreign weapon sounds like something out of *Resort-City Beat*.'

Hosokawa, though evidently thinking his proposition still had some validity, acceded to his superior officers' opinion with a bow. 'It was just an idea.'

Parry gave a kindly smile. 'Never be afraid to suggest an idea, Yoshi.' He glanced at his wristwatch. 'Ah. I should be on my way.'

'A busy night, sir?' said Hosokawa.

'The boss is off to a party at the Fuentes house,' said Johansen, waggling his eyebrows. 'He moves in important social circles, you know.'

'I didn't know you were a friend of Mrs Fuentes, sir.'

'An acquaintance. We met on the Civic Committee.' Parry quickly drained his glass. 'Listen, thanks, both of you. This has been very useful.'

Hosokawa manufolded INDULGENCE. 'Not at all.'

'Yeah, boss. No problem. Have a good evening.'

'You too. Hope you find those nice tourist girls.'

'Even if I don't, it'll be fun looking.'

24   FANDANGO

Beneath a sky the colour of a dusty aubergine, taxi-gondolas and
private launches, many of the latter piloted by uniformed chauf-
feurs, converged on the main gate of the Fuentes compound. People
in evening wear stepped out of the boats, men alighting first so that
they could assist their female companions, who were hampered by
long dresses and high heels. A doorman stationed at the gate
demanded to see hardcopies of invitations and checked names,
running his stubby finger down an alphabetized list.

Once inside the compound each guest was handed a flute of kir
royale. Clutching the ruby drinks, they filed up the brick pathway
to the house, laughing and chattering. Resident tax-exiles, NACA
officials, jet-setters who owned holiday homes in the city, proprietors of the swankier hotels, restaurateurs who ran the trendier
eating establishments, owners of the more upmarket boutiques,
plus a smattering of screen stars, TV personalities, and cigarette-
thin supermodels – these were the élite of New Venice and knew it.
Even those unfamiliar to each other exchanged grins of dazzling
complicity.

Parry, having taken a canal-bus part of the way here and walked
the rest, only realized as he was approaching the gate that he
needed a hardcopy invitation to get in. Cecilia had not sent him
one, or, if she had, had sent it to his home board, and he hadn't
been back to his apartment since breakfast. He thought he might
have to resort to flashing the badge about a bit – nobody would
refuse entry to an FPP officer – but it turned out that his name was
on the guest list, and the doorman waved him through without a
quibble. He joined the influx into the compound and, drink in hand
and speaking to no one, took his place in the straggling procession
up to the house. These were the same grounds he once used to pad
across as furtively as a cat burglar. Now, he strolled through them
at a leisurely pace, breathing in the warm garden scents of pine and
jasmine and the spicier artificial aromas of the perfumes and
colognes that drifted back from the people preceding him. Up to

the house he went and through an archway into the inner courtyard.

The courtyard enclosed a knot garden, entwined geometric patterns of shin-high hedges interspersed here and there with outcrops of shrub. Dwarf bay trees, topiaried into perfect globes or cones, arose at corners and intersections. In the middle, a goblet-shaped fountain played, its sides inlaid with an abstract mosaic of glass tesserae. Crackling garden flares sent up thin plumes of oily smoke and threw overlapping dapples of illumination on to the walls. Overhead, chains of fairy-lights were strung in a zigzag pattern between the columns of the cloister that ran around the upper storey.

Some of the guests stopped in the courtyard, but the general trend was onward, the current of people flowing towards the pair of studded oak doors that stood at the far end, opening on to the living room. Waiters flanked the doorway, holding silver salvers laden with canapés.

The living room had marble floors and textured-plaster walls with a dado of hand-painted tiles. There was a fireplace at one end and the voluptuous armchairs and sofas that normally occupied its centre had been rolled to the sides. A crystech chandelier, looking like a firework in mid-explosion, flooded the place with light. A rumble of voices echoed up to the high, raftered ceiling. Gathered in knots, the great and the good of New Venice laughed and glittered and talked about whatever it is such people talk about at these occasions – themselves and one another, mostly.

Parry saw no sign of Anna. However, the living room's four sets of sliding french windows were wide open and there were more guests out on the south terrace. She was probably out there. He took a sip of his kir, wrinkling his nose at the sweetness of it. An overrated drink, if you asked him. Fizzy pop for the posh. He set off across the room.

He had not gone more than three paces when a hand clamped around his upper arm, arresting his progress. He felt a squeak of irrational fear. He had been found out. Someone had spotted that he did not really belong here, that he was entirely the wrong class, the wrong background, a stranger, an interloper.

'Captain.'

The hand belonged to Muhammad al-Shadhuli. Unlatching it from Parry's arm, al-Shadhuli linked it with his other hand to form a SALUTATION. Parry tucked his champagne flute against his ribs in the crook of his elbow and awkwardly returned the greeting.

'I was hoping I might bump into you here,' said New Venice's NACA Liaison. He was a round-bodied and genial Tunisian afflicted, alas, with the worst teeth and breath Parry had ever had the misfortune to see and smell. Blissfully oblivious to his shortcoming, al-Shadhuli had a habit of thrusting his face up close at whomever he was talking to. He must have come to assume that it was common for those you were addressing to flinch and rear back.

'Now, sir, what is all this business with these Sirens?' he said, his nose mere centimetres away from Parry's. 'Céleste assures me you have it all under control.'

'The commissioner takes a slightly more optimistic view than I do, Mr al-Shadhuli. All I can say is I don't believe the situation is about to get any worse, at least not immediately.'

Before al-Shadhuli could reply, Parry raised his glass to his lips so as to block out the next gaseous gush from the NACA Liaison's gullet.

'I don't have to tell you,' al-Shadhuli said, 'the heads of the NACA nations are very concerned.'

Parry gulped down a swig of kir. 'I don't blame them. *I'm* concerned. Everyone is. I even had a Foreigner corner me last night and demand to know what's going on.'

'A Foreign representative approached you?' Al-Shadhuli looked clownishly distressed, his eyebrows raised, his mouth downturned. 'And what did you tell it?'

'That the FPP was working on the case, doing the best it can.'

'And was it, this Foreigner, able to offer any insight into the deaths?'

'It said nothing . . .' Parry hesitated, thinking of the golden giant's final manufolded remark, the indecipherability of which still bothered him: SUPERNAL, NEGATIVE. 'Nothing that was of any appreciable use.'

A society-column photographer respectfully butted in and asked the gentlemen's permission for a picture. Straight away al-Shadhuli threw back his shoulders, laid a hand lightly on the small of Parry's back and fixed his mouth into a broad smile that revealed his teeth in all their tumbledown, carious disarray. Parry, for his part, did his best to appear composed and at ease, but he could feel his expression tightening while the photographer fussed with his camera's exposure and focus controls. Eventually the photographer fired off three shots, thanked the gentlemen and moved on.

'You appear, if I may say so, Captain, uncomfortable having your picture taken,' al-Shadhuli observed.

'I've hated being photographed, ever since I was a boy. There I was, I'd be quite happily doing something, playing in the garden or on a beach or whatever, and out would come my dad's camera and he'd point it at me, and I'd just freeze and grimace. I can't act naturally when I know someone's filming me. I never know what the camera wants and always end up giving it what it doesn't want.'

'The ability to appear relaxed in front of the camera is a useful skill to possess. One that can seriously advance career prospects.'

'Well, that's undoubtedly true, but in my case I don't think it'd make a lot of difference even if I did acquire it. I think my career's advanced as far as it's going to.'

'You don't see yourself as a future commissioner, then?'

'I think that's more Raymond van Wyk's style.'

Al-Shadhuli was one of the people in positions of influence whose friendship van Wyk had assiduously cultivated. The two men shared an interest in chess and were sometimes to be found of an evening at a restaurant or café in the vicinity of FPP HQ, hunched over a game. More often than not van Wyk lost to the NACA Liaison, and Parry could not help but wonder whether this was due to artless chess-playing or artful politicking.

'You think so?' al-Shadhuli said. 'How interesting.'

'I'm not really commissioner material,' Parry added.

Al-Shadhuli clucked his tongue. 'You English. Underestimating yourselves is a national pastime. Céleste, I know, rates you very highly indeed, Captain. And this *shinju* business. *Insh' Allah*, you will get to the bottom of *that* soon and when you do . . . Well, I dare say it won't harm your chances of promotion when the time comes.'

'And if I don't get to the bottom of it?'

'I'm confident you will, Captain Parry.'

'Sir Jack!'

Suddenly Parry found himself enfolded in an enthusiastic hug.

'Zounds and gadzooks, thou hast made it to our revels!' Cecilia took a step back, examining him and herself. 'And looketh at us! We could be twins!'

She indicated his uniform and her dress, an ivory crêpe-de-chine shift with a gold-braid trim around the neck, offset with some very expensive-looking gold jewellery.

'Verily,' replied Parry.

Cecilia turned to the NACA Liaison, who appeared nonplussed by the peculiar English she and Parry had been using. 'Excuse me, Mr al-Shadhuli, would you mind if I borrowed the captain from you for something very important?'

Al-Shadhuli gave a courteous smile and bowed. 'Not in the least. You're well, Cecilia?'

'Very,' Cecilia said over her shoulder. She was already dragging Parry away, although, truth be known, Parry was not exactly resisting.

When they had put a few metres between them and al-Shadhuli, Cecilia leaned over and whispered in Parry's ear, 'Saved you, didn't I? You looked like you were about to pass out from boredom.'

'Or Mr al-Shadhuli's breath,' Parry replied.

Cecilia hooted. 'Sir Jack! How very unknightly of you.'

'Must be the booze talking.' Parry held up and squinted at his half-empty flute.

'You've hardly touched that. Come on. I bet you'd rather have a beer. Let's get you one and then we'll go find Ma.'

Linking her arm in his, Cecilia quick-marched Parry out of the living room and into the adjoining dining room, where catering staff were laying out stacks of crockery and rows of cutlery on a large table in readiness for a buffet supper. A bar had been set up in one corner of the room. Cecilia took Parry's unfinished kir from him, asked for a bottled Mexican beer, thrust that into his hand, and ordered a beer for herself as well.

'Cecilia . . .'

'Don't get your underpants in a knot, Jack. Ma said I could have one drink.'

'Really?'

'Would I lie to *you*?'

Parry looked at the bartender, who nodded. 'One drink for Miss Cecilia,' the bartender said, holding up a finger. 'No more.'

'There. See? The Alcohol Police already have their undercover operative in place.' Cecilia clinked the neck of her bottle against Parry's. 'Here we go, then. Chin-chin.'

'Cheers.'

Parry observed Cecilia out of the corner of his eye as she tilted back her beer bottle and took a sip. She was the image of her mother. It never ceased to amaze him how alike they were. She had the same colouring. The same wide eyes, with irises so dark brown they were almost black. The same lustrous sable hair worn, just like her mother's, centre-parted and shoulder length with a wave in it that sinuously described the line of her cheekbones. Cecilia was a few kilograms of puppy-fat plumper than Anna, and she had her father's nose, much more pointed and hawkish than her mother's little retroussé button. Other than that, everything about her – the pert, swaybacked posture, her mannerisms, the way she canted her head to one side when she laughed or was listening intently – was pure Anna. It was as though Cecilia was her mother in prototype, an incompletely formed version that, with the addition of a few years and a few social graces, would become a near-exact copy, just as gracious, just as elegant.

Cecilia belched and wiped her mouth with the back of her hand. There was still some way to go, obviously.

'All right then,' she said. 'Let's go track down the old dear.'

Anna was, as Parry had guessed, out on the terrace. She was wearing a silk slip-dress under a patterned chiffon blouse, both items black. Had she chosen the colour because it looked chic? Or to remind people that she was a widow? He hoped it was the former. Surely she had observed a sufficient period of mourning by now.

Surrounding her was a cluster of half a dozen people, all but one of them, he could not fail to notice, men. Were it not for Cecilia, he would have held back and waited for a more opportune moment, when there was less of an audience present, before approaching Anna. As it was, with Cecilia pulling him by the wrist, he had no alternative but to let himself be drawn into the centre of the assemblage. He felt all eyes on him as he was shoved in front of Anna like some kind of trophy.

'Look who I found!' daughter exclaimed to mother.

Parry directed an apologetic wince at Anna. She in turn, with a soft laugh and a long, sly blink, said, 'Jack,' and reached out with both arms to embrace him.

Her cheek against his.

The feel of her back muscles through lace and silk.

The musky, floral, oh-so-familiar fragrance of her.

The warmth her touch generated.

'How the devil are you?' she asked, ending the embrace.

'I'm well.'

'You *look* well.'

'And you look . . .' What? Exquisite? Intoxicating? Ravishing? What could he safely say in front of all these people? 'Well, as well.'

'I'm glad you could make it.'

She meant that, he was quite certain. She was not at all displeased to see him. She might not have invited him herself, but Cecilia would not have been able to get him on to the guest list without her say-so. He could only assume that the etiquette of Just Good Friends forbade Anna from asking him to come, but if her daughter did, then that was all right.

Anna gestured to the other guests around them. 'Have you met . . . ?' she said, and began making introductions. Parry shook hands, forgetting each person's name almost as soon as the physical contact was broken. He could see that they knew exactly who he was. A week ago he would have been any old FPP captain. A week from now, maybe the same. But this evening, less than thirty-six hours after the Dargomyzhsky footage first aired, he was *that* FPP captain. Such was the peculiar nature of fame, or rather the nature of the fame peculiar to him. He was the man of the moment, and naturally the half-dozen guests wasted no time in quizzing him on the *shinjus*. What was going on? What were those damned Sirens up to? Was this really some sort of bizarre suicide craze they had cooked up with the Foreigners?

He fielded the questions honestly, not afraid to confess ignorance when he genuinely did not have an answer but at the same time keen to impress upon these people that their city – his city – was in no immediate danger of going the way of Koh Farang. This, it soon emerged, was the principal concern among them: that, because of the deaths, Foreigners would start to shun New Venice, and incomes and property values would suffer as a consequence. The image of the ghost-city Koh Farang had become was the secret nightmare of every resort-city resident, especially those with sizeable financial stakes in real estate and the hotel and leisure industries. The fate of Koh Farang was a chilling portent of what might be, and while Parry could sympathize with the guests' anxiety, and even to a certain extent shared it, what he could not sympathize with was how comparatively little they were worried about the Foreigners themselves. The idea of Foreigners being upset or offended enough to desert New Venice seemed hardly to trouble them. The golden giants' peace of mind was, to them, a commodity of negligible value.

First Dargomyzhsky, now this lot. Anger stirred within Parry as the partygoers' questioning continued to develop its theme of jittery self-interest. It was all very well Captain Parry saying he didn't think New Venice would become a second Koh Farang, but what proof did he have? How did he know that Foreigners had not already begun a quiet, imperceptible exodus from the city? On the news this evening there had been a report of a decrease in the average Foreign population density.

Patiently Parry pointed out that the situations in Koh Farang and New Venice were not at all similar and that the decrease in Foreign population density was only a small fraction of a percentile, well within acceptable parameters for the time of year. Really, though, what he wanted to tell these people was to shut up and get their priorities straight. Losing money did not matter. Losing Foreign good will did.

Before he ended up saying something he might regret, Anna cleared her throat and interrupted the conversation. With such sweetness that no one could possibly have objected, she informed the half-dozen guests that there was somebody she wanted the captain to meet. If everyone would excuse them?

Taking Parry by the arm, she led him back into the house. Cecilia tagged along with them as far as the living room, then pretended she had spotted someone she wanted to talk to and veered off, leaving the two of them alone together.

'Thanks,' Parry said to Anna.

'For what? Getting you away from those people? I had to. I had to separate you from them before you started threatening them.'

Anna's East European roots seldom showed in her pronunciation of English, but she had a tendency to soften the diphthong 'th'. It was a trait Parry found inordinately endearing, and impossible to resist mimicking.

'I would never have started *surretening*,' he replied, 'although it's true I did feel like *sumping* a couple of *sem*.'

Anna smacked him playfully. 'Shut up, you. I did you a favour. Be properly grateful.'

'I'm sorry. Was it so obvious those people were pissing me off?'

'It was to me. But to be fair to them, they didn't know that Jack Parry comes with this huge red button marked "Foreigners". You press it at your peril.'

'Still, their attitude . . .'

'Is more common than you'd think, Jack. After however many years it is, the novelty has worn off for a lot of people. The golden giants have lost their lustre.'

'I don't believe that.'

'You choose not to believe that. But people can become accustomed to anything, however strange and wonderful, given time. Even a miracle can be taken for granted if it keeps recurring. Where you, Jack, still see golden giants, others, if they see anything at all, see just gold.'

'A few do, maybe. A few fools.'

'Oh, Jack.' She brushed fingers across his cheek, smiling. 'Faith like yours needs to be cherished. Protected. A rare orchid.'

Her fingers came to rest beside his mouth and lingered there, each tip a tingling imprint. There was only silence around them, a hundred people's mouths working but seeming to produce no sound.

If her face had moved towards his just a millimetre . . .

If her smile had been wider by just a tiny fraction . . .

If he had had just a scintilla more courage . . .

Then she took her hand away and the moment was gone. The roar of conversation flooded in around them once more.

'So,' she said, 'do you want to come and meet this person?'

'I thought that was just a pretext.'

'Well, it was and it wasn't. Come on. He's an interesting character and I think you'll find he's more on your wavelength than anyone else here.'

'Who is he?'

'Guthrie Reich.'

'Bless you.'

'Sorry? Oh. Oh, I see. Yes, I suppose it is a peculiar name.'

'Peculiar? It's downright cruel. Wasn't there a folk singer called Guthrie? Someone-or-other Guthrie?'

'I think so. And Guthrie's father was a musician. *He* probably chose the name.'

'So what about him? Should I have heard of this bloke? Is he famous?'

'No. But I have a feeling you'll like him. He runs a music revue. Traditional styles. Rock and jazz, mainly. Music from our youths. The sort of stuff Cissy can't stand. She thinks it's hideously boring.'

She glanced around. 'I don't see him here, but I've a pretty good idea where he might be.'

25   MIXED VOICES

They found Reich in the library, admiring Hector Fuentes's extensive collection of vinyl LPs. The only other people in the room were a couple of guests murmuring in low voices on a chaise longue in the far corner.

Reich was a tall, rangy, well-proportioned American in his mid-twenties, dressed in a fashion that had had its heyday at least a quarter of a century before he was born: a long black silk coat worn over a white shirt unbuttoned to the chest, a pair of black leather trousers, a pair of black leather knee-boots. Additionally, a black guitar plectrum dangled from his left ear, attached to the lobe by a fine gold chain and stud. His hair was a shaggy, blond-streaked mass and his skin had the even, burnished tone of someone who tanned himself regularly but with care.

He grinned and winked at Anna as she and Parry approached him. 'Boy, I knew Hector liked analogue,' he said, 'but I didn't realize how much till now.' He gestured at the long-players, individually racked, shelf upon shelf of them, each snugly protected in a transparent mylar sleeve. 'Must be at least a thousand of 'em here. Some white-label stuff I didn't even know existed. And a Borgstrøm and Olsen analogue hi-fi! Gravity counter-weighted turntable. Gold fascia and controls. Beautiful. Parts for a system like that don't come cheap. The styluses alone cost a fortune.'

'Luckily Hector *had* a fortune,' Anna said, with a laugh. 'Guthrie, I'd like you to meet a good friend of mine, Jack Parry.'

Only now did Reich take any notice of Parry. Until Anna made the introduction, his interest had been in the records and her. He had not even acknowledged that Parry existed.

'How you doing, Jack? Pleasure to meet you.' He shook Parry's hand as forthrightly as though he were working the handle of an old-fashioned town pump.

'Likewise,' said Parry.

'Love the uniform, by the way.'

'Really?'

'No, I mean it.'

The enthusiasm in Reich's voice struck Parry as insincere, but the expression in the American's grey eyes and healthy, angular face was generous and easygoing. Parry decided to give him the benefit of the doubt.

'That's a West Coast accent, right?'

'Correct, *dooooood*. Los Angeles. Wasn't born there, of course. Who is? I'm from San Diego originally, but my folks moved north when I was about three. My pop was chasing a career in the music biz. He never quite made it. You ever been to LA?'

'Afraid not. I'm not the world's most travelled person.'

'Well, you should go. It's a great old town. Least, it is now they've drained the place and crysteched it up. It wasn't such a great old town back when I was a kid. Third dampest city in the US, after New York and New Orleans.'

'You had some pretty bad epidemics there as well, didn't you?'

'Jeez, you kidding? All that stagnant sea water sloshing around, those streets *bred* fevers. People were falling sick and dying all the time. Yeah, it was a tough old place to grow up in, especially the neighbourhoods we lived in. But I was a tough old kid. I survived.'

'And what brings you here?'

'From Venice Beach to New Venice? You mean the lovely Anna Fuentes isn't reason enough?' Reich slipped an arm around Anna's shoulders and drew her to him. Parry could not decide which was worse: Reich hugging her in this way or Anna allowing herself to be hugged, giving no indication that she minded. 'Actually, I'm in the music biz myself. Kind of a promoter/agent type. Got a stable of trad musicians I represent. We're playing a few gigs here. With the help of the Fuentes Arts Foundation, God bless it.'

'Guthrie's agency gets a grant from the Foundation,' Anna said. 'Hector set up the Foundation as a tax deduction, but he honestly believed it was important to keep pre-Debut art forms, especially music, alive.'

'And you hear that garbage that's clogging up the hit parade and people dance to now, and you know Hector was right. The man with the money was *on* the money.' Reich gave Anna an extra-hard squeeze, then, to Parry's relief, let her go. 'I mean, in the States there hasn't been a song with lyrics in the Top Ten for the past year, and that just ain't right. All that warbling over a drum-loop. No song structure, no chord progression, no tune, no words, just Sirens making stuff up as they go. We gave away our music, man!'

We spent all this time creating beautiful works, songs, operas, sonatas, cantatas, chorales, and then we gave it all away!'

'It's a different way of doing things,' Parry pointed out. 'A new way.'

'Well, I'm all for adopting new ways, but not at the expense of the old ways. There's a whole long-standing tradition of music, decades of pop, centuries of classical, that most kids are growing up knowing nothing about. We can't just let it fade out and die.' Reich laughed. 'But hey. Don't get me started. I can drone on about this subject for ever.'

'I'm afraid, Guthrie, you're going to have a hard time convincing Jack that anything associated with Foreigners is bad,' Anna said.

'Ah, don't get me wrong. I've nothing against the big golden guys.' Reich gave Parry an amicable, magnanimous biff on the biceps. 'I like 'em. They're not the problem. We are. It's like, the day they came, we decided to rewind the tape and start again from zero. We wiped the past. And that's partly the reason I do what I do – so's we don't lose the past completely. You a fan of old music at all, Jack?'

'Some.'

'Then you should come to one of our shows. We opened here on Monday and my guys played up a storm, even if I say so myself. We got a few more dates lined up. Anna knows where and when we're on. Reckon you'd enjoy yourself.'

'I don't know. I have a pretty heavy workload on at the moment.'

'Oh yeah, that's right. All those Sirens and Foreigners dropping like flies. You're the guy has to sort all that out, ain'tcha?'

'Well, I think you've exaggerated the situation somewhat . . .'

Before Parry had a chance to finish the remark, a member of the catering staff appeared in the doorway to announce that dinner was being served. The appropriate sounds of hungry eagerness were made and they trooped out of the library.

In the dining room, polite but disorderly queues formed for the food table, while in a corner a quartet of Sirens – soprano, alto, tenor, bass – extemporized, their voices enfolding one another in sinuous random harmony. Amid the cluster and jostle of guests Parry became separated from Anna and Reich. He finished his beer shuffling slowly forwards. Reaching the table, he ran his eye over the copious array of foodstuffs before him. The caterers had laid on a spread of Anna's devising called *tapas gustări*, a mixed selection of Spanish and Romanian dishes that was something of a tradition at Fuentes parties. The combination worked well, the two cuisines being surprisingly compatible. There were stuffed cabbage leaves and cubes of maize polenta, meat-filled flaky pastries and ham-filled *bocadillo* rolls, rolled herrings and vinegar-marinaded anchovies, small potato omelettes and battered courgettes, plus a range of spicy sausages and salads. Parry set about heaping his plate high. Then, furnishing himself with a fresh beer, he headed out on to the terrace.

He ate alone to start with, perched on the terrace steps, gazing out into the benighted garden. A parade of umbrella pines, illuminated by spotlights at their bases, looked stark and flat, as though part of a stage set rather than real. Between them and beyond, there were intricate dark thickets of rhododendron.

He was used to eating on his own and in many ways preferred it. He had never quite mastered the art of filling his mouth and engaging in conversation at the same time. He offered no objection, however, when an elderly Englishman came up and asked to join him. Accompanying the Englishman was a woman young enough to be his granddaughter but too nubile and attentive to be anything other than his wife. Fourth wife, it turned out.

The two of them proved to be congenial company. The man was an expatriate of aristocratic lineage, almost a caricature of the breed, right down to his pronunciation ('orff' for 'off', 'ears' for 'yes'). He also dabbled in, as he called it, 'matters esoteric', and it wasn't long before he was regaling Parry with an account of his investigations into the crop circle phenomenon, to which he had devoted his twenties and thirties and a significant portion of his inheritance. His researches, he said, had led him to conclude that crop circles – genuine crop circles, that is, not the ones proven to have been humanmade – were an early attempt by Foreigners to communicate with the peoples of Earth. Having scrupulously measured the geometric shapes that constituted certain cerealogical formations, he had discovered that the ratios between the shapes' surface areas corresponded precisely to the harmonic fractions by which the notes in the diatonic scale were related to their tonic note. Each formation, looked at in this way, yielded a single musical note. And as the formations grew progressively more elaborate, so they yielded chordal configurations of increasing complexity.

'Do you see, old chap?' he said. 'The golden giants made them.

They were forewarning us of their arrival. Preparing the ground, as it were. Do you think it's any coincidence that crop circles have ceased to appear since the Debut?'

Parry nodded, although he had always thought that all crop circles were hoaxes and the reason they had stopped appearing was that the people who made them had simply ceased to do so after the Foreigners arrived. Who needed bogus extraterrestrial mysteries when there were genuine extraterrestrial mysteries around?

'And,' the expatriate continued, 'what better way to communicate with us than through the universal language, namely music. I know, I know, the universal language is supposed to be mathematics, but what is music, after all, but a refined form of mathematics?'

He went on in this vein, expanding his crop-circle theory to take in Pythagoras's observation that the distances between the planets of the solar system matched, with uncanny accuracy, the intervals between the notes of the diatonic scale ('The Music of the Spheres. Literally!'), and Parry interjected comments from time to time, but for the most part was content to listen, playing audience to the expatriate's lecturer. The nubile fourth wife, meanwhile, gazed at her husband with a fond, doting smile, looking as if she had been indulging him in his whims and fancies not for years but for decades.

Eventually, however, the expatriate brought the focus of the conversation around to the *shinjus*. He and his wife had been out of town for a couple of weeks and had returned yesterday to find all this hullabaloo going on. Perhaps the captain could explain what was up?

Parry did so as succinctly as possible, but as he spoke he could hear a certain testiness entering his voice, as it had done earlier. With no Anna on hand to intercede and maintain harmony, he felt it wise to curtail the conversation. As soon as he politely could, he made his excuses to the expatriate and his wife. Beg pardon. Call of nature.

Indoors, he fetched himself yet another beer, then began wandering from room to room, threading his way among the guests. Not in a mood to talk to anyone else just then, he adopted a purposeful air so that people would assume he was on his way somewhere, circulating rather than circling. He came across Cecilia, flirting flagrantly with a young man whom he recognized as an up-and-coming Hollywood actor and who was paying less attention to Cecilia than he was to smoothing an errant lock of hair repeatedly away from his face. Cecilia glanced away from the actor's bland, girlish features just long enough to flash a smile at Parry. The smile begged not to be interrupted, please, so Parry carried on.

He wound up back in the library, which, without actually being designated as such, was being used as the quiet room at the party, somewhere calm, a haven from the throng where people could talk without raising their voices. He whiled away a few minutes examining the shelves of LPs that had so impressed Reich. Anna had told him once how her husband would seldom listen to the records, as they were too brittle and valuable to risk damaging them by playing them, even on a top-of-the-range hi-fi. She had also told him how Fuentes kept a professional discophile on permanent retainer to scour the auction rooms of the world on his behalf, searching out rarities and classics and collectibles.

What must it be like, Parry wondered, to have so much money that you could buy things not because you desired them necessarily, or because they were of any practical use to you, but simply so that you could claim ownership of them? It had probably never occurred to Fuentes, a man to whom introspection was anathema, to ask himself this.

There are certain people who appear to have been born with a single purpose in life, human heat-seeking missiles who from the moment of launch hurtle unerringly towards their predestined target. Fuentes had been one. His career path described a smooth, upward trajectory from early apprenticeship to the worldly acme of material success and riches and power. He had started out at the age of sixteen working on building sites in and around Madrid, by the age of twenty had become a site foreman, and – such was his forcefulness and inner drive – by the age of twenty-three was managing a construction company of his own. There followed a crescendo of takeovers, acquisitions and expansions, until by the time he reached his early thirties Fuentes was Spain's foremost construction-industry mogul and fast becoming one of the most powerful and influential figures in the European business world, a man to whom other moguls looked in order to gauge their own next moves. His every decision seemed as astute as it was lucrative. To take just one example, his development of a rapid-setting, polymer-toughened concrete put him in a prime position to exploit the suddenly burgeoning demand for sea-defence technology. As the atmosphere warmed and the West Antarctic ice-shelf melted and the oceans swelled, brimming on to the land faster than anyone had predicted or suspected, prudent countries – not least the Netherlands and Belgium, which would otherwise have disappeared almost entirely – busied themselves erecting barriers to protect low-lying coastal regions. Fuentes, having foreseen this necessity, was quick to take advantage of it. He had also been one of the first to devise a practical, marketable application for crystech. When, not long after the Debut, the Foreigners presented every government on Earth with specimens of a type of crystal whose growth could be stimulated and manipulated through the use of sound, Fuentes was among the many pre-eminent industrialists and inventors entrusted with the task of experimenting with the stuff and discovering what it might be capable of. His R&D laboratories soon came up with a method of growing crystech subaquatically on a vast scale, and this process swiftly supplanted his own concrete as the basis-material for sea defences, as well as providing a straightforward and versatile means of laying the foundations of resort-cities, which were just then in the planning stages. Fuentes, therefore, was partly responsible for the construction of New Venice and its counterparts elsewhere in the world, and, in return, his role in the building of the resort-cities earned him a nickname – the Crystech Caballero – and several further huge sums to add to his already colossal fortune.

That, at any rate, was the official version of Fuentes's career. The unofficial version, which Parry had gleaned in dribs and drabs from Anna, was a less sanitized and salutary tale of back-door deals, intimidation of trade unions, blackmail, bribes, payoffs, payola. Fuentes had done nothing that could strictly speaking be described as illegal, nothing that was not commonplace in the world of corporate business, nothing that could be denounced as anything worse than sharp practice. Yet there was no doubting that he had in his time been a man who would stop at nothing to further his own interests and augment his income. That, as Anna had said, was how you had to be in order to survive and flourish in the world in which her husband had moved.

Yet, for all that he had achieved and accumulated (and setting aside for the moment *how* he had achieved and accumulated it), Fuentes had never struck Parry as a contented man. He had worked hard and relentlessly to extend his business empire and acquire wealth, but had seldom paused to enjoy the benefits of his work. As for his family, they had been almost incidental to his life, impinging on it without significantly affecting it. It seemed to Parry that, for Fuentes, Anna and Cecilia had been mere accoutrements – not the core of his existence, as they should have been, but just two more additions to his prestige, two more possessions that had been drawn into his orbit, two more moons orbiting the great Saturn of Hector Fuentes.

On one occasion Anna had confessed to Parry that it wasn't her husband's indifference to her and Cecilia that she minded, as much as the fact that they seemed so dispensable to him. It was as if Fuentes would have been happy to have any two people filling the roles of wife and child, so long as they were respectful and respectable and did not inconvenience or embarrass or compromise him. She was sure that he did love them both, in his own way, but he was a man who lived inside his head most of the time, absorbed with whatever deal or bid or project he was currently masterminding. Things that were happening in the wider world preoccupied him. Things that were happening immediately around him he barely noticed. His greatest passion was the thrill of being Hector Fuentes. Other interests, like his family, came a poor second.

Like his family, or like his LPs, Parry thought. Kept immaculately but not enjoyed, not cherished.

The obvious question, of course, was what had Anna seen in Fuentes in the first place. What appeal could such a man – so aloof, so self-obsessed – have had for her? When Parry had put this to her on one occasion, phrasing the question delicately so as not to sound incredulous, all she had said was that a man like him could not understand how attractive a man like Fuentes could be to women. Money, status, a few years' seniority and a certain dark streak of ruthlessness were all compelling traits, not least to the former Anna Enescu, who, born and brought up in a council slum on the southern outskirts of Bucharest, had scaled the cliff-face of European society from its very bottom to its very top using the only tools available to her, looks and sheer determination. The moment she met Fuentes, she had said, she had sensed in him something she recognized in herself, a kindred trait. And thereafter Parry had been reluctant to probe her any further on the subject, feeling he had strayed into an area he would rather remain ignorant about. There were aspects of Anna that did not tally with his preferred image of her and so he chose to disregard them.

Parry looked down to find the beer bottle in his hand empty. He had no memory of draining it. Time for another. He felt reckless, and knew that the alcohol was responsible and also that he had achieved the requisite level of inebriation not to care. Back to the dining room he went and, grabbing a fresh beer, coasted through to the living room, where he found, among others, Guthrie Reich.

The trad-music promoter was surrounded by a small gaggle of guests whom he was regaling with some anecdote or other. Probably telling them about his rough, tough LA upbringing, Parry thought acerbically. He moved away to a corner of the room and set to watching the jabbering faces of the guests, careful to avoid catching anyone's eye. The lingua franca here was English, but English spoken in such a range of accents and threaded through with strands of so many other different national tongues that, to his ears, nothing anyone was saying seemed intelligible. All he could hear was a gathered mass of superficially senseless sentences, a glossy, lulling glossolalia.

His gaze roved back to Reich, still in the throes of narration. No, he did not like the American. That smug, easy confidence. The way he had manhandled Anna like that. His familiarity with her. His intimacy.

Where did that intimacy come from? It might be that that was how Reich behaved with every woman. Equally, there might be more to it. Was it possible that he and Anna were more than friends? Could it be that—

'Earth to Jack? Come in, Jack.'

Parry blinked and twitched his head. Cecilia was standing in front of him, a bottle of beer in each hand.

'Verily, good knight, thou wast kilometres away!' She proffered one of the bottles to him. 'Here. For you.'

'And that other beer is the same one from earlier?' he said, taking the proffered bottle.

'Of course,' she replied, wide-eyed.

The identical patina of condensation on both bottles told Parry otherwise, but he let it pass.

'And I'm not even going to ask how you got *this* one,' he said.

'I have my ways.'

Naturally she did. Getting whatever she wanted was in Cecilia's genes.

'You know, you look like you could do with a bit of fresh air,' she said. 'How about a stroll?'

'Yes. Why not? A stroll would be nice.'

'Have you ever seen our marine feature?'
'Heard about it, never seen it.'
'Come along, then.'

26 NOCTURNE

They descended the steps of the terrace and moved across the lawn, away from the brightness and hubbub of the party, into the dark and shadowed hush of the grounds. It was the route Parry used to take after his trysts with Anna, although the circumstances now, of course, could not have been more different. This, if it was anything, was the opposite of a tryst. The anti-tryst.

As they joined a path that looped into the trees, he asked Cecilia about the young actor she had been talking to. Any luck? She replied that he was gay, and after a moment's pause qualified the assertion with: 'Well, probably. He certainly wasn't interested in *me*.' Parry averred that he seemed too interested in himself to be interested in anyone else, and added that if he wasn't gay he must be pretty stupid, to be oblivious to the charms of so beautiful and intelligent a young woman. Cecilia laughed, but not too scornfully, and said, 'Thou art *so* corny, Sir Jack.'

The path diverged. Right led to nowhere but the side gate. They went left. Enough illumination from the garden spotlights and the windows of the house filtered through the pines and rhododendra for them to be able to see their way and walk without stumbling. Soon they were approaching a wall of opaque black crystech about five metres high, its rugged, irregular planes glinting like onyx. The wall curved, and the path curved with it, terminating at the mouth of a tunnel. Here Cecilia touched a switch on a panel set into the crystech and uncertain blue light filled the tunnel from its further end, reflecting off the rough-faceted interior, rippling and restless.

The tunnel was tall enough to pass through without ducking, but broad enough to permit only single-file traffic. Cecilia went in first. Parry followed. They emerged at the other end on to a crescent-shaped strip of sand that rimmed one end of an oval pool of salt water. The sand, smooth and pale, sloped into the pool, continuing for a few metres before terminating at a narrow spiny reef of coral. The water was clear up to this point, then, suddenly and steeply deepening, went a murky turquoise.

The pool was approximately twenty metres across on its longest diameter. Its depths glowed with artificial subaquatic light and pulsed to the rhythm of hidden turbines which switched direction every few seconds, generating a sea-like swell-and-subside that sent delicate, frilly waves lapping up on to the sand. The crystech wall rose sheer around, forming an amphitheatrical enclosure.

The water teemed with life. In the shallows starfish fondled their way across the sand's rugose terrain, moving among darting shrimp and stolid molluscs. Above the fingers of coral, shoals of tiny silvery fish coalesced and dispersed and coalesced again, mercurial in both hue and disposition. Beyond the reef larger creatures lurked and circled, stirred from somnolence by the abrupt arrival of a false new day. A pair of thick-lipped, multi-coloured wrasse bumbled curiously around each other, nose-to-tail like greeting dogs, and something like a black dinner-plate with fins drifted gently around, as though in a state of profound cogitation. Anemones clung to the wall just below the waterline, some of them with their tentacles out and wafting, others budded as tightly as cherries.

'Pa had this built as his thinking place,' said Cecilia, smoothing the bottom of her dress and sitting down on the little beach. 'He came here whenever he didn't want to be bothered. By me or anyone else. Now I come here when I don't want anyone to bother *me*.' Slipping off her patent-leather pumps, she buried her bare feet in the sand and began flexing her toes. 'You too, Jack. Off with the shoes. Trust me, it feels great.'

Parry settled down beside her clumsily, his co-ordination not all it should be. He screwed the base of his beer bottle into the sand, then reached down, unlaced and removed his shoes, and peeled off his socks. He dredged his feet into the sand. The upper layer was cool, but beneath there was residual warmth, the stored heat of the sun, a memory of day. He wriggled his toes like Cecilia and felt the fine grains sift deliciously between them.

'This takes me back,' he said with a grin. 'I haven't played in sand since I was about nine.'

'What, back in the reign of Queen Victoria?'

'Oy, cheeky. Watch it. No, we used to go on beach holidays when I was little. Devon, usually, though a couple of times it was Wales. My sister and I had buckets and spades and we'd take it in turns to bury each other, then we'd gang up and bury my dad.

Funny, I was remembering beach holidays earlier when I was talking to the NACA Liaison.'

'Mr al-Shadhalitosis.'

Parry chuckled. 'That's a little disrespectful, Cecilia.'

'Oh, I didn't come up with the name. Ma did. She always calls him that behind his back. Once, by mistake, she even called him it to his face.'

'Oh dear. Did he notice?'

'I don't think so. But I nearly wet myself trying not to laugh.' Cecilia shuffled forwards on her bottom until the tips of her toes were just within reach of the waves. 'I didn't know they had beaches in the British Isles. Sandy ones. I thought they were all pebbly.'

'There used to be quite a few. Not so many now.'

'You don't miss it much, do you? England?'

'Sometimes. Not much.'

'Ma says you're more at home here than you ever were there.'

'Does she?' It was good to know that Anna discussed him with Cecilia. It was good to know that she talked about him when he was not there. 'Maybe I am. Which is odd, because you don't think of a resort-city as somewhere to put down roots.'

'You find that, too? I mean, I was born here, I've lived here all my life, on my passport card it has my nationality down as "New Venetian", but what does that mean? It means I belong in a place where everything's new and almost nobody's permanent. You know, other girls at school, they can say, "I'm Swiss", or "I'm Brazilian", or "I'm Malaysian", or whatever, and that tells you something about them straight away. It fixes them for you. "I'm New Venetian" – it doesn't really mean anything.'

'Not yet it doesn't. Maybe one day.'

'Though it does remind me of a joke. How do you make a New Venetian blind?'

'Presumably the same way you make a Venetian blind, which is—'

'Poke his eyes out!' Cecilia exclaimed, before he could pre-empt her on the punchline.

'Yes, yes. Very good. Update of an old, old, *old* joke, but never mind.'

'I could always say I'm half-Spanish, half-Romanian, I suppose,' Cecilia said, resuming the thread of her argument, 'but I don't feel Spanish or Romanian, and I can't speak either language except for the swear words I picked up from Ma and Pa. When I was small, they used to swear in their own languages to protect my innocent little ears. Ma still does sometimes, but mostly she doesn't bother any more, just uses English.'

'There's another way of looking at it, of course.'

'Swearing?'

'Being a New Venetian.' Parry found himself settling into a paternal, didactic frame of mind. It wouldn't do any harm to give Cecilia the benefit of his opinion. 'You said being whatever nationality "fixes" a person, and it does, but not necessarily in a good way. It pins them in place. It ties them to a certain set of conventions and values that have become fossilized over centuries. It binds them to certain patterns of thought, patterns of behaviour, certain traditions they can't always escape. And here you are, a mixture of two races, East and West Europe combined, living in a city designed by Italians and run by North Africans and filled with people from God knows how many different countries. As a New Venetian, no one can make assumptions about you based on race or cultural heritage. You're free of all that. You're a citizen of the world – the world as it is now, not as it used to be. You're the Foreign-era generation. The way forward. Independent of the past, the first step into the future. That's a great thing to be. An enviable thing to be.'

Cecilia peered at him, her face reflecting the dancing cerulean glow from the pool. 'Forsooth and i'faith, Sir Jack! "The first step into the future." Are you sure that's not overstating it a bit?'

'Yes, I'm sure.' He picked up his bottle and took a swig. 'Pretty sure.'

'Well, if you say so. At school they sort of tell us that, too – how different things are now. And when they teach us about the past it's always like, how awful it was. They teach History as if it's, well, *history*, and good riddance. As if we need to learn about it only so that we know what to avoid, what mistakes not to make. Kind of like the rape-awareness talk the headmistress gave us last term. You know: "This won't happen, but just to be on the safe side, these are the risks, this is what you've got to look out for . . ."'

'Not a bad comparison.'

'Was it really so awful? Before the Foreigners?'

Parry rested the rim of the bottle against his lips and mused for several seconds. 'I'd say so, yes. Things were pretty terrible towards the end. By "the end", I mean the end of the pre-Foreign era, but at the time we didn't know it was that and it still felt like it was the end. End, capital E. Of the world, of Civilization As We Know It. Everything seemed to be coming to a head at once. All the problems we'd created for ourselves. All the conflicts that had been simmering quietly away in the background, never really resolving themselves. All the bad things we'd stored up and ignored and hoped would go away. Suddenly it was all starting to get worse, much worse. I think it was the flooding that really opened the floodgates – if that makes any sense, which it doesn't, but *I* know what I'm talking about. When Bangladesh became uninhabitable and several Polynesian island chains disappeared from the map, and storm surges began inundating estuaries and destroying coastlines, that was when we finally realized that the warnings were coming true. Here at last was incontrovertible evidence of how seriously we'd fu—' He caught himself. 'Messed up the environment.'

'It's all right. You can say "fucked" in front of me. I have heard the word once or twice before.'

'Well, I'll try not to, if it's all the same with you. For my own peace of mind. Yes, the flooding. That was when we finally knew that the damage we'd done was irreversible. For the first time it became a real possibility that the planet might not be able to support us any more, and it seemed like the seas were just going to keep on rising and there'd be less and less land to go about and we'd have to head for the hills and climb and keep climbing while the water got higher and higher, lapping at our heels, and there'd be no escape and eventually we would all drown. That was how it felt. Honestly it did. And a kind of panic set in, and you know how people act when they're panicking. They'll do anything, tread on anyone, fight, claw, punch, kick, even kill, if they think it'll give them just that little bit better a chance of surviving. That was probably why so many wars flared up. Wars in places you'd never heard of, wars between countries you'd no idea hated each other. Wars fought over the most inhospitable and useless scraps of land you can think of, wars waged for the stupidest of reasons, wars that were about as pointless as wars can be, and that's pretty pointless. There's never been a war in your lifetime, Cecilia. Believe me, you don't know how amazing that is or how lucky you are. Every night on TV, to see pictures of yet more soldiers' corpses strewn on the ground, yet more civilians killed in crossfire, yet more towns burning and children sobbing and women telling stories of being rounded up and systematically raped . . . After a while, you just couldn't go on being appalled. You had to give up caring in order to stay sane. And then there were the Riots.'

Parry stopped and for a while the only sounds were the distant party and the soft cat-lick laps of the marine feature's waves. Cecilia, unsure whether to prompt him to continue, decided to keep silent and fixed her attention on a crown-of-thorns starfish that was crawling on its feathery frond-limbs toward her toes. Just before it reached them, she flicked her foot in the water and the starfish veered away. The sound of the splash also had the effect of rousing Parry from his verbal fermata.

'The Hunger Riots,' he said. 'But you don't want me to bore you about those.'

Cecilia detected a certain note in his voice, a certain need, and with a generosity that most would consider was beyond her years said, 'Go on. Bore me.'

'There isn't much to say about them anyway. The crops failed. No one's quite sure why, though everybody has an opinion.'

'Cross-pollination from a batch of wheat with a faulty terminator gene. That's what we were told. The final nail in the coffin of the whole genetic-modification thing.'

'Could have been. Could have been. Or it could have been some pre-existing crop blight that mutated, or it could just have been the fact that the weather was up the spout and there was so very little rain that spring. Whatever the reason, in Europe and America there were incredibly poor yields. It wasn't a complete wipe-out by any means. There was enough grain to go round. But we were used to super-abundance, we were used to an excess of food on the supermarket shelves, and suddenly that wasn't the case any more and we got scared. Other continents had bad harvests too, but ours were the worst affected, and it compounded the general sense of panic. All over the country there was hoarding of food, black marketeers were prospering, shops were getting looted, and in London there were protests on the streets, demonstrations against the government. Our leaders were telling us not to worry, you see, to stay calm, the situation was not as dire as it seemed, and that wasn't what people wanted to hear because back then it was automatically assumed that whenever politicians opened their mouths they were lying. And the protests went on for days and tempers frayed and then things turned violent.'

He took a long pull on his beer.

'The thing was, I could see their point. It was my job to help control the rioters, but I could see their point. We were sent in, the police, hundreds of us, to contain the situation, and we did eventually, but all the time I was thinking: I could be one of these people – the people I was staring at through my visor and shield, the people I was trying to stop damaging property and hurting one another and us. I could be one of them. Because we were all feeling it to some extent. The fear. The sense that civilization was slipping out of control, that things were falling apart, the centre not holding. If not for my job, my oath as a policeman, I could have been among of the crowds I was being ordered to charge at. Because they looked angry but they weren't. Not in their eyes. In their eyes they were just plain terrified. And then . . .'

His voice trailed away and, after several seconds of silence, he slowly turned his head to gaze at Cecilia.

'She was about your age,' he said softly. His eyes looked off-kilter in their sockets, beer-bleared.

'Who? Who was?'

'Perhaps a shade older.'

'Jack?' Cecilia had never seen Parry in anything other than full control of himself. Now he seemed to be drifting, his own centre not holding, and she was unnerved by the sight. And who was this 'she' he was talking about, this unknown female who had intruded into the conversation?

Parry raised a finger, then lowered it; opened his mouth, then closed it. 'No,' he said finally, and Cecilia was relieved to see him straighten up, sharpen, regain focus, recover self-governance.

'Old thoughts,' he said. 'Bad thoughts. I should really have put it all behind me by now.'

'It can't have been fun,' Cecilia said and immediately congratulated herself on having come up with the world's most banal statement.

'It wasn't. Any of it. They were dark days. Looking back you feel a bit foolish, but at the time it truly seemed as though we were on the downward slope, gaining momentum, a big chasm somewhere unseen ahead and nothing to stop us, nothing to save us. For once the sandwich-board loonies began to look as if they might be right after all. Apocalypse. Catastrophe. Cataclysm. Even the sanest of us were starting to have doubts. Even atheists were turning to the Bible, flicking through the last pages for clues. Room running out, food scarce, war everywhere . . . Without the Foreigners we might still have pulled through, who knows? Possibly. Sometimes I like to think that we would have. Most of the time I'm just glad we never had to try.'

The waves of the microcosmic ocean fell over themselves several times, struggling vainly up the sand.

'We'd got into a state where we were like a classroom full of children before the lesson begins,' Parry said. 'Chaos reigning. Ink pellets flying. Everyone yelling at the tops of their voices. Pigtails being pulled. And then in walks teacher, and all of a sudden it's hands on desks, spines straight, books out, and the room has gone so quiet that you can hear the last paper plane come skimming in to land on the floor.'

'Ink pellets? Books? When were *you* last in a classroom?'

Parry gave a rueful laugh. 'The point is, the Foreigners couldn't have chosen their moment better. What we needed right then was something that would force us to stop and take stock and start to behave again, and we got it. You know that religious movement based in Wyoming, I think it is? The one whose followers believe Foreigners are emissaries of God, sent to Earth to deliver us in our hour of need? I don't hold with that myself because it doesn't really fit the facts and because it's just a little too metaphysical mumbo-jumbo for my liking. But, annoyingly, there *is* something to the idea. If the golden giants had come any earlier, there's a chance we might not have appreciated them so much, and if they'd come any later, there might not have been any humans left on Earth to greet them. Deliberately or not, they arrived at exactly the right time. Our hour of need.'

'What *are* they, Jack? Aliens? Angels? What?'

'I don't know, Cecilia. The simplest, bravest, most honest three words any human being can say: I don't know. And I don't think we're meant to know, any of us. If Foreigners have some kind of higher cosmic purpose, and I don't believe they do, but if they do, then it's to keep us wondering, keep us guessing.'

He bent forward and started brushing sand from his feet.

'Anyway. Perhaps we ought to get back to the house. They'll be missing us. Missing *you*, certainly.'

27 SLUR

They washed their feet in the water, shook them dry and put their shoes back on. Cecilia patted sand from her skirt, while Parry briskly brushed the tail of his jacket and the seat of his trousers.

Outside, Cecilia extinguished the underwater light, and they waited as their eyes adapted to the gloom and the path glimmered back into visibility.

The return journey to the house was a slower, less sure-footed affair than the outward journey had been. Both of them were feeling the effects of the beer, and the surface of the path now seemed less even and the shadows that striped it hid all sorts of obstacles that had not been there previously. Each laughed whenever the other stumbled. Soon each was stumbling on purpose just to make the other laugh.

It pleased Parry that he and Cecilia got on so well. It also struck him as remarkable that two people who in so many ways were so utterly unalike should have sensibilities so similar. Here was she, fifteen years old, born into fabulous wealth, educated by home board as most children were these days until the age of eleven, then sent to boarding school so that she could acquire 'interpersonal skills' as well as further knowledge – and here was he, nearly fifty, a car-worker's son from Kennington, educated at state schools of the common-or-garden desks-and-teachers variety, a former copper, a Foreign Policy Police captain. Talk about chalk and cheese. It just went to show that . . .

Well, he could not think exactly *what* it went to show. But he liked the comfortable familiarity between him and Cecilia, and he felt that, were he presented with the opportunity, he would make a good stepfather to her, and he flattered himself that she, in turn, would enjoy being his stepdaughter. In an ideal world, it might come to pass. And this was, was it not, an ideal world? A world where the right things happened to the right people when the time was right? Yes, he believed that more firmly than ever. Infused with alcohol and *agapé*, he was convinced that everything would be resolved for the better. Even his current travails with the *shinju* deaths. It would all work out for the best.

Eventually the path brought him and Cecilia back through the rhododendron thickets and pines to the edge of the lawn. There was more than sufficient light to see by here, and thus no excuse any more to pretend to be clumsy. Both of them, as with one mind, straightened up and tried to look sensible and dignified, but the sight of each other doing so set them off laughing again. Still chuckling, heads bent together conspiratorially, they ambled across the lawn to the house.

Guests were on the terrace, clustered in knots. Parry spotted Reich standing there with two people – the NACA administrator with responsibility for transport in New Venice and the owner of The Gondoliers, one of the city's trendiest bar-brasseries. Reich was engaged in animated discussion with his companions but was also eyeing Parry and Cecilia sidelong as they approached, his face creased in squinting curiosity. Parry guessed that he and Cecilia were silhouetted against the tree spotlights and that Reich could not make out who they were. The trad-music promoter continued to watch them until they reached the foot of the terrace steps. Then the glow of the house lights revealed their identities and his look of curiosity was almost instantly replaced by a smile. Almost instantly. In the moment of transition between the two expressions, Parry saw – thought he saw – something else flit fleetingly across the American's features, something tight and cunning that vanished into the smile like a fox into undergrowth.

They climbed the steps, and Reich waved to them. 'Hey, you two. Where you guys been?'

'Just having a wander,' Parry replied.

'Fine night for it.'

'Yes, it is.'

'We heard some laughter out there. Guess it must have been you.'

'Guess it must have,' said Parry, unable to prevent a slight Californian drawl from entering his voice. Normally, to avoid the risk of offence, he was punctilious about maintaining his native accent. This was a particularly important skill in a city where English could be heard in such a broad range of inflections and pronunciations. Emulating an interlocutor's speech patterns was an easy trap to fall into. That Parry had just done so showed just how far his inhibitions had been lowered.

241

Reich, if he noticed Parry's slip, gave no indication of it. 'So what were you up to that was so funny?'

'Oh, nothing. Just a game we were playing.'

'Yeah? What kind of a game?'

'Well, not even a game really. We were just having fun.'

'Is that so?' Reich leaned close to Parry, dropping his voice. 'Only – and you know, Jack, I don't mean any disrespect by this – but the way you two came out from the trees like that, it kinda looked like . . .' He winked. 'If you know what I mean.'

'I beg your pardon?'

Reich leaned back. 'That's how it looked, is all.'

Parry paused for a second, assessing what he had just heard. Was Reich really implying what he appeared to be implying?

'But you know, I wouldn't blame you,' Reich added. 'If I were you, hey, I'd do the same.'

'I think you'd better take back that remark,' said Parry. Every word of the sentence was rimed with ice.

'Jack.' Reich shrugged. 'It was just an observation. I'm not saying anything was going on. I'm simply telling you how it looked.'

The owner of The Gondoliers and the NACA administrator were looking on with interest, as was Cecilia. None of them had heard the content of Reich's *sotto voce* aside to Parry. They had seen the American murmur something to Parry and Parry bristle, but they had no way of knowing what had sparked the antipathy – the palpable crackle of resentment – that was now radiating from Parry towards Reich.

As for Parry, the sense of wellbeing that had filled him just a couple of minutes earlier was gone as if it had never existed, and outrage had come rushing in to fill the vacuum left by its departure. That Reich would dare say such a thing! That he could even think it!

'Apologize,' he said simply, hoarsely. 'Now.'

'Whoa, Jack,' Reich replied, half-laughing. 'Easy there.'

Easy there? *Easy there?*

An aquifer of pure frigid fury surged through Parry, welling towards the surface, speeding up through cracks and crevices. He urged himself to stay calm. His hand was up almost before he realized it. A hunk of Reich's shirt front was clutched in his fist, cloth screwed over knuckles, and he was dragging the music promoter towards him. Gasps came from all around and Reich's eyes were wide and startled, but in them a steady amusement continued to flicker, like a pilot light that will not, no matter what, go out.

'Listen, you tosser,' Parry said, his voice a grunting, guttural hiss. 'I'll say it just once more. Apologize. You're sorry, you regret ever opening your mouth, you're a stupid arsehole and it won't happen again. Do that and maybe I won't shove your teeth down your throat.'

'Jack. Please.' Reich had his hands up like someone at gunpoint, but he was grinning. The physical intimidation did not appear to worry him at all. 'There's no call for this.'

'Say. You're. Sorry.'

'OK, Jack, OK. Whatever. Sorry. I'm sorry. Peace.'

Parry stared into the American's eyes. He saw no trace of regret *there*. But what was he going to do? Was he going to punch Reich? In front of all these people? In full view of the *crème de la crème* of New Venice?

And just like that his anger was gone, and he felt empty and deflated and foolish. He relinquished his grip on Reich's shirt, and Reich shook out his collar and smoothed out his shirt front and began crooking his head from side to side as though his neck bones had been thrown out of alignment.

'Hell, Jack,' he said, sounding vaguely pained, 'I was only having a little fun.'

'Fun?' Parry echoed weakly. He was conscious of dozens of pairs of eyes on him. Interest in the altercation had rippled out through the crowd on the terrace. Conversations had dwindled and heads were now turned towards him and Reich. He looked to Cecilia for support, and found her trying to appear amused, unconvincingly.

'Sure,' said Reich. 'Jerking your chain a little. Course, if I'd known you were going to react like *that* . . .'

'Jack?' said a female voice.

Parry swung round. He had thought the situation could not get any worse, but there – as if to prove him utterly wrong – was Anna, and beside her, further compounding his embarrassment, NACA Liaison al-Shadhuli. It was impossible to know how much of the incident either of them had seen. All Parry could be certain of was that they had seen enough to be appalled at him.

'Jack, what *is* going on?' Anna demanded.

'Nothing,' Reich interjected quickly. 'Nothing's going on. Just a little misunderstanding between me and the captain. A little difficulty in interpretation. How's it go? "Two nations divided by a common language"?' He turned to Parry. 'So, no hard feelings, Jack.' He held out a hand. 'Huh, buddy?'

Numbly, dumbly, Parry reached out and shook Reich's hand. Then, muttering, 'Excuse me,' and entangling his fingers into a brief APOLOGY, which he aimed at no one in particular, he turned around, looking for the nearest and most convenient exit route. The terrace steps. He trotted down them and headed, once again, out across the lawn, feeling the weight of silence and several dozen gazes on his back.

Hot-faced into the warm, resinous night air he went, heading for the trees and the anonymity of the dark, cursing himself every step of the way.

28 LAMENT

FPP HQ on a Saturday morning was a subdued, hollow husk of itself. A quarter of the usual workforce was on duty, and whereas on weekdays the building busily bustled, now only the occasional voice or set of footfalls could be heard. The susurrant sibilance of the air-conditioning was plainly audible in every corridor, like a sigh of relief.

For a man nursing a mild hangover and a heavy dose of remorse, there were worse places to be.

In his office, Parry had the *shinju* folder open on his work-board screen. Ostensibly he was reviewing the facts of the case in the light of his conversations yesterday with Quesnel and Johansen and Hosokawa. Actually he had scarcely read a word of the data in front of him, but sitting at his desk pretending to be doing something was preferable to sitting at home doing nothing at all.

He had hoped work would take his mind off the events of last night, but his thoughts returned again and again to the topic like a dog to a much-scented lamp-post. In particular he dwelled on his unfortunate set-to with Reich. Had he overreacted? It was quite possible that he had. Certainly he should not have grabbed Reich. Whatever the provocation, however drunk you were, however badly someone rubbed you up the wrong way, there was no excuse for behaving like a thug, least of all when you were an FPP officer. Then again, Reich should not have suggested, not even light-heartedly, that there had been something improper going on between him and Cecilia. Parry did not consider himself a prude, but there were some things you simply did not joke about.

So, yes, he should have curbed his temper, but by God, the events of the past few days were enough to have worn anyone's self-restraint thin! It seemed whichever way Parry turned he was being confronted by obstinacy, cynicism, resentment, selfishness, mockery, anger. Van Wyk and Dargomyzhsky and MacLeod and Reich and even Quesnel, with her demands for a speedy resolution to the case – since setting foot in that room at the Amadeus, he had encountered nothing but the worst human traits. It was almost as if he had returned from his holiday in England to a parallel dimension New Venice, where all the gains that humankind had made since the Debut had been mysteriously erased. The Siren deaths and Foreign losses had torn away a façade and exposed a squirm of venality beneath, like worms under a stone.

Was the decency of the post-Foreign era really nothing more than a shell, one so thin and brittle that it cracked under the slightest pressure?

He did not think he wanted to know the answer to that question.

And there was a second source of shame from yesterday evening – something he had done after fleeing from the terrace and before letting himself out by the side gate.

A bruise on the left lobe of his forehead was a small memento of *that* episode. He probed the swelling gingerly, his fingertips triggering a smart of pain. To the touch the bruise felt as large as a tennis ball, but in the bathroom mirror earlier that morning he had seen that it was not much bigger than the yolk of a fried egg. It was all the colours of dusk, and had a thin scabbed cut down the middle like the slit of a cat's eye.

Though Parry remembered perfectly well how he had obtained the bruise, how he had ended up back at the marine feature in the first place was nothing more than a dim memory. He had followed the path, intending to take the turn-off that led to the side gate, but had somehow missed it. All at once, as the wall of black crystech loomed, he had become aware of the need to urinate. His bladder, full and tight from all the beer, throbbed urgently, and he had known that if he did not relieve himself straight away . . .

He was not sure what impelled him to go inside the marine feature, but modern manners – or some atavistic, animal need – demanded he seek seclusion. He recalled trying and failing to locate the panel mounted at the tunnel entrance that housed the switch for the underwater light, and then deciding he was probably better off without artificial illumination anyway; less likely to be discovered that way. He had groped through the tunnel, and on the crescent of sand had unzipped his trousers and shuffled to the water's edge.

As the urine began jetting from him in a hot golden arc, spattering into the marine feature's shallows, he had had a thought which he remembered finding bitterly hilarious at the time.

I'm pissed. I'm pissed off. I'm pissing.

Greeting this cunning play on words with a ferocious chortle, he had continued urinating for what felt like an hour. There had seemed to be no end to the contents of his bladder, and standing there waiting for the flow to abate he had had plenty of opportunity to contemplate the marine feature by the light of the stars and moon, to observe the silken, silvery heave of the water, the obsidian shine of the encircling wall. With the flooding, the sea had become a source of fear, the enemy of humankind, and this place – this tamed, neutered ocean-in-miniature – was, it had occurred to him, a kind of revenge. An act of defiance, almost. How much must it have cost to build? And how much did it cost to maintain, to keep the water clean and oxygenated, the fish fed? What a thing of arrogance and extravagance! Pure Hector Fuentes! So why not piss all over it? He had, after all, pissed all over Fuentes in another way, had he not? By screwing his wife?

At the time, drunk, these thoughts had felt entirely natural and proper. Now, sober, Parry cringed. For one thing, he had not actually hated Fuentes while he was alive. He had envied the man and felt sorry for him at times – the adulterer's compassion for the cuckold. He had even feared him. After all, should Fuentes have found out about the affair, it would have given him absolute power over Parry's life and future. But hated him? He did not think so. Nor had he embarked on the affair with Anna for any other reason than that he was utterly beguiled and besotted. He had loved her and she, incredibly, had reciprocated that love, and whom she was married to had not figured in it at all. Once or twice he might have felt a flicker of furtive satisfaction that by sleeping with Fuentes's wife he was, in however small and secret a way, subverting the Crystech Caballero's track record of success, but almost immediately he would disown both the thought and the emotion.

Last night, however, with his pride badly damaged, he had drawn a savage comfort from the act of besmirching the marine feature. It had been a small, cheap victory. He had relished it to the full.

Fate's revenge had been as immediate as it had been inevitable. Having finally finished urinating, he had tucked himself away, zipped up, turned around and headed confidently towards the spot in the wall where he believed the tunnel mouth to be. A sharp, violent pain in his forehead informed him that he had miscalculated its position by a few crucial centimetres. Clutching his head, he had spun around and stamped his foot and grunted obscenities till the smart of impact had simmered down to a dull sting. Then, very cautiously, he had groped for the outline of the tunnel entrance and fumbled his way through.

One useful by-product had come from the self-inflicted blow. Hitting his head had had the ancillary effect of clearing it, so that there had been no further mishaps on his journey out of the grounds. Pain: not only was it the great teacher, it was the great soberer.

Enough of that. Parry removed his reading spectacles, rubbed his eyes, repositioned the spectacles on the bridge of his nose and told himself to concentrate on the matter at hand. To ignore the ache at the back of his skull and the dry, clotted feeling in his mouth and the manifold embarrassments of last night and *think*.

The *shinjus*. Triple-X. Propaganda slayings.

Perhaps there was some pattern he was supposed to be perceiving, some link between the Amadeus and Debussy incidents over and above the fact that in each instance a Siren had died and a Foreigner had been lost. If these were killings designed to make a point, then the perpetrators might have strung some tiny cohesive thread between them, some subtle, mischievous indicator of organization behind the apparent randomness.

The locations, for example. Both hotels were in the same district. Was that pure chance?

Most likely. After all, if the *shinjus* were simply suicides, then the probability that the second would occur in the same district as the first was only one in eight. Not terrifically long odds. Now, if there was a third *shinju* – and Parry sent up a small prayer that there would not be – but if there was and it, too, took place in the South-West, then not only would it be a pretty clear indication that the *shinjus* were *not* unconnected suicides, but it would give him good reason to suspect that his district had been chosen deliberately, and even that he himself was, for some reason, being targeted.

Was that a possibility? Were the *shinjus* an indirect attack on him? Did Triple-X harbour a grudge against him?

He could not see why. Had all this been happening in the East District, Captain Roldán's wedge, then that would have been a different matter, for it was Captain Roldán who had negotiated the departure of the Triple-X cell last year, smoothly convincing the Triple-Xers that staying in the city might not be in their best interests and backing up his argument with the threat of releasing the names and likenesses of the cell's members to the local media and thus exposing them to public opprobrium. This Constitution-ally unexceptionable FPP tactic had achieved its goal, but never the less Parry could imagine the Triple-Xers resenting not merely the fact that they had been run out of town but also the fact that the only weapon Roldán had deployed against them had been words. They might well want to get their own back on Roldán ... but surely not by carrying out murders in the South-West. Why pick as their theatre of operations a district overseen by a captain who had had no involvement at all in ousting them? And why not directly attack the captain himself?

No, Parry decided, the *shinjus* were nothing to do with himself personally. There was no point pursuing that paranoid line of reasoning any further.

But still, the locations. If this was a Triple-X plot, was there something in the choice of hotels? Some clue in the lives or, perhaps more likely, deaths of the two eponymous composers?

Aware that a certain amount of clutching at straws was going on here, but feeling that even a straw was more solid and substantial than anything else presently within his grasp, Parry summoned up Search mode on the work board and input the words 'Mozart' and 'Debussy'. He tightened the search parameters to biographies only and specified a thousand-word limit. Within seconds assembled text sketches of the lives of the two composers were up in front of him.

There were similarities between the precocious Austrian prodigy and the wayward French modernist, but only insofar as both composers had been esteemed during and after their lifetimes and were acknowledged by posterity as versatile innovators who contributed significantly to the development and advancement of classical music. In less basic terms, Parry could discern little in common between them. Mozart far outweighed Debussy in prolificacy of output and musicological significance, and also had led a far more frenetic and profligate life. As for their deaths, even Parry, no expert in the subject of classical music, was aware that Mozart had met his end under murky circumstances, possibly poisoned by a rival. Had Debussy likewise been the victim of foul play? It seemed not. Debussy's promotion to the ranks of the Choir Invisible was the result of natural causes. Cancer brought him to the Final Chord.

A swift subsidiary search provided Parry with a list of each composer's complete works, and it was while perusing these that he made what he at first thought to be the breakthrough he was looking for. His eye was drawn to the surname of the man who provided librettos for three of Mozart's operas, Lorenzo da Ponte. Dagmar Pfitzner had been found at the Ponte da Ponte. Was the bridge named in tribute to the librettist? A quick consultation of an annotated New Venice tourist map confirmed that it was. Excitedly scanning the lists of works for further such conjunctions, he found that one of Debussy's orchestral pieces was entitled *La Mer*. Was it not in sea water that Dagmar Pfitzner had met her end?

This spark of connection, so rapidly kindled, was just as rapidly doused by a sprinkling of common sense. No murderer, however artful, could have guaranteed that Dagmar Pfitzner's shoe buckle would snag on kelp on one of the Ponte da Ponte's piles. She might have ended up attached to any bridge on that canal. Equally, she might have floated under them all, unhindered, and ultimately been discovered kilometres away from the scene. The da Ponte link was coincidence. Had to be. And the same for the 'sea' link. Coincidence. Random correspondences. Meaningless synchronicities. These things happened. Once, back when he was in the Met, Parry was called to three death scenes in the space of a single day. The three people involved had all perished in differing circumstances – a car crash, a stabbing, a heart attack – but the peculiar thing was that all three had shared the same name, or at any rate a name that was spelt differently but sounded the same. The first was a teenager whose first name was Lee, the second was a Chinese woman whose family name was Li, and the third body belonged to a man with the surname of Leigh. It wasn't *so* bizarre, but it had his colleagues at the station whistling spooky TV theme-tunes at him for weeks afterwards.

Well, he thought as he leaned back disappointedly in his chair, it had been worth a shot. Detective work was about narrowing down options, eliminating possibilities. Now, if nothing else, he could confidently say that he was not chasing after some cunning master criminal who was leaving a trail of clues in order to taunt and tantalize his pursuers. This was real life, after all, not bloody *Resort-City Beat*.

All right. He had amused himself. Now was the time to think realistically.

Thinking realistically, Parry realized he was no further forward with the investigation than he had been two days ago when

Dagmar Pfitzner's body was discovered. Apart from acknowledging that the *shinjus* could be Triple-X actions, he was still, essentially, stymied. Bogged down. Dead in the water.

Like Dagmar Pfitzner.

The joke brought a mirthless twist to his lips.

So, what now? Having searched for some kind of thematic motif running through the two *shinjus* and found none, what should he do next?

The only answer his baffled, beleaguered brain could come up with was talk to Quesnel. He was floundering and he knew it. To be brutally honest – and hangovers had a tendency to make him brutally honest with himself – he had been floundering from the outset, pretty much. He had been confident that the case was within his ability to clear up. He was beginning to see how ill-founded that confidence had been. He had believed that even within the restrictions of Foreign Policy he could, through persistence and open-mindedness, achieve some sort of resolution to the situation. He was beginning to see how simplistic that belief had been. If the *shinjus* were suicides, then MacLeod was right: how could the FPP stop them happening? Of their own accord they would either continue or not continue. If they did catch on and become a macabre fad among Sirens and Foreigners, then the FPP could only sit tight and wait for the craze to run its course. And if that meant New Venice gained a reputation with the golden giants as the venue for a dubious Foreign/human practice and their numbers fell as a consequence, then that was what had to be. Likewise, if the *shinjus* were a murderous Triple-X protest, the FPP was also severely limited in its range of possible responses. It lacked the powers to prosecute a murder inquiry to the fullest possible extent, and the last time there had been a Triple-X cell active in the city the FPP had been able to unearth it thanks solely to Toroa MacLeod's predecessor as head of the local Xenophobe chapter. Right now another cell could be at work within New Venice, but unless its presence was betrayed by a tip-off, the FPP had no means of locating it, lacking both the resources and the authority to perform a thorough investigative sweep of the city. Triple-X knew this. Its members continually took advantage of the loopholes in Foreign Policy that enabled them to lurk within a resort-city like maggots in an apple, industrious yet unseen. It seemed they were caught and handed over to the mainland authorities only if the FPP got lucky and they were shopped by an insider or else the Triple-Xers themselves got unlucky and were discovered *in flagrante*. Parry could hope that either of these things might happen, but he would be foolish to count on it.

So this was what it came down to. He was stuck. He was stumped. He was out of options. The pressure he was under was taking its toll. And it was about time he said as much to Quesnel. He could ask her to assign another captain to help with the case (though not van Wyk, please). He could even ask her to take the investigation off his hands altogether and bring in someone fresh to tackle it (though, again, not van Wyk). The main thing was, he ought to let her know that he had run into a wall. There was no shame in that, surely. She would understand. He wasn't giving up on the case, merely acknowledging the impossibility of the position he was in.

Was the commissioner at HQ today? Like him – spouseless, solitary, unattached – Quesnel often worked at weekends. He picked up the telephone receiver on his work board, summoned up an internal line from the onscreen menu, selected 'Quesnel', and was put through to the commissioner's extension. He heard the busy signal, and the screen offered him the 'Voicemail?' prompt. He hung up, stood up, and, with a certain heaviness of tread, made his way to the lift.

The lift disgorged him on Floor Upper C and he walked to the end of the corridor. Outside the door to the commissioner's office, he stopped and put an ear to the wood panelling. He heard a voice, very faint. He knocked and opened the door, preparing his hands for an APOLOGY for the intrusion.

The manufold never manifested. It was not Quesnel on the phone at her desk. It was van Wyk. The Afrikaner was seated in the commissioner's chair and was looking quizzically across the room at Parry, one hand masking the speaking end of the telephone receiver.

'Yes?'

Parry glanced around the room. There was no sign of Quesnel. 'I came to see the commissioner. Mind telling me where she is?'

Van Wyk gave an insouciant shrug. 'Not here, obviously.'

'Then what are you doing at her desk?'

With a sigh, van Wyk removed his hand from the receiver and spoke into it. 'As a matter of fact, Muhammad, the man himself has just walked in. Yes. OK, I'll call you back later. *Salaam.*' He set the receiver back in its cradle, then leaned forward, resting his elbows on the desk and steepling his fingers. 'Well, well, well. Captain Parry. Or should that be "Battling" Jack Parry, the Drunken Party Pugilist?' He mimed a punch. 'How are we feeling today? Somewhat the worse for wear, I should imagine. The NACA Liaison was just filling me in about yesterday evening's little fracas *chez* Fuentes. That's quite a bump you have there on your forehead. I trust the other fellow came off worse.'

'Have I missed something?' Parry retorted. 'Have you been appointed commissioner and no one told me?'

'Not at all, Parry, not at all. I often sit in for Céleste. I'm surprised you don't know that. It reassures the commissioner to know that her desk is being manned when she herself can't be there.'

'Is that a fact? And you just sit in her chair and happily make phone calls?'

'As it happens, it was the NACA Liaison who phoned *me*. Or rather, he was phoning Céleste in order to report your, as he himself put it, puzzling behaviour last night. Really, Parry. In uniform and all! Hardly a credit to the badge, I should say. I suppose that's why you came to see the commissioner. To explain yourself.'

'No, I came to ... Actually, it's none of your business why I came. Are we expecting the commissioner at HQ any time today?'

'She should be in later. Around midday.'

'I'll talk to her then.' Parry turned on his heel.

'Oh, by the way, Parry.'

Parry looked round.

'Good job on the *shiatsus*.' The Afrikaner's eyes twinkled like two malevolent stars. 'Telling Céleste there was nothing to worry about. Nicely done.'

You odious little ...

Parry steadied himself. 'Van Wyk,' he said, 'you have no idea how complex and difficult this case is. You have not the first inkling what I'm up against.'

'The Constitution. That's what you're up against.'

Parry, of course, had been coming to this unwelcome conclusion himself, but he would rather have had both hands lopped off than admit it to van Wyk. 'It's simply that this case has no precedent in FPP history and no obvious explanation. Given which, I think any captain in my position would be experiencing the difficulties I am.'

'Any captain except one who's convinced these are murders.'

'Not this again. Van Wyk, I've never said these *aren't* murders.'

'But you remain reluctant to accept the possibility, and while you continue to do so, your investigation continues to limp along like a lame horse.'

'I've dealt with this investigation to the very best of my abilities.'

'Letting Céleste stand up in front of the press and make a fool of herself? You call that the very best of your abilities?'

'What went wrong there was due to circumstances beyond my control . . .'

The words tailed away.

Could it have been? Yes. Yes, it could have.

Narrowing his eyes, he aimed an index finger at van Wyk. Suddenly it was all perfectly clear to him. 'It was *you*, wasn't it?'

'I beg your pardon?'

'*You* did it. *You* erased the message from her work board.'

'I don't understand.'

'Oh, do me a favour. The message I left Quesnel early Thursday morning advising her to abort the press conference. What, did you sit there and listen to it as it was coming in and then think, I'll get rid of that?'

'I honestly have no idea what you're on about. Thursday morning?'

'Why, van Wyk?' Parry was moving towards the desk. 'Why would you do such a thing?'

'Really, Parry, this is ridiculous.'

'Why would you try and sabotage me like that?'

'Sabotage?'

'To make me look stupid? A liar?'

'Parry . . .'

Parry halted at the desk. A two-metre width of dark-blue crystech separated him from van Wyk. The Afrikaner was looking perplexed. Perplexed and – yes, was that not a flicker of guilt in his eyes?

'But you must have realized I'd speak to Quesnel later and tell her about the message,' he said. 'You must have realized she'd believe I left it, even if I didn't have Shankar and Hosokawa as witnesses. So if you were trying to make me look incompetent, it was a pretty half-arsed attempt.'

'But why would I want to make you look incompetent?'

'Do I have to spell it out for you?'

'I think you do.'

'Because you want this investigation for yourself. You've wanted it right from the start.'

Van Wyk lifted his shoulders and spread out his arms, the gesture of an eminently reasonable man. 'Parry. For one thing, although we may not see eye to eye on many subjects, I am, I assure you, on the same side as you. I want to see this situation resolved as much as you do. You have to believe that. And that's why all this talk of me sabotaging you is absurd.'

'It may seem absurd to you, but—'

'For another thing—'

'But to me it's—'

'For another thing,' van Wyk said, firmly, 'on Thursday morning I came into HQ *after* Céleste. I popped in to see her when I arrived and she was already at her desk. You can ask her. I'm sure she remembers.'

Parry opened his mouth to respond, but could think of nothing to say.

'Yes. You see? So you should be a little more careful, I feel, before you go bandying about this sort of baseless accusation. But then, on current showing, "careful" is a word that can hardly be applied to you. It's clear you're under a lot of strain, Parry. You might wish to consider a session with one of the in-house counsellors. I could set up an appointment for you if you're too English to do it yourself.'

Parry seethed with contempt. 'Screw you, van Wyk.'

'How eloquent.'

'No, really. Screw you, you sycophantic turd.'

'Parry, I think you should leave before this becomes any more unseemly.'

'"Unseemly." I should give you "unseemly". Right here and now. I should give you a right "unseemly" seeing to.'

'Oh dear.' Van Wyk shook his head like a disappointed teacher. He did not believe the threat. Neither did Parry. 'This is exactly what I was talking about. The strain. Perhaps I should recommend to Céleste that she take you off the investigation.'

Parry slapped the desk. 'I can handle the investigation. I am *going* to handle the investigation.'

'Not if you continue with this inappropriate behaviour, you aren't.'

'Just watch me.'

'Oh, I am, Parry. I'm watching you very closely indeed.'

Parry, leaning across the desktop, glared at van Wyk. Van Wyk returned the glare with a look of calculated contempt.

Very slowly, Parry nodded, then broke the eye-contact, turned and left the room.

29 RESOLUTION

On the way down in the lift, he reflected ruefully on what he had just done.

Screw you, van Wyk. Piece of genius, that was.

He had played right into the man's hands. Van Wyk now had more than ample evidence to present to Quesnel in order to get Parry removed from the *shinju* case (and himself, doubtless, put in charge of it in Parry's stead). In fact, even if van Wyk *had* resorted to the chicanery of erasing the voicemail message, he really need not have bothered. Parry, it seemed, was quite capable of appearing incompetent without help from anyone else.

But, said a small voice in the back of his mind, wasn't this what he had wanted anyway? To be absolved of responsibility for the investigation?

No. Not like this. Not by being forced to surrender up the case just because of a couple of lapses in judgement.

Indeed, perversely, bloody-mindedly, Parry was now more determined than ever to stick with the investigation. He would struggle on with it, and if Quesnel tried to take him off it, he would fight tooth and nail to remain involved. He refused to give van Wyk the satisfaction of seeing him fail. Absolutely *refused*.

He re-entered his office, fired with renewed zeal, ready to re-examine the facts of the case once again, turn them upside-down and inside-out and back-to-front, scour them like a prospector panning an already well-sieved portion of stream-bed mud for the few grains of hidden gold it might yet contain.

His good intentions were derailed by the voice message that was waiting for him on his work board.

Not even a message, exactly. More a summons.

30 SUSPENDED CADENCE

Anna did not take her Bononcini sunglasses off as the waiter ushered Parry to the table. She kept them on as Parry sat down opposite her. She kept them on even after the waiter had brought over menus. The sunlight was intense up on the Alto Rialto, but the Touching Bass, one of a dozen restaurants and brasseries on the concourse, benefited from the protection of a large canvas awning, stretched trampoline-tight overhead. Parry realized, therefore, that he was being punished. By screening her eyes from him with the Bononcinis, depriving him of the sight of them, Anna was consigning him to a kind of inverse purdah.

'Hungry?' she enquired.

'What do you recommend?'

'The steak's good here.'

'It's a bruise, not a black eye.'

'I'm sorry?'

'A raw steak's supposed to be good for . . . Never mind.'

Now was obviously not the time for humour, however inept. Parry bent forward and inspected the menu. He tried to make sense of the words in front of him but was unable to concentrate. All he could see were lines of print, nothing intelligible. Knowing Anna, she would prolong this. Make him suffer before she forgave him. But she *would* forgive him, he was in no doubt about that. He had disgraced himself but not, he thought, irredeemably.

'I could do with something a bit lighter anyway,' he said.

'Yes,' Anna replied. Neutrally. Inscrutably.

The waiter returned a minute later to take their order.

'I'll have the goat's cheese filou parcels, please,' Anna said.

'Certainly, Mrs Fuentes. Sir?'

'Yes. Me, too.' Parry disliked goat's cheese – nothing to do with the taste of the stuff, just the fact that it originated from so unappealing a beast – but he could not think of what else to have, and hoped, somewhat pathetically, that ordering what Anna had ordered might in some small way ingratiate him with her.

'To drink?'

'Mineral water for me,' said Anna. 'I imagine the captain will have the same.'

Parry nodded.

The waiter left, and a silence fell between Parry and Anna. Parry felt it was best to wait for Anna to speak. She, however, showed no immediate inclination to do so. She toyed with the handle of a spoon for a while, rubbing at an imagined smear, then turned to gaze across to the Alto Rialto's balustrade-hemmed perimeter. The Alto Rialto was a square concourse fixed between the summits of four central hotels, cantilevered on slender, cross-braced struts. It was said that you could see all of New Venice from here, although from the centre of the concourse, where the Touching Bass was, only ocean and sky were visible, two sharply delineated swathes of dark and light blue.

Parry preferred not to contemplate the fact that all that was keeping him from a multi-storey plummet to the ground was a few worryingly thin struts and an architect's calculations. Never the less, while Anna maintained her silence, his thoughts turned repeatedly to the gulf of empty air beneath him, so that there was a literal dimension to the state of suspense in which Anna was holding him.

At last Anna spoke.

'Have you ever done something that you truly, truly regret, Jack?'

The phrasing of the question and the weary wistfulness of its tone took Parry by surprise. If Anna was referring to that thing last night with Reich, as she seemed to be, then she had chosen an odd way to do so.

'I have, yes,' he said. 'Many things. Including my behaviour at the party.'

She appeared not to hear the last part. 'I remember you telling me once that there's a lot you did as a London policeman that you aren't too proud of.'

'Did I?'

'Planting evidence. Lying to suspects, telling them you had incriminating testimony you didn't have. Getting a bit, I think the word you used was "heavy-handed", in the holding cells.'

'Well, yes, that did happen from time to time. I – we – weren't above bending the law to suit us. In my defence, I only ever got involved in that sort of stuff with someone who I *knew* was guilty, but I didn't have enough hard evidence to pin on him and I knew he'd get away with it if something wasn't done. That was then, that was the way we coppers did things then, had to, and I'm sorry about it, and I know being sorry about it doesn't make it any better, but it does make me all the more determined that the FPP should never be like that. *Will* never be like that.'

'What I'm thinking of particularly is the Riots. The girl?'

He had forgotten till then that, in the aftermath of sex one night, he had told Anna about the girl. He had had few secrets from her in the confessional of her marital bed. Lying beside her, he had been naked in every way.

'She . . . yes. She's the one thing in my past that I will never ever forgive myself for. I mean, God knows how many other people I hurt that day. It took us till midnight finally to bring the whole thing under control, and we only managed that through being even more violent than the protesters. I think things had got to the stage where that was the only way to do it. Even so . . .'

'Even so, there was no excuse for what you did to her. Even though you had no choice.'

'It was pandemonium, Anna. How I imagine war must be like. At times I felt like I was outside my body, looking down at myself. It was as though someone else was doing these things, these terrible things.'

'Pandemonium,' Anna said, nodding. 'That's it. You think you know yourself, you think you understand yourself, you think you're in control of all you believe and do, but then when the chaos comes you realize that that's just an illusion. And a fragile illusion, too.'

'Anna, what's this all about? Why are we talking about my police career?'

The waiter reappeared, bearing a bottle of mineral water and two ice-filled glasses. A moment later he returned with plates.

'Enjoy your meal,' he said, and left.

Parry eyed the food unenthusiastically. Although his hangover was just about gone, he had little appetite on him. Even if one of his favourite dishes had been set before him – a nice juicy lamb cutlet, for example, or a bubbling lasagne – he would have tucked into it with minimal relish. It did not help, either, that the filou parcels reminded him of Dagmar Pfitzner's drawstring purse. There was, at least, a helping of wild rice on the side of the plate, along with a heap of salad leaves. He concentrated on those, masticating with herbivore listlessness.

Another long silence stretched, with his question dangling clumsily in the air like some rearview-mirror novelty.

Finally Anna said, 'It's about us.'

'Us.' Parry spoke the word with as little inflection as possible. Inside, a part of him was thinking: This is it, she's ready to start again. Another part, larger and less exuberant, was thinking: That's it, it's all over.

For a second time, Anna wrongfooted him.

'Hector knew.'

The chewing motion of Parry's jaws slowed to a halt. Numbly he gulped down the mouthful of food.

'Knew?' He kept his voice low; resisted the urge to gesticulate. 'When? When did he know? How long for? From the start? Jesus, Anna . . .'

'Calm down, Jack.'

'I *am* calm. All things considered, I'm being very calm indeed. But, for fuck's sake, Anna – your husband knew what we were up to! Your husband, one of the wealthiest and most influential men in New Venice, *knew*.'

'You're getting aggressive. I thought this might happen. I shouldn't have told you.'

'Well, I'm glad you did. And I'm not getting aggressive.'

'Oh no?' She pointed to his right hand. It was clenched around the handle of his fork, the knuckles bulging like large white marbles beneath the skin.

Parry, forcing forbearance on himself, laid the fork down.

'All right, I'm a little tense,' he admitted. 'But it's hardly surprising, is it? Hector could have ruined me. Ruined *us*.'

'Could have but didn't. And before you say any more, I want you to hear me out. Please. Listen to what I have to say, and then you can be angry or shocked or bitter or whatever you want to be. OK?'

'OK,' said Parry, briskly. 'Fine. Go ahead.'

Anna tilted her head forwards a couple of degrees, as though collecting her thoughts. Parry imagined her eyes closing behind the Bononcinis. Then she raised her head again, and he saw himself in each lens of the sunglasses, reflected distantly and darkly.

'It was after,' she said. 'After Hector fell ill. After you and I stopped seeing each other. Because of the cancer, Hector and I found ourselves spending a lot of time together – a lot more time than we ever had before. And we found ourselves talking a lot more, too. The way a husband and wife are supposed to talk. You know, two people chatting, saying whatever comes into their heads. Until then everything had been formal between us. Formal and distant. Sometimes we'd barely see each other or speak to each other during the day. Hector would already be working at breakfast. He'd have a portable extension of his home board set up on the dining table and be typing into it or making calls from it while he ate his *huevos rancheros*. Then he'd go to his study until dinnertime and then maybe we'd be out at a party or over at friends' in the evening and it's just not done, is it, to have a conversation with your own spouse at a social function. Also, he'd be away on business trips a lot. A week could go by and the only contact I'd have with him would be a single phone call, if that. I didn't mind. I'd accepted when I married him that this was how it would be. We'd had a bargain, of sorts. He was Hector Fuentes, first and foremost. Then he was my husband and Cissy's father, second. Cissy and I were just two small compartments in his life. Cissy loved him, of course, in spite of how he was. She grew up not knowing anything else about fathers except that this was how they were – aloof, uncommunicative, often absent. It was only when her home-board tuition ended and she went away to school and began comparing notes with the other girls there that she realized a father was supposed to be warm and caring and involved in his daughter's life. It didn't make her love him any less, but it did make her a bit sad to think that she was missing out on something – something most of her schoolfriends took for granted. But anyway. This isn't about Cissy.'

Anna considered the possibility of eating more of her meal, decided against, and took a sip of water instead.

'When he discovered that he was dying, Hector was forced to take stock of his life. I honestly believe he'd thought he was immortal up until then. Invincible, certainly. Finding out that he was just as vulnerable as anyone else, and moreover that it was his own body that was killing him . . . Well, he took it as a personal insult. No matter how many times Dr Lü said that his condition was incurable, Hector wouldn't believe him. He fought against the cancer. Raged against it. He thought that through sheer will, with nothing but the power of his mind, he could beat it. But of course the cancer was *in* his mind, in a sense, so he was fighting a battle he

262

couldn't win. The cancer was destroying the best weapon he had against it, his brain. And once he learned to accept that, which in the event he did quite quickly, he turned into another person. He became gentler, more reflective. He started asking me questions. "Have I lived decently?" "Have I been a fair man?" These things suddenly matter when death is breathing down your neck. And it was from there that we began to talk more openly with each other, discussing things we would never have dreamed of discussing before. How we were. How we thought and felt. Things that went to the heart of who we were. Things that came from the heart of who we were. In those weeks, Hector and I grew closer than we had ever been. I'd always admired him. Respected him. I'd had a great affection for him right from the start, and of course he had given me my beautiful daughter, for which I would be forever grateful to him. But it wasn't until then that I loved him. Really, genuinely loved him. And that, I suppose, was the first time I ever felt guilty about you and me.'

'And so you told him.'

'Not just like that. I didn't just blurt it out. But as he got iller and iller – is that an English word? "Iller"?'

Parry shrugged, not caring.

'As his cancer got worse, anyway,' said Anna, 'my guilt got worse, too. It was as though, like him, I had something malignant festering inside my head. And as he got thinner and feebler, I just felt more and more sorry about what you and I had done. I wanted to tell him about it so that I could get it off my chest. I wanted – what is it called in church? Absolution. I wanted absolution from him. And I didn't want him to die not knowing. That would have been unbearable for me.' She let out a shuddering sigh. 'How selfish I am.'

Though he was still angry with her, appalled by what she had done, Parry could not let such self-denigration go uncorrected. 'Not at all. You aren't selfish, Anna.'

'I am. It didn't even occur to me that I might make Hector miserable by telling him. All I cared about was my own misery. It was the chaos, you see. That pandemonium I was talking about. My life was in turmoil and I couldn't see straight, couldn't think straight.'

'There you go. So it wasn't your fault.'

'All the same.'

A gust of wind caught Anna's hair and drove a lock of it into the space between her left eye and one hinge of her sunglasses. She pushed the glasses a little way down her nose in order to extricate the errant lock, and Parry was at last given a glimpse of her eyes. They looked tired, and he noticed (it seemed like for the first time) just how embedded in wrinkles they were, not least at the corners, where crow's feet scored the skin, showing up pale against her tan.

'It must have been three, four weeks before he died,' she said. 'He was dreadfully weak. He could barely get out of bed. It was a still evening. I'd been reading to him by his bedside. He liked me to read to him, as you know. Poetry. Short stories. I'd finished a story – Borges, I think it was – and he said how much he had enjoyed listening to it and what a kind and generous woman I was, and that was it. I couldn't hold back any longer. Out it came. He lay there, listening, not saying anything. I just went on talking, telling him about us. About how we'd met at the Civic Committee. About how we'd arranged our meetings. About what we'd done in the very bed he was lying in! God! But Hector said nothing, just heard me out, and when I'd told him everything and there was nothing left to say, he thought to himself for a while, and then do you know what he said? "Thank you, Anna." That was all. "Thank you." And he moved his hand to pat mine. His hand was so thin by then. So feeble. A hand that had once held such power. A hand that had built up an industrial empire. I hardly felt it touching mine. It weighed less than a sheet of paper, less than a moth. Tap, tap. Then it slid back on to the bed, exhausted.'

'There were no repercussions? No recriminations?'

'None.'

'There must have been.'

'He took it with absolute' – she searched for the right word – 'equanimity. If he hadn't been dying, it might have been different. That was partly why I felt it was safe to tell him. He had become such a reasonable, philosophical person.'

'And he never mentioned it again?'

'Never. Not once. He just seemed to absorb the information, accept it, and that was that.'

'That's a little odd, don't you think?'

'Not really. He was *dying*, Jack. I think he had more important things on his mind. And besides, because he and I had never been that close, at least not before those last few weeks, then maybe it didn't seem like such a betrayal to him. Anyway, I've never believed that he was perfectly faithful to *me*. Maybe he was, but I wouldn't be surprised if, while he was away on business trips, he didn't go to bars and pick up floozies and take them back to his hotel. I've no proof he ever did anything of the sort, but I strongly suspect he did and it didn't bother me. Why should it? Why should I care if every so often he had a discreet little one-night stand? If it was meaningless to him, why should it mean anything to me? And if I'm right about him having these flings, then it would have been hypocritical of him to resent me for being unfaithful to him, and Hector was many things but he was not a hypocrite. So that's why I think he didn't mind about you and me. That and, like I said, because he was dying.'

A thought occurred to Parry, and he dismissed it as quickly as possible. Could Anna have initiated the affair with him as a way of getting her own back on Fuentes for his supposed infidelities? He was ashamed even to have had the idea. He knew that Anna had loved him. He believed that implicitly.

'But,' Anna said, 'I still felt I had not been properly forgiven. It preyed on my mind all through those last few weeks. Hector was starting to get his affairs in order. That's such a dark euphemism, isn't it? "Get your affairs in order." So innocent-sounding, so pragmatic, and yet what it's really saying is you're getting ready to die. And that meant there were lawyers coming in and out of his room, and he'd spend a lot of time on his home board, when he could, going over his assets and investments, making sure everything was secure, his finances were in good hands, Cissy and I were going to be well provided for, all that. He seemed to have less and less time for me. He was working, he was sleeping, he was sedated . . . What I'm saying is that I wanted to talk some more with him about you and me, but I never seemed to get the opportunity. Not only that; I was scared to bring the subject up again. It had taken all the courage I possessed to tell him that one time. I kept hoping he would save me the trouble and bring it up himself, but he didn't. And the days slipped away, and soon he was just this thin, wheezing thing with tubes stuck into him, this grey-faced, suddenly old man who needed a pipe down his throat to keep him breathing and who could barely hold his eyelids open, it was so much effort. And I'd lost my chance. I would never hear him say, "I forgive you."'

Her voice went hoarse. She steeled herself.

'Cissy and I sat up with him on his last night. We knew he didn't have long. All the nursing staff had told us so. Around midnight

Cissy fell asleep, right in the chair beside the bed, and I spent the rest of the night talking to him, holding his hand. I doubt he heard a word I said. He would roll his eyes occasionally, move his head, open and close his mouth. He was full of painkillers. Barely conscious. I could almost feel him fading, through his hand. Feel the warmth leaving him. The life. By dawn he was gone. Lying there, so still, so hollow. I disentangled my hand from his and the last words I whispered to him were "I'm sorry". And I went downstairs and out into the garden, and it was a beautiful cool morning, I remember, and there was mist rising from the grass and everything was so quiet. And I wept. Not just for Hector. I wept for myself. Because I hated myself. I hated myself because the Hector I had got to know while he was dying was a far better man than I had ever believed he could be and if only I had made a bit more effort while he had been alive then maybe I could have found that man earlier. If only I had *tried* with him, instead of being so damn superficial. I had got everything I expected from him – comfort, security, a family – but I could have had love, too. I could have had it all, and I had just been such a shallow, stupid, superficial fool.'

She might have been crying then. Her eyes might have been moist. Parry had no way of telling. Tentatively he reached across the table to touch her forearm. He allowed himself the briefest moment of contact, his skin on hers, then withdrew his hand.

'It wasn't your fault,' he said. 'You know that. He was as much to blame as you. More so. You yourself said how cold he was, how preoccupied. He didn't let himself be any different until he became resigned to the fact that he was dying. I doubt there was anything you could have done before then that would have changed him.'

'I know.' She heaved in and let out a breath, controlling herself. 'I know you're right. But after he died, after the funeral, for a long time I could feel nothing for myself but utter contempt.'

'It's natural, isn't it? Part of the grieving process.'

'Is it? To despise yourself? To feel that you're worthless as a human being?'

'To regret missed opportunities, that's for sure.'

'This wasn't just that. This was about everything I'd done. The way I'd conducted my life. The compromises I'd made to get to where I was. When I was a little girl in Bucharest, we lived in that god-awful apartment block. I've told you about it, haven't I? That disgusting place. It was on the edge of a great concrete wasteland, the site of Ceauşescu's Civic Centre which, thank God, that monster never finished building, and it smelled and it was noisy and it was infested with rats the size of cats and cockroaches not much smaller, and there were five of us – me, my parents, my two brothers – crammed into two small rooms and never any privacy, never any peace. And almost from the day I was old enough to think for myself, I dreamed of a better existence. I dreamed of one day living in a big beautiful house like the type I saw in American soap operas, and having servants and the very best clothes and a husband who adored me and whom I adored. I vowed to myself that that was the life I would have when I was grown up. But of course I had no idea what it would take to get there, what sacrifices I would have the make along the way. "Be careful what you wish for, you might just get it." Isn't that what they say? I soon learned, the hard way, that I wasn't going to achieve what I wanted if I wasn't ruthless. If I didn't use people. So I did. Men, mostly. I took them for what I could, then abandoned them when they were no longer any advantage to me.'

'Anna, you don't have to go on if you don't want to.'

'But I *do* have to, Jack. You have to know what kind of a person I am.'

'I know that already.'

'No, you don't. You think you do. There's a big difference. The kind of person I am is an opportunist. An exploiter. If someone can't help me, I want nothing to do with them. Like my family, for example. My parents, my brothers. Do you know when the last time I had any contact with them was? Over twenty years ago. Twenty years! I don't know where they are now. I assume they're still in Bucharest, but I'm not sure. I don't even know if they're alive or dead. As soon as I could escape from life with them, I did. I left them without a second thought, without a backward glance. I didn't fall out with them. I simply didn't need them any more. And that's how it's always been with me. How it's *had* to have been. You don't advance in life by making sentimental attachments. Sometimes I even think of myself as a vampire. I know, I know. Romanian. How clichéd. But that's a good description for the way I've behaved. Like a vampire. Find victims, suck them dry, move on.'

'Everyone uses other people to some extent.'

'Do you, Jack?'

'I think so.'

'I don't.'

'Anyway, all these bad things you've supposedly done – they're in the past. They don't matter now.'

'They're in *my* past, and my past makes me who I am now.'

'No, how you act now makes you who you are now. A past is something that can be wiped clean. The Foreigners showed us that.'

'Really, Jack? Can you forget the girl at the Riots? Can you wipe *her* clean?'

Parry momentarily foundered. 'All right, no. But I can make her a lesson to learn from. A mistake not to repeat.'

'Well, maybe not everyone's like you. Maybe not everyone can learn.'

'Look, Anna, I still don't understand. What are you getting at? Are you trying to make me despise you? Because you'll have to try a lot harder than that if you are.'

'What I'm trying to do is set things straight. I haven't been treating you fairly this past year, Jack. I'm trying to explain what's been going on in my head. You see, it wasn't adultery, you and me, until after we had to stop seeing each other. It wasn't adultery, as far as I was concerned, because you were supplying the one thing missing from my dream life, the one thing Hector was not giving me. The adoration. Adoring me and being the man for me to adore. You were the missing piece of the puzzle. So in that respect I was using even you, the last person on Earth I would ever want to use.'

Parry laughed, and how querulous it sounded, how brittle. 'I think I was quite happy to be used like that. I think I still would be.'

'Regardless,' Anna said, brushing this aside. 'I saw nothing wrong in what we were doing until Hector and I, so late in the day, thawed to each other and I realized how I had underestimated him and how, in a different way, I had underestimated myself. It's a shock to be confronted with your own failings, particularly if they're as great as mine. It's a shock to discover you're a self-centred, calculating, manipulative bitch.'

'Anna—'

'Yes, yes, you'll leap in chivalrously here and tell me what you feel I need to hear. But face it, there must have been times this past year when you've thought exactly that about me. "What a bitch. Cutting me out of her life without giving any good reason why. Letting me hang there, close to her but just out of reach." It would have been easier for both of us if I'd simply said we could never meet again, but the trouble is I like you. I like you too damn much for that. I like talking to you. I like your certainty, your positiveness. That's me being selfish again. And there's Cissy, of course. She brags about you to her friends at school, did you know that? "My mother's friend, the FPP captain. He's really cool." Actually, I think she considers you as much her friend as mine. So that has complicated everything, you being so damn nice. So damn dependable. So damn trustworthy.'

'You make them sound like bad qualities.'

'That's just it. In my world they *are*. If I could bring myself to hate you for even a second, then my problems would be solved. But I can't, I just can't.'

'Not even after last night?'

'Of course not. Although what happened last night has a lot to do with why I've decided to say all this to you now. I'm still not clear what made you attack Guthrie out on the terrace. I only caught the tail-end of it. I know you didn't much like him from the start. I imagine he said something crass about Foreigners or Sirens or New Venice or the FPP and you'd been getting so tightly wound up all evening by everyone else asking you about the *shinjus* that you finally snapped. Was that it?'

'There was a bit more to it. Quite a bit more.' Could he repeat to her Reich's comment about him and Cecilia? He felt he ought to, simply so that he would look less like the villain of the piece. Then again, what difference did it make? No matter what Reich had said, he should never have grabbed him and threatened him. He should have just walked away. 'But, well, yes. He made a remark, a thoughtless remark, and I lost my rag. And I'd had a bit to drink, too, of course. You must know I'm deeply embarrassed about what happened.'

'I'm sure you are. You're so principled, Jack. And that's why you're not the sort of person I deserve to be with and why you should steer clear of me. I could be very dangerous for you.'

'I think you should let me be the judge of that.'

'Oh, so you know me better than I know myself?'

'No, but I know myself better than you know me. Look, I'm not the saint you seem convinced I am. I'm a lot harder than I appear.'

'You're hard on the outside, but not on the inside. And I'm the opposite. You wouldn't like what you found if you got to know me really well.'

'But I love you, Anna.'

The words came out unbidden, startling him. He could scarcely believe he had said them, but at the same time he knew he had been going to say them all along, ever since receiving Anna's message instructing him to meet her for lunch. Somehow, whether or not an appropriate moment in the conversation arose, he had known he was going to admit to her how he still felt about her.

Abruptly Anna's face became as immobile and unreadable as a Foreigner's mask.

Then, softly and sorrowfully, she said, 'I know.'

A year ago it would have been *I love you, too*. Today: *I know*.

Inside Parry, something cracked like glass in a furnace. Cracked and started to fall away in fragments.

'And I'd thought you might have ...' Anna frowned. 'Not "grown out of it", that's the wrong phrase. Kicked the habit? I don't know. But last night when Guthrie put his arm around me in the library, I saw the way you stiffened, the little flinty flash that came into in your eyes. That's the look a man gets when he sees another man staking a claim on a woman he considers *his* property.'

Parry wanted to tell her she was mistaken. But she wasn't, was she? Not really.

'I pretended to ignore it, of course,' Anna went on. 'I'm very good at pretending to ignore things, especially at parties. I know how to keep my sweetest smile on. But then when I came out on to the terrace and found you and Guthrie at loggerheads, it was obvious to me what was really happening.'

'So *is* there something going on between you two?' Parry felt bitterness eating away at him like an acid. 'You and Mr Bighead from LA?'

'Is it any business of yours if there is?'

Christ, that was cold of her. Shockingly cold.

'Perhaps not,' he said. 'But surely I have the right to ask. Surely you owe me that much.'

'But this is what I've been trying to get across. If you could just listen to your voice, Jack, could just see the look that's on your face ... This is why you should have nothing to do with me.'

'I deserve an answer.'

'Do you? After all, even if there *is* something going on between me and Guthrie, what difference does it make to you?'

'All the difference in the world. To our friendship, if nothing else.'

'If you really thought we were just friends, then the idea of me having a relationship with another man wouldn't bother you.'

'And if we really were just friends, you wouldn't be avoiding answering my question.' Parry was half-convinced, half-hoping that what he was involved in here was nothing more than a negotiation. He did not want to believe that Anna was finally, after all this time, pulling up the drawbridge for good. Rather, he had to believe that this was a challenge to his talent for persuasion, something for which a successful outcome could be achieved through the diplomatic skills which made him such a good FPP officer. 'So, come on. *Are* you and Reich involved?'

'What do you want me to say? What do you want to hear?'

'The truth, of course.'

'All right. No. We aren't.'

'Well, then. There you are.' He sat back, satisfied.

'You believe me?'

'Why shouldn't I? I never thought he was your type, anyway.'

'Not my type?'

'Too young, too dumb.'

'I'd have thought that made him ideal for me. I know plenty of women my age and in my situation who've taken "young, dumb" men as their lovers. And actually, Guthrie may be young but he isn't stupid. He's passionate and extremely articulate.'

'And conceals it well behind a mask of utter crassness.'

'You're still jealous of him, aren't you? Even now. Even though I've just told you there's nothing going on between him and me, you still feel the need to assert yourself over him.' She shook her head. 'Sometimes I really wonder about men.'

The waiter, concerned that sir and madam were evincing so little interest in their food, came up to their table and enquired if everything was to their satisfaction.

'Everything's fine,' Anna informed him, 'but I think we're done here.'

'Of course, Mrs Fuentes. Will there be anything else? Dessert? Coffee?'

'Just the bill, please.'

With an impassive bow, the waiter picked up their barely pecked-at meals and glided away.

'Anna . . .'

'What?'

He had to know. He hated himself for asking but he had to

know. 'Just tell me. Tell me straight. Is there still a chance? For you and me? Any chance at all?'

A pause. 'It's not that simple.'

'Do you want me to change in some way? Because I will.'

'No, you idiot. No! That's just it. I want you to stay exactly as you are. I want you to continue being the Jack Parry I know and . . . like.'

'But?'

'I don't know if there *is* a but. I only know that I've made a mistake. I should have done this much earlier. Cleared the air between us.'

'I doubt it would have made any difference.'

'Not to you, perhaps.'

The waiter returned with the bill. Normally Parry would have wrangled with Anna over which of them should pay, both knowing that he would concede to her in the end, but both also knowing that it was important for his peace of mind that he didn't do so without putting up a fight. Today there was none of that. He could not summon the energy to offer so much as a token protest as Anna brandished an IC card at the waiter. He did not even propose to pay the tip, as he sometimes did. He just sat there and looked on as Anna invited the waiter to add a more-than-generous gratuity to the total, in response to which the waiter wrung his hands in a prolonged and unctuous GRATITUDE.

Anna rose from the table and shouldered the black leather backpack she often carried with her as a handbag. Parry, not knowing what else to do, rose also, and together, Anna walking just a pace or two ahead, they left the Touching Bass and headed across the Alto Rialto in the direction of one of its quartet of supporting hotels, the Da Capo.

Many of the sightseers and restaurant patrons on the concourse turned to watch Anna as she passed, some of them recognizing her, others (it goes without saying, mainly men) simply admiring her looks. She drew their gazes like a magnet draws iron filings, as heedless of them as they were attentive to her. Glances were directed at Parry, too, but few rested on him for long. Even if anyone recognized him, the beautiful woman with him was incomparably more interesting. Aesthetically, she was out of his league. That much was obvious to anyone who looked at them. But she was out of his league in another way, too. This he understood now. Within Anna there were complexities that were beyond his ability to fathom and perhaps beyond the power of their feelings for each other to surmount. The ambition that had driven her on since childhood, impelling her to take the course through life she had taken, was, it appeared, a source of perplexity and distress to her, and this was something he would be able neither to comprehend nor to alter. At the heart of her lay a whirling core of confusion that would always send him spinning centrifugally away whenever he came too close to it. For this reason, she would remain essentially unknowable to him. She would always be, in the least specific sense of the word, foreign.

Neither said anything to the other until they were traversing the short walkway that bridged the gap between concourse and hotel. Halfway across, Anna broke the uncomfortable silence.

'I suppose I can't not ask.' She tapped the area of her forehead where the bruise was on Parry's. 'This?'

Parry felt a blush threaten and fumbled out some excuse about not switching the light on in his bathroom last night and then stumbling in the dark and striking his head on the door jamb.

'Oh dear,' Anna said, and her mouth crinkled at one corner. It was the closest she had come to a smile since arriving at the restaurant, and though it was half-hearted and short-lived, Parry was inordinately glad to see it.

Then they were atop the Da Capo, and as they approached the staircase that led down to the lifts, both heard strains of a sinuous, eerie, lilting music, carried to them across the rooftop on the breeze. It was faint and enchanting, the sort of sound one might imagine fairy music to be.

Parry saw his opportunity. 'I think I'll stay up here a little longer,' he said, nodding in the direction of the music.

Anna looked relieved, as though, like him, she had not been relishing the prospect of the journey down, the two of them penned together in a lift car for over a minute. 'Yes, why not? It's a lovely day.'

'You take care,' Parry said.

'This isn't goodbye, you know, Jack. I don't know what it *is*, but it isn't goodbye.'

Parry nodded, yet to be convinced.

Anna was halfway down the stairs when, remembering something, she about-turned and came trotting back up.

'I nearly forgot.' She unslung the leather backpack, delved inside and took out a square of paper which she handed to Parry.

It was a flyer, and it consisted of a blank sleeve, inside which was a circle of card printed to resemble a seven-inch vinyl single, complete with textured grooves. On one side of the central label, around the hole stamped in the middle, were the words:

The Trad Music Revue!
New Venice Residency

The other side of the label bore a list of dates, times and venues for all of the performances of Guthrie Reich's bands in New Venice.

'And what do I want this for?' Parry asked, eyeing the flyer as he would have a forged banknote.

'I don't know. I thought perhaps you might want to go to one of Guthrie's concerts. To show him there aren't any hard feelings.'

'And if I don't?'

'This isn't a test, Jack. It's a chance to patch things up if you want to, that's all. It might surprise you to learn that, in spite of everything, Guthrie doesn't hold a grudge against you. In fact, after you stormed off last night, his first words were, "That guy has spunk." '

'As a compliment it loses something in the translation.' Parry reinserted the 'single' into its sleeve, then folded the flyer in half and slid it into his inside jacket pocket. 'Well, I'll think about it.'

'How kind of you.'

'Don't mention it.'

Anna, having furrowed her brow at him for a moment, turned and made her way back down the staircase. At the bottom, she went left and was lost from view.

Moments later, Parry was on the other side of the rooftop.

The Da Capo's famous wind garden consisted of several dozen crystech 'instruments', weird and outlandish sculptures of every shape and size – tall and short, slender and squat, solid and hollow, vaned and tubular, squared and curvilinear, geometric and quasi-organic, some resembling worms, others like elaborately spined and finned deep-sea fish, others reminiscent of a child's construction blocks, others vaguely harp-shaped, others akin to nothing else on Earth. Each was of a different hue, so that together they formed a sparkling, sun-catching assemblage of ruby and emerald and sapphire and topaz and citrine and amber and aquamarine and more. And around them, into them, through them, over them and under them, the wind blew, its irregular pulses and ebbs eliciting strange hums and keening hoots and abstract tinkles and undulating whistles and flittering trills and vibrant, shivery drones. The notes were of various pitches and keys that shifted according to the intensity of the wind, so that sometimes they clashed discordantly and sometimes they merged together into a muddy, meaningless blare, but sometimes, just occasionally, through some adventitious gust, some quirk of the breath of the breeze, they massed into a single, brilliant, shimmering chord that swelled to a majestic crescendo, as though drawing strength from its own sonority, resounding like the trumpets of heaven, thrilling to the soul.

There were several humans other than Parry here, sitting or strolling, enjoying the random anemogenic performance. There were also, as Parry had hoped there would be, Foreigners, two of them stalking about, each tracing its own path among the instruments.

Taking up a position at a corner of the garden, he watched the two golden giants wander. Every wail and whine of the instruments caused them to quiver, but it was the moments when the wind inspired a fortuitous euphony that really set them going. A tremor-racked ecstasy overcame them for as long as the chord endured, their shudders subsiding as it faded.

On any other day, Parry would have found observing the Foreigners consoling; he would have derived a vicarious delight from their pleasure. Today he quickly discovered that this usually reliable source of consolation was denied him. Watching the golden giants, he felt nothing. No emotion was stirred. Whatever it was in him that responded to Foreigners, like a string resonating in sympathy to the plucking of another identically tuned string, was, at present, absent.

He told himself that all was not lost. He told himself that Anna had not completely dashed his hopes.

He would almost have believed this, too, were it not for the dull, sick ache in his belly – an ache that had nothing to do with hunger – and the hot, damnable pricking in his eyes.

INTERLUDE

One Month Ago . . .

His apartment's almost empty. You've seen jail cells with more furniture. There's some kind of Zen thing going on here, you think. Contemplative space. What a loser.

The guy is as anal as his surroundings. So anal, in fact, it's a wonder he can ever stand up after he's sat down. He comes across like a bit of a faggot, too. Maybe is a faggot.

But you pour on the charm anyway. Pour it on all the more intently because you think he might've taken a fancy to you. You're not above using your looks in this way. You know what you've got. You've seen what it can get you, this gilded exterior of yours. You can make anyone like you if you want to. Admire you. Love you. But no one's ever allowed past the outside. No one ever gets to see how you are within.

'Listen,' you say, 'I know you still have your doubts. It's asking a lot of you. I understand that. But think about what you stand to gain. As someone once told me not so long ago, you don't get reward without risk, or words to that effect.'

'But if I'm caught . . .'

'You won't be. Trust me. You won't be doing anything that'll make people suspicious. You'll just be going about your business as usual. If you keep your head, no one'll be any the wiser.'

'I'm not a good liar.'

'You don't need to be. You only need to be a good actor. You only need to be able to play yourself. And anyone can do that. We do it all the time, don't we? Playing the person we want everyone to think we are. It'll be a piece of cake.'

'It sounds easy.'

'It is easy! This day and age, everyone's prepared to take you for what you are. People aren't geared to look for cheating and duplicity any more. They see what they see and they're content to leave it at that. Which makes life much simpler for those who are a bit smarter, who can play a cleverer game.'

'Why me? Why, of all the people you could have chosen, did you choose me?'

Here, you lay on the doe-eyes. You lean forward. Your voice is all sincerity.

'Because I wanted someone my age. I wanted someone who has ambitions but maybe hasn't gone the right way about starting to realize them. I wanted someone eager, hungry for more from life.'

And you wanted someone who has yet to make his mark in this city and therefore knows he has less to lose. Someone young and impressionable. You've had access to news files and official documents. It wasn't hard to zero in on a suitable candidate.

'You realize how much I'm trusting you here,' you add. 'Already I've put this much faith in you. I wouldn't have done that if I didn't believe there was some kind of bond between us. I feel we share similar aspirations, similar goals. From the moment I first got in touch with you, I felt here was a person I had a lot in common with. Someone who understood me as I understood him. Maybe you got that impression also?'

He bobs his head a little, looking shy. The hook's well and truly embedded. Now to reel him in.

'You promise I can't get caught?'

'Hey, I guarantee it. You're smart, you're quick-witted, unlike the rest of the dopes you work with. You'll run rings around them.'

'And once it's over?'

'You can stay, you can leave – it's up to you. Since no one'll know you were involved, no one'll care what you do afterwards. The money's in blind trusts. Live on it unobtrusively, spend it carefully, and there's no reason anybody'll ever link you to this.'

'Blind trusts,' he murmurs. He looks at you. Gazes hopefully. Longingly.

You gaze back.

Blind trust.

FOURTH MOVEMENT

31 ANTICIPATION

Parry awoke in the still small hours of Sunday morning and knew, with an awful visceral certainty, that bad news was on the way.

Lying on his back, sprawled diagonally across the bed with the top sheet corkscrewed around his torso, a sure sign of a restless night, he waited for the sense of foreboding to subside. Around him he could hear a faint hum and whisper and hiss within the walls, the noise of the building's circulatory and nervous systems carrying on their ceaseless surreptitious activity. Snug-fitting window blinds shut out all external light, so that he was surrounded by a darkness that was seamless and absolute. The bedroom wombed and cocooned him, and he told himself that there was nothing to worry about. He must have had a bad dream, that was all – a nightmare that had evaporated at the moment of waking, leaving no memory of itself, just a residue of anxiety behind.

He told himself this, but as the minutes passed the sense of foreboding would not go away. He felt it as a weight beneath his solar plexus. As an itch in his fingers. As a dry ache at the back of his throat.

In the end, there was nothing else for it. He knew he was not going to go back to sleep. Sighing, he groped for the bedside-lamp switch.

After putting on a bathrobe and emptying his bladder, he went to the kitchen and switched the kettle on. The clock on the electric stove read a quarter to five. He stood there, blearily eyeing the line of empty beer bottles that were waiting by the sink to be washed and sent down the recycling chute, like a row of condemned prisoners lined up for execution. It had been a bit of a session last night. He had visited Britten's for Britons on the way back from the Da Capo, bought a brace of four-packs of stout, and spent the rest of the afternoon and evening working his way through them while at the same time spinning aimlessly through the almost unending range of TV channels and e-ther feeds. By about six he had become physically numb. By eight he had become mentally numb as well.

He could barely recall undressing and getting into bed. Surprisingly, he did not feel too hung-over now. Perhaps it was too early for that. Possibly he was still drunk. The main thing was that thanks to the beer he had been able to stop thinking about Anna for a while, and about the *shinjus*; he had been able to blank these painful preoccupations from his mind and be, if only temporarily, just a simple, untroubled man once more.

The kettle bubbled to the boil and Parry, every action stupor-slow, warmed the teapot, scooped in tea leaves, poured in steaming water, grabbed a mug and a carton of milk, placed them with the pot on a small woven-rush tray, and carried the tray into the living room. As he slid open the balcony windows one-handed, tendrils of chilly air seeped in, snaking around his bare calves, spurring his leg hairs to rise like quills. He took the tray out on to the balcony and laid it down on the small plastic table there, then pulled up a chair and, drawing the bathrobe's lapels tight together under his chin, sat.

All around him the city lay silent and dreaming, motionless in the pre-dawn dark, static beneath the icy spindle of the fading stars. There were lights on outside front doors and in the heads of lamps along the canal and bridges, their glows blurry, faintly hazed. The surface of the canal itself had a perfect, gleaming smoothness, as though its water were black glass, solid enough to walk on. Palms with their firework bursts of frond stood frozen in the breezeless air. Paused between the hurly-burly of late-night escapades and the gummy-eyed stirrings of a new day, poised as though mesmerized and ready to come round on command, New Venice waited. Refreshed and cleansed by the night, it waited like a shriven penitent dressed all in white. Innocent again, for now.

The only thing moving in the stillness was the steam from the teapot spout, which rose hypnotically in a twisting, self-wrapping wisp that dissipated into invisibility some twenty centimetres above its point of origin. And gazing at it, Parry found his thoughts drifting inexorably back to another sleepless early morning.

Although the Debut had been almost exactly a third of his lifespan ago, he remembered it more vividly than he did any other event in his past, with the possible exception of the Hunger Riots. He imagined the same must be true of every human being who had been old enough at the time to be aware of what was going on. He could recall the entire experience in immaculate detail, starting with being roused by a neighbour, one of the gay marrieds who owned the flat below his (a couple of night owls, they were almost always out clubbing after dark and seldom got to bed before three a.m.). He remembered the gritty prickle in his eyes and the woken-too-soon heaviness in his head as he was wrenched from sleep by a hammering on the main door to his flat and a male voice calling out, 'Mr Parry! Mr Parry! Turn on your TV! Now!'

His first thought, as he groaned out of bed, was that it had finally happened: one of the world's many nuclear powers had finally gone and done it. That was the only reason he could think of why a neighbour would wake him at – Christ! – half-past three and tell him to watch television. So who had dropped the Bomb on whom, he wondered as he stumbled grimly out of the bedroom, struggling into the first item of clothing that came to hand, a pair of sweatpants. Korea on Japan? Pakistan on India? Israel on Iraq? Brazil on Mexico? Burma on Thailand? Russia on one of the satellite republics with which it was constantly skirmishing? Those were chaotic days, before the Debut. As he had told Cecilia, it was hard not to believe that an End was on its way.

In the living room he had fumbled with the On button on the television remote control, expecting that no matter which channel the TV happened to be tuned to, it would be transmitting fuzzy, shuddering images of devastation: firestorms, charred bodies, shattered buildings, roads crammed with frantic evacuees, the terrible grey snow of fallout, perhaps even (if someone had had a camera to hand and the presence of mind to use it) a shot of a distant mushroom cloud on the horizon, like a gigantic fist clenched against the sky. What now? he remembered thinking as the wallscreen ignited into life. What will become of us now? The genie is out of the bottle. If one country has pressed the button, others won't think twice about doing so. This is the first step down the long, slippery slope.

But of course what appeared on the TV screen was not images of humankind's final, irredeemable descent into Hell. What appeared was almost diametrically the opposite.

The reports were coming in from Sydney and Guadalcanal, where it was mid-afternoon, and from Lhasa and Rangoon, where it was mid-morning, and from Manila and Beijing, where it was midday. They were coming in from Hawaii and Tahiti, where dusk was gathering in the west, and from Aden and Johannesburg, where rosy-fingered dawn was creeping in from the east. They were coming in from Seattle and Vancouver, where it was late evening, and from Washington and Lima, where it was close to midnight. They were coming in from the Canaries and the Azores, where it was just a little earlier than London, and from Rome, Madrid and Tel Aviv, where it was just a little later, and from London itself, too. All across the planet, British foreign correspondents and local English-speaking reporters were relaying the news, those with handheld microphones gripping them tightly, and all of them talking in tingling, incredulous tones.

'It appears as if it could be some kind of publicity stunt . . .'

'Nobody is exactly sure what time the first one was sighted . . .'

'All I can say is, it's approximately two-and-a-half metres in height, and . . .'

'And as you can see, it's just wandering around, looking around. I say "it", but it could be "he", it could be "she" . . .'

'So far there's been no word from the White House or from the United Nations, where the ten-nation Security Council has just convened an emergency session . . .'

'Incredible, absolutely incredible . . .'

'People are scared to approach them, but as far as I can see, they are not hostile. I repeat, so far these creatures, these *beings*, have not acted in any way whatsoever that could be perceived as hostile . . .'

'The feeling among people I've been talking to here is that this must be a practical joke of some sort, but if so, no one has any idea who might be responsible, and I think if you look at the images we're sending you, you'll be able to see quite clearly that this cannot be a joke, this has to be something else altogether . . .'

It all unfolded at a strangely leisurely pace, like the telling of some old familiar legend. Indeed, there were times when Parry felt as though what he was witnessing *was* something which had happened years ago; that the entire broadcast was a lavish, documentary-style recreation of some famous historical event. This sense of *déjà vu* came and went throughout the morning, and he wondered if it had anything to do with the fact that numerous science-fiction films had dramatized various versions of this scenario, the arrival on Earth of beings from beyond, so that the scenes on television – the satellite-bounced reportage, the faces of the studio presenters as they strove to keep their expressions impassive and unperplexed, the politicians with their mantra of no-comment-at-this-time, the shots of the non-terrestrials themselves – echoed images that were ingrained in the collective unconscious.

Perhaps humankind had rehearsed this fable so often in its celluloid imagination that, now that the fable had actually become fact, everyone involved seemed to be playing a part, spouting lines of dialogue from a script, copying gestures and expressions that had been perfected by actors. Life, in other words, imitating art, and faithfully, but with little spontaneity.

That was not to say it was not exciting. It was. It was thrilling to see the footage of these 'golden giants', as one commentator dubbed them, swishing here and there in a world-spanning variety of locations, and to hear the quiver in the reporters' voices (that quiver, more than anything else, confirmed that what was going on was way out of the ordinary). It was thrilling, but alarming, too, for of course no one had any idea what the creatures wanted, what they were here for. They looked peaceable enough, but again, science-fiction films had warned of the possibility that a race of non-terrestrials might have sinister designs on good old Planet Earth. There had been no death-rays as yet, no demands to be taken to Earth's leaders, no attempt to grab hold of bystanders and start snacking on their brains, but that did not necessarily mean the tall golden visitors' intentions were honourable. These first arrivals could be merely a scouting party, here to reconnoitre the terrain while the invasion fleet loitered somewhere beyond Earth's atmosphere, cloaked against detection, ready to swoop once the signal was given.

And yet somehow it was obvious that these humanoid beings were not inimical, nor likely to be so. With their slightly stooped posture and their laboured way of walking, they did not have the bearing of fearsome, anthropophagous conquerors from the stars. On the contrary, there was a distinct gentility about them. Everywhere they went, they looked around them with donnish bemusement, as though everything they saw was new and different and ever so fascinating. When they gathered together in those gaggles of two or three, they really looked as though they were conferring, comparing notes, silently recommending one another to go in a certain direction to view a certain sight. Parry was not the only person to draw the conclusion, on the strength of the television footage alone, that the creatures' reason for coming here was nothing more insidious than curiosity. They were checking the place out. They were, quite simply, tourists.

Few people went to work that day. Some stayed at home because they feared the end of the world was nigh, but most stayed at home simply so that they could continue watching television. Parry, while as keen as anyone to keep abreast of the situation, felt that keenness outweighed by a sense of duty. He knew he really *ought* to show his face at the station, and so around seven-thirty, the usual time, he reluctantly got dressed in his customary sports-jacket-and-trousers ensemble and left his flat, walking out into an autumn morning that was brisk and bright but with just enough of a chill snap in the air to augur yet another long, harsh winter.

He had never, not even on Christmas Day, seen a London so quiet or so still. It was as though some apocalypse *had* taken place after all. The streets were empty apart from the occasional taxi or bus, whose engines, blatting echoingly between the buildings, sounded inordinately loud in the hush. The urban birdsong, by contrast, was muted, as though its participants were so stunned by the lack of competition from traffic that the most they could muster was the odd timid peep or warble. Parry came across several dogs trotting around untended, their owners presumably having let them out for a walk and neglected to let them back in again, and he passed a front garden where a pair of children, too young to understand the full import of what was going on, were bouncing solemnly up and down on a wooden seesaw. Whenever he did encounter another adult pedestrian, it was either a tramp too crazed or booze-blitzed to register that there was something unusual about the city today, or else someone like him, trudging unwillingly to work. In the latter instance he and the other commuter might exchange a remark as their paths crossed, something to the effect that there was no rest for the wicked, or they might simply share a rueful look. Either way, in the phlegmatic British manner, neither made reference to the phenom-enal events that were taking place, except obliquely, by indicating the fact that, for *some* people at least, life had to carry on as normal, no matter what.

On average the walk from his flat to the station, door to door, took Parry half an hour. That morning, with few other pedestrians to circumambulate and no traffic to wait for at junctions, he managed the journey in two-thirds of the time.

Only a handful of the day shift had bothered to make it in, and most of them were congregated, along with some remnants of the night shift, around the wallscreen in the recreation lounge. Parry had had an idea that it might be, to say the least, a slow day, but he quickly discovered that there was in fact nothing at all to do. No calls were coming in, other than from citizens who assumed that the police, being authority figures, must have some explanation for the golden giants. There were no domestic emergencies occurring or crimes beings committed anywhere. And so Parry, having helped himself to a cup of tea from the vending machine, sat down with his colleagues to watch the continuing news broadcasts, which had displaced all other programming.

Everyone in the recreation lounge had a tale to tell about what they had been doing when they had first heard about the creatures, and there was, quite properly, plenty of speculation as to what the beings were and what they were after, but for the most part Parry and his colleagues stayed silent and let the television do the talking. Anxiety was evident on one or two faces, but by and large Parry thought that everyone else in the room was feeling what he was feeling. It was too embryonic an emotion to be given a name, at least not yet, but if allowed to grow and develop unhindered, it might just conceivably be called hope.

Around eleven, the prime minister stepped out into Downing Street to deliver a statement. He said nothing that the US president and the Russian premier and the president of the EU and China's first lady and the secretary-general of the UN and even the mayor of London had not already said, namely that the situation was being monitored closely and that so far there was no apparent cause for concern. He added that the country's armed forces were on emergency standby, ready to respond if 'developments should prove disadvantageous to national security', and concluded by saying that he intended to remain in touch with other world leaders and would take no action precipitately and without the full and unified consent of the international community.

This was greeted with scorn by the assembled company.

'Typical,' sneered a DI, rolling his eyes. 'It was the same when the crops went. "Everyone says there's nothing to worry about, so there's nothing to worry about." That wanker doesn't have an idea of his own in his head. He probably wouldn't know he needed to take a shit if his advisers didn't remind him.'

'Well, you've got to admit he's better than the last one, isn't he?' said a constable. '*He* didn't listen to anybody. Everyone kept telling him we needed sea defences and what happened? 'Bye-bye, East Anglia!'

It was this same constable who, minutes later, proposed a trip out in a squad car to look for one of the creatures. Two of the curious (in both senses of the word) beings had been sighted in Hyde Park and another one at Kew Gardens. He asked if anybody wanted to come along with him. Parry was surprised to find that his was the only hand raised. Everyone else appeared content to experience the event through the medium of television rather than at first hand. Perhaps it seemed more real to them that way.

Driving along the South Circular, Parry and the constable passed several groups of citizens who had had the same idea and were out and about on creature-seeking expeditions. The mood of the groups was boisterous, like that of people on a scavenger hunt or a pub-crawl. Near Vauxhall Bridge they encountered one lot who seemed to be less rowdy and more purposeful than the rest, and Parry observed that one of them was carrying a portable radio. He tuned the squad car's shortwave to several different news stations till he found one which was broadcasting a live commentary phoned in by a man who was tracking one of the golden giants through Battersea Park. The constable hit the accelerator and moments later he and Parry were hurtling past the Dogs' Home and pulling up in front of the gates at the park's south-eastern corner.

They found the creature and a handful of onlookers – about a dozen of them all told, including the man with the phone – at the Buddhist shrine that stood halfway along the park's northern perimeter, directly next to the Thames. The creature was circling slowly around the monument, seemingly unperturbed by, or unaware of, the attention it was drawing. The constable, who was the officious type, the type who thought a uniform gave you a licence to throw your weight about, ordered the onlookers to stand back and not crowd the creature – unnecessary advice, since everyone was keeping a good, wary distance from it anyway. Parry, meanwhile, separated himself not just from his fellow policeman but from his fellow humans, edging sideways until he was in a position where the only animate object in his line of vision was the creature.

His first direct, unimpeded, unmediated view of a Foreigner . . .

Seeing: the brightness of the day, the whiteness of the shrine, the rippling shimmer of the creature's garments.

Hearing: the nervous shufflings and murmurings of the onlookers, and the man with the cellphone still quietly, urgently narrating.

Feeling: the cool, light wind on his face and a heart-quickened trickle of sweat running from one armpit down the side of his ribs.

Tasting: a nervous, electric tang on his tongue, mingled with the lingering savour of his recent cup of tea.

Smelling: the grey leaden odour of the brimful river and the simmering, carbonized pungency of city air.

Whenever he recalled that moment, it was as a combination of all these five impressions, his senses working like the instruments in a quintet, eyes and ears carrying the melody, skin and tongue adding harmonic layers, nose providing the underpinning bass tones. It was as though the memory was imprinted not just in his brain cells but in his entire physical structure. He would never – *could* never – forget it. Nor would he ever forget the emotion evoked in him by the creature, the spiritual product of the pan-sensory concert. It was a feeling quite without precedent in his life, a feeling of being suffused with utter, unvanquishable gladness.

Everything is going to be all right.

The creature, its appearance, its behaviour.

This I understand. Everything is going to be all right.

And he knew that this was a moment he would look back on as pivotal in his life. Even as he was marvelling at the Foreigner, some small part of him was telling him that he was never going to be the same again. A new phase was beginning for him, right here, right now. He could sense his past detaching itself, pulling away like a train from a station. The worst of him was aboard that train. All the stupid little jealousies and desires, the ambitions and the frustrations, the vices, the vexations, all the petty, lazy traits that had accreted to his character over the years like mud on a tractor tyre, lumbering him, encumbering him – he was shedding them. From here on (and this was not a vow, simply a statement of fact) he was going to be a different man. A better man. In this creature in front of him, this meandering, inexplicable golden-robed entity, he sensed transformation. He sensed metamorphosis. He sensed himself, not as he was, but as he could be.

And then the Foreigner disappeared. Just like that. It did not precisely vanish; rather, Parry happened to take eyes off it for a moment and it just sort of slipped away, unobtrusively. One moment it was there, and then it was no longer there and seemed to have been absent for quite some while. When Parry asked members of the crowd if any of them had seen what had happened to it, they all said the same. They were not aware of it leaving, only aware that abruptly, without their noticing, it had left.

And this, it would turn out, was how Foreigners always came and went – silently, unobtrusively, without anyone noticing.

When you considered the Debut, as Parry was doing now, you could not help but find it remarkable that events passed off so peacefully that day. Given the general volatility of the world at the time, things could have gone horribly wrong. The military in one of the more fractious and unstable regions of the globe could have launched pre-emptive commando strikes against the golden giants. Panicking, paranoid civilians could have turned vigilante and done the same. Anywhere, it was possible that uncertainty could have bred fear and fear bred violence against the visitors, and then doubtless the Foreigners would have turned tail and fled, departing *en masse* as suddenly and mysteriously as they had arrived, having decided on the evidence of the indigenous population's initial response to their arrival that this planet was too backward and barbaric to warrant further visitation. For a while, without realizing it, humankind underwent a kind of test. The choice was hostility or hospitality. And the Foreigners' beauty and apparent benignity notwithstanding, the fact that the people of Earth chose hospitality was something to be lauded. Indeed, for a species with a history of almost invariably taking the wrong path instead of the right, to have displayed such wisdom and self-restraint was little short of miraculous. Somehow, when it really counted, humankind found in itself the collective will to behave responsibly. And somehow, in that crucial hour, it earned the right to continue and survive and prosper.

All this would become apparent in retrospect. But during the Foreigners' first hours on the planet, most people were conscious of just two things: that the question of whether humankind was alone in the universe had been answered with a thunderous, resounding *NO*, and that as a result, whatever the immediate future might hold, nothing would ever be as it was before.

For some, no other explanation than this would be necessary to account for the spate of improvements that followed, once the shock of the Foreigners' arrival had died down. Now that humankind knew for sure that it formed part of an immeasurably bigger picture, it simply could not continue with its internecine struggles and its plunder and despoliation of its home planet. And so, all at once, warring factions began suing for peace. Treaties were signed, truces declared, statutes proposed and enacted. International debts were cancelled. Technologies were shared by the richer countries with the poorer. The trade in arms declined, the trade in alms boomed. A great constructive effort was made to *change*.

Parry himself was of the opinion that the provision of proof that humankind was just one race among many was indeed part of the reason for the worldwide outbreak of common sense, but he was also of the opinion that the principal reason was the Foreigners themselves. In the presence of such sublime creatures, anything less than the noblest behaviour seemed a crime.

It was a tenet he adhered to firmly, and came across nothing to contradict, in the ensuing months. When it was decreed that the term which was most commonly used when referring to the creatures, Foreigners, was to become their official nomenclature, he considered this to be an appropriately dignified and inoffensive choice. When it became apparent that Foreigners were chiefly attracted to ocean shores and beautiful architecture and warm climates, he thought this fitting and heartening, since the humans they met in those environments would be at their happiest and most congenial. When the Japanese commenced construction of a city designed specifically to appeal to and accommodate golden giants, and several other nations announced their intention to follow suit, Parry greeted the news with approval because it seemed a considerate, altruistic gesture. And when the UN decided that these new resort-cities needed some kind of nominal police force, Parry was among the first to submit an application to join.

He had never once regretted the decision.

Until, perhaps, now.

Now, when he was sitting on his balcony in the pre-dawn chill, filled with the unnerving certainty of imminent misfortune.

And what could that misfortune be? What else but that the already messy and convoluted *shinju* investigation was about to become even messier and more convoluted? His subconscious had noted the three-day interval between the first two *shinjus*, had extrapolated from this fact that a third, if it was going to occur, would have occurred last night and be discovered today, and had imparted this information to him in the form of a dream he could not remember and the lingering sense of impending disaster that he was still feeling.

And if there *was* a third *shinju*, and it came exactly the same number of days after the second as the second had after the first, *then* what?

Then he would have little choice but to abandon his belief (his hope?) that the deaths and losses were not double murders. Such regularity of timing would be stretching coincidence too far. He would have to accept the unpalatable truth that there were killers on the loose in New Venice and that the killers were in all likelihood Triple-Xers.

In one way that would make his life easier. In another way it would make it more complicated. It would mean he would at last know for sure in which direction to steer the investigation, but it would also mean he was faced with the task of finding two or perhaps three individuals in a city with a population of several tens of thousands – an ever-changing roster of inhabitants who flitted in and out of town, leaving little trace of their comings and goings beyond a name at Customs. The proverbial needle in a haystack.

The flow of steam from the teapot spout had diminished to a faint, dispirited thread. Parry wanted to reach out and pour himself a cuppa, but found that he could not rouse himself to move. Despite the chilliness of the air and the hardness of the chair, he was feeling oddly languid and comfortable.

He closed his eyes and opened them, and the sky had lightened. He closed and opened them again, and the sun was just clearing the rooftops. He wanted to stand up and go indoors, but his eyelids descended again, and then suddenly he was warm and there were boats on the canal and people out on their balconies and the sun was well above the rooftops and beaming brightly.

Morning. Day.

He was still conscious of the sense of foreboding, but it had diminished considerably. What had seemed intense and portentous during the cold and dark and stillness of the small hours now seemed, in the warmth and brightness and bustle of full daylight, foolish and false. If he had had a bad dream, then that was all it was – a bad dream.

He had just about managed to convince himself of this when the telephone rang.

His joints were stiff from sleeping outdoors, sitting upright. He creaked and limped and winced across the living room. He slumped at his desk and picked up the receiver.

It was Avni.
It was the bad news he had been expecting.
It was worse than he had been expecting.

32 TREBLE

Forty minutes later, a far-from-happy Parry was being admitted by a far-from-unhappy van Wyk into Room 707 of the Hannon Regency in New Venice's North-West district.

Had he been in a more objective frame of mind, Parry might have discerned a certain irony to the situation, namely that it was almost a direct inversion of the situation at the Amadeus six days ago. Then, it had been he presiding calmly over the scene of a *shinju*, with van Wyk intruding intemperately into the room and drawing startled looks from Dr Erraji and a pair of mainland criminalists as they unpacked their equipment and prepared to get down to work. Now the roles were reversed and van Wyk was the calm presider, Parry the intemperate, criminalist-startling intruder.

Irony, though, is usually lost on those whom it disfavours, and almost always lost on someone whose mind is seething with emotions such as indignation or anxiety.

In Parry's case, indignation *and* anxiety.

No sooner had van Wyk opened the door to his knock than Parry strode into the room, ready to demand that control of the scene be relinquished to him immediately. Unfortunately, in his forthright haste he neglected to prepare himself for the room's Foreign-scale proportions. All at once the world loomed large around him, and he faltered and staggered and had to reach out for the nearest wall (closer to hand than it appeared) in order to anchor himself. As van Wyk leaned behind him to shut the door, Parry swayed. His head swam. He felt about a metre tall.

As though from far away he heard van Wyk saying, 'Parry, you look pale.' There was a sweet-sounding, almost paternal note of concern in his voice. 'Perhaps you'd better sit down.'

Parry waved the suggestion away. Squeezing his eyes shut, he imagined an even larger room, with a chest of drawers higher than his head and chairs that had to be climbed into and a bed like something out of a fairy tale, fit for several kings at once.

(The Foreigners, he thought fleetingly, make children of us all.)

Once he had the image of the larger room firmly established in his mind, he reopened his eyes, and clear-headedness was restored, along with awareness of his own correct proportions.

He peered at Erraji, then the criminalists, then van Wyk, all of whom were looking solicitous, all but one of them genuinely so. He knew he had just fumbled his best and perhaps only chance for gaining the upper hand. Everything about the situation here was to van Wyk's advantage, and he had hoped that by storming in and blustering he might be able to catch the Afrikaner off-guard and outmanoeuvre him, and now that hope, thanks to one moment of carelessness, was gone.

'Where are they?' he asked. The question was a stalling tactic. He needed time to think, time to come up with a fresh way of handling van Wyk.

Van Wyk gestured towards the bathroom door. 'In there. It's a nasty sight.'

'A Siren?'

'A Siren and a Foreigner.'

'How were they discovered?'

'Same as at the Amadeus: a wake-up call wasn't answered. And before you say any more, Parry – I know. I know. Another *shinju*. And you think that it should be yours to handle. But let us consider one simple, salient fact. This is the Hannon Regency. The Hannon is in the North-West district.' Van Wyk folded his arms. To the tips of his brush-stiff flaxen hair, he was the picture of gloating triumph. 'My wedge, Parry. *My* wedge.'

'But the commissioner—'

'I've already discussed it with her. She feels as I do. It's time another captain took on the investigation. And happenstance has decreed that that captain should be me.' He leaned closer to Parry. 'And a good thing too, because I am going to get results, Parry. Believe you me, I am.'

Parry struggled against a mounting, engulfing sense of impotence. He must be able to salvage something from this. He did not know what direction van Wyk was going to take with the investigation, but whatever it was, he knew it was going to be drastic and unsubtle. He recalled van Wyk's suggestion for an alternative method of resolving the problem at Koh Farang: *a quick, hard crackdown on the perpetrators would have sorted everything out in no time.*

He took a deep intake of breath, drawing on every gram of self-control he possessed, every last reserve of reserve. 'All right. As you say, happenstance has brought you in on the investigation. Can I ask what you propose to do?'

'You can ask. I don't see why I have to tell you.'

'Because the previous two *shinjus* were in my district. And because I've been on the case for nearly a week.'

'Without any notable success.'

'Never the less, in that time I have gained some insight into how local residents and Sirens feel about what's going on.'

'You think you're the only one who's been getting feedback from the public? So has everyone who wears this badge!'

'But I'm still the FPP officer everyone associates with the investigation.'

'The FPP officer everyone associates with an inability to solve it.'

'Van Wyk, just tell me what you're going to do. Please.'

'Oh well, since you said the magic word . . .' Van Wyk turned to Erraji, who, along with the criminalists, had been doing his best to pretend not to be listening. 'Doctor? Would it be all right for me to show my colleague the remains?'

Erraji considered, then nodded. 'Please avoid touching anything if you can.'

'Thank you. We'll be careful. Parry? Over here.'

Van Wyk led Parry across to the bathroom door, which he opened with a small flourish.

The bathroom had no windows. Light from the main room illuminated its interior dimly. Parry, at van Wyk's invitation, stepped forward into the doorway. The reek of blood, thick and sickly, filled his nostrils. He saw two haphazard heaps of clothing on the floor, one of them glinting. There was something occupying the bath, something bulky and pallid and shapeless and streaked with black. There were marks on the wall above it – a pattern of smears, black also.

Van Wyk ran his hand over the light-switch sensor. Lights flickered on. Black became vermilion.

The two heaps of clothing were a pile of human garments and the remains of a Foreigner. The thing in the bath was a naked man. Although the bath was Foreign-scale, the man was so grossly, grotesquely overweight that it looked the appropriate size for him. He was lying on his back, his head wedged against the mixer tap, his chin thrust down into a half-dozen doughy rolls of neck fat. His eyes were open, their irises misted, one upper eyelid drooping.

There was blood all over him. Blood marbled his bulbous belly and his lumpen legs and his squashed, flabby pectorals. Blood strung his body hairs in tiny coagulated blobs. Blood seamed the folds in his lily-livid flesh. Blood had collected in a pool at his crotch, making a neat island of his genitals. It was blood which had been released from within him via a ragged slash in each wrist – wounds gouged with the pocketknife that was now clasped loosely in the fingers of his right hand. And there was so much of it! So much blood that it seemed scarcely feasible a single corpse, even one as corpulent as this one, could once have contained it all. So much blood that it was as if the dead man had been attempting to wash himself in his own lifestuff rather than water.

And on the wall tiles above this ghastly sight, this veritable bloodbath, Parry could see that the pattern of smears was in fact a sentence – words formed in sloppy, multi-fingered strokes of blood.

In a limp, nerveless voice he read the words aloud, as though by speaking them he might deprive them of some of their unwelcome and uncompromising significance:

'Don't Let This World Become The New World.'

A slogan.

A well-known slogan.

And beneath it there were three crosses in a row, like some sinister love-token:

$$X \; X \; X$$

'So you see, Parry?' said van Wyk. 'There's no question any more, is there? No doubt about what's happening. Triple-X. They did this. How I'm not sure. My guess is the autopsy will show that they drugged him, then dumped him in the bath and opened his wrists for him. The main thing is, it's clear that the perpetrators *are* Triple-X and they've been waiting for us to come after them. They *want* us to come after them. They've got fed up with us wallowing around without a clue. They've put their signature to their handiwork because they want credit for these killings. This is a direct challenge from them and I've accepted it.'

'But how?' was all Parry could think of to say. 'How do you plan on finding them?'

'How else? The local Xenophobes have *got* to know who they are and where they are. Kyagambiddwa did, didn't he?'

'But Kyagambiddwa volunteered the information. You can't just go waltzing into Free World House and force the Xenophobes to tell you where the Triple-Xers are.'

'Can't I?'

'It's unConstitutional.'

'Measure Nine, Parry.'

'But the public good—'

'– *is* threatened, as far as I'm concerned. Law is about interpretation, after all, and I interpret the presence of a Triple-X cell in our city – a *murderous* Triple-X cell – as a danger to everyone here.'

'I really can't stand by and let you do this, van Wyk. I'm going to talk to the commissioner right away.'

'It wouldn't do you any good. Céleste has already sanctioned the arrests.'

'Then she can *un*sanction them.'

'Parry, don't you see?' Van Wyk shook his head pityingly. 'It's too late. Weren't you listening to me just now? I said I've accepted Triple-X's challenge. Accepted, past tense. Officers are already on their way to Free World House. In fact, I'd be surprised if MacLeod and his cronies aren't being shipped to HQ even as we speak.'

'Shipped to—? For God's sake, van Wyk! Do you know how much trouble this is going to cause?'

'I said I'd get results. I bet by lunchtime we'll have the names of these Triple-X maniacs and where they're hiding.'

'And if the Xenophobes don't know?'

'They know, Parry. Believe me, they know. And by the time I'm through questioning them, they'll be begging to tell me.'

33 CHAMBER

Floor Lower B, the basement of FPP HQ, consisted of a bunker-like corridor with a row of cubic chambers along one side, hollowed out from the building's crystech foundations. The walls, floors and ceilings were plastered and painted white, except the outer walls of the chambers. These were left unrendered and, being transparent, provided a source of light and a view, at least during daytime, although the view was of the depths of the Fourth Canal and the light was consequently filtered and dimmed by water. What you could see was entrancing anyway. Through a metre of clear crystech you could see fish swimming amid the jostling subaquatic shafts of sunlight. You could see the miniature tornadoes of bubbles that trailed the shadows of passing surface traffic, whip-whirling in the wake of propeller turbulence. If you looked upwards, you could even see the canal surface itself, a rippling, flexing membrane between worlds.

The chambers – no one called them cells – were not uncomfortably furnished, and their doors, in keeping with the rest of HQ, were without any form of retaining mechanism other than a spring-loaded catch. In theory, anyone escorted down to the basement was free to depart at any time. In practice, this seldom happened. The majority of people detained by the FPP knew that one of three fates awaited them: a trip to the airport, a trip to the mainland, or simply the extraction of a promise not to repeat your misdemeanour. Since none of these was too fearsome a prospect, there was nothing to be lost by staying put and availing yourself of the FPP's hospitality.

Here were sequestered the three Xenophobes – MacLeod, Greg and the Tibetan monk – who were permanent residents of Free World House. (The other two whom Parry had seen at Free World House, the Native American woman and the Mexican Indian, worked there but, it transpired, lived elsewhere.) When invited by van Wyk's officers, very politely, to return with them to HQ, the three men had complied demurely and without demur, as any law-abiding citizen would, and now each was ensconced in a separate chamber and showing neither any inclination to leave nor, unfortunately for van Wyk, any inclination to speak. Indeed, the Tibetan monk had taken himself off to a corner and was sitting there cross-legged, hands on knees, eyelids shut fast, sunk into a state of meditation so profound that you could have screamed in his ear and he would not have noticed. The Xenophobes had, it appeared, a prearranged policy on what to do when arrested by the FPP. Acquiescence up to a point; thereafter, mute defiance.

Van Wyk had found the defiance entertaining at first. He relished a challenge. By the time Parry joined him down on Floor Lower B, however, he had been questioning the Xenophobes for the best part of an hour without managing to extract so much as a syllable from any of them. He was, therefore, no longer in a particularly agreeable frame of mind.

During that hour Parry did two things. First, he phoned Johansen at home and asked him to come in to HQ. Johansen, bless his loyal socks, did not ask why he was wanted but simply said he would be there as soon as possible and hung up. Next Parry went up to see Quesnel to ask permission to continue to play a part in the *shinju* investigation.

The request surprised the commissioner. 'I wasn't aware you were *off* the investigation, Jack.'

'But I thought, you know, because van Wyk was at the Hannon . . .'

'Then you thought wrong. Yes, Ray is on the case now. He has to be. I can hardly hand you responsibility for an incident in his wedge, can I? But I never said anything about you not staying involved with the investigation as well. In fact, I said just the opposite to Ray when I gave him authority to round up the Xenophobes. I told him you and he would be working together from now on. Equal partners. I guess he didn't mention that to you, did he?'

'It . . . didn't come up in the conversation.'

'Damn it. Ray's a basically decent person, but ambition gets the better of him sometimes.'

'Sometimes, ma'am?' Parry said, with a certain – he hoped forgivable – rancour.

'OK, a lot of the time,' Quesnel conceded, 'but you shouldn't resent a guy for trying to get ahead.'

'Not unless he does it at someone else's expense. He lied to me so as to have some time alone with the Xenophobes.'

'He didn't lie, Jack.'

'He deliberately omitted to tell me something, knowing I'd assume he'd been handed sole charge of the investigation. It amounts to the same thing.'

'Maybe it does. In the long run it doesn't make much difference. Ray is how he is. Deal with it and move on.'

'Ma'am, forgive me for saying this, but why are you always so ready to defend him? You know as well as everyone else in this division that he's short-tempered and has a pretty cavalier attitude regarding the Constitution. I mean, here he is, invoking Measure Nine in order to justify hauling the Xenophobes in and he's no proof they're connected to Triple-X!'

Quesnel dropped her voice, becoming quietly, imperiously stern. 'Jack, Ray is a good officer, a good captain. He's forceful. He gains respect. If he's short-tempered, well ... I could name another captain who's been a bit deficient in the anger-management department recently. In fact, while we're on that subject, I hope you have a good explanation for what went on at the Fuentes place, night before last.'

'There's nothing I can say. I was out of line.'

'Goddamn right you were. And I'm only going to overlook what you did because I know how these *shinjus* are running you ragged and because I know that, if you want to hold on to your job, you won't be so stupid as to ever do anything like that again.'

'I understand, ma'am. Thank you.'

'But getting back to Ray. I may not always approve of his methods, but I trust him. I trust him like I trust you, although for different reasons. You I always know are going to do the decent thing. He I always know is going to do the correct thing – correct as in best but not necessarily most desirable.'

'Ma'am ...'

'Let me finish. Decent doesn't always work, Jack. A few days back you sent me a report saying the first *shinju* was a double suicide. You believed that. So did I. Maybe we wanted to believe it a little too much. I don't know. The upshot is we got skewered. And now we know for sure that this business is a Triple-X action, and it so happens they chose to stage this new atrocity in a hotel in the North-West, which means Ray has to be dealt in on the game and frankly I think that's no bad thing. I think you and he together, and I stress together, may be able to crack this. You're opposites; you complement each other. Ray has good gut instincts. You've a good heart. That makes for a good combination. So I want you, Jack – well, no, I'm ordering you: swallow your pride and suck up your resentment and work with him.'

And if I refuse to obey that order? Parry thought. But the spark of insubordination fizzled out swiftly. 'Of course, ma'am. Yes.'

'Ray may be wrong about the Xenophobes, but equally he may not. The link between them and Triple-X is historically strong – strong enough for there to be reasonable grounds for bringing them in. I have my misgivings, but I gave Ray the go-ahead, and that's my decision, my call. You will respect that.'

'Yes, ma'am.'

'And Jack.' Quesnel's eyes were blue lightning. 'You will never, ever query my judgement again. In anything. Is that understood?'

Understood and remembered and never to be forgotten. Parry left Quesnel's office feeling chastised and to a lesser degree chastened, and headed downstairs to wait for Johansen in the entrance atrium. It aggrieved him to have been sidelined on his own case, and he had that never-comforting sensation of events slipping out of his grasp. He felt buffeted about, as though he had spent the past week in a lifeboat on a stormy sea. Nothing was certain any more, it seemed. There was nothing he could count on.

Then Johansen arrived, and seeing the Norwegian – who had agreed to come without having to be asked twice, without wanting to know why – Parry felt his spirits lifting somewhat.

Down in the basement, the two of them made their way along the corridor to where van Wyk's day-shift sergeant, a Czech woman by the name of Fibich, was standing.

'Captain,' she said, offering them SALUTATION. 'Lieutenant.'

'Is Captain van Wyk in there?' Parry asked, pointing to the nearest door.

Fibich nodded.

Without knocking, Parry and Johansen went in.

Toroa MacLeod was sitting in a chair that was positioned to face the viewing wall. Van Wyk was standing beside him, twitchy and exasperated, his hands clasped tightly together behind his back as though each was restraining the other from lashing out.

'Parry,' van Wyk said, neither pleased nor surprised.

MacLeod turned his head to give Parry and Johansen a cursory glance. His eyes flicked up briefly to the bruise on Parry's forehead, which overnight had begun to spread and fade like a clot of smoke being dispersed by wind. His face showed no expression except that lent it by his tattoos. Whatever the arrangement of MacLeod's features, implicit aggression was ever-present in the tattoos' swirl and roil.

'And I see you've brought along your pet yeti for moral support,' van Wyk added.

'Let's keep it civil, shall we?' Parry said. 'So – what's the news?'

'Mr MacLeod here and his friends have been keeping shtum. Which, as I see it, can only mean they have something to keep shtum about.'

'Or that they know they're under no obligation to talk,' said Johansen. The 'pet yeti' crack had not gone down well with him.

'No legal obligation perhaps, Lieutenant,' van Wyk said tersely, 'but how about a *moral* obligation? These people know who's killing Sirens and Foreigners. Don't you, MacLeod?' MacLeod, who had resumed gazing out into the canal, did not respond. 'They know their names and where they're hiding. And as residents of this city and as human beings, they cannot in all conscience withhold that information from us. They have no right to.'

'Perhaps if *I* were to have a chat with Mr MacLeod?' Parry ventured. 'Alone? He and I have already established a certain . . . understanding.'

'No, Parry,' said van Wyk. 'No. You've had your shot. Had it and blown it. It's my turn now.'

'I feel I shouldn't have to remind you that the commissioner has stipulated that we work together and get on together. Or perhaps I *do* have to remind you.'

The barb found no purchase in van Wyk's thick hide. He merely shrugged. 'Then get on with me by leaving me to get on with this.'

A soft, low chuckling began, forestalling any comeback from Parry. MacLeod, the source of the sound, was shaking his head slowly like someone who has just heard a familiar but still amusing joke.

'Yes?' van Wyk snapped. 'Something you wish to share with us?'

The Xenophobe looked round, mirth and malice glittering in his black-pearl eyes. 'You lot. No wonder no one takes the FPP seriously. Listen to you – squabbling over who's boss. Like children in the school playground.'

'Captain Parry and I are discussing certain administrative adjustments,' van Wyk said, 'which are none of your business.'

'Hey, you asked me if I had something to share with you.'

'And now I'm asking you to keep your comments to yourself.'

'A couple of minutes ago you were desperate to get me to talk, now you want me to shut up. What is it with you? Make up your mind, man!'

'MacLeod . . .' van Wyk growled threateningly.

'Don't, van Wyk,' Parry said. 'He's just trying to get a rise. It's his way.'

'Then I would advise him not to. I'm a dangerous man to provoke.'

'I'm really scared,' said MacLeod, sounding not in the least bit scared at all. 'What are you going to do? Beat me over the head with a rolled-up copy of the Constitution?'

'Don't tempt me.'

'Oh, come on, Captain! Do you think I'm just some stupid *kaffir*? Do you think I actually believe you'd dare lay a finger on me? I know your precious Constitution as well as you do!'

'Never mind what you believe, MacLeod.' Van Wyk laid a hand on each arm of MacLeod's chair and leaned towards him till their faces were less than a handspan apart. 'What do you see in my eyes?'

'I see,' MacLeod said, staring back placidly, 'an FPP officer who's overstepping the rules and who's picking a fight with a bad man to pick a fight with.'

'Van Wyk,' said Parry, 'if I were you I'd back off. Now.'

'Stay out of this,' van Wyk warned, not taking his eyes off MacLeod.

'Don't be an idiot. You so much as touch him, and he'll be crying police violence to every bloody media source in this city.' Not to mention, Parry thought, you start a fight with MacLeod and he'll kick your arse to kingdom come. Not that that's something I wouldn't like to see.

'He's protecting them,' van Wyk said, with a jab of his head at MacLeod. 'You know it. I know it. He's protecting these Triple-X bastards and they're getting away with murder because of it.' He looked back at the Xenophobe. 'Just one name, MacLeod. That's all I ask. One name.'

'You want a name?' MacLeod grinned ferociously. 'All right, I'll give you a name. Stupid South African dickhead.'

Van Wyk's face flushed red and his eyes screwed to puckered slits. Parry could see how it was all going to unfold in the next few seconds: van Wyk grabbing MacLeod, MacLeod retaliating, an ugly scuffle being played out here at FPP HQ, at the very heart of law and reason in New Venice . . .

He gestured to Johansen and the burly Norwegian, needing no further invitation, hurried across the chamber to intervene. Before van Wyk knew what was happening, Johansen had seized him about the chest and was bundling him away from MacLeod.

'What are you doing?' van Wyk yelled. 'Let go, you oaf!' He strained and flailed, but Johansen had him in a powerful bearhug. Van Wyk was not getting free till Johansen let him free.

MacLeod, looking not at all ruffled by anything that had just occurred, rose to his feet. He glanced at the two FPP officers struggling, then turned to Parry. 'Well, that's that then. Time I was off.'

He made for the door. Parry moved to intercept him.

'Mr MacLeod, I'm sorry about all this. Truly I am. Perhaps if you were to come up to my office, we could discuss things in a more civilized manner.'

'Oh no, Captain. No, I've done my bit. I've played the good little citizen. And you know what I'm going to do now? I and my colleagues are going to leave this building, and then I'm going to contact the news media and let them know about the way the FPP have harassed Xenophobes and abused their civil rights. Again. Just like at Koh Farang. I imagine a lot of people will be interested in that story, don't you?' He skirted around Parry and opened the door.

Van Wyk broke off from railing at Johansen to call out, 'Sergeant Fibich! That man is not to leave the basement!'

Fibich obediently accosted MacLeod as he exited into the corridor, but there was little she could do other than ask him to return to the chamber, a request MacLeod blithely ignored. She offered Parry a helpless shrug as he strode out of the chamber in pursuit of the Xenophobe. 'Sir, I—'

Parry swept past her, perfunctorily manufolding INSIGNIFI-CANT. He caught up with MacLeod just as he was knocking on the door to the next chamber.

'MacLeod,' he said, 'listen. You do understand that by going to the media you'll be making an already volatile situation much worse.'

'Of course,' MacLeod replied. 'What better reason for doing it? This is the opportunity I've been waiting for, Captain. Everyone's frightened that New Venice is about to become another Koh Farang and now, thanks to your Captain van Wyk, I have fuel to add to the fire.'

'And there's nothing I can say that'll—'

'– dissuade me? Nothing at all.'

The chamber door opened and out stepped the aborigine, Greg.

'Greg, all well?' MacLeod asked.

'No worries. I liked watching the fishes.'

MacLeod laughed and set off for the next chamber along to rouse the Tibetan monk.

Within a minute all three Xenophobes were in the corridor and trooping towards the staircase at the far end. Van Wyk, still in Johansen's clasp, could be heard roaring and cursing, the noise echoing within the confined space.

As the Xenophobes reached the stairs, Parry stirred himself to one last effort.

'MacLeod. Any of you. Please. If you know anything – anything at all – about the deaths, for heaven's sake help us. Foreigners are being lost. Sirens are dying. If you can do anything to stop it, you should. You know you should. This isn't about politics or beliefs. Those are important, but this is even more important. I'm not asking you to betray your cause. All I'm asking is for you to be human.'

At that, MacLeod, who had climbed as far as the third stair, halted and peered over his shoulder.

'Captain,' he said, 'it's precisely because we're human that we're Xenophobes.'

And with that simple, softly spoken assertion, he resumed his ascent.

At a loss for anything further to say or do, Parry stood and watched the other two Xenophobes follow their leader up the stairs.

The Tibetan monk was last in line. As he placed his hand on the steel banister, he paused, then looked round at Parry. His face appeared inexpressive, but there was, Parry thought, something in his eyes – a significance, a meaning, intended for him. Pity? Regret? The look lingered, but Parry could not interpret it, and the monk, seeming to realize this, bowed slowly and low, then turned again and proceeded after the others, rising step by step until the hem of his saffron robe, then his calves, and finally his sandals disappeared from view.

34 FRET

There could have been recriminations. Parry could have bombarded van Wyk with I-told-you-so's. He could have gone straight back up to Quesnel's office and reported the whole sorry episode in the basement and entrusted it to the commissioner to mete out discipline where it was deserved.

He could have, but frankly he could not be bothered. What difference would it make? Things had been thrown so severely out of kilter that the small measure of vengeful satisfaction he would gain from ensuring that van Wyk got his come-uppance would barely begin to redress the balance. Besides, settling scores and apportioning blame matter only to those who care, and Parry just did not care any more. He felt like a boxer who has soaked up one too many blows from his opponent. He could carry on with the fight, but what would be the point? He wasn't going to win. Better to sink to the mat and wait for the count of ten and an end to the punishment.

On the news that lunchtime the lead report was on the Hannon Regency *shinju*. An employee of the hotel had leaked the story, no doubt in return for a handsome tip-off fee. Much was made of the grisly Triple-X graffito and all that it implied. Much was also made of the fact that this third set of deaths coincided with the announcement of a significant decrease in the numbers of Foreigners visiting New Venice. The downturn first registered on Friday had steepened severely, and no longer could the drop in the figures be dismissed as a statistical blip. Foreign population density was now at ninety per cent of seasonal average. 'These are very sensitive beings,' commented François-Joseph Vieuxtemps, once again being called upon to give the benefit of his expertise. 'As I clearly state in my book *Foreigners Are Neither from Venus Nor from Mars*, one cannot predict what human actions they will consider offensive. Nor can one predict what steps they will take to avoid such actions in future.'

In a subsidiary report it was revealed that, according to well-informed sources, Sirens were starting to drift away from the city too. For most of them money was a stronger motive for staying than the remote-but-pertinent possibility of violent death was a motive for leaving, but dozens none the less had headed off for pastures new and more would surely soon follow. When it came down to it, one resort-city was much the same as another to a Siren, and a resort-city where you were not likely to be ambushed and murdered by Triple-Xers while plying your trade was understandably more appealing than one where you were.

There was a sour, nervy atmosphere in the city as Parry walked home from HQ that afternoon. He was reminded of London in the run-up to the Riots. It seemed almost everywhere he went he heard flashpoints of argument, voices frayed at the edges. Strangers' glances were furtive, clouded with mistrust. And if people were not succumbing to their anxiety, they were overcompensating for it, masking it too strenuously. Holidaymakers were braying when they should have been laughing. Stallholders were bragging about their wares instead of simply selling them. Café proprietors and restaurateurs were patrolling their outdoor tables, slapping backs, laying on the bonhomie with a trowel. Universal unease, and Parry, as he walked, wallowed in it, drawing a perverse comfort from it. He even nearly laughed when he caught sight of the headline on a copy of the *Clarion on Sunday* that someone was reading: 'New Venice Sunk?'

That evening he went out, in plain clothes, to attend Sirensong. His hope was that he might overhear something useful, might eavesdrop on a conversation that would provide a lead to the Triple-X cell. The chances of this happening, though, were slim, and he knew it. The real reason he was going out was to observe how the Foreigners were behaving.

And they were behaving in a manner that could only be described as agitated. Their movements were rapid and awkward, not at all elegant, and they were perceptibly less confident than usual as they negotiated with Sirens (who themselves were drinking and smoking too much, talking loudly, affecting an air of exaggerated nonchalance). At each location where he loitered, Parry got the impression that the golden giants were there against their better judgement, impelled by urges they could not contain or control. That made him think that he had been wrong about their love of the human voice. (He had been wrong about so much else. Why not this?) What impulse could override common sense, could drive you to take excessive risks, could surmount even the fear of death? Not aesthetic appreciation, that was for sure. What else could it be but lust? The Foreigners' desire for singing was nothing more than the heedless, insatiable hunger of the libido. Maybe they were able to convince themselves that the pleasure they derived from singing was more than merely physical. Or maybe for them, as for many humans, there was little distinction between lust and love, the latter a euphemism for the former. He had always given them the benefit of the doubt before. They were such immaculate creatures that even to think of them as possessing sexuality was somehow wrong, tarring them with the brush of human traits. They were above such concerns as gold is above dross. Yet now, as he watched them haggle with Sirens, he saw being acted out over and over again the prelude to a more intimate transaction, the financial foreplay of the world's oldest profession. For all the dissimilarities – the terminology, the nature of the service being provided, the fact that the participants did not belong to the same species as each other – at the end of the day (literally) it was still just whore and client, trick-turner and punter, hooker and john.

Throughout the following day, Monday, Parry's disenchantment deepened while the mood in New Venice grew edgier and more unsettled. He did not go in to work. Unable to face all those searching looks, all those pairs of eyes seeking from him a reassurance he would not be able to give, not to mention all the comments he was bound to get about his forehead, which still bore a faint bluish bruise – unable to face the prospect of any of this, he called in sick, something he had never done before, not even when genuinely feeling under the weather. He phoned Johansen's work board and lied about having a cracking headache, and then stayed indoors all day watching TV and hating himself for his cowardice. Concerned calls came in from Johansen and from Avni, and he listened to them while the home board recorded them and then he erased them. The morning slipped by and his beloved city continued to writhe in pain. Through the television, as though through a window, distanced, he observed its suffering. What could he do? Nothing. Was there some way of solving this mess? None whatsoever. He thought several times about calling Anna, just to share some of his misery with her. But given the way they had parted after their lunch at the Touching Bass ... No.

On at least a dozen occasions that day the commissioner and

NACA Liaison al-Shadhuli appeared on television, sometimes as a duo, sometimes separately, to deliver messages of reassurance. They spoke soothingly, but neither of them was able to offer much more than a promise that the culprits would be caught using all Constitutional means available, and neither, when pressed by members of the press, sounded wholly convincing in their denials that New Venice was about to go the way of Koh Farang. As the day wore on, both officials grew appreciably less patient with their questioners. Wearily they made their points again and again, striving to generate new permutations of the same old answers.

Then, in the evening, Toroa MacLeod entered the fray, as he had vowed he would, and the platform from which he did his best to foment the unrest in the city was none other than *Calliope*.

The programme, recorded during the afternoon and aired at the primetime seven p.m. slot on NVTV, had been trailed extensively throughout the day as a 'Crisis in New Venice' special, and as the opening credits ended the camera found the show's presenter in sober, sombre mode. None of the usual bounding on to the stage with her arms raised while the studio audience whooped and cheered and clapped. Instead, with the audience observing a preordained silence, the lights went up to reveal Calliope seated centre-stage in a white armchair, dressed in a plain, dark trouser suit. The camera dollied in for a close-up. Calliope was possessed of a face that appeared to have been stretched vertically between the mouth and eyes, resulting in an artificially long nose. She was beautiful in a lofty, patrician kind of way, but when her hair was tied back, as it was today, depriving her features of their usual softening frame of jet-black ringlets, she looked hawklike and severe.

'Good evening,' she said, as the camera came to rest, 'and welcome to a special edition of the show. It can't have escaped the attention of anyone in this beautiful city of ours, or in the wider world, that New Venice is currently facing the most serious crisis to have befallen any resort-city since Koh Farang. Last Monday . . .'

And after giving a potted version of the events of the past seven days, Calliope continued: 'As usual on this show, it is not our intention to cast aspersions or draw attention to mistakes. What we hope to do in the next hour is make a frank and honest assessment of the situation and see if we can come up with any solutions. To help us do this we have a number of guests in the studio, and I'd like you to welcome the first of them now. He's the head of the local chapter of the Xenophobe movement – Toroa MacLeod.'

MacLeod strode onstage to polite applause. He was wearing a pair of khaki slacks and a loose-fitting, lilac-coloured shirt. After greeting his host with a brief handshake, he settled down into another white armchair positioned at right angles to hers.

'Toroa? Did I pronounce that right?'

'Impeccably, Miss Papaioannou.'

'Calliope.'

'Calliope.'

'Toroa, first off, before we get to serious matters . . . This is the first time we've had you on the show, and I feel I have to mention those tattoos of yours. They're very striking.'

'Thank you.'

'They're known as "moko", aren't they?'

'That's correct. Score one for your researchers.'

'Can you tell us a bit about them? Do they mean something?'

'Well, you said "before we get to serious matters". To me my moko *is* a serious matter. It symbolizes my connection to my people and to the *Maoritanga*, my people's way of life. In the early days, Maori men would draw marks on their faces in charcoal before going into battle, to make themselves look more ferocious. At some point – no one's sure when – it was decided to make the marks permanent. I wear them now to remind me of my heritage, but also to remind me that I am engaged in a battle myself, one no less fierce or important than, say, the Taranaki wars of the 1860s. Just as my forebears did their best to resist the encroachment of white settlers on to their land, so I am determined to resist the encroachment on to our planet of a race of outsiders whom I consider no less insidious and destructive.'

'You're referring to Foreigners.'

'Of course. The *Pakeha*.'

'"*Pakeha*"?'

'It's the Maori word for anyone who isn't Maori. Specifically it's come to mean a white person, but I feel it applies just as well to the golden giants.'

'And you regard the golden giants as "insidious and destructive". Some might find that a somewhat . . . unusual view.'

'Not at all. As a matter of fact, I think you'll find it's quite a common and widely held view. Not everyone is prepared to come out and say it as we Xenophobes are, but most people in their heart of hearts know it's wrong the way we've let the *Pakeha* take over and dominate our world. It's wrong that we invest so much time and effort in ensuring that they're happy. It's wrong that we've focused so much of our culture around them that, in our eagerness to please them, we've lost sight of our own best interests, and even of our own humanity. All of us, if we're being honest with ourselves, feel that the adoration of Foreigners and all things Foreign-related has got out of hand, but because that's an unfashionable sentiment, most of us are reluctant to voice it. What I'm saying is, there's a huge silent majority out there who agree with the basic tenets of the Xenophobe movement, and in that respect, I feel that with my opinions I am merely the spokesperson for a vast, unseen legion. An "anti-Foreign legion", if you will.'

'"Dominate our worlds." You think that's something the Foreigners have set out to do deliberately?'

'Can you say that they haven't?'

'They seem benevolent.'

'They do. Perhaps they themselves even think they're benevolent. But then that's the way with all colonialists. White Europeans in the eighteenth and nineteenth centuries believed they were helping the "savages" of the New World by making them wear clothing and learn the Bible. They probably even believed they were helping them by turning them into slaves and stealing their land and slaughtering them when they rebelled.'

'I take your point, but the comparison isn't strictly accurate, is it? The Foreigners haven't forced us to do anything we don't want to do. No one *makes* Sirens sing for them. No one *ordered* us to build resort-cities.'

'Which merely renders our enslavement all the more shameful. We voluntarily put our necks in the collars. We held up our hands and asked for them to be manacled. Or should that be – ha ha – manufolded?'

'Then what about the obvious improvements the Foreigners have brought?'

'What about them?'

'We have endlessly renewable, non-polluting power sources.'

'Comp-res? Non-polluting? *Noise* is pollution. Besides, who knows if comp-res cells don't have harmful by-products that we just don't know about yet? We could be irreparably damaging our bodies every time we get in a vehicle or turn on a portable radio. Remember the saying about Greeks bearing gifts, Calliope.'

'I'll choose not to take that as an insult.'

'Oh, it really wasn't intended as one.'

'Anyway, I doubt you could disagree with the fact that the world now has an international political consensus of a kind that would have been inconceivable before the Debut.'

'You know, someone else tried out that argument on me recently. Someone who's utterly, unthinkingly in thrall to the *Pakeha*. And I'll tell you what I told him. It's not a consensus. We've just lulled ourselves into a false sense of security.'

'Meaning?'

'Some people claim that we're living in a Golden Age. We aren't. At best this is an Indian summer. Throughout history there have been eras like this. Uneventful interregnums. Outbreaks of peace and order and prosperity. Camelots. They never last. This one won't, either. Soon enough, you mark my words, things will return to how they used to be.'

'And you'd be happy about that? You'd be happy to see the human race lapse back into its old ways – international hostility, corporate greed, systematic destruction of the environment?'

'I'm not saying any of those things are desirable, but they *are* human, and that's what's important. They're natural, inevitable consequences of the human condition. Just as crime is a natural, inevitable consequence of the human condition. All crime, including murder, which is, don't forget, as old as Cain. These things are a part of us and by pretending the urge to steal or kill no longer exists we are limiting ourselves as human beings. We are limiting our spirit and making ourselves less than men.'

'Or more.'

'No, we can never be more than what we are. That's an illusion, just as this whole "Golden Age" is an illusion. An illusion like Christmas, with all the tinsel enthusiasm and artificial good will and camouflaged greed that that entails. Consensus and kindliness and orderliness, you see, Calliope, are simply not the human way. The absence of a necessary element of chaos in our lives causes tension, and since the Debut that tension has been bubbling away beneath the surface, buried, suppressed, unexpressed. The pressure has been building. The cracks, as we are seeing here in this city, are starting to show. And very soon, I feel, this whole charade of good behaviour we've been putting on is going to collapse and all manner of pent-up frustrations and desires and angers are going to come through.'

'But this is my point, Toroa. You would welcome that?'

'I'd welcome it as a restoration of the proper order of things. Of course, given that nature's way is for a situation to swing from one extreme to the other before equilibrium is achieved, I suspect that the transition back to our former state will be a difficult one, a violent one even, and not everyone will survive it. But in the long run, once the transitional state is over, life will be better for us all. Better as in more human.'

'That's a very pessimistic outlook.'

'I disagree. I regard it as positive. Pessimism, anyway, is just another word for realism, and I'd rather be a realist than an optimist. The optimist is destined always to be disappointed.'

'And on that note, perhaps we can turn to the issue we're concentrating on in this edition of *Calliope*. If you've just joined us, I'm talking to Toroa MacLeod, head of the New Venice Xeno-phobes, about the *shinju* murders that have rocked this city during the past week. Toroa, it's become apparent that Triple-Xers—'

'If I can just stop you there a moment, Calliope. I'd really appreciate it if you wouldn't use that word.'

'Which word?'

'*Shinju*. I know everyone's using it as a convenient shorthand, but it's racist, patronizing, socially divisive and, strictly speaking, inaccurate.'

'I see. What would you suggest I say instead?'

'You could call them "statements". Or maybe "gestures".'

'I take it you condone them, then.'

'Did I say that?'

'"Statements" would seem to imply that you regard them as a legitimate form of protest.'

'That, Calliope, is your view.'

'But Triple-X has traditionally been regarded as an adjunct of the Xenophobe movement, its militant wing. It stands to reason that you might not disapprove of what they get up to.'

'How so?'

'Well, Triple-X is sort of the hammer of the movement, isn't it? The blunt tool that gets results when fine words don't.'

'Not a description I would necessarily agree with.'

'Have you ever met a Triple-Xer?'

'I can't say that I have.'

316

'But you might have.'

'You know, Calliope, if I wasn't such a fan of your show and didn't know better, I'd say you were working your way towards accusing me of being an accessory to these acts.'

'Not at all.'

'I should hope not. In fact, while I'm here, I'd like to state for the record that neither I nor any Xenophobe resident in this city has any knowledge of the identities or whereabouts of the perpetrators of these deeds. A fact the Foreign Policy Police seemed unable to grasp yesterday when they unceremoniously and unConstitutionally arrested us and held us in their cells.'

'Yes, I understand you've lodged a complaint with the FPP Council. Why the Council? Why not Commissioner Quesnel?'

'Quesnel sanctioned the arrests. I can only assume she also sanctioned the way we were treated by her officers in the cells – subjected to an intense interrogation and exposed to abuse and violence. So what good would complaining to her do?'

'Abuse and violence? A lot of people would have a hard time believing that of the FPP.'

'A lot of people underestimate the depth of resentment among FPP officers towards Xenophobes.'

'But don't you feel the FPP had *some* justification for bringing you in?'

'What justification? Because Triple-X has some notional affiliation with Xenophobia? No, the way I see it, harassing Xenophobes has become an accepted FPP tactic. It happened at Koh Farang, now it's happened here. If there's trouble in a resort-city, blame the Xenophobes. And that's victimization, pure and simple.'

'But why would the FPP wish to victimize you?'

'The FPP can't stand us because we're a dissenting voice, because we upset the consensus that they're so keen to maintain and that they, more than anyone else, represent. So if they have an opportunity to make us look like villains, they take it. They round us up and then later they release us. "Oh sorry, our mistake." Meanwhile, the damage to our reputation has been done. But the thing is, the public at large are cleverer than that. They know that if the authorities are trying to smear you, then what you have to say must be worth listening to.'

'You mentioned Koh Farang. Do you see other parallels between that situation and this one?'

'Of course. Here, as there, someone wants the *Pakeha* to leave.

And their plan – these people, whoever they are – appears to be working. What was the percentage drop recorded on Sunday? It was on the news this morning.'

'Thirteen per cent.'

'While on Saturday it was ten. Word is spreading among the *Pakeha*.'

'And if the *shinjus* – forgive me, if the "statements" stop, do you think Foreigners will start coming back?'

'Who knows? Though if Koh Farang is anything to go by, the answer is no.'

'You don't seem entirely displeased.'

'I'm a Xenophobe. One day I hope to see the world completely liberated from the influence of the *Pakeha*. If they abandon New Venice, as they may well, then I can hardly look at it as anything other than a step in the right direction, can I?'

'And I'm afraid that's where we're going to have to leave it for now. A controversial viewpoint. Some might say a pragmatic one as well. Toroa MacLeod, thank you very much.'

'A pleasure, Calliope.'

'After the break, a vox pop from the plazas, and then an expert on the Foreign Policy Constitution gives us his verdict on how the FPP is handling the crisis and what steps they might take to bring it to a speedy resolution. *Calliope* – in tune with public opinion. We'll be back in just a few short minutes. Keep watching!'

And most viewers did as Calliope commanded, but Parry was not among them. He stabbed the remote control's Off button in disgust and sat there staring at the pearlescent blankness of the wallscreen, upon which an after-image of MacLeod's face hovered, picked out in retinal shades of red and yellow, riven with tattoo lines like the visage of some gloating, scarified demon.

He felt sick. Sick and resentful. Granted, Calliope had tackled MacLeod with, for her, an unaccustomed incisiveness. Normally she spent her interviews agreeing with her guests and offering them gentle, leading questions that allowed them to say nothing more than they had come there to say. With MacLeod, apart from that initial compliment, she had been atypically challenging (hinting, perhaps, at a certain depth of dislike on her part). Yet it had not been enough. A more stringent interviewer would have torn holes in MacLeod's arguments. Calliope, for all her best efforts, had allowed him to emerge looking justified and – worse – plausible.

He had done damage. He knew it. Parry knew it. The wound inflicted on New Venice by the *shinjus* had just been aggravated.

But was it a mortal wound?

Parry's father, that builder of cars, that mender of musical boxes, that occasional dancer of deliriously daft dances, used to have a saying: 'There's nothing that isn't fixable.' It was a motto the old man had been able to apply to almost anything, from a rust-locked mainspring to a boy's broken collarbone to a hostile international dispute, and it was the closest he ever came to an expression of life-philosophy. Whatever went wrong was never irreparably wrong. Right up until his death, this belief had kept him cheerful in spite of any obstacles fate had put in his way, and after he was gone Parry had felt that the onus was now on him, as though a mantle were being passed on between the generations, to keep the paternal flame of optimism burning. This had not been easy at first, since he was innately of a cynical disposition (something that suited him for, and was fostered by, a career in the police, since it brought him repeatedly into contact with the worst elements of society). Not only that but the death of his father was in itself the ultimate disproof of the old man's upbeat creed, for here was something that was resolutely *not* fixable. Here was an absence in Parry's life that would not be filled in. Here was a pain of grief that would not, it seemed, ever mend.

His mother's illness and death, following on so soon after, did little to change his mind. During that embattled, embittered year, which fell between the year of the Hunger Riots and the year of the Debut, Parry became convinced that his father had been mistaken, perhaps even deluded. Nothing was fixable. Life was a series of accumulating losses which could never be recovered, which could only be adjusted to and tolerated. The future was decay. Human-kind was damned.

The arrival of the Foreigners changed all that, confirming at a stroke that his father had been correct all along. A man's soul could be purged. An entire planet could be redeemed. Finally Parry was able to embrace his father's creed wholeheartedly, and it felt like discovering a beaten-up old radio whose batteries should have run down years ago and switching it on and finding that yes, by God, it still worked, the music coming through loud and clear.

Quietly, without making a great fuss about it, without proselytizing, he had lived thereafter by his faith in the fixability of things. And now that faith, that armour against the slings and arrows, was all but eaten away. The *shinju* investigation had acted on it like dripping acid, and MacLeod's performance on *Calliope* provided the final corrosive trickle, penetrating through.

Going to his home board, Parry sat down, slapped on his reading spectacles, called up mail-composition mode, and set about drafting a letter of resignation.

Even as he typed in `Dear Commissioner Quesnel`, he could scarcely believe what he was doing. His nerves shrilled with abhorrence, but the abhorrence served only to confirm the rightness of the action. He could never have tendered his resignation casually. It was meant to be hard to do, therefore he must be doing the correct thing.

In the event, he did not get any further with the letter than those first three words. While he was deliberating over the phrasing of his opening sentence, the doorbell buzzed, announcing not only a visitor but – though Parry had no way of realizing it then – the start of a process whereby his father's dictum would prove to have some value in it yet.

35 INCIDENTAL

'Yoshi. This is a bit of a surprise.'

Hosokawa bobbed his head briefly, nervously. 'I would not have troubled you at home, sir, but you weren't at HQ today and . . .' The sentence trailed off. Hosokawa seemed unable to meet Parry's gaze. A minute earlier, on the condominium's front doorstep, he had likewise been unable to meet the gaze of the entry-intercom camera.

'Well, what is it?' On any other day Parry would have been more patient. He would have waited until Hosokawa was ready to say what he had to say. On any other day.

'I shouldn't have come.' Hosokawa manufolded APOLOGY and started back towards the apartment door.

Parry felt a pricking of conscience. Lack of charity, though under the present circumstances understandable, was never forgivable. 'No, wait. Hold on. If there's something you want to talk about . . .'

Hosokawa slowly halted. Without turning round, he said, 'I was told you're not feeling well. I'm embarrassed that I came here without calling first. This could perhaps wait till tomorrow.'

The *perhaps* told Parry that it could not. 'No time like the present. Can I get you something to drink?'

'No, thank you.'

'Then shall we sit?' Parry steered Hosokawa by the shoulder into the centre of the living room, away from the vicinity of his home board. The words Dear Commissioner Quesnel were still onscreen, and he did not want to risk Hosokawa catching sight of them, even though the young man would probably not guess what they implied.

Seated, Hosokawa fidgeted and cogitated for a full minute before finally he spoke again. 'Things are getting bad, aren't they?'

'You mean New Venice? You could say that.'

'A week ago, this hardly seemed possible. Foreigners leaving. Sirens, too. Do you think, sir, that it's gone too far to reverse?'

'It may have,' Parry admitted reluctantly. 'Even if by some miracle we find these Triple-Xers before they strike again, I don't know. Once the Foreigners have got it into their heads to go, how can we stop them?' He sighed, not expecting the exhalation to sound so shaky. 'But I'm sure you'll be able to find employment elsewhere, if that's what you're worried about. Smart young fellow like you – shouldn't be a problem.'

'No, sir, really, I'm not concerned about that at all. It's just . . .' A kind of spasm passed across Hosokawa's face, as though he had suffered a twinge of arthritic pain. He looked across at Parry, at last staring directly at him. 'Captain, it's not my place to say this, but I'm aware how this *shinju* business has been affecting you. I don't normally pay attention to rumours, but it's been going around at HQ that you were in a fight a couple of nights ago and that you and Captain van Wyk have clashed quite seriously.'

'Exaggerations.'

'I'm sure. But I have always considered you an honourable man, sir. I wish that somehow you might have been spared all this.'

'Believe me, I wish that too,' Parry said, with feeling. 'I've got to look at it objectively, I suppose. Eight wedges in New Venice and Triple-X picked a hotel in mine for its first atrocity. It was just the luck of the draw.'

'Yes,' said Hosokawa uncertainly. 'You also had the misfortune that I was on hand at the Amadeus. If I hadn't mentioned *shinju* to you, perhaps you might have cleared the whole matter up by now.'

'Forget it, Yoshi,' Parry said, although a certain small part of him snatched greedily at the idea that the blame for his woes lay, at least to some extent, with Hosokawa. 'You saw what you thought you saw. I believed what I wanted to believe. We were both misled, but the difference is, I'm the one who misled himself. By the way' – he was keen to move on to another subject – 'anything happen at HQ today that I should know about?'

'The commissioner called an Ensemble.'

'Probably not before time. What did she say?'

'She told us to be on the alert, ask around, speak to people we know, generally keep an ear open for leads to the Triple-X cell, but be subtle about it. She said that you and Captain van Wyk were jointly in charge of the investigation and that if we got wind of any suspicious behaviour or heard a rumour, we were to report it to either of you, however trivial it might seem. Oh yes, and if another *shinju* happens, no matter whose wedge it happens in, it's to be considered under your and van Wyk's jurisdiction. What else? She told us to stay calm.'

'Do people at HQ look to you like they *aren't* calm?'

'I think there's a lot that's not being said. You know, everyone putting on a brave face, while underneath . . .'

Parry nodded. In a way he was glad he had missed the Ensemble. It was an occasion – all the officers in the division congregated in the main hall at HQ, with him, the other seven captains and the commissioner seated before them on a dais – which made him uncomfortable at the best of times, and he could just imagine the looks that would have been fixed on him today had he been there. Disappointed. Pitying. Accusing. A sea of heads in front of him, officers from every district, and he had let them down. All of them.

Dear Commissioner Quesnel . . . He would get back to his resignation letter as soon as Hosokawa had gone.

'What about you, Yoshi?' he asked. 'How do *you* feel about all this?'

'I feel . . . I feel that something can still be done to pull us back from the brink.'

'Really? I admire that. A couple of days ago I might even have agreed with you. Now, frankly, I think we should be prepared for the worst.'

'But if it were possible to catch whoever is doing this and somehow demonstrate to the Foreigners that the problem had been cleared up?'

'Didn't work at Koh Farang, did it? The FPP paraded those cultists around the city, showing them to the few Foreigners that remained and trying to get them to manufold APOLOGY. They just refused. I'm sure it would be the same with the Triple-Xers.'

'But it might be worth a try.'

'Well, maybe. If we can nab the bastards.'

'"Nab"?'

'Apprehend. Arrest. Catch. Yoshi?'

'Sir?'

'I'm going to read between the lines here, and I may be wrong, but might you have some idea where the Triple-Xers are? Because if you do, why beat around the bush like this? Why not just tell me?'

'It's not that, sir.' Again, a pained spasm fleetingly contorted Hosokawa's face. 'It's . . . I was just wondering. Triple-X. What if it isn't Triple-X doing this?'

'Who else would it be? The writing on the wall at the Hannon was something of a giveaway, after all.'

'But could the writing not have been a – what's the phrase? A red herring.'

A blood-red herring, Parry thought. 'It might have, I suppose,' he said, 'although I think it a little unlikely.'

'Of course, sir. All the same, you acknowledge that it's a possibility.'

'Triple-X fit the frame, Yoshi. They have the incentive.'

'But Triple-Xers aren't the only ones with a grudge against Foreigners.'

'Aren't they? I can't think of anyone else who'd be prepared to cause Foreign losses simply to make a point.'

'There are some people,' Hosokawa said, hesitantly, 'who are of the opinion that Foreigners have changed certain aspects of our culture for the worse.'

'There are,' Parry replied. 'There are indeed. But I'm sure even those people realize that a small compromise here or there is nothing when set against the benefits that the Foreigners have brought. If they didn't realize that, they'd have to be mad.'

'True, sir. You can never discount the possibility that there's a madman in our midst.'

'Several madmen. Called Triple-Xers.' Parry could not keep a note of impatience from entering his voice. He was tiring of the conversation. Hosokawa, though he could not be faulted for trying to help, was not actually achieving much with this attempt to reassess the case. There was no point in reshuffling the pieces of the jigsaw when the puzzle was already almost completed. 'Listen, Yoshi, I appreciate your coming round and everything,' he said, 'but if you wouldn't mind, I'm still not feeling brilliant.'

Hosokawa took the hint.

At the door he said, 'I apologize for taking up your time, sir.'

'No problem.'

'You told me the other day that I shouldn't be afraid to suggest an idea. You'll give some thought to what I've said?'

For what it's worth, Parry thought, but said breezily, 'I will.'

'Thank you, sir.'

Parry closed the door on the young officer and stood for a moment shaking his head. He was touched by Hosokawa's visit, but felt a little patronized by it, too. The kid had meant well, but he appeared to have forgotten that his captain was an old pro, a man with fifteen years of police experience under his belt and almost as many years again of experience in administering Foreign Policy.

The latter period, of course, about to come to an end.

With a weary grimace, Parry settled back down in front of his home board and lodged his spectacles back on his nose. The screensaver had kicked in – a pair of golden hands drifting lazily around, shifting between manufolds and every so often pausing and standing still for a spot of thumb-twiddling. He hit a key, and up came `Dear Commissioner Quesnel`.

First line. In the light of recent developments . . . No. In *view* of recent developments.

There are some people, Hosokawa had said, *who are of the opinion that Foreigners have changed certain aspects of our culture for the worse.*

Off the top of his head Parry could think of no one he knew who felt like that.

`In view of recent developments`, he typed, `I have come to the conclusion that I have no alternative but to`

Not 'alternative'.

`no choice but to`

Certain aspects of our culture.

Such as?

In the States there hasn't been a song with lyrics in the Top Ten for the past year.

Guthrie Reich in the library at Anna's.

The image leapt into Parry's mind as though it had been crouched like a greyhound in the trap, trigger-tight, waiting to be sprung. Reich's plectrum earring twirling as he moved his head. Reich losing, for a moment, that easygoing manner of his as he voiced a long-held and deep-felt grievance.

You hear that garbage that's clogging up the hit parade and people dance to right now.

And then it all came tumbling forth in a great connective rush, and Parry could almost hear doors flying open, bang bang bang, one after another in quick succession, as the logic-surge sluiced through.

We gave away our music, man!

Oh Jesus, was that it? Was that your Triple-X cell right there?

He examined the idea that he had just formulated, inspired by Hosokawa's remark. He examined the idea as though it were an actual object in space which he could walk around, look under, over, inspect from every angle. He felt its size, its shape, its awkwardnesses, its possibilities.

Then he went to the bedroom to find his uniform jacket.

Then he made a phone call.

Then, tucking his FPP badge into his pocket, he headed out.

36 CONCERT

As a taxi-gondola (costly but expedient) carried him across town towards the OZ Club, the certainty Parry had felt when leaving his apartment began to fade. With every side-slipping judder of the boat in the water, every wave-slapping lurch of its bows as it rode the swell of another vessel's wake, conviction ebbed and was replaced by doubt. What had seemed, when first thought of, incredibly plausible, now seemed, upon further consideration, not so plausible, just incredible.

Consequently, as the taxi-gondolier guided his craft down the narrow backwater where the OZ Club was located, Parry was tempted to ask the man to turn about and take him back home. But he knew he could not do that. He could see Johansen up ahead, plain-clothed like himself, waiting outside the entrance to the club. That, he realized, was why he had instructed the lieutenant to meet him here rather than at his apartment. Knowing subconsciously that he might have second thoughts on the way over, he had arranged things so that it would be hard for him to back out.

Hard, but by no means out of the question. He could simply tell Johansen the truth. He had changed his mind. Sorry. Just some crazy brainstorm he had had. Best forget about it. Johansen would understand.

The taxi-gondolier throttled down and hove to, easing the boat in alongside the club entrance with practised precision, stilling the last of its forward momentum with a foot braced against the canalside walkway. Parry paid and tipped him, then accepted Johansen's proffered hand and was pulled – virtually hoisted – ashore.

The club entrance was an open doorway in the side of a hotel. Above the lintel, picked out in a glowing wriggle of neon tubing, was the club's name, derived from the initials of the surnames of its American co-owners, Messrs Osterburg and Zimmerman. Amplified music could be heard emanating from within, as though from the bottom of a deep-sunk mineshaft, a dense seismic throb of

327

sound. What instruments were being employed, what tune was being played, it was impossible to make out.

'*God aften*, boss,' Johansen said. 'Headache better?'

'Yes, thanks.'

'I have to admit, you've got me stumped. What are we doing here?'

On the phone Parry had told Johansen nothing more than to go to the club; he would explain things there. Now, he hesitated. This was his last chance to hit the eject button. Should he take it? Or carry on?

Part of him felt as though he were a shipwrecked mariner, desperate enough to grasp at anything, the least flinder of flotsam, in the hope of staying afloat. Another part of him . . .

Oh, what the hell. He had come this far.

He told Johansen about Hosokawa's visit to his apartment, and about the young officer's seemingly offhand remark. It was possible that Hosokawa had merely been airing a view, with no thought as to its deeper ramifications. Equally, it was possible that the entire purpose of his visit had been to drop the remark into the conversation and see what effect it had on his captain. Hosokawa might have developed a fresh theory about the *shinjus* which, unsure of its worth, he had wanted Parry to ponder on and, if he saw fit, act upon. Either way, deliberately or inadvertently, Hosokawa had jogged Parry's brain, setting loose an idea – and that was why he and Johansen were here at the OZ.

'So wait a moment,' Johansen said, working it through in his head. 'Musicians? The perpetrators of the *shinjus* are musicians with a grudge against Foreigners? And they're trying to pass their crimes off as Triple-X actions?' A slight narrowing of one eye said it all: he was sceptical.

'Not exactly, although that's what I thought of at first. After all, the Foreigners have made most non-Foreign styles of music, if not obsolete, then at least less relevant. That could be a source of resentment to someone who enjoys and performs traditional human music, especially the kind of music that needs charity funding to survive. But then it occurred to me: what if it's the other way round? What if it's Triple-Xers trying to pass themselves off as musicians? And then I realized that the *shinjus* started shortly after this lot arrived in town.'

And he produced from his back pocket the flyer which Anna had given him at the Da Capo and which had since then been lodged in the inner pocket of his uniform jacket.

Johansen took the flyer, unfolded it, smoothed out the crease, slid out the 'single', perused the label on one side of it, perused the label on the other, returned it to its sleeve, and passed the flyer back to Parry.

'Well,' he said, shrugging, 'what's that phrase your mother always used to use? The one about "shy bears"?'

'Shy *bairns*,' said Parry, mimicking his mother's soft Yorkshire cadences. 'Shy bairns get nowt.'

'That's the one.' Johansen made an ushering gesture towards the doorway. 'So let's not be shy, then.'

Directed by a painted arrow on the wall that was helpfully inscribed 'THIS WAY', Parry and Johansen followed a dimly lit corridor that burrowed through the side of the building and terminated at a descending flight of stairs, the edges of which were picked out with embedded strips of tiny lights. At the foot of the stairs another corridor angled off to the right, shorter than the upstairs corridor and lower-ceilinged. A second arrow encouraged them to continue. With every step they took, the music grew louder and gained definition, as though it were the solution to a cryptic puzzle, revealing itself in increments, becoming clearer the closer you drew to it. First, drums – a four-on-the-floor backbeat. Then a voice, rasping, intense. Then what lay between, the bulk of the music: crunchy phased guitar and plump, thudding bass.

They arrived at a pair of swing doors, next to which stood a no-necked bouncer in evening wear. Looking bored, the bouncer pointed the two of them towards a booth, where a young woman sat, also looking bored. She took money from them, gave them tickets and pointed them back towards the doors.

'Busy night?' Parry asked the bouncer, raising his voice to be heard above the music.

The bouncer, whose kind were rarely required to exercise their talent for queue-control and troublemaker-pacification in New Venice, gave a rueful roll of the eyes and pushed one of the doors open.

Out came sound.

Echoing, volcanic.

Sound loud enough to be a physical force.

Sound loud enough to distend the corneas and vibrate loose clothing.

Sound you almost had to walk against, like a high wind.

Heads lowered, Parry and Johansen entered the main part of the club.

The OZ was, usually, a well-frequented nightspot where the latest Siren hits were played over relentless, chattering drum-machine patterns, with a disc jockey mixing different kinds of songs together, cross-fading among anything up to a dozen tracks at once, and so creating, in the manner of the Da Capo wind garden, a shifting musical collage that was sometimes infernally discordant and sometimes celestially melodious. A skilled Siren DJ was intuitively able to draw together the right voices singing the right phrases in complementary keys so as to generate moments of choral harmony. He or she could also, if desired, deliberately generate moments of choral cacophony in order to provide a necessary relief from the sweetness, since sweetness soon becomes cloying unless leavened by a modicum of sour. In this respect the true virtuosos of the craft of Siren DJ-ing were artists in their own right, masters of randomness, and their deftness with a mixing desk was rewarded by the adulation of large crowds of club-goers, who would throng the dance floor, surrendering to the rhythm and the unfamiliar cadences and concatenations the DJ served up, responding to the changing moods of the music, letting themselves be stirred and jarred, startled and moved, surprised and entranced, while their sweat flew and their bodies gyrated and their hands fluttered and manufolded. It had been known for Foreigners to attend such sessions, passing among the dancers and being accorded a respectful distance, a no-contact zone roughly a metre in radius. They did not, though, visit nightclubs often and, when they did, seldom stayed long. Xenological wisdom had it that the music, for all its attractiveness to the golden giants, was too loud for their tastes, or else engendered in them a sensory overload, evoking too many emotions too rapidly. That certainly might account for the fact that most of them, as they retreated, manufolded APOLOGY and EXCESS.

Because venues like the OZ Club prospered by playing Siren music throughout most of the week, it meant that on slow nights – and nights did not come much slower than a Monday night – they could afford to showcase forms of Euterpean entertainment with a more eclectic appeal. Hence tonight the OZ was playing host to the Trad Music Revue and, from the looks of things, the evening's takings were going to be well below par. All told, there could not have been more than a dozen paying punters on the premises, not counting Parry and Johansen. They were grouped at the bar, predominantly elderly, predominantly male, leaning with drinks in their hands and gazing across a gulf of empty, unilluminated dance floor to the stage where, normally, the Siren DJs held court and where, now, a four-piece hard-rock band – like its audience, elderly and male – was conjuring up a sonic hurricane.

The stage was not large, so the band were cheek by jowl, the bassist nearly sitting on the drummer's low tom, the guitarist having to angle himself away from the vocalist so as to avoid jabbing him in the ribs with his instrument's head. Yet within the restricted space they managed to perform dynamically, or at least as dynamically as men of pensionable age are able. The guitarist thrashed and windmilled, the drummer flailed, the vocalist postured and shook his fist as he sang, and only the bassist kept stock-still, observing that unwritten law of bass-playing which forbids any greater expenditure of physical resources than that required for the plucking of plectrum on string. If you watched them carefully, you might notice that the guitarist winced whenever he bent to wring out a power-chord, and you might infer from this that he was being given trouble by a touch of lumbago; you might see the drummer look pained as he tried to twirl his sticks between beats, his fingers not as dextrous as once they were; you might see the redness of the singer's cheeks and be concerned that he was dangerously overtaxing himself. And you would not have to look closely at all to discern that the four of them, with their outfits – assorted combinations of spandex, leather, silk and stretch denim – and their lank, scanty hair looked, quite frankly, ridiculous, like characters from some ghastly pantomime, the sort of haggard, prancing, tatterdemalion figures that could incur bad dreams in a small child. None the less, in spite of their many physical impediments, you could not deny that they were giving it their all. The song that was exploding out from the speaker stacks behind them – a raucous enumeration of a female sexual partner's most alluring attributes – was a triumph of effort over circumstances, not to mention imagination over reality. They were putting as much into their music as if there was a stadium filled with ten thousand screaming fans in front of them and not just a near-empty nightclub and a handful of nodding cognoscenti.

The song, which to judge by its most often repeated line was entitled 'That's What I Want from Her', reached its climax in a tumult of chords and a cascade of cymbal crashes. This was followed by a squalling, terminative wail from the vocalist. Then the drummer seemed to strike every piece of his kit at once, and the guitarist and the bassist joined him in pounding their instruments simultaneously, once, and again, and one more time, and then one more time for luck, and then the vocalist screeched 'Yeah!' and there was another all-for-one pounding of instruments, which seemed to signify that this was truly the end of the song, but then the guitarist wrenched out one more chord, and the drummer hit his snare, and the bassist twanged his E-string, and the singer yelped, and the guitarist tweaked off a high note, and the drummer, determined to have the very final word, hit his snare with both sticks . . . and at last, after many false endings, there was silence.

The cognoscenti at the bar put down their drinks and applauded lightly. There were a couple of thin cheers.

'Thank you!' the vocalist gasped. His efforts at the microphone had left him so short of breath that, were this a hospital, you might have expected to see an orderly rushing off to fetch a cylinder of oxygen. 'You've been (wheeze) wunnerful audience. Love to (wheeze) home with us. We're (wheeze) the Burning (wheeze) Red-Hot Lovers. Thank you. G'night.'

There was another patter of applause as the vocalist staggered offstage and the guitarist and bassist unplugged their instruments and followed him, filing out through a side door. By way of a triumphal parting gesture, the drummer, as he stood up from his stool, lobbed his sticks towards the audience. The throw was clumsy and the sticks landed well short of their intended target, clattering on to the dance floor and rolling to a halt. When, eventually, an audience member went to pick them up, it was not as an eager souvenir-seeker but rather with the air of someone tidying up a piece of litter that could be a hip-breaking hazard to the unwary.

A trio of roadies – hirsute, cumbersome, dressed in leather waistcoats, black T-shirts and black jeans – came out and set about preparing the stage for the next act on the bill, wrestling a digital piano to the fore. Meanwhile, Parry and Johansen found themselves a table at the edge of the room.

'So what did you think of them, boss?' Johansen asked, with a nod of his head in the direction of the stage.

'I've heard worse.'

'Yeah. OK if you like that sort of thing. But actually what I meant was what did you think of them as Triple-Xers? Because I tell you, they looked way too old to me.'

'Old, but still quite sprightly. Besides, I know you get your younger Triple-Xers, your student reactionaries, but mostly they're people who were around long before the Debut.'

'Maybe the next lot will fit the bill better.'

'Yes. Or maybe . . .'

The roadies had finished rearranging the stage, and as they ambled off Parry saw someone emerging from a dark corner beyond the bar. Lithe and leather-clad, the man bounded across the dance floor, hopped up on to the stage and took the microphone.

'Good evening again, my friends,' said Guthrie Reich, grinning against the spotlights. 'Didn't I tell you the Lovers would rock your socks off? Yeah! And now, with our last act tonight, a change of pace, not to mention perspective. She enthralled music-lovers for over twenty-five years with her extraordinary songwriting ability and her laceratingly confessional lyrics. She's been retired for a decade, but we're proud and privileged that she's performing again and she's on our bill. A goddess of the piano keyboard with songs like candy-coated cyanide, she's here tonight with her band. Please put your hands together and welcome . . . Miss Leni Foss and the Three A.M. Sessioneers!'

Out came four men, not one of whom would see his fiftieth birthday again, followed a moment later by a frail-framed woman of similar vintage, with long wiry copper hair and startled bush-baby eyes. Leni Foss (for this was she) approached the stage and her piano stool timidly, as if having to coax herself every step of the way. Yet once Reich had stepped aside and surrendered the microphone stand to her, she underwent a transformation, taking charge, straddling her stool, adjusting the mike stand. She then shouted out a greeting to the audience, gave the title of a song ('Men's True Hate'), counted the band in, and launched into a harsh bluesy riff on the piano which her drummer complemented with a lolloping 12/8 beat and plenty of hissing high-hat action, while her bassist provided the underpinning with some sinewy travelling-arpeggio work.

No sooner had this middle-of-the-road vibe been established, however, than Leni Foss hurtled off down some extraordinary vocal byways, singing a lyric about sex during menstruation in a banshee soprano that looped and skirled around what would otherwise have been quite a pretty melody, adding jagged edges to sustained notes and making her quavers quiver. She sang about 'twisted sheets and tangled bodies', about 'a trickle of scarlet on her lover's thigh', about her lover's fearful rush for the bedroom door, about the blood that meant that 'I'm living, not you're dying', and it was abundantly clear that she relished the discomfort her words were inducing in the men present and her voice was inducing in everyone present irrespective of gender. She grinned ferociously as she scratched and slammed at the piano keys, while riding her stool like an unbroken stallion. She was compelling to watch and at the same time unsettling, for her commitment to her song was so absolute that she seemed almost naked, a creature of nothing but rage and music.

When the song ended, the ensuing applause was as much of relief that the song was over as of praise for its content and the way it had been performed. Leni Foss thanked the audience and began to introduce her band members, whom she referred to as her 'boys'.

Parry decided that now was as good a time as any to make his move. He signalled to Johansen to accompany him, and they stood up and walked past the bar to the corner to which Reich had returned after his bout of emcee-ing.

'Guthrie Reich?'

Reich, who was sitting with his feet up on a table and his chair canted on its rear legs, looked round and furrowed his brow, apparently confused to have been addressed by name by a complete stranger. Then he executed an almost textbook double-take, and broke into a smile.

'If it ain't old Jack "shove your teeth down your throat" Parry,' he exclaimed. 'Well, well. You're a different man out of uniform. What you doing here? Come for the show?'

'Not exactly.'

'No? I kinda thought it might be your thing. Not Leni, maybe, but some of the other guys.'

'I'm not here for any kind of entertainment at all. Mr Reich, I'd like to ask you to return with me to Headquarters to discuss a matter of FPP business.'

Reich's eyebrows shot up.

'You are under no obligation to comply with my request,' Parry continued. 'However, refusal to do so may count against you at a later date. You may defer compliance to a more convenient time, which is to be not less than twenty-four hours from now.' He was doing this by the book, reeling out the standard FPP rote, keeping firmly within the guidelines, staying formal and expressionless – yet it could not be denied that secretly, guiltily, he was enjoying himself. 'Should you wish, we can arrange for a mainland lawyer to be in attendance while we interview you, although you must bear in mind that this is not, in the legal sense, an arrest.'

Reich still looked astonished.

Leni Foss commenced her next number, a little ditty she called 'I'd Rather Die'.

Parry folded his arms. 'Well, Mr Reich? What's it going to be?'

Finally Reich said, 'Leni's the last act on the bill. Just let me see her off at the end, then I'll come with you.'

37 INDETERMINACY

At night the chambers of Floor Lower B were not as agreeable and welcoming as they were by day. With no sunlight to illuminate the canal water, the transparent outer walls showed nothing but blackness. There was no sense of distance or perspective. Fish could not be seen. There was nothing but a void out there, a dark weight of water, glowering, impenetrable. You could not help but think that you were deeper than you actually were. You could not help but imagine that you were down in the colder fastnesses of the ocean, the trenches where the nightmare creatures lurked – the X-ray crustaceans, the surly coelacanths, that whole benthic bestiary of evolutionary by-products and offcasts and dead ends, blind and gaping and skeletal and snaggle-toothed.

'I'm telling you, Jack,' said Guthrie Reich, not blind, not gaping, well fleshed, with perfect dentition, 'they're artistes. They're passionate about one thing and one thing only, and that's their music. OK, from time to time they might gripe that these days it's Sirens who get all the attention and most of the money. But come on, who of us doesn't bitch from time to time about the guys who earn more than we do, the guys who get the glory we think we deserve? That's just how people are.'

'And yourself, Mr Reich?' said Parry. 'Do *you* gripe about Sirens?'

'Sure, I've been known to. Now and then. You heard me at Anna's. So I don't like what they sing. That makes me a critic, man. Not a psycho-killer.'

'And Foreigners?' said Johansen.

'What about them?'

'Do you hate them?'

'No way. Like I told the captain the other night, I've got nothing against them at all. They're kinda fun to have around. They get on and do their thing, I get on and do mine, that's OK. So long as no one's giving me grief, I'm a live-and-let-live kind of person, you know what I'm saying?'

'Never the less, Mr Reich,' said Parry, 'it seems an odd coincidence, don't you think, that the first *shinju* murder occurred two days after the Trad Music Revue turned up in New Venice.'

'"Odd" because it was two days? Should it have been a shorter length of time? Longer? What are you getting at, Jack?'

'Mr Reich . . .'

'So it's a coincidence. Coincidences happen. If they didn't, nobody'd have invented a word for them. Anyway, when was the first *shinju*? Sunday night?'

'The early hours of Monday morning.'

'Sunday night, I was with the bands. We were rehearsing.'

'Till when?'

'Late. Midnight, at least. You can check. We were using an empty storage area down on the waterfront. East district. We were making enough noise. People nearby got to have heard us.'

'How about Wednesday night?' said Johansen.

'Gig. A place called The Tempo Zone.'

Parry remembered the name of the club from the flyer. 'And how late did that go on?'

'Pretty late. I can't say exactly *how* late. Thing is, the guys in the Revue? I don't know if you noticed, but they're none of them what you might call spring chickens. Even playing a short set takes it out of them. Afterwards, all they want to do is go to bed and go to sleep. Like the Burning Red-Hot Lovers. You saw them? Forget about burning red-hot love. A nice rubdown with warm liniment is about the most exciting thing *those* guys can handle.'

'So there's no one young on the Revue?' Johansen said. 'No one at all?'

'It's a senior citizen's game,' replied Reich. 'I'm the youngest person involved by a coupla decades.'

'And why is that?' said Parry. 'Why is someone like you, someone your age, involved in trad music?'

'Why not? It's my thing. It's what I do.'

'Not much money in it, though.'

'So? Some of us don't have any choice about what we dedicate ourselves to. We just find what we like, what we're best at, and do it. Some people still collect old books, don't they? Some people won't watch any television that wasn't broadcast before the turn of the century. Some people breed cats or koi carp or whatever. I like trad music, and that's how I've chosen to make my living, such as it is. Could be because my dad was a musician, a son of the rock'n'roll generation, and I grew up listening to the old stuff he liked. I don't know, and it doesn't matter. We are what we are, aren't we? You're a Foreign Policy cop. I'm a trad music promoter. Whatever life fits us out for, that's what we become.'

'Mr Reich,' said Johansen, 'have you at any time had any association with the Xenophobe movement?'

'The Xenophobe movement? That bunch of whiny windbags? No way. Uh-uh.'

'What about Triple-X?' said Parry.

'Yeah, like, even if I *was* a Triple-Xer, I'd say so.'

'But Triple-Xers certainly aren't "whiny windbags", are they? Xenophobes talk, but Triple-Xers *do*.'

'You know what? I'm not sure you have the right to be asking me these questions.'

'We have the right to ask them. You don't have to answer them if you don't want to, that's all.'

'Well, I've been answering, haven't I? And I think that says a great deal. Tell me, Jack, did someone put you up to this?'

Parry frowned. 'What makes you say that?'

'Well, OK, I realize you don't like me much. I don't know *why* you don't like me, 'cause I think I'm a pretty likeable guy, but I guess something about me rubs you up the wrong way. Thing is, I can't believe you'd let that be your sole reason for suspecting me and my artistes of being . . . well, hell, for want of a better word, *terrorists*. So I can only assume that someone else pointed the finger at us. Said, "Try those Trad Music Revue dudes. They're kinda hinky." Maybe even suggested we were killers. Am I right?'

'I admit, the idea wasn't entirely mine.'

'There you go. Whose was it? Some Siren? Some of those guys have got a real grudge against trad musicians. Probably because trad musicians have stuck to their guns. They've kept their integrity and Sirens haven't.'

'Actually, it was one of my own officers.'

'One of your own officers.'

'Whom I don't think has anything particularly against trad music.'

'Young guy, is he?'

'Relatively young.'

'Well educated?'

'Yes.'

'Kind of stuffy?'

338

'I wouldn't really call him stuffy.'

'Yoshi's a *bit* stuffy,' Johansen said.

'Big fan of Foreigners?'

'I wouldn't know.'

'There's a certain type of person, you see, Jack, who just wants to do a Stalin number on the past and erase every trace of everything that happened before the Debut. And things like my Revue piss that sort of person off. I'm not saying this officer of yours is like that exactly, but if he pointed you in my direction, without any solid evidence, just as a suggestion, then you've got to ask yourself why he did it. What does he have against something like the Revue? It's got to be some kind of a personal grievance, doesn't it?'

Some kind of a personal grievance. Parry wasn't sufficiently well acquainted with Hosokawa to know whether or not he hated trad music and its practitioners. He was, however, rapidly coming to the conclusion that a personal grievance *had* played a part in his decision to arrest Reich: his own dislike of Reich. It was he, after all, who had inferred from Hosokawa's vague, generalized comment a specific reference to the Trad Music Revue. It was he, too, who had divined a deeper significance to Reich's complaints about Sirens at Anna's party.

Damn it. Reich was right. Something about him *did* rub Parry up the wrong way, and he had allowed it to influence his decision-making. Animosity had clouded his judgement. He had not been *thinking*. He had only been *feeling*.

He looked at Reich, looked at him long and hard, with resentment and a certain amount of shame, and finally he said, 'You're free to go.'

'What?' said Reich. 'Interview over? Just like that? You sure?'

Johansen's face was exhibiting a similar sentiment.

'You may leave,' said Parry. 'You are at liberty to depart. The door is open. How many other ways can I put it?'

'I sort of had the feeling I was here for the night.'

'Lieutenant Johansen will escort you upstairs and arrange for transport to take you back to the OZ Club, or to your hotel if you'd prefer.'

'Well, that's very nice of you, but—'

'Mr Reich, do you or do you not want to go?'

Reich got to his feet. 'I guess this means we're innocent, then. We've got the alibis.'

Parry did not reply.

'Ah, come on, Jack, no need to be like that. You're only doing your job, right? Can't fault a guy for that.'

Parry made a gesture, something between a jerk of the thumb and a swat at an imaginary fly. 'Enjoy the rest of your time in New Venice, Mr Reich.'

'I surely will, Captain. And thanks.'

'For?'

'Oh, nothing really. Just thanks.'

When Johansen and Reich had gone, Parry went to the chamber's outer wall and pressed his hands to it. The crystech felt smooth and neutral, neither cold nor hot, neither pliant nor unyielding. He gazed through its transparent thickness into the jet-black canal, into the unseen currents, the hidden motion. The canals had been dubbed 'the veins of New Venice', which, like most travel-brochure clichés, was unimaginative but not without a certain basic truth. Through his palms, through the crystech, Parry could faintly detect what felt like a pulse. He did not think he was imagining it. It was definitely there – a sluggish thing, a slow, steady, tidal push-and-pull, an echo of the immense surges of the ocean around the city.

After the Foreigners were gone, after people were gone, after the city's hotels and towers were abandoned to bleach and rot in the sun, there would still be this heartbeat. New Venice would continue to be nourished by Mother Mediterranean. The sea would continue to imbue the city, this stillborn dream, with a kind of life.

It was something, at least.

'Boss?'

Snapped from reverie, Parry realized he had been standing, leaning against the crystech wall, for a good quarter of an hour. 'Yes?'

'Looks like you did the right thing releasing him.'

'Well, I still have my doubts, but his alibis seem sound.'

'Very sound. Because we're one of them now.'

'What?'

'There's been another *shinju*.'

'You're kidding.'

'The desk-duty officer just told me. The call came in about twenty minutes ago. Captain van Wyk's already on his way.'

'Where?'

'The Scroll.'

38 FOURTH

Of all the hotels in New Venice, the Scroll was the most unusual-looking and, since distinctiveness confers cachet, the most expensive. It was a slender, helical building, in effect a coiled strip of rooms that had been drawn upward from the centre till, fully unfurled, it formed a cone a kilometre high. A funicular lift served the interior, cabling up and down a spiral track, and the penthouse suite, known as the High Den, a split-level turret with an encircling panoramic balcony, was almost entirely kitted out with crystech decor – crystech floor-tiles, crystech bathroom furniture and fixtures, crystech dining table and chairs, crystech cutlery and crockery and glassware, crystech wall mosaics, crystech bar, even a crystech refrigerator. Designed for human occupancy, to spend one night in this dazzling eyrie cost the equivalent of the price of a modest-sized family home. For the mega-wealthy, no other hotel room in New Venice would do.

The Scroll, in short, was an extraordinary edifice. Unique. There were even rumours to the effect that the building – resembling, as it did, that fairly well-known symbol of phallic potency, a unicorn's horn – augmented the sexual performance of those staying in it, not to mention the vocal performance of Sirens singing there for Foreign residents.

What lay in a shadowed side alley at the Scroll's base, however, was neither as unique as the hotel, nor as lovely to behold. Indeed, what lay in a shadowed side alley at the Scroll's base – a human body and a set of Foreign remains – was something that had become (for Parry, at any rate) all too horribly humdrum, all too depressingly routine.

When he and Johansen reached the scene, they found that a small crowd of onlookers had formed at the alley's mouth. Close enough to see what was going on but not so close that they could see too much, the onlookers were murmuring to one another, strangers exchanging opinions as frankly as old friends. They did not move aside when asked, so Parry and Johansen, with their FPP badges clipped to their shirt pockets, had to shoulder their way through, Johansen offering an excuse-me here and there, Parry in too grim a mood to bother.

A few metres along the alley there was a vent in the side of the hotel from which emanated a plume of steam and the smell of laundering. Next to it stood a sparkling-clean garbage container, lid firmly sealed so that no odours could escape. The two sets of remains, Foreign and human, lay beside the garbage container. As ever, the one was shining and markless, the other brutally damaged, both deprived of the life they had contained.

Parry took stock of the scene. A little further on along the alley van Wyk was standing, engaged in conversation with a woman in a chambermaid's uniform. The woman was describing something, pointing and gesticulating to illustrate what she was saying.

Slowly, wearily, Parry approached the pile of Foreign clothing. Mask, gloves, robe – no different from the three sets of Foreign remains he had previously encountered. He wished he was more disturbed by what he was looking at, but repetition had begun to inure him. What had, at the Amadeus, seemed appalling, a crime against nature, now was no more than saddening, like the sight of a small bird lying dead on the ground, frail and insignificant.

He moved on to the corpse, which belonged to – strictly speaking *had* belonged to – a small, dark-haired man of indeterminate age.

Immediately, he saw that there was no way in the world that the man could have killed himself. His head was battered and broken, one eye bulging from its socket, the other buried beneath swollen, plum-purple lids. Several of his fingers were mangled, twisted, crushed. Blood had poured from his ears and nose, caking his mouth and hair. His mashed lips resembled sun-dried tomatoes. This person, quite clearly, had been beaten to death.

All the while, the crowd of onlookers was growing restive and more vocal. Parry heard his name mentioned a couple of times, and then someone said, in a loud, direct voice, 'You FPP. You're just letting this happen. Why are you not *doing* something?'

Another of the onlookers joined in, made brave by the boldness of the first: 'Yeah, why don't you let someone else take over? Someone competent like the mainland police.'

A third added, 'This is all your fault!'

The rest, roused by these denouncements, uttered growls and grumbles and mutterings in a variety of languages, a polyglot murmur of discontent, the words different, the sentiments alike.

Parry turned and examined their faces, and saw in them a look he knew well, a look he remembered vividly from the Hunger Riots: the fury of fear.

He turned to Johansen. 'Pål, would you mind having a word with that lot? Try and calm them down a bit?'

Johansen went over to the crowd and attempted to convince them that there was nothing of interest to them here and that they should disperse and return to their hotels. Parry, meanwhile, made his way over to van Wyk and the chambermaid.

'Natives getting restless, eh, Parry?' said van Wyk.

'As well they might. Who is this?'

Van Wyk introduced him to Senhora Coutinho, a member of the Scroll's janitorial staff. She was a stout, squat, thickly bespectacled Portuguese. Shock and consternation were writ large in her face.

'Senhora Coutinho is the one who made the call to HQ,' van Wyk said.

'And you were also the one who discovered them, Senhora?' Parry asked.

'*Sim.*' Senhora Coutinho pronounced the last letter of the affirmative as a glottal rather than a labial, so that the word sounded not unlike *sing*. 'I walk this way, along here, for the bus to take me home, and I find them.' She indicated the lost Foreigner and dead Siren without actually looking at them.

'Perhaps you could tell the captain what else you saw, Senhora,' said van Wyk.

'I see a man running away.' Senhora Coutinho aimed a stubby finger towards the other end of the alley, which opened out on to a walkway beside a narrow canal. 'I come around corner from the hotel entrance, hear feet, pit-pat. See the man running.'

'Definitely a man?' said Parry. 'Not a woman?'

'Definite a man. The shape of him, how he run. Then I see the dead ones, the man and the *Estrangiero*.'

'Can you tell me what he looked like, the man, the one running?' Parry could scarcely believe it. An eyewitness. Some good luck at last. 'Was he European? Asian? North African?'

'I see nothing of how he look like.'

Crestfallen: 'Nothing at all?'

'I see only his back. And it is dark. I see only a shape like a man, you understand?'

'A silhouette.'

'*Isso! Silueta*. And my eyes' – the senhora circled an index finger at her spectacles – 'are not so good. At night, *very* not good.'

'Well, was he tall? Short? Anything you can remember seeing, Senhora, anything at all will help.'

'It's no good, Parry,' said van Wyk. 'I already asked her all of this. All she saw was a man who appeared to be of average height and medium build, and that's it. Which gets us absolutely no nearer finding these Triple-Xers.'

'Damn!' Professional decorum prevented Parry from venting his frustration with a coarser expletive.

Senhora Coutinho turned to van Wyk. 'You have not tell him the violin.'

'The violin?' said Parry.

'The senhora,' van Wyk said, making a face, as if this was some ridiculous childish fancy he was being expected to indulge, 'seems to believe that the fellow was carrying a violin.'

'*Sim*. It was this shape . . .' Senhora Coutinho used both hands to mime the outline of a string instrument – the long narrow neck, the voluptuous curves, the waist-like indentations.

Parry frowned. The Triple-Xer had used a *violin* to batter the Siren and the Foreigner? What good was that as a weapon? Senhora Coutinho had to have been mistaken. As she herself had said, her night vision was not good.

Offering her a cursory GRATITUDE, Parry excused himself and strode off along the alley in the direction the fleeing killers had taken.

Triple-X had been here. Less than three-quarters of an hour ago, one of them had been here. He was passing through the air the man had passed through, breathing the very molecules he had exhaled. So close. So bloody close! And yet still, damn it, not close enough.

He reached the canal at the end of the alley. He braced his hands on the walkway guardrail. Opposite was the NVTV building, a huge blank-sided cube topped with a crewcut of aerial masts. Close by, to his right, was a line of mooring posts. The Triple-Xer could have had a boat tied up there, perhaps with an accomplice waiting in it, keeping the engine idling. The killer could have climbed in and made a quick and easy getaway, the canal waters erasing the boat's wake, smoothing out tracelessly.

It was a bit insulting, actually, when you considered it. The Triple-Xers were no longer bothering to try to make the murders look like double suicides. So confident were they that the FPP wasn't going to catch them, they weren't even going to the trouble of hiding in hotel rooms and carrying out their crimes in soundproofed seclusion. They were simply waylaying their victims in alleys and clubbing the hell out of them there, just like the cultists had at Koh Farang.

Bastards!

Overcome by a fit of rage, Parry banged his fist against the guardrail.

Bastards! Bastards!

He banged his fist again, then started banging it repeatedly, pounding and pounding the guardrail till he thought he might fracture a metacarpal. The impacts echoed dully along the guardrail's hollowness. Soon the pain became too great and he had to stop. Wincing, he held up his hand and examined it, peering at it as though it were not a part of him but some throbbing, painful parasite that had fastened itself to the end of his arm. He thought of the victim's hands. He had been holding them up, hadn't he? That was how his fingers had ended up so bashed and mangled. He had been trying to ward off the blows. The blows that had been inflicted with . . . a violin?

It could not have been a violin. Something that looked like one, maybe, but not a violin.

Then it came to him.

It came to him in one of those subtle, silent instants of clarity. No thunderbolt from heaven. No lightbulb popping on. Just sudden understanding emerging from within, fully formed, entire. Like a map being unrolled, revealing the full lie of the land.

Seconds later, he was back at van Wyk's side.

'Van Wyk, I know who did this.'

'Oh really?'

'Yes really. This and all the other *shinjus*. And we have to go and arrest them right now, before they can dispose of the murder weapon.'

'Right now?' Van Wyk grinned superciliously. 'But Parry, surely we need authorization from the commissioner.'

'Never mind that.'

'Well, what about the Constitution? Measure Five forbids—'

'Van Wyk, I never thought I'd hear myself say this, and I know *you* never thought you'd hear me say this, but to hell with the Constitution. And to hell with the commissioner. We may already be too late, but if we don't move now, we may never get a chance like this again.'

'Well now.' Van Wyk eyed Parry appraisingly and with a certain amount of approval. 'You've certainly changed your tune.'

'I'm just fed up with these wankers giving us the runaround. We can stop them, right now. You, me and Johansen. How about it?'

'You know who they are?'

'I do.'

'Definitely?'

'I'm sure of it.'

Van Wyk grinned. 'Then enough chitchat. Let's get moving.'

INTERLUDE

One Day Ago . . .

You should've known this might happen. In a way you did *know, so it doesn't matter so much. You were sort of prepared for the possibility. It was one of the many variables you had to take into account, so you already know what countermeasures you need to deploy.*

In your hotel room, he sits on the edge of the bed and wrings his hands. An inarticulate manufolding.

'I can't go on,' he says.

'Yes, you can.'

'I can't stand it any longer. The lying. The deception.'

'You've been doing great so far.'

'I think he knows.'

'He doesn't have a clue.'

'And I . . . I like him. I feel sorry for him.'

'Don't. He doesn't deserve your sympathy.'

'I want out.'

'There isn't much more to do. Just a few more days, that's all. Everything's running fine. Better than fine! We just have to keep our nerve and keep going. We can do this!'

'But I'm scared all the time. Scared someone's going to catch me. I'm risking so much!'

'You're risking so much?*' It's time for some judicious anger. Time to set him straight on a couple of things. 'Compared with me you're risking nothing!'*

'I'm an accessory.'

'And I'm the fucking criminal! You think you *could get into trouble? Look what* I'm *doing! You think what* you're *doing is hard? Try walking in* my *shoes, my friend! Christ, I thought you were stronger than this. I thought you were more of a man.'*

He flinches, as though whipped. He stops wringing his hands. He goes slack, subdued.

'I'm sorry,' he says, limply. 'I'm sorry. I don't find this easy, that's all.'

349

You soften, too. Forgivingly. Like a parent with a child.

'Hey, I understand.' You touch his shoulder. 'It isn't easy. But if it was, I'd have asked someone else to do it. I wouldn't have chosen you if I didn't think you were up to the challenge. We're a team, man. We're partners. You and me – we rely on each other. That's how it works.'

He doesn't say anything for a while. Your hand remains on his shoulder. If he stands up and tries to kiss you, you'll kill him. There's a hunting knife in the drawer of the bedside table, on top of the Bible. You'll gut him in one swift stroke like a fish. You'll slice him up like fucking sushi.

But he doesn't try anything. He just sits there, then says, 'Of course. Forgive me. A team. You're right. I'm sorry about all this. I let the pressure get to me. I don't know what I was thinking.'

You pat him once, then let go of him. 'It's no big deal. Just a few more days, then it'll all be over.'

'I can manage that.'

'Good. Good fellow.'

After he leaves, you know that at some point you are going to have to kill him. Once he's outlived his usefulness (as the saying goes), he's dead. You can't afford to have him roaming around, obsessing over his complicity. Eventually his conscience will get the better of him and he'll crack, and then he'll sell you out. You're quite certain of that. Guy like him, he won't be able to stop himself.

That's OK, though. Killing him won't be a problem.

You didn't really want to have to share the loot anyway.

FINALE

39 ATTACK

'Give them a bit longer,' said Parry, peering through the bars of the gate into the darkened garden. The gravel path shone like a meandering moonlit river. Free World House rose at the end, a tall, pale oblong inset with black squares of unilluminated window. 'They live there. There *must* be somebody home.'

'Do you want me to try the bell again?' said Johansen.

'Leave it just another moment.' Parry stared at the house, willing a light to come on. The Xenophobes had to be in. This was their stronghold, their lair. Where else would they run to? He glanced back at the launch that was tethered outside the gate. In the days of combustion engines, he would have been able to tell if the launch had been used within the past half-hour by laying a hand on the motor housing. Comp-res engines, however, generated negligible quantities of heat, so there was no simple way of telling if the boat was the getaway vehicle the Xenophobes had used to return here from the Scroll. He was almost certain it was, though.

'Looks to me,' said van Wyk, never one to miss an opportunity to carp, 'as if we've had a wasted journey.'

Parry ignored the comment and was about to tell Johansen to press the bell button again when a downstairs window abruptly filled with brightness. Seconds later, a wary voice issued from the intercom speaker.

'Yeah? Who is this? And d'you know what bloody time it is?'

It was the aborigine. What was he called? Greg.

'Evening, Greg,' Parry said, leaning towards the intercom microphone, falsely breezy. 'Foreign Policy Police. I was wondering if we might have a word.'

'Pretty late for a social visit. What's this about?'

'Can we come in?'

'Hold on.'

There was silence from the intercom for a while. Parry exchanged glances with Johansen, then with van Wyk. The

353

lieutenant gave him an encouraging wink. The Afrikaner had still to be impressed.

'Captain Parry?' Now the voice from the intercom speaker was the rich, sinewy baritone of Toroa MacLeod.

'Mr MacLeod.'

'To what do we owe the pleasure?'

'I'm here with two of my fellow officers. We'd like to speak to you.'

'Again? What's it about this time?'

'I'd prefer we didn't do this standing out here.'

'You can at least tell me what it is you want to discuss.'

'A matter of some importance. The sort of thing that's better said face to face.'

'I'm not even going to think about letting you in until you state your business, Captain. I've told you before, I know my rights and I know my Constitution.'

'But you know me, too, Mr MacLeod. You know what sort of person I am. You know that you can trust me, but also that I'm persistent.'

'And that's supposed to be some sort of threat, is it?'

'All I'm saying is, I'm prepared to stand out here all night if I have to. Do you want that? Do you want me standing out here, leaning on the doorbell button every five minutes?'

There was a pause, then MacLeod said, 'Harassment.'

'It's only harassment if you have nothing to hide.'

MacLeod laughed. 'Can I really be talking to Captain Jack Parry? This doesn't sound like him at all.'

'Will you let us in, Mr MacLeod?'

Another pause, then heavily, calculatingly, the Xenophobe said, 'All right. Very well.'

The intercom buzzed. The gate clanked open, and as it did so, Parry noticed that there was a bolt fitted to its outer upright, pointing vertically downwards. When the gate was fully open, the bolt could be lowered into a socket embedded in the edge of the path.

Without knowing quite why – sensing, perhaps instinctively, that a clear exit route might be necessary – he waited until the gate had swung through the full ninety degrees and come to a rest against its stop, then bent down and shot the bolt home. There was a click as the gate's automatic closing mechanism disengaged. With a glance at his two companions, Parry started up the path, van Wyk following him, then Johansen.

They were halfway to the house when a floodlight mounted above the front door came on, bathing the garden in brilliance. As Parry raised a hand to shield his eyes against the sudden dazzle, he heard the front door open. The next thing he heard was a familiar tick-tack pattering, the sound of dog claws on gravel.

He had warned van Wyk and Johansen on the way over to expect the Alsatians. He had also told them what they should do in order to stay safe – keep to the path. He was confident Johansen would heed the advice, but van Wyk he was not so sure about. There was no guarantee that the Afrikaner might not attempt something rash.

Against the flare of light, Parry glimpsed Pinkerton and Butterfly hurtling towards him in a series of long, hunching lunges, their paws kicking up small scuffs of gravel behind them. Their heads were hung low, their ears were flattened, and as they drew closer he could see that the muzzles of both of them were split by great brutal grins.

All at once he was certain that, this time, the dogs had been sent out not to provide an escort but to attack.

He stopped dead in his tracks. Behind him, Johansen and van Wyk did the same. There was no time to run and even if there had been he doubted he would have been able to move. His body had seized up, leaving him locked inside himself, a prisoner in a statue-stiff shell, petrified. Thoughts flashed. How much pain would there be? How bad would the injuries be?

At the last possible instant, almost as if they had never had any intention of stopping, the Alsatians came to a halt, skidding on the gravel. They stood in front of Parry, angled towards him like the hands of a clock at ten-to-two. Their bodies were rigid, their heads raised, their teeth bared. Their eyes defied him to move, to so much as twitch a finger. He remembered how intimidating their silence had seemed the last time he had encountered them. It was worse now, when they were showing him their fangs, clenched and snugly interlocking sickles of bone, exposed clear to the gums. A growl from either of them would have been, in a strange way, welcome. It was not normal, this inculcated muteness. It was eerie, unnatural. Machine-like.

'Well, well, what do we have here?' Out through the front doorway came MacLeod, rubbing his hands together. Greg emerged behind him. 'Captain Parry. And friends. Captain van Wyk. And the big Aryan poster-boy, what's your name again? Jonsson? Jorgensen? Something like that.'

Johansen let out a huff of displeasure, which he would have followed up with some kind of surly retort had Parry not interrupted him with a raised hand. 'Pål, I'll handle this. Mr MacLeod, I think it'd be better for all of us if you were to send the dogs back indoors.'

'For all of us? What would *I* gain from it?' MacLeod strolled a few paces down the path, then halted, fists on hips.

Parry glanced down at Pinkerton and Butterfly – poised, pointed, patient, primed. There was no doubt in his mind that the dogs were ready to attack on command. One word from MacLeod and they would be on him. Those teeth! The question was: would MacLeod dare give that command? And the answer was: if Parry's guess was right, if MacLeod *was* the one responsible for the *shinjus*, then yes, he probably *would* dare. He had nothing to lose, after all. He must realize why the FPP were here. He must sense that the game was up, and that although he might have succeeded in bluffing them yesterday at HQ, he wasn't going to be able to do so again, not this time, not now.

'I just thought that a man like you wouldn't need to hide behind guard dogs,' Parry said, selecting his words as carefully as a watchmaker selects components. He knew that he had embarked on one of the most important negotiations of his life. Maybe even a negotiation *for* his life.

'Meaning what, exactly? That I'm a coward?' MacLeod chuckled, a lightless sound, like coal tumbling into a scuttle. 'Try and see it from my point of view, Captain. You come to my premises, my home, unannounced, in the middle of the night. You ask to be invited in without giving a reason for your presence. You bully your way in as though you're, I don't know, let's think. The Stasi? The KGB? Someone like that. I, for my part, have a legitimate form of security, a means of protecting myself and my colleagues from just this kind of unwarranted intrusion. I'd be foolish if I didn't use it.'

'I understand that. Nevertheless, you strike me as a man who prefers to be on an equal footing with his opponents. A man who likes a level playing field. Which this' – Parry risked a tiny nod at the Alsatians – 'is clearly not.'

'Ah yes. That's me, isn't it? The noble savage.'

'Don't put words into my mouth.'

'I don't have to. I know what you think of me. A jumped-up primitive. Little better than a missionary-boiling cannibal.'

'I think you need to believe that that's how people think of you. It gives you something else to feel aggrieved about. In a way, you'd hate to be thought of as civilized. But of course that's exactly what you are.'

'Right, yes. How flattering. "Civilized." And the civilized thing to do would be call the dogs off, am I correct?'

Parry nodded.

'It would also be the unwise thing,' said MacLeod, folding his arms, intransigence personified. 'Only an idiot fails to use all the advantages at his disposal, and Pinkerton and Butterfly are definitely my best advantage over you.'

'Parry?' said van Wyk. 'Parry, let's just turn and go. We can come back later. With reinforcements.'

'Yes, yes, very sensible of you, Captain van Wyk.' MacLeod twiddled a finger in midair. 'Turn and go.'

And, thought Parry, then what? While they were walking away, MacLeod would set the dogs on them. Or he would not, but by the time they returned (with, as van Wyk had suggested, reinforcements, including people to handle the dogs if necessary) MacLeod would be gone. On to the mainland. Over the hills and far away. He would be found eventually, and brought to justice and convicted, but in the meantime he would be free to commit more crimes and Parry could not allow that. MacLeod had to be arrested today. Right here. Now.

He fixed his gaze on MacLeod. The floodlight tinged the Xenophobe's head with a corona of yellow radiance. His tattooed face was cast into shadow. Amid the shadow, his eyes, small in their sockets, glinted blackly. Here he was. The man who had killed four Sirens and committed four Xenocides. The man who had sullied the sanctity of New Venice. The man who had poisoned the place for Foreigners, so that now word was spreading among them – *steer clear*. The man who had ruined the city. Here he was. And Parry knew he was never going to get another chance like this. And so he knew that he had no choice.

He raised his right foot. Brought it forward. Let the sole of his shoe come to rest again on the gravel – a soft, biscuity crunch.

The Alsatians blinked. He could almost have sworn it. Blinked, as though unable to believe what they had just seen.

He took a second step, placing his left foot ahead of his right.

357

His left thigh was now less than ten centimetres from the tip of Pinkerton's nose. Pinkerton twitched a glance at MacLeod, the erect black triangles of his ears ever so slightly, just perceptibly, wilting. You could see what he was thinking. *This is all very perplexing. Should I attack? Surely I should be attacking.*

'I'd advise you not to come any closer,' said MacLeod. 'They're trained to restrain, not to kill, but you know how dogs are. There's no guarantee, if I set them on you, that they won't get . . . over-enthusiastic.'

Parry stared straight at MacLeod, deep into the black pearls that were his eyes. It was a look that said, *I'm not bluffing.* A look he was able to make convincing only because he really was *not* bluffing.

He took a third step and a fourth, and the fabric of his trousers brushed Pinkerton's muzzle, and Pinkerton jerked his head back, no longer looking puzzled, now looking downright distraught. The expression on Butterfly's face was the same. Why were they not being called upon to defend the household? These three men were unquestionably interlopers. They should be chased off the premises.

'Final warning,' MacLeod intoned. But wasn't there the tiniest tremor of uncertainty in his voice? As if Parry's insane defiance was the last thing he had been expecting?

'Parry . . .' There was no mistaking the emotion in van Wyk's voice: anxiety. He could see Parry getting all three of them hurt with this behaviour.

Nevertheless: another step. Both dogs were behind Parry now and MacLeod was just a few metres ahead. A couple more paces and it would be possible to reach the Xenophobe with a running jump; take him down before he could give the dogs the attack command. Parry's mouth was dry, his belly was knotted and he could feel his heartbeat in his teeth. He could not believe what he was doing and yet at the same time he knew he could not do anything else. By deploying the dogs, MacLeod had thrown down a gauntlet, and against all sense and reason Parry had picked it up. Challenge accepted. How about *that*, MacLeod? What are you going to do *now*?

Another step.

'Very well, then.' MacLeod squared his shoulders. There was resolution in his stance. Finality.

Oh Christ, thought Parry.

Then—

'Hey! Doggies! Here, doggies!'

Parry wheeled round.

Johansen was off the path and waving at the Alsatians with both arms. 'Look! Look where I am! Come and get me!'

'Pål, no!'

But it was too late. Pinkerton and Butterfly were off like bullets from a gun. MacLeod yelled something to them, but they did not hear. Their canine minds registered one fact only: a non-resident of the house had broken the cardinal rule of the garden and stepped off the pathway. That transgression overrode all other concerns.

As soon as he was sure that the Alsatians were coming for him, Johansen turned and made for the gate. Quite clearly he thought he had a chance of outrunning the dogs. He was not, however, with his tree-trunk torso and thick, lumbering limbs, a person built for speed, and, although accelerating as fast as he could, he managed fewer than a dozen strides before Pinkerton caught up.

With a leap, Pinkerton snagged Johansen's shirtsleeve with his teeth. Johansen stumbled but carried on running, lugging the dog after him. Then Butterfly came alongside and lunged for Johansen's leg, sinking her teeth into the meat of his calf. Johansen cried out, staggered, but kept on going, dragging himself along with his other leg. Pinkerton relinquished his hold, reared back, and went for the same spot on Johansen's forearm, and this time his fangs closed on flesh as well as fabric. Again Johansen cried out, but still, remarkably, he persevered. Momentum and sheer brute strength propelled him on towards the gate, with both Alsatians clinging on to him and blood now visible, spilling out over his hand and his ankle. Reaching the gateway, he lurched through, taking the dogs with him, and as he did so, he twisted his head round and yelled, 'Boss!' It was not a plea for help. He had done his part. Now Parry must do his.

Parry, looking on in startlement and horror, could only nod. He was pretty sure his lieutenant did not see this, for Johansen was already moving away from the gateway. Bleeding profusely now, still jaw-gripped by the unrelenting Alsatians, he was making for the canal. Butterfly, as if sensing what her quarry intended to do, planted her paws on the walkway paving and pulled harder than ever in the opposite direction, and Johansen let out an appalling howl as something in his leg – something intrinsic, something crucial – *tore*. Not even this, though, could prevent him from reaching the edge of the walkway. He teetered beside the canal, just next to the prow of the Xenophobes' launch, and for a moment Parry thought he was not going to succeed. Both Alsatians were resisting him now, backpedalling, tugging at him, yanking, trying to bring him down. It was a battle of wills as much as of strength, and had Johansen lost heart and relented and fallen back on to the walkway, one or other of the dogs would have surely gone in for the kill, ripping his throat out.

But Johansen was stubborn and had bulk on his side. He strained forwards till he was leaning over the canal, and once he had passed a certain angle of declivity, gravity took over. He toppled, and the dogs, to whom it did not even occur to let go, went with him. With an immense splash he hit the water, and Pinkerton and Butterfly plunged in alongside him, headfirst.

What happened thereafter, Parry was unable to see. There was a sound of thrashing and churning in the canal, but the walkway was a metre higher than the water's surface, and Johansen and the dogs were hidden from view.

He felt an impulse to rush to Johansen's rescue. But Johansen had drawn the dogs away for a reason. In depriving MacLeod of his canine edge, he had evened up the odds. He would be annoyed if Parry let his effort and self-sacrifice go to waste.

So instead Parry rounded on MacLeod and levelled a finger at him. 'You,' he snarled, 'are fucking *dead*.' And he charged at the Xenophobe, powering towards him over the gravel.

He would have wagered good money on MacLeod standing his ground. MacLeod, however, for no immediately obvious reason, did the opposite, turning about-face and heading for the front door. Parry sprinted after him, but was intercepted by Greg, who tackled him around the waist and brought him crashing to the ground. The two of them thumped on to the grass, with Greg on top, a position he swiftly capitalized on by straddling Parry's chest, pinning his arms down. Parry writhed and strained, but Greg leaned forward with all his weight on his knees. Parry's heels scrabbled but could not gain any purchase on the grass, and so he could not obtain any leverage with which to buck Greg off. Where the hell was van Wyk? He saw Greg drawing back his fist. He saw the fist – a burled, grey-knuckled, gnarly thing – come hurtling towards his face. He braced himself for the blow . . .

. . . and then Greg's weight was no longer on him, and Parry heaved himself on to his side, and there was Greg prone on the grass, and there was van Wyk, knee planted squarely in the small of Greg's back, forcing Greg's left arm up between his shoulder-blades in an agonizing half-Nelson. Greg yelled, Greg lashed backwards at van Wyk with his right hand, but Greg was not going to break free of the hold any time soon.

'Well, go on!' van Wyk shouted to Parry, with a jerk of his head. 'Don't just lie there. MacLeod! *MacLeod!*'

Parry scrambled to his feet, took a moment to orient himself, then set off for the front door. Things had got badly out of hand, but there was no time to dwell on that. Right this moment, what was or was not Constitutional did not matter. What mattered was MacLeod. Getting MacLeod. Making him pay. For the *shinjus*. For the chaos he had brought to New Venice. For the aggravation he had caused Parry personally. For Johansen.

The front door was half open. Parry barged through. The hallway, with its array of ethnic artefacts, was empty, MacLeod nowhere to be seen. Swiftly Parry scanned the walls, searching for an absence. There. Next to the knobkerrie. A pair of empty brackets where Senhora Coutinho's 'violin' had hung. The odd-shaped club he had seen on his previous visit to Free World House. There it had been, in plain view. How amusing that must have been to MacLeod – to have invited Parry over, knowing he would have to walk through a room containing the club and that his gaze might even come to rest on the item itself, completely unaware that it was the weapon responsible for the Xenocides and the most recent homicide. The sheer bloody nerve of the man.

Footsteps.

Parry spun round.

MacLeod, running at him from the direction of the staircase. He had been hiding there, behind the stairs.

In his hand – the selfsame violin-shaped club. A few smeary bloodstains on its striking surface.

There was no time to think. MacLeod was coming too fast. Parry brought his arms up reflexively, covering his face. He twisted sideways, hunching himself. The club whirred through the air, and there was a dull detonation just below his right shoulderblade. He reeled from the impact. There was an instant of numbness, then a sudden sunburst of pain, shooting up through his ribs and along his arm. He gasped. Hissed. Gritted his teeth. Looked up. The club was on the backswing, MacLeod's muscle-clustered forearm drawing it behind his head. Parry recalled the self-defence techniques drilled into him years ago during his police training. How to deal with close-combat weapons. Instinct was to back away, but the best method of rendering a close-combat weapon ineffectual was to do the reverse and move in, getting inside the arc of use.

With a desperate growl, he threw himself at MacLeod. It was like colliding with the flank of an ox – sheer meaty solidity. He grabbed MacLeod around the chest with his right arm. With his left hand, he seized MacLeod's wrist, halting the club on the downstroke. The wrist twisted and turned in his grasp. He dug his fingers in hard, then lowered his head and shoved, thrusting MacLeod bodily backwards at the nearest wall, sending him thumping shoulders first against a woven rug of some kind, richly coloured and patterned.

Still struggling to control MacLeod's clubbing arm, he began punching him in the side. Ribs. Waist. Hip. Again and again he drove his knuckles into MacLeod. MacLeod took it. He rammed a knee into MacLeod's thigh. MacLeod did not flinch. He aimed a jab at MacLeod's solar plexus. MacLeod grunted at the blow.

Then, in a lofty, lordly manner, MacLeod began to laugh, and all at once it was clear to Parry that he was being toyed with here. MacLeod, like a schoolyard bully, was allowing him to get a few licks in so that his punishment, when it came, would be all the more deserved and all the more severe. Still, there was nothing for it but to keep hitting him. Stopping now would be tantamount to admitting defeat.

MacLeod tolerated the assault for a few moments longer, then, deciding enough was enough, he grabbed the back of Parry's shirt collar with his free hand, yanked Parry backwards and, with a grin, kicked his legs out from under him. As Parry sagged, MacLeod held him by the collar, supporting his weight. Parry saw MacLeod's head rise and go back. He saw neck tendons tensing, jaw muscles tightening, and he knew what was coming. There was no way to avoid it. The best he could do was try to limit the damage.

It came like a violent nod, a gesture of agreement perverted. Aiming for the bridge of Parry's nose, MacLeod delivered the headbutt with all the force he could muster, but just as the blow descended Parry brought his own head forwards and down, and so instead of brow meeting cartilage, brow met brow, bone against bone, a hollow, teeth-clacking collision that stunned both him and

MacLeod. Losing their grip on each other, the two of them stumbled apart. Scarlet-and-gold catherine wheels flew across Parry's vision. He clutched the top of his forehead, staggering. A field of pain flared through his skull. He tasted bile at the back of his throat. He swallowed hard and searched through screwed-up eyelids for MacLeod.

MacLeod, hunched over, was also clutching his forehead. Looking up, his gaze met Parry's, and his mouth elongated into a sneer.

'Fucking *Pakeha*,' he snarled and lumbered towards Parry again, club aloft.

He's going to kill me, Parry thought, even as he braced himself for this new assault. He's not going to stop until he's fucking killed me.

In every violent situation Parry had been in during his Met days there had always been at least one other police officer at his side and the security of knowing that back-up was on its way. Not only that, but more often than not his opponents had been drunk or out of their heads on drugs, and therefore clumsy and easy to outwit. MacLeod was none of those things. MacLeod was a born fighter, and physically outclassed Parry as a pitbull outclasses a Yorkshire terrier. Not only that, but Parry was on his own. Van Wyk had his own Xenophobe to handle, and even supposing he was able to come to Parry's assistance, would it make any difference? MacLeod was more than a match for the two of them. *And* he had a weapon.

These thoughts flashed through Parry's mind in the space of less than a second, and then MacLeod was on him. He blocked a clout from the club with his forearm, and Jesus Christ it *hurt*, pain jangling along his ulna and radius like vibrations along the twin tines of a tuning fork, but then he had his hand on MacLeod's face and he was clawing at it, sinking his fingers in. He felt the moistness of mouth and the roughness of eyebrows and the resilient protrusion of nose, and he imagined MacLeod's face as a piece of paper he was scrunching up, and he clenched his fingers tighter, and he heard MacLeod yell out in pain, and then he himself was the one yelling out in pain as something struck him hard on the side of the head, MacLeod's fist, and struck him again, his ear going numb and thunderously deaf, and again, his skull shaking atop its vertebral stem, and he let go of MacLeod's face, and MacLeod was growling, and almost by feel alone Parry found the club and tried to wrench it out of the Xenophobe's grasp, because that was the real danger here, fists could hurt but the club could truly harm, and then he and MacLeod were grappling over the weapon, and then (he did not know how it happened – maybe MacLeod tripped him, maybe he tripped MacLeod) they were on the floor, lying on their sides on the zigzag-pattern parquet, still grappling over the weapon, pressed against each other like lovers, grunting, furious, Parry kicking MacLeod, MacLeod pummelling Parry with his free hand, and Parry was prising hard with his fingers and at last he felt the handle of the club coming loose, and all of a sudden the club was free and skidding across the floor, and Parry thought he glimpsed feet, bare feet, just where it fetched up, and then he realized that MacLeod must have let go of the club on purpose, probably because it was not so easily wielded while they were both struggling on the floor, and then he understood the real reason why MacLeod had let go as he felt both of MacLeod's hands clamp around his neck –

– what an exposed portion of the anatomy a neck was; how terrifyingly vital, vulnerable, it was –

– MacLeod's hands like pincers, squeezing, crushing –

– Parry flailing his fists against MacLeod's arms, and they were girder-thick, implacable –

– Christ, he couldn't breathe –

– head bloating with blood –

– a sound in his ears like a torrent of water –

– chrysanthemum-bursts of colour in his vision –

– couldn't breathe –

– this was it –

– flailing, failing –

– Anna –

Inhale!

Sharp, sweet air. Coughing, choking, and his windpipe feeling ragged, lined with broken glass. Inhale! Another wheezing in-gulp of air, and yes, he was breathing, he was able to breathe, his throat was no longer constricted, he could *breathe*. MacLeod had let go. MacLeod had spared him?

MacLeod?

Nearby. Sprawled on the floor like a sleeping infant. Blood glistening in his hair. Blood?

Beyond him, the violin-shaped club, dangling from a man's hand.

Parry blinked. Logical thought was beginning to return, comprehension dawning.

The Tibetan Xenophobe, clad in a striped cotton dressing-gown, was standing over MacLeod, clasping the club loosely as if unsure whether to keep a hold of it or drop it. On his face there was a look of grim revulsion, whether directed at MacLeod or himself it was hard to say.

Parry struggled up to a kneeling position. His head was ringing. His throttled throat throbbed. 'Sir?' he said. The word came out as rough as sandpaper.

'Is he dead?' the monk asked, not looking up.

As if in answer to the question, MacLeod moaned softly.

The monk's shoulders sank and the club fell from his fingers, hitting the floor with a clunk.

'Karma,' he murmured to MacLeod.

Parry clambered to his feet.

'Phone,' he croaked to the monk.

40 SPIRITUAL

The ambulance pulled away from Free World House and nosed slowly and carefully past a trio of tethered FPP launches. In clear water beyond, it picked up speed and its roof-mounted emergency lights came on, enclosing it within a whirling, hectic cocoon of reflected red. Parry watched it make a right turn and disappear from view. It would be at St Cecilia's within a quarter of an hour. There, emergency-room doctors were waiting. The paramedics had reassured him that both the injured men aboard the ambulance would receive immediate and first-rate medical attention, the very best that any resort-city had to offer. The wellbeing of MacLeod, who according to the paramedics was suffering from concussion and possibly a fractured skull, Parry was not so worried about. Johansen, though, was a different matter. If for any reason *he* didn't pull through . . .

He told himself not to think that way. Not only was Johansen in good hands, but he was fit, strong, healthy. In fact, barely twenty minutes ago, Parry had been marvelling at his lieutenant's might and tenacity. This was when he emerged from Free World House after summoning the ambulance, to find Johansen clinging to the side of the Xenophobes' launch, one arm hooked over the gunwales, kicking with his good leg to stay afloat. The Alsatians, by this time, had extricated themselves from the canal by means of a nearby slipway and were sitting on the walkway, sodden, bedraggled, and looking not at all vicious or threatening – more sheepish than German Shepherd. Their dunk in the water had had a chastening effect on them, and when the monk called to them from the gateway, they responded only too eagerly, hurrying ahead of him up the path, glad to be returning to the warmth and the dryness and the certainty of indoors.

With some effort, Parry managed to haul Johansen around the boat and, with Johansen's groaning assistance, out of the canal and on to the walkway. The lieutenant had lost a lot of blood, and was losing still more rapidly. It was spilling from his wounds, mingling pinkly with the rivulets of water pouring from his clothing. He was going into shock, starting to shudder, burbling incomprehensibly in Norwegian. Kneeling, Parry undid Johansen's trouser belt, slid it off and tied it around Johansen's thigh as a tourniquet, then pressed a wadded-up handtowel, which the monk fetched from the house, to the deep ragged dog-bite in Johansen's calf. It seemed to work, the flow of blood abating, but Parry could not have been more relieved when, at last, the paramedics appeared and took over. He stood back and watched them set to work with quick, cool efficiency – giving oxygen, administering morphine, inserting a plasma drip, binding wounds – and he sent up a small prayer of gratitude that these men and women existed. You seldom gave them a thought until they were needed, until they were saving the life of someone you cared about.

As the ambulance's wake settled, Parry turned away from the canal, passed back through the gateway and followed the path up to the house. Although Pinkerton and Butterfly were locked up inside, he still could not bring himself to take a direct route to the front door, straight across the lawn. Silly, but there you are. Every step he took triggered a fanfare of small agonies. His neck hurt the worst of all, with the top of his forehead coming a close second. His right latissimus dorsi muscle, just below the shoulderblade, was beginning to stiffen up as a consequence of the clout it had received from the club. A great oval bruise was welling on his left forearm. Various other aches and abrasions, too many to count, added to his suffering. One of the paramedics had suggested that he should come to the hospital too, but he had refused. Though everything seemed pretty much sorted out here, there was still work to be done, and as long as he felt fit enough to do it – which he did, just barely – then he had to remain. The paramedic had given him an analgesic patch, and he had attached it to the underside of his wrist but it had yet to take effect.

In the hallway, an officer from van Wyk's district was keeping watch over the club, which lay on the floor where the Tibetan monk had dropped it. The club, which Parry now knew to be a Maori weapon called a *patu*, was the crucial piece of evidence in the *shinju* case. Blood samples taken from it, and a comparison between it and the injuries inflicted on the Siren found in the alley next to the Scroll, would determine if it had been the murder weapon. Van Wyk had ordered that it was not to be moved or even touched until the criminalists came.

Upstairs, in the Xenophobes' campaign office, van Wyk was attempting to interrogate Greg and not having much joy. The aborigine sat in silence, massaging his left shoulder and keeping his gaze truculently lowered, refusing to meet his questioner's eye. As Parry glanced in through the doorway, van Wyk threw him a look of exasperation. Parry nodded noncommittally. Not his concern. He had someone else to talk to. He carried on up to the next floor, where, in the conference room in which he had first met MacLeod, the Tibetan monk was now waiting for him.

The monk was still wearing nothing but the striped dressing-gown, and it looked incongruous on him, too mundanely modern for a man whose customary attire embodied a centuries-old spiritual tradition. He looked round when Parry entered the room, and as his head turned, his cap of fine hair-stubble caught the glare of the downlighters with an iridescent ripple.

'Your lieutenant,' he asked, 'how is he?'

'As well as can be expected,' Parry replied. His voice was a laryngitic rasp, hoarse and strained.

'And Toroa?'

'He'll recover.'

'I'm glad. For his sake *and* for mine. The Buddha holds that all life is sacred. To take life is absolutely forbidden.'

'Well, I think you're safe on that count. And you prevented the taking of *my* life, which has got to balance things out, surely.'

'Possibly.' The monk gave a half-smile. 'It could almost be a *koan*, couldn't it? Something for the novices to ponder. "Should one be prepared to kill in order to prevent killing?"'

'If it helps, I'm very grateful to you for intervening.'

The monk waved a hand, as if to say, *It's nothing.*

Parry sat down opposite him, lowering himself gingerly so as not to jar his neck. 'Listen, you haven't told me your name . . .'

Either the monk did not hear, or heard but did not think the matter important, for he said, 'I could have prevented more death tonight, Captain. I was aware what Toroa and Greg were planning. I could have told you yesterday at FPP Headquarters what they were intending to do. I am ashamed that I did not, but my loyalties were in conflict.'

Parry recalled the significant look the monk had given him as the Xenophobes were leaving the basement.

'I have my religious beliefs, you understand,' the monk continued, 'but also my political ones. Mostly the two coincide, but sometimes they do not. You perhaps wonder why someone like me has thrown in his lot with the Xenophobe movement.'

'It had crossed my mind.'

'The reason is very simple. I was born, Captain, in a country under siege, a country occupied by a nation hostile to its people and traditions and religion. I grew up watching Chinese soldiers break up peaceful demonstrations with tear gas and guns. I saw members of my own family imprisoned for daring to voice opposition to Beijing. Resistance to occupation and adherence to faith were all but synonymous then. And as I come from such a background, it would be hard for me, both as a Tibetan and a Buddhist, to stand back and do nothing while the entire world suffers a similar kind of occupation. China attempted to stamp out Tibet's native culture and religion and even its language, and almost succeeded, and the Foreigners, as I see it, are doing something similar to our planet, not with violence, nor it seems with any degree of deliberate intent, but no less effectively for that.'

'I'd dispute that point, but my voice just isn't up to it.' Parry tried to laugh, but all that emerged from his windpipe was a rough hiss.

'Though there might appear to be a contradiction between the tenets of Buddhism and Xenophobia, Captain,' the monk went on, in his measured, accentless English, 'to my mind there is none. To be a Xenophobe and engage in non-violent protest against Foreigners does not run counter to the teachings of the Buddha. Indeed, when it comes to Foreigners, there is no Buddhist doctrine at all. At least, no official doctrine. Perhaps you are aware of a belief held by certain denominations of my religion, a belief not sanctioned by the Dalai Lama but popular none the less, that Foreigners are brahma deities. You have heard of this?'

Parry shook his head, or rather moved it a few degrees to the right then stopped because it hurt. 'No,' he said.

The monk sat forward in his chair, pressing his hands together in the manner of one zealous about explaining. 'In Buddhist cosmology, Captain, there are many realms of existence. The second highest of these is the *rupa-dhatu*, the realm of form. It is the home of lesser gods, those who still have a connection with events in the lower cosmological strata, unlike the gods of the *arupa-dhatu*, the realm of formlessness, the highest realm, who spend their long lives in the deepest levels of yogic trance and are beyond all earthly concerns. According to our myths, the gods of the *rupa-dhatu* enter the lower realms at the time of earthly cataclysm, which recurs periodically through the ages. As the destruction takes hold, in the form of a flood that deluges the land and wipes out the human race, they come down to take up residence. From them the next race of humans is descended.' The monk held up a hand, as if in anticipation of a question. 'Of course, doubtless you are thinking: if the Foreigners are these gods, why are we not all drowned and dead? And you are right. What has happened this time round – or so, at any rate, those who hold this belief say – is that the gods of the *rupa-dhatu* have taken pity on us and come down early. Their timely arrival has averted the flood and broken the cycle of destruction and creation. It is for this reason that this belief is considered in some quarters heretical, since it runs counter to accepted Buddhist teachings. Although there is, I must admit, other evidence that would seem to give it some credence.'

'Other evidence?'

'Music, especially chanting, plays an integral part in Buddhism, more so than it does in any other religion, I think. Our sung mantras enable us to control various hidden energies within ourselves, and each of the eight main musical instruments we employ in our ceremonies has a counterpart sound within the body, so that the one can be used to arouse the other for devotional purposes, through sympathy between the outer and the inner. Music and the body, in other words, are intimately interrelated. You see? Then there are the *mudras*, the conventional gestures employed by artists in visual representations of the Buddha. These involve the positioning of the hands, each position having a specific significance. The parallels are intriguing, are they not? Although they could of course be nothing more than coincidence.'

'They could,' Parry said, thinking: The Foreigners as Buddhist deities? Well, he had heard stranger theories before. 'Listen, this is all very interesting, but—'

'But what is the point I am making? The point I am making, Captain, is this. I do not hate anyone or anything, and therefore I do not hate Foreigners. What I object to is the effect they are having on the world. If they are gods, which I doubt, but if they are, that is still not a reason to let them take over our lives and divert our individual and communal destinies in the way they have. Some say they have brought us to paradise. I say that is false. Escaping *samsara*, extracting oneself from the continual flow of transitory existence, moving beyond the ego and the miseries of living – in short, following the dictates of the Eightfold Noble Path and achieving *nirvana* – is a matter for each of us alone. Ethical behaviour can originate only from within the individual. It cannot be imposed from without, by gods or by anyone, and if we believe we have become better people thanks to the Foreigners, then we are mistaken, for all we have really done is found a means of convincing ourselves that we do not need to examine our lives any more or make the effort to improve. Saying we have achieved a paradise does not make it so. On the contrary, it makes it less likely than ever that we will achieve the perfection we are looking for.'

'Because someone's taken that responsibility away from us. Because we've become complacent.'

'Precisely so,' said the monk, sitting back, satisfied that he had got his point across. 'So now you understand how I feel about Foreigners, and why. I feel strongly that they have taken away an element of self-determination from us and caused us to become, as you say, complacent, self-deluded. But, for all that, I remain a Buddhist first and foremost. I cannot under any circumstances condone violence or killing. I have, therefore, been experiencing a conflict of interests this past day or so, ever since I learned what Toroa was up to. A conflict of interests which I was unable to resolve until just now, half an hour ago, when I heard the disturbance downstairs and came down and found Toroa viciously assaulting you. I saw him attempting to kill you and I realized I had to make a choice one way or the other, politics or religion. I chose religion.'

'For which, again, I'm grateful. So *is* MacLeod a Triple-Xer?' This was what Parry had been hoping he would be able to ascertain, beyond doubt, from the monk.

'He and Greg both are, in as much as anyone can be described as a member of that group. There is no formal initiation into Triple-X, no official roster of membership, no set of rules or conventions. One becomes a Triple-Xer simply by choosing to behave like a Triple-Xer. One's deeds define one's allegiance. You are aware of this, of course.'

'The definition has always been a little vague to me. You've made it clearer.'

'Good. But what you must also be clear about, Captain Parry, is that Toroa and Greg only became Triple-Xers on Saturday.'

'You mean Saturday a week ago. Before the first *shinju.*'

'No, I mean last Saturday. The day before yesterday. That was when they finally decided to commit murder in the name of their cause.'

'The day before yesterday?' Even if Parry's throat had been in full working order, there was every chance the words would still have emerged as a whisper, constricted by incredulity.

'Captain, neither Toroa nor Greg had anything to do with the first three *shinjus*. This is what I wish to explain to you most of all. I can vouch for their innocence. I live in this house with them, and I can attest to the fact that both of them were here on the nights the first three *shinjus* took place. Only on Saturday did Toroa begin openly to entertain the notion of committing one himself. The Triple-X slogan at the scene of the third *shinju* gave him the incentive. He thought that, since Xenophobe extremists were responsible for the crimes, there was no harm in joining in and contributing a similar crime of his own. And, of course, another *shinju* would only add to the atmosphere of fear and mistrust in New Venice and further alarm the Foreigners, perhaps even provide the final push necessary to get them to leave here for good.'

'MacLeod didn't commit the first three?'

Parry longed for it not to be true. He longed to believe that the monk was lying.

The facts, though, when considered in the light of what he had just heard, seemed to bear out the monk's claim. The modus operandi for the first three *shinjus* differed from that of this evening's in certain crucial aspects. The first three were in hotel rooms; this evening's took place outdoors. The first three were mocked up to look like suicides; this evening's was unarguably murder. The first three had been carefully planned and staged; this evening's was opportunistic and comparatively crude in its execution. He had thought the reason for the change in tactics was simply that the perpetrators had become lazy, made arrogant by the FPP's inability to catch them. In fact, it was the perpetrator who was different. MacLeod had merely jumped on the *shinju* bandwagon, that was all. Added a further storey to an edifice erected by someone else.

So whoever was responsible for the first three *shinjus* was still out there, roaming free. Parry had believed that the whole nightmare was over. He had thought the battle at Free World House just now marked the climax of the investigation. He had allowed himself the possibility of the hope that New Venice's sufferings, and his own, were at an end.

372

Wrong.
Wrong, wrong, wrong, wrong, *wrong*.

41 DISSONANCE

An hour later Parry finally felt able to leave Free World House. Everything seemed to be in hand. Greg had been taken to HQ and would be held under close guard in the basement until the mainland police came to fetch him sometime tomorrow morning. As for the two other New Venice Xenophobes, the Native American and the Mexican Indian, the monk had assured Parry that they were innocent of any involvement in MacLeod's schemes, and Parry had asked him, as a favour, to contact them and tell them to visit HQ as soon as they could in order to provide statements. He had then phoned Quesnel at her home and, without apologizing for waking her, brought her up to speed on recent events. She had told him that she would see him and van Wyk in her office in the morning at nine sharp, and offered him tentative congratulations on a job well done. When informed that MacLeod had been responsible only for the latest *shinju*, she had said, 'Well, it's still good news anyway, eh?' After that, he had made a call to St Cecilia's, but had been able to ascertain only that MacLeod and Johansen had arrived there and that the lieutenant was presently undergoing surgery.

By the time all this was done, he was left feeling drained and exhausted, hollow as a shucked husk. The lateness of the hour and his fight with MacLeod had taken their toll. His reserves of energy were low, his thoughts were sluggish, and when van Wyk advised him to go home, saying that he could handle things here by himself, Parry, who had never thought he would have cause to be grateful to Raymond van Wyk, thanked him and did as he had suggested.

One of van Wyk's officers chauffeured him to his apartment in a launch. In his kitchen, he made himself tea and carried the cup through to his bedroom. There he removed his clothes, which were sticky with Johansen's blood, and, leaving them in a heap on the floor, crawled sighingly into bed. Sleep stole over him before he could even think about drinking the tea. It was absolute sleep, like anaesthesia, deep and dreamless. He awoke from it shortly after seven in the morning, all stiffness and ache. He shuffled to the bathroom like an arthritic old man. The Jack Parry who blinked back at him from the mirror above the basin was a battered parody of himself – empurpled neck, swollen temple, red-raw bruises everywhere. Blood encrusted his hands; there were dried-dark crescents of it beneath his fingernails. Ruptured capillaries pinkened the whites of his eyes.

'You look a right sight,' he told his reflection.

His voice, at least, was no longer so hoarse.

He washed, stuck on a fresh analgesic patch, made and drank some tea and then went through the torture of getting dressed, forcing his uniform item by item on to his suffering body. His right arm gave him the most trouble. Any action that involved raising it, whether inserting it into a sleeve or doing up buttons above the level of his navel, was met with a painful, clenching protest from his latissimus. Putting on his tie was the stiffest, sorest procedure of all, but it was inconceivable that he go around tie-less. While in uniform? Never.

At HQ, there were congratulations to be fielded. Word had got around. Every officer he encountered on the way to his office greeted him with a grin and EXCELLENCE. Some, noting his injuries, tendered SYMPATHY as well.

In his office he called St Cecilia's and eventually was put through to one of the interns who had attended to Johansen last night. The lieutenant, he was told, was doing fine. Sedated but in a stable condition. The injury to his leg, particularly his Achilles tendon, was of some concern, but chances were good that the damage was remediable and Johansen would soon be walking again. Parry enquired after MacLeod, strictly out of professional interest, and was told that the Xenophobe was still unconscious and that a couple of FPP officers, along with a mainland policeman, were stationed by his bedside, keeping an eye on him. As Parry hung up, he made a mental note to visit Johansen that afternoon.

He had expected that Quesnel would tear a strip off him and van Wyk, if for nothing else than for failing to seek her authorization before making their visit to Free World House. But the commissioner, when the two of them presented themselves in her office at nine as scheduled, mentioned this lapse only in passing, dismissing it as an error born of necessity. Other than that, she had nothing but praise for them. They and Johansen had acted with great initiative and, when required, great courage. They should be proud of themselves.

And one of them, van Wyk, most decidedly was. He preened as Quesnel spoke, smug to the very tips of his ears, and Parry could just imagine the thoughts that were parading through his brain: visions of grandeur, Raymond van Wyk as saviour of the city, mighty catcher of villains, the man who had helped unearth (no, in van Wyk's head it would be played a pivotal role in unearthing) a Triple-X cell. But then van Wyk wasn't the one who had been beaten up by a club-wielding terrorist, nor the one who had watched a friend of his being savaged by guard dogs. Van Wyk could afford to exult. Parry had lost too much, not merely last night but over the past week, to feel that apprehending a pair of Triple-Xers was a success worth celebrating.

'Ma'am,' he said, while Quesnel was still in full commendatory flow, 'much as I hate to be a spoilsport, I feel obliged to remind you that we still have murderers, possibly another Triple-X cell, loose in this city.'

'I am aware of that, Jack.' Quesnel was, as he had hoped, in too good a mood to take umbrage at the interruption. 'You can allow an old girl one small moment of triumph, can't you?'

'With the greatest respect, until whoever's responsible for the first three *shinjus* is in the hands of the mainland police, I don't feel I can allow anyone anything.'

'Parry, isn't it just conceivable that you're being over-cautious here?' said van Wyk. 'If you ask me, MacLeod is behind all of the *shinjus*. I know what that Tibetan told you, but who's to say he's telling the truth?'

'Why would he lie?'

'To protect MacLeod. Or to protect *himself*. After all, if he knew what was going on and didn't tell us, that makes him an accessory. If he claims he sincerely didn't know what MacLeod was up to until a couple of days ago, then he's still an accessory, but it doesn't look nearly so bad.'

'I believe him.'

'You'd take him at his word? A Xenophobe?'

'I don't think he's capable of lying.'

'Listen, guys,' Quesnel interjected. 'I appreciate there's more work to be done on this. Right now, though, the main thing is that we have two felons in custody, which means we have good news to give the city. Speaking of which ... I've scheduled a press conference downstairs in about an hour's time, and I want both of you there with me. I want you to get the credit you deserve.'

'Can I ask, ma'am, what you intend to say?'

'At the press conference, Jack? What do you think? I'm going to let everyone know that the FPP has scored a great success.'

'You'll say that the problem's only been partly resolved?'

'I'll say that we have *shinju* perpetrators under arrest.'

'But you'll make it clear the investigation is still ongoing.'

'Well, sure.'

There. Her eyes had cut slightly to the left, before returning quickly to look at him. The merest flicker of a movement, but it told Parry everything he needed to know.

'You're going to make out as if it's all over,' he said, levelly, 'aren't you, ma'am?'

'I'm not going to lie, if that's what you're insinuating.' Quesnel was still sounding cheery, but the subtext was unmistakable: *Don't you dare presume to question me.*

'No, not lie. But you're going to – how shall I put this? – neglect to mention that MacLeod is responsible for one of the *shinjus* only. You're going to phrase things in such a way that everyone will assume he committed them all.'

'I'm going to say that we have, thanks to the efforts of three of my best officers, uncovered and arrested a Triple-X cell in our midst. I'll let everyone know that the investigation isn't complete, that there are still a few loose ends to be tied up—'

'But you won't explicitly state that there are other Triple-Xers still out there,' Parry insisted. 'That's what it comes down to, doesn't it? You're going to let everyone believe everything's all right again.'

Quesnel fixed him with a hard, glittering stare. Van Wyk was also staring at him, quite unable to fathom where this insolence had sprung from, this insubordination. How on earth could Parry talk to the commissioner in this way? What had got into him? Had he gone mad?

But it wasn't madness. If Parry had been sufficiently self-aware at that moment, able to step back from himself and examine objectively what he was doing and why, he would have perceived that what was motivating him was nothing other than a frayed, soul-deep weariness. He was weary of all the games, weary of all the etiquette and double-speak his job forced him to employ, weary

377

of being polite and saying what he thought others should hear and of other people saying what they thought others should hear. What did all these circumlocutions and circumventions achieve? Nothing. They wasted time and got no one anywhere. All this *talk* mired and muddied and muddled, and he was sick of it. Sick and tired. It was time for some honesty for a change. Time for some plain speaking.

'Captain,' said Quesnel (and Parry could not remember the last time she had addressed him by his rank), 'I can't believe you don't realize what a precarious state this city is in right now. New Venice is this close' – she held up a thumb and forefinger, squeezing half a centimetre of air between them – '*this* close to the abyss. I don't know if you caught the news this morning, but Foreign population density's down by nearly a quarter. The drop in numbers is accelerating, people are anxious, very anxious, and anything I can say – anything – to put minds at ease I *will* say. Anything I can do to lower the level of concern in this city I will do. And if that means finessing the facts, then goddamn it I'll finesse them, and I'm sorry if that doesn't sit right with you, but there's a lot more at stake here than just Jack Parry's peace of mind.'

Parry came right back at her, with a fearlessness that would have been inconceivable a week ago. 'And what happens when we find a fifth *shinju*, right after you lead everyone to believe there won't be another one? What then? Wasn't it bad enough last week, you on TV saying the Amadeus deaths were a one-off while I was sitting in a room at the Debussy with a set of Foreign remains on the balcony and a dead woman floating in the canal below? Didn't that little episode teach you something?'

'New Venice needs to hear it's safe again,' Quesnel retorted, with steely, incisive calm. 'Foreigners need to feel they can continue coming here. Sirens, too.'

'Even if New Venice isn't safe?'

'If the atmosphere in the city improves, Foreigners will pick up on that.'

'You mean you hope they will.'

'Yeah, OK. I *hope* they will. What else can I say? I can't be sure their numbers will go up again, but if people here relax, if Sirens feel it's OK to stay, then maybe it'll happen.'

'But what if—'

'And in the meantime,' Quesnel said, overriding him, 'the investigation goes on. We question MacLeod and his buddy, find out everything we can from them, and we continue looking for the other bunch of Triple-Xers. Quietly. Keeping it nice and low-key. Not making a song and dance about it. And if the other Triple-Xers assume that the heat's off them, then who knows? Maybe they'll decide now's a good time to stop the attacks, lie low, maybe even leave.'

'Or a good time to step up their campaign. Ma'am, I can't be a part of this.'

'No one's asking you to stand up and say everything's peachy and wonderful, Jack. All you have to do is be there next to me at the press conference and let me tell everybody what a good job you've done so far. You could maybe even smile, if you think you could manage it. And then you can get back to hunting for the other perpetrators. Just a few minutes in front of the cameras, that's all I'm asking from you, while I do what I can to pull this city back from the brink and maybe buy you some time into the bargain.'

'I can't,' Parry said, shaking his head as emphatically as his traumatized neck would allow. 'I *won't*.'

'Sometimes, Parry, you have to be prepared to compromise a little,' said van Wyk.

'Exactly,' said Quesnel.

'Well, in that case I have no choice.' Parry's hand went to his badge.

'Oh no.' Quesnel stabbed a stern, admonishing finger at him. 'Don't you try that on me. Don't you even think about pulling *that* stunt. I won't have it. I won't have you flouncing off like some snitty teenager who can't get his own way. You don't get off the hook that easily. You have a job to do, Captain, and you're damn well going to do it!'

'Then,' said Parry, his hand falling away from the badge, 'help me do it, Commissioner, by being absolutely honest at the press conference.'

'I've told you what I'm going to do. I'm not going to change my mind, and *you* are not going to change it for me.'

'Then don't expect me to support you. Don't expect me to stand beside you and endorse a lie.'

So saying, Parry spun about on his heel.

'Jack.'

He marched to the door.

'Jack!'

He hauled the door open.

'*Jack!*'

Without a backward glance, he exited Quesnel's office.

42 SCALE

Down in his office, he sat at his desk with his head in his hands, trying to work out whether what he had just done had been terrifically principled or terrifically pigheaded. Either way, one thing was certain: tactically, it had been a serious blunder. He had antagonized the commissioner, a friend, an ally, at a time when friends and allies seemed in drastically short supply. It was obvious what he should do. He should head straight back upstairs, apologize and agree to attend the press conference. It would only be a few minutes of his life, a small act of silent complicity, for the greater good of the city. Would that put *such* a strain on his conscience?

Well, yes, it would. He could see Quesnel's point, of course. Right now, soothing the city's fevered brow was of paramount importance. The need for the FPP to act with perfect integrity came second to that. Besides, her decision to 'finesse' the facts could be justified, broadly, under the terms of Measure Seven and, for that matter, Measure Nine, so it was not even as if the Constitution was being contravened, at least not in the letter. There was nothing wrong, in other words, with what Quesnel proposed to do. None the less he felt that she had, in some indefinable but fundamental way, betrayed him. By asking him to stand beside her in front of the cameras, she had invited him to play a visible role in a conspiracy to mislead. Worse, she had baited the invitation with an appeal to his ego: *Let me tell everybody what a good job you've done so far.* As if he was in this for fame and acclaim! As if that was the only reason he had joined the FPP!

He wondered if he was judging the commissioner too harshly. But then she herself judged others by the severest standards. And she must have been aware what an awkward position she had put him in. Must have.

So it went, round and round in his head, reason and resentment on a whirling carousel, the one chasing the other, till at last, growing impatient with his own indecision, he told himself to stop

381

farting around and make a choice. Either go upstairs and grovel to Quesnel and then show up for her damn press conference, or else stick to his guns, accept that he had done nothing wrong, and get on with doing his job.

For once, in a tussle between common sense and pride, pride won. He would get on with doing his job. Right. Great. That was *that* sorted. So what should he do?

Well, one possibility was to go downstairs to the basement and have a word with Greg. Perhaps he might succeed where van Wyk had failed and be able to winkle out what Greg knew – assuming Greg knew anything – about the other Triple-X cell.

On the other hand, he could go and see if Hosokawa was still at work and, if so, try to get him to elaborate on that hint he had dropped last night (if indeed it *had* been a hint).

The latter seemed potentially the more profitable of the alternatives, so he left his office and made his way to the operations room.

Grins and claps and cheers greeted his entrance. With as much graciousness as he could muster, he batted down the applause, using both hands spread flat, as a conductor does when quietening the orchestra. He felt fraudulent. He had done nothing to deserve this. His small and very hard-won triumph at Free World House was a tick in the plus column, certainly, but it barely began to offset the many, deeply scored minuses he had racked up over the past few days.

He crossed the room, glancing sideways at Johansen's empty cubicle as he went (the 'NORWEGIAN FROM HELL' slogan on the chair-back seemed bleakly vainglorious just then). Near the far end was where Hosokawa usually sat. Being a junior officer, Hosokawa did not have a cubicle and work board exclusively his own but time-shared with equally junior officers on different shifts.

He was not occupying the cubicle right now. Another officer was in his place.

Parry turned to Avni, whose shift officially ended half an hour ago but who was still at her desk, catching up on filework.

'Is Yoshi around?'

'He didn't come in last night, sir.' Avni could not resist a wry, insinuating raise of one eyebrow.

'Didn't come in? Well, did he call in sick?'

Avni shook her head. 'I tried ringing him at home several times. His board was in answer mode.'

'Try him again, would you?'

Avni punched up and dialled Hosokawa's home number. 'Still in answer mode,' she said, replacing the receiver.

'Then where's he got to?'

'I was wondering that myself, sir.'

Parry knew Hosokawa to be a conscientious young man. If unwell or otherwise indisposed, he would have contacted Avni in order to inform her of his absence from work. That he had not done so, in conjunction with his visit last night, started an itchy tingle at the back of Parry's brain. Neither event, last night's visit or this morning's absence, was in itself particularly untoward. Together, however, they added up to . . .

To what?

Parry could not say. Somehow, though, he had the feeling not only that the two events were linked, but that they amounted to more than the sum of their parts.

'Rachel, I realize you're off-duty, but would you do me a favour?'

'Of course, sir.'

Ten minutes later, Parry and Avni were aboard an FPP launch, pulling out from the vehicle pool at the rear of HQ. Parry was ensconced in the stern and Avni was at the helm. She guided the launch along the subsidiary canal that ran behind HQ, then eased to a halt at the junction with the Fourth Canal. Traffic was busy on the Fourth, lines of boats streaming in both directions. Their wakes churned up such a chop that, in order to hold the launch in place while waiting for a break in the flow, Avni had to keep the propeller gently turning and make continual small adjustments to the rudder.

As the launch idled and bobbed, Parry's attention was drawn towards the steps of the Piazza Verdi, where a small crowd of men and women was gathering. Journalists. He watched them checking their equipment and chatting amongst themselves, and he thought of the impending press conference and felt a flush of shame. He was running away. That was what it boiled down to, wasn't it? This journey to Hosokawa's apartment was nothing more than a pretext – and a slim one at that – for avoiding rather than facing up to a problem. He was worried about Hosokawa, yes, no question. But so worried that he had to go and check up on him straight away? So worried that he couldn't put off doing so till after the press conference?

He contemplated telling Avni to turn the boat around, but at that moment the sergeant, spying a gap in the traffic, gunned the throttle, and the launch lurched forwards and the opportunity was lost.

Through New Venice's waterway web they warp-and-wefted, travelling for the most part along subsidiary canals, side routes and rat-runs and doglegs and cut-throughs, until eventually, five kilometres west of Hub Lagoon, they arrived at Scriabin Heights, a complex of residential blocks that afforded sea views – or rather between-building sea glimpses – for its upper-storey tenants with west-facing windows. Tying up at a communal mooring area, they continued on foot, following colour-coded signs to the block where Hosokawa lived, F# White. There, Avni pressed the bell-button for Hosokawa's apartment. After several tries had failed to obtain a response, she turned to Parry with a shrug. 'Well, sir? What now?'

'If he's not in, he's not in. Nothing more we can do, I suppose.'

'But if he is in?'

'That's just it. That's what worries me.'

'If you really need to know if something's happened to him, I could always break in.'

'Break in? You mean pick the lock? Kick down the door? I don't think that would be appropriate.'

'No.' Avni took a step back and peered up. 'Whenever I've locked myself out of my apartment – it hasn't happened often, I should add – what I do is I ask my next-door neighbours to let me in, then climb along from their balcony to mine and get in through my window.'

Parry frowned up at the building. F# White, like every block in Scriabin Heights, was of a chunky, utilitarian design, its balconies divided one from the other by thick, jutting partitions.

'Do you really think you could manage it?'

'Sure. I don't see why not.'

'What if Yoshi's window's locked?'

'Who locks their balcony windows?'

'Fair point.'

Hosokawa lived on the fifth floor. There was nobody home in the apartments on either side of his. The occupant of the next apartment but one, however, *was* in, and when Parry explained to him that they needed to use his balcony, he – a grizzled but genial Welshman – was only too happy to be of assistance. He ushered the two FPP officers through his living-cum-dining area, out on to the balcony.

There, Avni clambered smartly over the balustrade and reached, first with one arm, then with one leg, around the partition that separated the balcony from the one belonging to the residents who lived between the Welshman and Hosokawa. Having established a handhold and toehold on the other side of the partition, she then (in a manoeuvre which, just watching it, made Parry's palms go cold and his balls crawl) began inching her way around, hugging the partition tightly, until the majority of her body – head, torso and hips – was on the far side. Her other arm and leg followed, one at a time, and then she was easing herself over the balustrade and stepping down on to the neighbour's balcony tiles.

'All right?' Parry said, leaning around the partition.

'Of course, sir,' Avni replied.

'Ah, the magnificent confidence of the young,' said the Welshman, who had been standing at Parry's shoulder all this while, looking on. 'They never have any reason to doubt themselves physically. Not like us oldies, eh, Captain?'

Parry nodded without looking round, none too happy to have been bracketed as a fellow 'oldie' by someone who was at least a decade his senior.

'It's that Oriental lad you're after, is it?' the Welshman went on. This episode was clearly going to be the highlight of his day. 'I don't know him very well, see. Keeps to himself. But he's one of you, isn't he? I see him coming and going in his uniform.'

Parry nodded again.

'I don't suppose this has anything to do with these awful murders.'

'Just an FPP matter.'

'I'm glad to hear it. That's a bad business that is, those murders. A bad, sad business. I hope you catch the bastards quickly, that's all I can say. Although I've a horrible feeling that however soon you get them it's going to be too late.'

Parry refrained from commenting. By now Avni had walked the length of the neighbour's balcony and was on the outside of the balustrade again, preparing to negotiate the next partition. He watched her feel around the partition with one hand and grasp the lip of the balustrade to Hosokawa's balcony. He watched her foot go next, questing for the gap between balustrade and balcony floor. Then she was sliding herself around the partition, shifting her weight from one side of it to the other. There was a drop of four storeys beneath her, with nothing to break her fall at the bottom except a paved courtyard floor. He envisaged one of her hands losing its grip. He envisaged her plummeting.

Then Avni was on the other side of the partition. Then she was bringing her other limbs around it. Then she was clambering over the balustrade.

'Safe and sound,' said the Welshman, with a relieved sigh.

'See anything, Rachel?' Parry called across the intervening balcony.

'The drapes are drawn,' came the reply. 'I'm going to try the window.'

There was the rumbling roll of a window sliding open, then, for a brief while, silence.

And then Parry heard Avni say, just audibly, 'Oh no.' And then, louder, urgently: 'Sir? Sir!'

Parry ran back through the Welshman's living area and hurried out of the apartment and along the corridor.

43 FINGERING

Hosokawa's apartment was minimalist heaven. The carpet was the colour of fresh mushrooms, the walls and ceiling were painted with white eggshell, and a full inventory of furniture would go as follows: one standard wallscreen, one black-lacquered coffee table, one matt-black anodized-steel lamp, one buff-coloured armchair, one pair of ash-framed etchings, and – on a shelf, providing a much-needed dash of brightness – one stem vase containing one silk tulip (scarlet). Hosokawa's home board was tucked out of sight in a corner alcove, and his uniform jacket hung on a hanger on a coathook next to the front door, the last item of clothing to be donned each morning as he left for work. Everything in the room was spaced out, positioned just so, with an artful eye, meticulously, attesting to an orderly life. A life planned out. A life undisrupted.

But death disorders. Death unplans. Death disrupts.

Hosokawa was slumped in a kneeling position by the door, naked except for a pair of white Y-fronts. A noose fashioned from a kimono sash ran from his neck to the same coathook from which his uniform jacket was suspended. His face was grey-tinged and, with its protruding tongue and bulging sightless eyeballs, gargoylesque. His hands were clasped tightly together in his lap, and the sash was stretched to its full length, the noose forcing his head back, so that there was an air of penitence about his posture. Upraised face, interlinked fingers – it was a ghastly garrotted genuflection.

'Oh fuck me,' Parry breathed, as he gazed down at the body. 'Oh you poor bloody sod.' He looked round at Avni. Her face was set hard, her lips compressed together. 'Rachel?'

'I'm sorry, sir. He wasn't a friend or anything. It's just . . . Someone you know.'

'Makes a difference, doesn't it?'

'I tried not to be unfair to him. I don't think I was ever unfair. That "college boy" stuff was only . . .'

'Humour in the ranks. Everyone does it. For heaven's sake don't go beating yourself up over this.'

Easy to say, but Parry himself was experiencing similar feelings. It occurred to him that he might bear some of the responsibility for what had happened to Hosokawa. When Hosokawa came to his apartment yesterday night, had it been merely to make vague insinuations about the Trad Music Revue, or had there been a more complex motive? Could it have been that he was trying to indicate that his life was threatened, either by some other person or by some inner demon? Asking, in a shy, oblique way, for his captain's help?

If only he had paid a little more attention. If only he had listened to Hosokawa a little more closely. If only—

No. If-onlys like those led you nowhere good. If-onlys like those led you along a path Parry was all too familiar with, a lonely, downward-spiralling trail of self-recrimination and self-disgust. A long time ago, in another country, he had caused the death of a young person, someone not dissimilar in age to Hosokawa. (*Probably* caused that young person's death, but then in the mind of a guilt-stricken and conscientious man there isn't much difference between probably and definitely – the one bleeds easily into the other.) For weeks after the Hunger Riots, months, years even, he had agonized over the girl he had so ruthlessly battered. He had seen her in his dreams, falling at his feet, blood-streaked, silently screaming. Time and time again he had spotted her face in crowds, or thought he had. For a while, almost every girl of comparable age he encountered had resembled her in one way or another, so that scarcely a day went by when he wasn't reminded of what he had done. The horror of it had taken a long time to fade, and now, as he looked down at Hosokawa – someone he perhaps could have saved, perhaps *should* have saved – all the old feelings, the bad feelings, were coming back to him, welling up inside. A guilt like his never really went away, did it? It just retreated to some hidden cave in memory and hibernated there, waiting till for the right time to wake up and spring forth, fresh and undimmed.

No. Don't think that way!

'Sir?'

'Yes?'

Avni was looking quizzical.

Had he murmured it aloud? *No. Don't think that way!* He had done, hadn't he?

'Right, yes.' He struggled to regain his composure, to claw himself back together. 'Well, we should take a look around, shouldn't we? See if there's some clue lying about. A note, maybe. Eh?'

'Yes, sir,' said Avni, uncertainly.

'Come on then.'

Apartments in Scriabin Heights were not large, so it didn't take them long to give the place a thorough going-over, especially since Hosokawa favoured such spartan decor. In a chest of drawers they found socks in rolled rows and folded shirts with sharp creases. In a wardrobe they found shoes and coats and the kimono from which the strangulating sash had come. In kitchen cupboards they found cooking utensils racked and crockery stacked and groceries organized systematically. No item did not have a location in which it rightfully belonged. The only thing in the entire apartment that seemed untidy and thus inconsonant with its surroundings – other than the corpse, of course – was Hosokawa's FPP badge, which, instead of being pinned to the lapel of his uniform jacket as one might have expected, was perched on his home board, propped against the screen. Parry pointed this out to Avni. She agreed with him that it was an odd place to put your badge and wondered if Hosokawa had left it there to remind him to do something.

Parry looked back at the corpse, stiff and still and silently awful. Why? That was the question, wasn't it? That was always the question. Why had this happened? And why strangulation? Why the kimono sash? Why the near-nakedness and the clasping-together of the hands? Everything had to have a reason. A death like this did not occur without some logical justification.

The hands . . .

He looked more closely.

Christ, how stupid not to have noticed that immediately.

Hosokawa's right index finger was locked around the lower joint of his left little finger. The remaining three fingers of each hand were wrapped tightly around the opposite hand. His thumbs were buried between his palms, out of sight.

A hand-symbol. Clenched at the moment of death. Fixed in place by rigor mortis.

TRUST.

Parry looked from the hands to the badge on the home board; from the badge on the home board back to the hands.

A couple of seconds later, he was at the home board. He picked up the badge, moved it to one side of the screen, and struck a key. The home board awoke from dormancy.

Onscreen there was text.

The first few paragraphs of a letter.

Addressed to him.

Locating, unboxing and putting on his spectacles would have meant several seconds' delay. Instead, Parry bent close to the screen and, squinting to counteract his presbyopia, started to read.

Good morning, Captain Parry.

If all has gone as I hope, you will be reading this on your work board, with Guthrie Reich under close guard downstairs. Perhaps you will have managed to extract a confession from him already. In fact, I wouldn't be surprised if, as soon as you arrested him, he started to brag about what he has done. I think, from my acquaintance with him, that he's that type. If I'm wrong about that, then ask him where he was while his bands were rehearsing the Sunday evening before last. If he tells you he was with them, he is lying.

I'm sorry about this. I'm taking the coward's way out. I should have told you everything when I went to see you yesterday evening, but when we were face to face I found I just couldn't. I couldn't bear the thought of what I would see in your eyes when you heard what I had to say. Contempt, but worse than contempt, disappointment. I don't think I'm flattering myself when I say that I feel you had high hopes for me. I deeply regret that I've let you down. I've let myself down too, if that's any consolation.

I used to consider myself an honourable person, modest in my wants and ambitions. But we never truly know ourselves, do we, until we are tested. And I was tested and found that what I thought I was far exceeds what I actually am. Here is someone who used to believe that becoming an FPP officer was the best thing he could ever do, someone who chose the job because he had all sorts of noble ideals about improving the world, serving the public, helping Foreigners, being a paragon of honesty and respectability. Selfish ideals, I can see now, but at the time heartfelt. And here I am, having betrayed all that I believed in because of an ideal much stronger and more alluring. The ideal of a life of moneyed luxury, enough wealth never to have to work again, a future of endless leisure and pleasure. The materialistic ideal that we all, I think, from time to time dream of. Even maybe you, Captain. An existence much like that of a Foreigner, gliding from one sun-kissed location to another, pursuing recreation without a care in the world.

If I seem to be rambling, I apologize. I have this urge to explain myself to you properly and in the clearest possible terms (praise be to Chambers software) so that you might at least understand why I did what I have done, if not sympathize with it or even forgive it. That, I realize, is what this letter is – part justification, part confession.

Guthrie Reich first contacted me last autumn. At the time I had no idea who he was or why he selected me rather than anyone else. He told me later that mine was the personality type best suited to what he needed. Even now, I don't know whether to be flattered by that or ashamed.

It started out with an exchange of e-mails, Guthrie dropping hints here and there about what he wanted from me and what he was offering in return, saying just enough to keep me interested, leading me on, tantalizing me, until, without realizing it, I was already half committed before I even knew what I was committed to. He made it sound so unambiguous, so easy. All I would have to do was say a few things at the right time, follow his instructions, let him know what was going on at HQ, smuggle out a few necessary items – in short, be the worm inside the apple. He made my part in his scheme seem vital but

391

at the same time simple. I would have to do so little and for such a huge reward!

He was highly plausible even over the e-ther. In person, he was ten times more persuasive. We met just the one time, a month ago. He came here to my apartment and we talked for several hours, and when we were done we had made a deal. And he thanked me. I will never forget that. As though I had done him a favour. Yet he also made me feel as though I was the one who should be grateful to him. He won me over, Captain Parry, utterly and completely, and I believed I never would have a qualm about doing what he told me to do.

That morning at the Amadeus, however, when I was confronted for the first time with the horrific consequences of what I'd become involved in . . . Well, you recall how I vomited. But it wasn't merely at the sight of the Siren's body. It was at the realization of the part I had played in his death. I was sick not just to my stomach but to my soul. And it was then that my conscience, which I had managed to wrap up in cotton wool and put away somewhere where it wouldn't bother me, escaped from its hiding place and began to badger me. I carried on doing what I was supposed to, being Guthrie's puppet, speaking the lines he gave me, misdirecting you, sabotaging your investigation, but all the time the voice in my head was getting louder, saying, 'What are you up to? Why are you betraying this man, this captain whom you so admire? Why are you

The letter ended, abruptly, with that truncated sentence. Parry tried scrolling down further, but there was no more. Leaning back, he exhaled, frowned, and ran a hand backwards across his scalp, smoothing flat what was no longer there to be smoothed flat.

'We had him,' he said at last, voice low and hard. 'Damn it, we *had* him and we let him go.'

'Who, sir?' Avni had been reading the letter over his shoulder. 'This Guthrie Reich person?'

'Down in the basement. Christ, and Hosokawa thought we'd keep him there. He thought he was safe. He thought we'd have Reich all neatly confessed up and bang to rights, and he could write this letter and then sneak out of town before anyone could find out he was Reich's accomplice, his inside man.'

'But this is a suicide note, sir, isn't it?' Avni scrolled back through the text to the second paragraph. 'Yes. Look. "I'm taking the coward's way out." That's classic suicide-note language.'

'This isn't a suicide note. Yoshi wanted me to know what he'd done so he wouldn't feel so bad about himself. "Part confession." Confession in the telling-the-vicar-about-your-sins sense. He was a coward only because he chickened out about saying all of this to my face. He planned to write this, send it, then pack up a few belongings and get the hell out of New Venice. But he couldn't finish it.'

'Because his guilt got the better of him and he gave up writing it and went and hanged himself.'

'No, he couldn't finish it because he never got the chance. He was interrupted. Someone came round. Someone he wasn't expecting to be at liberty any more. Someone who had come to kill him, for no other reason than sheer spite.'

'Guthrie Reich.'

'None other. Reich turned up on his doorstep, and Yoshi had no idea Reich knew he had shopped him. He must have assumed I'd arrested Reich but had to release him, or else that I'd not got the clue he gave me and hadn't arrested Reich at all. Either way, he'd no choice but to let Reich in. Otherwise it would have looked suspicious. So he put his board to sleep and welcomed Reich in and tried to act as though everything was normal and hunky-dory. But at some point he must have sensed that something was up, that Reich was here for more than a social visit.'

'Why, sir?'

'The badge, Rachel. He could even have put it there on his home board *before* he let Reich in. I think it's possible Yoshi knew what Reich was here to do. I think he may actually have wanted to die.'

'So his hands . . .'

'To make absolutely sure that whoever found him would also find the letter and know who his murderer was.'

'But sir, surely you didn't tell Reich that Hosokawa was the one who had put you on to him. Did you?'

'As a matter of fact . . .' Parry slid a thumb and forefinger over the bridge of his nose and dug them hard into the inner corners of his eyes. 'I did. Not exactly. Not in so many words. But Reich asked us some questions while we had him in the basement at HQ, and damn it, Lieutenant Johansen actually said Yoshi's name. He couldn't have known that Reich knew exactly who "Yoshi" was. And besides, by that stage the bastard had managed to convince us that he was innocent. We didn't really have any evidence against him other than Hosokawa's word, and his alibis seemed credible. I should have checked them, but then that fourth *shinju* turned up and there was no way Reich could have done it because Pål and I were talking to him when it happened. For God's sake, Hosokawa picked such a bloody roundabout way to implicate Reich! And I wanted to give Reich the benefit of the doubt. I'd taken this sort of knee-jerk dislike to him when we met and I wanted so badly to be wrong.'

'But what does it mean in the letter . . . Where is it? This bit. Here. "Misdirecting you, sabotaging your investigation."'

Parry remembered Hosokawa mentioning *shinju* to him in the lift at HQ; remembered him at the Bar Brindisi, talking about weapons designed to kill Foreigners. There was your misdirection right there, the first attempt successful, the second not so. And sabotage? How about his phone message to Quesnel from the Debussy, the one that went astray? It was Hosokawa who erased it from the commissioner's work board. After Parry called HQ, Hosokawa asked Kadosa to sit in for him at the front desk and went upstairs, entered Quesnel's office and wiped the message. Early morning. Hardly anyone around to see him. Not *such* a difficult trick to pull off, not in a building without locks, and not for someone in uniform in that building, someone who had a perfect right to be there.

'Like the letter says, he didn't have to do much,' he said in answer to Avni's question. 'But what he did was more than enough. Anyway, we can sort all that out later. What we need to concentrate on right now is the fact that I've fucked things up and they need to be unfucked. So let's go get Reich. Agreed?'

'Agreed.'

'No matter where he is or what he's doing, the bastard is coming back to HQ with us.'

The only slight problem was, Parry had no idea where Reich was staying. He did, however, know someone who might.

Snatching up the phone receiver from Hosokawa's home board, he dialled a number.

Three rings.

Be in, he thought. Please be in, Anna.

A fourth ring. Then: 'Hello?'

'Anna.'

'Jack. You sound strange. What's up? Do you have a sore throat?'

'Listen, I'm sorry, Anna, I need to be quick. Reich. Guthrie Reich. Which hotel's he staying at?'

'Um, now which did he say it was? The Górecki, I think. Yes, the Górecki. Why do you want to know?'

'You're sure it's the Górecki?'

'Yes. Sure.'

'Thanks.' Parry made to hang up.

'But you won't find him there right now. Jack? I said you won't—'

'I heard. Where is he?'

'Off on a trip.'

'A trip? Where?'

'What's going on? What do you want with Guthrie all of a sudden?'

'A trip *where*, Anna?'

'El-Ghaita.'

'The hum farm?'

'He said he's never been to one before. He wants to see what it's like.'

'When did he leave?'

'I've never heard you like this before, Jack. What has he done?'

'Anna, when did he leave?'

'He came by about an hour ago. I let them borrow the launch to get to the mainland. They're going to rent a car from there.'

'"They"?'

'Cissy's gone with him. He asked her if she would. I don't think she wanted to very much, but then again she doesn't visit the mainland often and she's never seen a hum farm either, so I think she was curious. Guthrie said they could stop by one of the souks as well, and you know how Cissy is about shopping. Any chance she can get.'

'Christ.'

'"Christ"? Why "Christ" like that, Jack? What's happening? Something's wrong, isn't it?'

'Nothing's wrong, Anna.'

'Tell me!'

'Everything's going to be fine. Trust me.'

'Jack? Tell me, Ja—'

He put the receiver down.

He looked at Avni.

'Sergeant. Take me to the mainland. Now.'

44 TRANSPOSITION

The strait between New Venice and the mainland was relatively calm that morning and they made the crossing in a little under twenty minutes. The FPP launch, not designed for open water, lurched and lolled clumsily in the ocean swell, but Parry, remembering the advice of an old song, kept his eyes on the blue horizon, and suffered the odd queasy twinge but successfully staved off full-blown seasickness.

Halfway across, Avni broached the topic of FPP jurisdiction on the mainland, or rather lack of same. She chose her words carefully, knowing she was drawing attention to a fact of which her superior officer was already perfectly well aware. She asked him if the proper thing to do in the circumstances would not be to alert the mainland authorities and leave it to them to locate and apprehend Reich.

Parry's reply was curt. 'Of course it'd be the proper thing to do, but frankly, I don't care. As soon as I'm on the mainland, it's as if I'm not wearing this uniform.'

Avni nodded, understanding. 'Then what would you say if I volunteered to accompany you to El-Ghaita?'

Parry looked at her and she could see he was touched by the offer. 'I would say I appreciate it very much, but getting me this far is more than enough aiding and abetting. I can't ask any more from you. Silly for both of us to lose our jobs over this, eh?'

And that was the end of the discussion.

Situated on the point on the mainland closest to New Venice, the port that was their destination looked as if it had stood there for several decades, but in fact it antedated the resort-city by just a couple of months. Before then, there had been only cliffs, a promontory, a spit of beach which the rising sea-levels were steadily encroaching on, a few fishermen's dwellings. Then two great curving crystech breakwaters were planted, like a pair of embracing arms, and inland access roads were constructed, and an entire service infrastructure was put in place to meet the logistical requirements of New Venice's creators and builders: wharves for the loading of freight barges, moorings for the ferries that took workers to and from the site, restaurants, cafés, a small hospital, cheap accommodation. Without design, at random, all manner of domed, rounded, white-stuccoed buildings sprang up along the breakwater like some fungal growth, while two kilometres away across the water something far more delicate and elegant and intentional began taking shape.

It had been anticipated that once the whole mighty city-raising enterprise was over, the port, having fulfilled its purpose, would quietly fall into disuse. However, some entrepreneurial types spotted an opportunity. Visitors to New Venice might want to venture on to the mainland, mightn't they? And what about those who had jobs in the city but did not live there? They would need a place to embark from and return to every day.

And so the port (which had no name, but then things that birth themselves seldom have names) gained a second lease of life as ferry companies established themselves there, tour operators took over buildings and set up offices, car-hire agencies likewise purchased premises, and souvenir vendors moved in too, erecting their stalls along the length of the seafront promenade, until soon the port was given over almost wholly to commerce of one sort or another. This did not make the place any lovelier to the eye – if anything, the opposite – yet in its bustling, dusty functionality there was a certain vigorous charm. The port faced New Venice across the strait unblinkingly, not pretending to be anything other than what it was, the supermarine metropolis's lesser cousin, conveniently situated, there for a purpose, utilitarian where New Venice was utopian.

Avni steered into the calmer waters of the manmade harbour and hove to in front of the promenade. As Parry stepped out, he looked round at her. He started manufolding GRATITUDE, but then thought better of it and, unclasping his hands, said simply, 'Thanks.'

A few moments later, having run the gamut of a half-dozen eager souvenir vendors, Parry entered the seafront premises of a well-known international car-hire firm. The clerk on duty, a slim, limpid-eyed North African woman, was efficient and helpful, and in no time at all Parry's passport card and credit card had been swiped and he had leased a Volkslied coupé for the day.

'And do you have an itinerary planned, sir, or are you just going to go where the mood takes you?' the clerk asked.

'El-Ghaita hum farm. There and back. That's it.'

'Really? El-Ghaita? How unusual. You're the third person this morning. It's not normally such a popular destination.'

'The third person?'

'I had a couple come in, about an hour ago.'

'A young man and a teenage girl, travelling together?' It wouldn't be *such* a coincidence, would it? After all, there were only so many car-hire agencies in the port that Reich and Cecilia could have visited.

'That was them.'

Parry's next question elicited a puzzled frown from the clerk. 'How did she seem to you? The girl?'

'She seemed . . . fine. Smiling. Perfectly normal. Why?'

'No reason. It's just that I know them.'

But he was glad. If Reich had anything sinister planned for Cecilia, Cecilia did not know it yet. It could, of course, be the case that Reich had nothing sinister planned for her at all and that this trip they were taking was just what it appeared to be, a tourist jaunt. Reich might not know that Parry was on his tail again.

None the less, there was *something* worming away in Parry's belly, a feeling without form or name, something that was a little like anxiety and a little like dread.

Out in the car-hire agency's backlot a score of vehicles waited in the sun – saloons and multi-passenger transports mostly, perched lightly on their axles, their profiles sleek and streamlined apart from the bulbous roofs (designed that way to provide sufficient headroom for Foreigners, who, though they themselves never drove, did sometimes go on road-trips with Sirens and private tour guides). Parry's Volkslied coupé was by far the most compact car present and consequently the fastest. The standard output for a comp-res engine was around 40 kilowatts, and no automobile manufacturer had yet worked out a way of putting more power than that beneath the bonnet without the engine becoming unviably large and, perhaps more important, piercingly noisy. Speed, therefore, meant less weight, and the Volkslied, with its stripped-down interior, molybdenum-alloy bodywork, negligible suspension and legal-minimum engine soundproofing, was capable of up to 85 k.p.h. That was why Parry had chosen it, and he was especially pleased by his choice when he ascertained from the clerk that Reich and Cecilia had hired a Merbecke-Bentzon tourer, a boxy four-seater, comfortable but far from racy, which could manage 70 flat-out with a tailwind. There was no chance the Volkslied's speed advantage would enable him to catch up with Reich and Cecilia before they reached the hum farm, but he could at least whittle away a portion of their head start.

The clerk switched on the Volkslied's ignition and, while the battery busied itself building up a charge, invited Parry to sit behind the wheel so that she could go over the controls with him, showing him which switches and stalks did what. It had been years since Parry had driven a car, and when the time came for him to shift out of neutral and guide the Volkslied out of its parking space and on to the main road, he did so in a gingerly fashion. Having grown accustomed to boats, which were subject to their own particular set of laws of momentum and inertia, it took him several minutes to get the hang once again of a vehicle that didn't bank when it turned a corner, didn't suffer from rear-end drift and could stop dead at the touch of a pedal. The first kilometre of his journey, from the rental-agency backlot to the slip-road that fed on to one of the lesser inland highways, was slow, erratic going, and on one occasion only the alertness of another road user averted a collision. By the time Parry was on the highway, however, his confidence had grown and he felt comfortable taking the Volkslied up to 70 k.p.h, 75, 80, and soon above 80.

With velocity came renewal of purpose. Parry gripped the steering wheel and kept the accelerator flattened, letting the two-lane highway of sun-faded tarmac carry him, kilometre by dusty kilometre, towards his objective.

The highway was edged on both sides with loose scree, parallel margins of overlap, neither road nor desert but something in between. The red landscape that spread around it was rough and ragged and hard-baked, flat all the way to the horizon on the left, flat as far as the foothills of a distant mountain range on the right. There were outcrops of scrubby bushes, like clumps of burnt hair on singed skin, and cacti that had grown into poses reminiscent of soldiers being strafed with gunfire, canted backwards, arms outstretched. There were groves of apple and olive trees, planted in rows, and every now and then Parry would see a camel wandering beside the road, browsing, apparently unowned. He passed the shells of petrol stations, lost to rust and uselessness, and – with increasing infrequence the further inland he went – awning-covered stalls manned by cloaked and turbaned North Africans who would stand up as the Volkslied approached and beckon to him, begging him in a masque of imprecation to stop and buy their wares: fresh fruit, locally made trinkets, bottles of water or soft drink. Sometimes he spied villages huddled in the middle distance, connected to the highway by rutted tracks. A line of electricity pylons strode alongside the road, shouldering their load of cable. The sky was vastly blue.

He had not entered another country so much as, it felt, another medium. An environment as sparsely populated and given over to soil as New Venice was densely inhabited and given over to water. Arid where New Venice was irrigated. Empty where New Venice teemed. And onward the Volkslied glided, and soon there were no more petrol stations and villages and stalls and camels to be seen, only desert, the pylons and the unmoving mountains with their marbling of snow. The highway was almost exclusively Parry's. Every once in a while he overtook, or passed coming the other way, a bus or a container truck. Otherwise he was on his own, one man inside a cooled car-shaped capsule, encircled by emptiness. He pressed on relentlessly.

Shortly a road sign appeared, its message conveyed in both Arabic and English:

El-Ghaita
20 Km

Beneath was the NACA logo, a white silhouette of the upper half of the African continent with the alliance's acronym banded in blue across the middle in Roman script and the ornate Arabic equivalent.

Twenty kilometres. Roughly another quarter of an hour.

The feeling that was worming away inside Parry began to writhe with greater urgency, as if, though still formless, it sensed that some kind of confirmation of its reason for being might be drawing near. The desert was becoming rockier and more rugged, and it had been a long time since Parry had seen another vehicle, or indeed any sign of civilization other than the highway itself and the pylons. Of the latter there were several lines now, stitching across the landscape near and far, many of them converging and running alongside each other companionably, their cables dipping and rising repeatedly. The sun was immense, burning all shadows away. The only sounds Parry could hear were the huff of the

Volkslied's air-conditioning, the rubbery thrum of tyres on tarmac, and the comp-res battery's constant dual-pitched whine.

The final remaining kilometres counted down, and now there were more power lines than ever, marching in from all across the region, drawing together to their point of origin like strands of a gigantic metal spider-web. Then Parry got a glimpse of something dark and huge and shapeless hunkering on the horizon, quivering in the heat haze like a mirage. As he drove closer, the mirage resolved into buildings, a good twenty of them, each like a gigantic aerodrome hangar, laid out in a grid pattern across a hundred hectares of desert.

He arrived at a junction signposted with the hum farm's name and turned off on to a narrower, less-well-made strip of road which bundled bumpily along, its unevenness little mitigated by the Volkslied's unforgiving shock absorbers. A chainlink perimeter fence came into view, demarcating the hum farm's limits. Road and fence joined up and, side by side, shared a course.

Half a kilometre on, the first of the hangar-like buildings loomed, and Parry saw a white car parked at the roadside, next to the fence. A Merbecke-Bentzon tourer.

He braked and pulled in behind the Merbecke. Its rear window sported a sticker identical to the one in the rear window of the Volkslied, showing the car-hire agency's name and logo. There was no one inside.

He killed the engine and got out of the Volkslied, entering a breezeless, ferocious heat. As the whine of the engine faded, a faint, intermittently rhythmic buzzing reached his ears, like the drone of contented bees in their hives. The sound of the hum farm, the sound of energy being produced and reaped. He walked over to the Merbecke. There were footprints in the roadside dirt, leading from the car to the fence. One set was large, made by a man wearing boots with a thick corrugated tread. The other set was smaller, and the pattern in them was that of the sole of a woman's trainers, incorporating a brand-name imprinted repeatedly in the dust. At the fence, the footprints were scuffed and overlapping. There were more of them, also scuffed and overlapping, on the other side.

It had been Reich's idea, no doubt. Instead of continuing on to the hum farm's entrance, he had stopped the car here and suggested to Cecilia that they climb in over the fence. Parry could imagine him telling her it would be more fun this way. They wouldn't have to join one of the boring official tours. They could take their time looking around and not have to listen to some over-informative guide droning on about output levels and charge manifestations and other such technical blather. And he could imagine Cecilia, reluctant at first, being persuaded to go along with the idea. It would be exciting, wouldn't it? And what was the worst that could happen to them if they were caught? They would be thrown off the premises. No penalty was imposed for trespassing on NACA property, since it was generally considered that most people were responsible enough and sensible enough not to do so. In fact, for this very reason, security at hum farms and other such places was next to non-existent. You might have a couple of uniformed guards on patrol. Other than that, nothing but a fence like this one, a token gesture, barely four metres tall, less than twice the height of the average man, with no barbed wire on it. A barrier even a less-than-agile person could clamber over without much difficulty.

Yes, Parry could see Reich talking Cecilia into sneaking in over the fence with him. He could see it happening quite easily.

He could also see Reich forcing her to. At gunpoint, or maybe knifepoint, or simply with the threat of physical violence. He could see Reich turning on her as he stopped the car, his mask of affability slipping away, his voice hardening, his smile as cruel as cancer. *This is where we get out, little rich bitch. We're going for a stroll.*

He knew what Reich was capable of. He had shot a Siren at point-blank range, pushed another off a balcony, slashed the wrists of a third and written on a wall in the man's blood. Savage, pre-meditated, cold-blooded murder.

He also knew that there was no good reason for Reich to kill Cecilia. No good reason for him to harm her in any way.

The thing in his belly shifted and slithered uncertainly, not wanting to be what it was, longing to be anything other.

The footprints continued beyond the fence, two sets side by side, traipsing across the gravelly red dust towards the nearest building.

Parry reached up, inserted fingers into the chainlink and started to climb.

45 SNARE

Close to the building, the bee-like drone deepened to a low, dense throb that you could not only hear but feel through your skin. Every few seconds, the comp-res array reached a cyclical frequency peak and there would be an especially low pulse and the dust would shiver and dance on the ground. Parry remembered the last time he had visited El-Ghaita, shortly after the hum farm had come onstream. The place was somewhat dustier now, the buildings no longer gleaming in their newness, but otherwise little had changed. He remembered feeling an excitement that bordered on wonder. A safe, clean, never-ending supply of energy! Now, as he approached the building, he felt only dull anxiety, an empty, metallic-tasting unease.

The footprint trail left by Reich and Cecilia led to a large personnel-access door. Parry grasped the lever-handle, pressed down and heaved. The door, heavy with soundproofing, rolled reluctantly open, and immediately the throb increased to a loud rumble, pouring out from the doorway. He entered a kind of antechamber, a bare rectangular room painted entirely in vivid green. On one wall there were pairs of orange ear-defenders hanging from pegs, beside which was a notice in several languages, the text preceded with a drawing of hands twisted in WARNING and followed by a drawing of hands clenched in GRATITUDE.

Danger!
Unprotected exposure to array is hazardous.
Ear-defenders must be worn at all times.

Sound advice. Parry took a pair of ear-defenders for himself and slotted them over his head. They were a snug fit, almost painfully tight. Once they were properly in position, the rumble was muffled to a grumbling murmur. He noted that two of the other pairs of ear-defenders were missing from their pegs.

At the opposite end of the room lay a set of swing doors fitted with safety-glass portholes. Parry walked over and glanced through one of them. The wire-latticed pane was dusty and what lay beyond ill-lit. He could make out nothing except a few smeary flashes of light. He pushed the door and side-stepped warily through.

Size.

Space.

Power.

In the dim illumination provided by frosted skylights set into the rib-reinforced roof, six huge comp-res cells stood, one ranked beyond the other in a row reaching all the way to the far end of the building, a distance of some three-quarters of a kilometre. The cells' paired crystals, each of them the size of a three-storey house, were mounted on wheeled flatbeds that could be pushed or pulled along tracks by means of oiled pistons as thick as sequoia trunks. All the pairs were resonating madly, shivering in mutual frisson with their partners, their multi-faceted contours blurring, defocused by vibration.

At the centre of each cell hung a conducting rod, a long, tapering stalactite of metal suspended from a lofty gantry. Light-forms played around the rods' spherical tips – branching crackles of static mostly, every now and then amoebas of lambent plasma that would wriggle and flow then dissipate, and sometimes pinkish-blue halos that would form around the entire tip, brighten, then pop like punctured soap bubbles. The air smelled of electricity, of burnt-out fuses, iron filings, and shivered so intensely with the density of sound being given off by the array that it became thick and watery, almost tangible.

Parry took all this in at a glance – impressive, but not why he was here – and then began scanning for Reich and Cecilia.

No sign of either.

He started to move. Heading right, he proceeded past the first comp-res cell. He kept to the side of the building and peered around him as he went, on the alert for any activity that was not the shimmer of the crystals or the glowing writhe of a charge manifestation. He was only too aware that he was restricted to a single source of sensory input. Rendered effectively deaf by the ear-defenders, vision was all he had to rely on, and so he stared around him owlishly, almost scared to blink in case, in that split-second of sightlessness, he missed something.

He had gone almost half the length of the building when he

glimpsed, to his left, movement. A person. Someone all the way over on the other side of the array, passing across the gap between two of the cells, heading the opposite way from him. He thought he had seen blond hair, but was not sure. He backtracked hurriedly.

Through the next gap between cells he caught sight of the person again. Striding swiftly, purposefully towards the exit. Tall and leather-trousered and carrying a canvas rucksack on his back. Even with his head partially obscured by ear-defenders, still unmistakably Guthrie Reich.

Breaking into a run, Parry reached the first comp-res cell and the antechamber, then turned right, traversing the width of the building. His plan was to intercept Reich, heading him off before he reached the end of the array. He was deliberately not thinking about why Reich was on his own. He was deliberately trying to ignore what that might mean.

He came around the corner of the array, expecting to see Reich walking towards him.

No one in sight. Reich was gone.

Slowing his pace, Parry proceeded past the first cell. Reich *had* been here. Definitely. So where the hell was he?

A flicker at the periphery of his vision, and then Reich was standing directly behind him, holding a hunting knife up to his throat. Reich had spotted him. Reich had ducked behind the comp-res cell. Reich had him at his mercy. The power to bring about his death was in Reich's hands.

Parry knew then that it was over. He waited, almost impatiently, for the cut – the cold kiss of the blade through his skin and flesh and throat, the hot rush of blood.

Not even fifty, he thought, absurdly. And then: Carol. Someone'll have to break it to poor Carol. And Anna.

The knife remained in place, but the cut did not come. Gradually, the blade moved away from his neck. He watched it, a wicked half-smile of stainless steel, glide out past his right shoulder. A hand clamped on his other shoulder and he was turned around.

Reich stepped back three paces, the knife still out and pointing towards Parry. He motioned with it, indicating that Parry was to stay where he was, not move a muscle. Then, slowly, deliberately, he lowered the knife and tucked it into his trouser belt. He took his hand away from the hilt and, in another mime, showed Parry how swiftly he could reach for the knife if necessary. One quick, clean manoeuvre, like a gunslinger going for his six-shooter. *Watch out,* was the gist of this dumb-show. No sudden moves, or the knife would be out again, fast as a blink.

Parry nodded, demonstrating that he understood.

Now Reich brought his hands together at waist-height and, after some fumbling, manufolded TRANQUILLITY.

TRANQUILLITY?

Peace. A truce. He was asking for a truce.

Parry's instinct was to respond with NEGATIVE, but then he thought of Cecilia. He had to know where she was, what Reich had done with her.

ACCEPTANCE, he replied. Then: FEMALE, INTERROGATIVE.

Reich, evidently feeling that hand-symbols were inadequate to the task, shook his head and reached up for his ear-defenders. He pointed at Parry, indicating that he should do the same.

The two men simultaneously slid their ear-defenders back over their heads, down to their necks.

Thunder.

Stunningly loud.

Like the lowest pedal notes of a thousand cathedral organs being played in unison. A continuous moaning roar that crammed the otic canal, penetrating tympanum, stapes, cochlea, pressing in hard all the way to the nerve-receptors. A sound like earthquakes and tidal waves. Tectonic tumult. An aural *Götterdämmerung* on a scale not even Wagner had dreamed of. The noise that might accompany planets cracking asunder, heavens fissuring, suns going nova.

Head swimming, dizzied by the din, Parry looked across at Reich. Reich was grinning, as though relishing the discomfort, both Parry's and his own. He shouted something to Parry. In the midst of the comp-res roar, his voice was a mouse's scratch, the words unintelligible.

Parry yelled back, 'Can't hear!'

Reich replied at the top of his lungs, 'I said, "Count yourself lucky I'm not supposed to kill you!"'

'What does that mean, "not supposed to"?'

Reich either did not hear the question or did but did not see fit to answer it. 'I bet you're wondering where she is!'

'If she's dead, Reich, I swear to God, so are you!'

'She isn't dead, Jack! Not yet! I admit you—'

407

The rest was lost amid a sudden temporary swell in the sound from the array.

'What?' Parry shouted.

'You came earlier than you were meant to!' Reich bellowed. 'But that's OK! This past few days, improvisation's just about become my middle name!'

'Where is she?'

'Somewhere in the building! You shouldn't have much trouble finding her, but you better start looking now! She's tied up and she isn't wearing her set of these any more!' He tapped his ear-defenders. 'I've been watching her squirm without them! Kind of beautiful, in a way!'

'Bastard!' Parry took a step towards him.

Reich's hand flashed to the knife hilt. 'Listen, Jack! I meant for you to find her deafened, maybe even dead! This way, at least you've got a chance to save her! Only thing is, you can save her or you can try to arrest me! One or the other! And I'm not going down without a fight!'

'Give up, Reich! Take me to her and then come back with me to New Venice! I'll put in a good word for you, say you co-operated!'

'No way, Jack!'

'I mean it! Do you really expect to get clean away? Someone'll catch you eventually! Help me now, and local law will go easier on you!' Parry's voice was starting to fail. His damaged throat was finding it a strain to keep bawling at this level.

'No one's going to find me! I'm going to slip away and no one'll have the first clue where I am or even *who* I am! It's all planned out, Jack! There are still places on this planet where a man can disappear, especially a man with enough money to cover his tracks!'

'*I'll* find you!'

'Yeah, yeah! Big talk! Now come on! Clock's ticking! Are you going to try and tackle me, or are you going to go rescue your little girlfriend before she goes completely Quasimodo? It's up to you! Bear in mind I'm the one with the knife, and even without it I'd still kick your scrawny English ass! So you can sacrifice yourself or you can save Cecilia! It's an either/or deal! Me or her! One or the other of us but not both!'

Parry thought of charging at him. Thought better of it.

'So who's it to be?' Reich yelled. The grin on his face was now so broad it was almost a leer.

I could take you, Parry thought. Knife or not, I know I could take you down.

'Quick, Jack! Make up your mind!'

But then Cecilia's only chance . . .

'Me or her? Time's a-wasting!'

A teenage girl.

'Choose, Jack! *Who's it going to be?*'

CODA

They had arranged to meet at a café and briefly, for a minute or so, it was as though nothing had changed: the two of them sitting down at a table together, her ordering coffee, him tea. But then a silence fell between them, a silence magnified by the lack of patrons at the tables around them, the unfrequentedness of the once-busy plaza on which the café was situated, the thinness of the traffic on the canal beyond. A silence that was just one of many now occupying the city, one of the increasing number of absences and emptinesses that were taking over as life and noise and activity in New Venice day by day abated.

'How are you, Jack?' Anna asked.

'Bearing up. You?'

'Fine.'

'Cecilia?'

Anna made a glum face.

'But the specialist said her hearing *might* get better.'

'No sign of that so far. The ringing is still there. It drives her mad sometimes.'

'But she can still hear.'

'Most things. But it's not just the deafness. What he did to her, pulling a knife on her like that, tying her up . . .'

'I know.'

'She has nightmares about it. She sleeps with me now. We always have to have a light on in the bedroom. The therapist is trying to help, but I wonder whether she'll ever truly get over it.'

'She will, I'm sure.'

'Maybe.'

'Does she still blame me?'

'Partly.'

'What if I were to go and see her?'

'Not a good idea, I think.'

'I could tell her I'm sorry. That might make a difference.'

'Possibly. Possibly not. Don't take it to heart, Jack. Whatever

Cissy thinks, it wasn't your fault. Any of it. If it was anyone's fault, it was mine. I let her go off with him. I shouldn't have, but then I had no idea about him. He seemed so decent, so trustable.'

'He *seemed* a lot of things.'

'But you feel you should have known somehow, don't you? You feel you should be able to sense when someone is that dangerous, that insane.'

'I used to meet people like him all the time, back before the Debut,' Parry said. 'Smiling rapists. Baby-faced child-killers. Butter-wouldn't-melt wife-beaters. Blokes you'd have happily had as friends if you didn't know they broke kneecaps for a living. I thought they'd become extinct. Their time had been and gone. That's what living here too long does to you.' He shook his head, an old man weary of the ways of the world. 'Cecilia told me a joke the other day. How do you make a New Venetian blind?'

'That's one of her favourites. "Poke his eyes out."'

'The real answer is: you don't have to. Chances are he's blind already.'

'You hated Reich from the start, though,' said Anna. 'You saw through him. You saw what he was.' She no longer referred to Reich by his first name. She, like the reporters and commentators on television, preferred the monosyllable of his surname. You could say it like a dog-bark, or like hawking phlegm from your throat.

'Not hate him. At your party, he just . . . got to me. He knew which buttons to push. Christ, did he know which buttons to push!'

'But maybe if I'd listened to you . . .'

'Wouldn't have made any difference, I don't think.'

Their drinks arrived. The café owner himself brought them and then took up a position at the edge of his territory, mournfully surveying the plaza and its dearth of potential customers. There was sweat shining on the back of his neck and dampening his shirt in great crescents below his armpits.

Parry stirred milk into his tea. 'I just wish he'd come after me directly. I just wish he hadn't involved anyone else.'

'Why did he do it, Jack? Take against you like that? Why did it suddenly become so personal for him?'

He gave her the explanation he had given Quesnel, Muhammad al-Shadhuli, the FPP Council, anyone who asked. The glib, bogus explanation which, because it came from such an unimpeachable source, and because no one but he and Reich knew the full truth, had so far not failed to convince.

'Someone like that needs an enemy, a face that can become the focus for his hatred and paranoia. Plus, criminals often get to feel that they're engaged in a personal war with the cops pursuing them. Reich decided I was his main opponent, and as the net tightened around him he decided to lash out against me. He'd become mad with what he'd achieved so far, drunk on success. He thought he could do anything he liked. Never mind that Cecilia wasn't part of his original plan. He wanted to harm me in the worst way he could think of – by harming her.'

'God.' Anna shuddered. 'God, I want to hurt him so badly. When they find him, I'm going to ask to be left alone in a room with him for half an hour. I'll bribe whoever I have to. I won't kill him. I'll just leave him wishing he was dead.'

'They won't find him, Anna.'

'You say that with such conviction.'

Conviction, or hope? 'They won't. He's a clever bastard. He'll have changed his appearance, and he'll be hopping from place to place, resort-city to resort-city, never staying anywhere long, never doing the same thing twice, never drawing attention to himself.'

'But how will he manage it? Surely he'll run out of money soon.'

Oh, I doubt it, Parry thought, but said, 'He'll manage. We're talking about someone who pulled off three vicious and audacious murders, someone who manipulated an entire city into self-destructing. He'll stay one step ahead of the law until the fuss has died down, and then he'll quietly settle somewhere and blend in and no one'll know who he is or anything about him apart from he's the nice new neighbour who moved to the area recently.'

'But you want him caught too, don't you?'

'Of course,' he said, but he didn't, not really. Good though it would be to see Reich brought to justice, he knew that if Reich was caught, then inevitably the whole story would have to come out, the real reason why Reich had done everything he had done. And then . . . Well, then everyone would know what at present only the two of them, he and Reich, knew. And Parry had no desire for Anna to suffer any more than she had already. He wanted her to be spared the exquisite torment that he was going through. He wanted the pain, for her sake, to be his and his alone.

'What are you going to do?' she said.

'About Reich?'

'Generally. Now that . . .'

'Now that there are so few Foreigners left in New Venice and most Sirens have buggered off too and those that haven't are making plans to go and soon there'll hardly be anyone here at all?' He sighed. 'Stay. That's all I *can* do. I don't belong anywhere else and the FPP will keep its division open for as long as there are people here, a core presence. I can be a part of that. Everything's uncertain, but for the time being I can hang on. What about you?'

'I . . . I think I may be "buggering off" myself.'

'Yes?'

'Back to Romania most likely, with Cissy. Make a fresh start there. I can introduce her to my side of the family. All those relatives she's never met before. And it'll be a different culture, a whole different environment, and that'll be good for her. No bad memories. I'll sell up here if I can. Frankly I don't think there'll be anyone willing to buy the house, and even if there is, it won't fetch a fraction of what it's worth. But that's not the point. Cissy and I have more than enough to live on.'

'I think that'll be a good idea,' Parry said, after a moment's pause.

'Do you?'

He nodded. 'There's nothing really here any more, is there?'

She seemed as though she was about to say something important just then, but thought better of it. They finished their drinks and paid the bill and parted with a light kiss on the cheek and a hollow goodbye, and as Parry walked home he wondered if she had been going to ask him to come with her and Cecilia to Romania and be a part of her 'fresh start'; and he was glad that she had decided against doing so, so that he hadn't had to turn her down.

Litter bins on plazas and esplanades were overflowing, and grateful seagulls were greedily snacking on the spilled morsels of edible matter, the crusts and rinds and peels and leftovers. Fine shoots of grass were poking up between paving stones, and seaweed was proliferating in the canals, unchecked. The smell of salt water, characteristic of the city, was somehow more prevalent these days, pungently briny where once it had been mild and tangy and invigorating. It was a slow death. A death by desertion and neglect. New Venice withdrawing from existence by degrees. A long, lingering diminuendo.

You could count the remaining Foreigners and Sirens in their dozens rather than in their hundreds. A golden giant wending its way through the gathering dusk to Sirensong was a rare sight, and Sirensong itself was a depleted, desultory affair, more motet than chorale, a handful of voices, none of them trying their hardest. Sometimes Parry wished that it could just be over with, finished, done; that New Venice could be put out of its misery like a lame horse, a bolt through the skull, that's it, goodnight. At other times he regarded the continuing presence of Foreigners and Sirens as an encouraging sign, hinting that the city's decline was reversible and that Foreigners might start visiting again in their droves and departed Sirens might return and everything would end up as it had been before. It was not often that he felt such a miracle was possible, but at least he still had his moments of optimism. Brief the moments and faint the optimism, but at least, even after all that had happened, he still had them.

He took his time as he paced through the ailing, failing city, and he thought of Reich and Hosokawa and how, between them, they had achieved this. It had been a scheme as elaborate as it was ruthless, designed with the express purpose of ruining New Venice and, in ruining the city, ruining Jack Parry as well. Piecing it together had taken time, but once Parry had managed to slot all the elements in place he had been able to perceive the full ingenuity of the plan and even, in a bitter way, to admire it. Perhaps its cleverest aspect had been how Reich had manipulated him throughout, using his own hopes and preconceptions against him. Assisted by Hosokawa, Reich had toyed with Parry from the start, letting him think he was making decisions for himself when all he was doing was heading in whichever direction Reich chose to steer him. It was hatefully brilliant.

That the first three *shinjus* were murders staged to look like suicides had become apparent soon enough. What Parry had failed to realize – even after that Foreigner accosted him and manufolded SUPERNAL, NEGATIVE – was that no Foreigner was lost in the first three. The Foreign outfits left at the scene were genuine enough, but no Foreigners had worn them in a while. They had come from the storage units at HQ, smuggled out by Hosokawa and replaced with accurate replicas. The only golden giant involved had been Reich himself. Reich impersonating a Foreigner. Reich in stacked-sole shoes and a fake mask, like one of those actors in *Resort-City Beat*. Reich lurching along, Foreigner-fashion, to Sirensong and getting hooked by a Siren and taking the Siren back to a hotel room he had booked into earlier in the day (also in his Foreign guise), and then killing his victim and leaving a set of Foreign clothing at the scene in a pose suggestive of a loss, and then, still dressed as a Foreigner, making his getaway. Anywhere other than a resort-city, such a plan would have had a limited chance of success, but here, a place where, until recently, Foreigners were a common sight, if you had an accurate disguise and a pocketful of Foreign currency you could pass yourself off as a golden giant and the deception was not likely to be noticed.

All this Parry had been able to deduce on the strength of two pieces of evidence. The first was the rucksack which he had seen Reich carrying at El-Ghaita and which had been found in the boot of the white Merbecke-Bentzon (the car had turned up, abandoned, on the outskirts of Marrakesh). Inside the rucksack, as well as ropes for tying up Cecilia, Reich had been carrying his fake Foreign outfit, including the built-up shoes and a mask that looked indistinguishable from the real thing but could come apart into two halves, dividing along a seam hidden among the corrugations of its 'hair', and be worn over the head. Behind its golden eyes there were one-way lenses; between its golden lips, a tiny slot to facilitate breathing. Unless you peered very closely at it you would never spot the trickery, and who, in the normal course of events, peered closely at a Foreigner's face? There was never anything to see there. All golden giants were blankly identical. You looked at their hands to gauge their mood, not their masks.

The second piece of evidence was the simple fact, confirmed by the forensics laboratories in Tangier, that three of the Foreign outfits at HQ had been replaced with copies.

So much for the How of Reich's scheme. The Why had been established, to most people's satisfaction, by the various journalists who had made enquiries into Reich's upbringing and background. Their researches had turned up the fact that Reich's father, an aspiring rock musician, had killed himself when Reich was fourteen. Reich senior had had the misfortune, or the lack of commercial nous, to attempt to make a name for himself as an old-school rock'n'roller just when Siren music was becoming the rage, sweeping aside all other musical artforms. He had persevered with his style of songwriting and performance, but no one had wanted to know. Thwarted in his dreams, and unwilling or unable to adapt to suit the times, he had lapsed into a profound depression and taken his own life. His son, after spending several years of his adult life futilely promoting the cause of traditional music through his revue, had decided to state his beliefs in a much more demonstrative and violent manner. The *shinjus* were an act of vengeance upon Sirens, the people he had borne a ten-year-long grudge against, the people who had, in his view, deprived him of his father.

That was what everyone now thought, at any rate, and, as motives went, it seemed credible enough. But as with the explanation for Reich's kidnapping of Cecilia, there was more to it than that. Why did Reich choose New Venice rather than a resort-city closer to home – Bridgeville, for example, or Baja Beach? And where had he come by the money to fund his enterprise and bribe Hosokawa? So far not many people had seen fit to ask these questions, and even fewer had attempted to answer them.

But Parry thought he knew.

Hearing an airship overhead, he paused and looked up. It was nosing its way eastwards, heading out over open sea. These days, whenever you saw an airship, it always seemed to be heading out to sea, its destination elsewhere. Anywhere so long as it was elsewhere. And its engine note was a forlorn, mournful drone, a dirigible dirge.

The airship passed out of sight and Parry resumed walking. Perhaps tonight he would go and visit Johansen at St Cecilia's. Johansen's leg was healing well and in general he seemed to be in good spirits. A couple more operations on the tendon were required, and Johansen found the physiotherapy painful and a chore. Prevented from keeping up with his weightlifting routine, he was missing his daily endorphin hit and was running to fat, and he griped about all these things, but his sense of humour remained largely intact. He and Parry had taken to sitting out on the hospital's terrace of an evening and chatting or just silently watching the sunset. Parry would give him regular updates on the goings on at HQ, providing verbal snapshots of life under the new regime of Commissioner Raymond van Wyk.

Quesnel had handed in her resignation shortly after Reich escaped. She had justified the decision to Parry by saying that an important head should roll, and he had opined that it ought to be his, and she had replied that she was the one ultimately responsible here, and besides, maybe a high-profile sacrifice might make a difference. So she had shouldered a burden of blame that was not rightly hers and gone back to Canada.

And of course it had made no difference at all.

As anyone could have predicted, van Wyk was appointed her

successor, and immediately he set about drafting changes to the Constitution which he submitted to the FPP Council under the heading of sensible precautions for preventing the *shinjus*, or anything like them, from occurring again. The changes involved amplified powers of arrest and detention, the right to carry out surveillance operations, and the right to expel from a resort-city anyone deemed, by very loose criteria, undesirable or a threat to stability. He also proposed the implementation of tighter entry and exit controls at Customs. They were policing practices from a bygone age. Antediluvian. Rumour was, the Council and the UN were going to ratify them.

Parry, naturally enough, resented being professionally answerable to van Wyk, but not as much as he had expected he would. He realized he had developed a grudging, ironic respect for the man. You had to hand it to van Wyk. He had been right all along, more or less. About the *shinjus*. About the Xenophobes. A cynic like Raymond van Wyk and he had been right all along.

NACA, meanwhile, was doing its best to woo back tourists and, more importantly, Sirens to New Venice. Huge sums of money had been spent on an advertising campaign in every medium, extolling the city's virtues and buffing up its tarnished image by means of such slogans as 'New Venice, the Jewel in the Mediterranean' and 'New Venice – Still the Place to Come!' and 'New Opportunities, New Horizons, a New Beginning . . . New Venice'. Promotional chemotherapy, but so far the patient was not responding to treatment. The much-publicized arraignment of Toroa MacLeod and his accomplice on counts of murder and Xenocide had not helped, either. Yes, it showed that the law was working, but it also served to reinforce in people's minds New Venice's associations with murder and anti-Foreign sentiment.

Onward Parry went, head down, barely looking where he was going. He was thinking now about Hector Fuentes, and wondering just how intensely the man must have loathed him to have wrought this much death and desolation on his behalf. Or perhaps Fuentes had *not* loathed him. Perhaps Fuentes had looked down, like a god, and decided to crush his wife's lover just because he felt like it, just because he could. Whatever the reason, hatred or mere spite, Parry was almost certain that Fuentes was the true architect of his and the city's downfall. Lying on his deathbed, Fuentes had reached out his mighty hand and imperiously, impetuously, arranged for New Venice to be humbled and brought low, and Parry with it.

Fuentes had not spent his final few days, as Anna had put it, 'getting his affairs in order'.

He had been getting *her* affair in order.

And in Guthrie Reich he had found a more than willing agent to execute his posthumous revenge. Reich had carried out Fuentes's wishes to the letter and with gusto. Too much gusto, in the event. Fuentes, of course, would not have wanted Cecilia hurt. By that stage in the proceedings, however, Reich had ceased to differentiate between what Fuentes desired and what he himself thought was necessary. Sensing that he was running out of time, and wanting to deliver one last devastating blow to Parry, Reich had turned his sights on the only person in New Venice to whom Parry was close, other than Anna and Johansen. Cecilia had suffered because of her friendship with Parry. Would probably suffer for the rest of her life. You could say that that was her father's fault, and also Reich's, but in the end, Parry knew it was really only his own. His own and Anna's. And that was the awful truth which Anna must never know. That he and she together were the ones who had triggered all this off. That their affair, begun in perfect innocence, had been the catalyst for the entire tragedy.

Count yourself lucky I'm not supposed to kill you, Reich had said at the hum farm.

Parry counted himself *un*lucky. Killing him might have been the kindest thing Reich could have done.

He walked on through the abandoned city, a tired, broken man carrying a secret around inside him, heavy as a boulder.

Would Reich be found?

Would Foreigners return to New Venice?

Would he ever see Anna again?

There was only one answer to any of these questions.

I don't know.

The simplest, bravest, most honest three words any human being can say.

I don't know.